D0354448

MYS
OSTER   Oster, Jerry
            Fixin' to die

FIXIN' TO DIE

FIXIN' TO DIE

JERRY OSTER

BANTAM BOOKS
NEW YORK · TORONTO · LONDON
SYDNEY · AUCKLAND

FIXIN' TO DIE

A BANTAM BOOK / MARCH 1992

Grateful thanks to Lily Stein Oster for permission to use her original poem, "Know."

Grateful acknowledgment is made for permission to reprint an excerpt from "Baby Can I Hold You" by Tracy Chapman © 1988 EMI APRIL MUSIC INC./PURPLE RABBIT MUSIC. All rights controlled and administered by EMI APRIL MUSIC INC. All rights reserved. International copyright secured. Used by permission.

Library of Congress Cataloging-in-Publication Data

Oster, Jerry.
    Fixin' to die / Jerry Oster.
        p.   cm.
    ISBN 0-553-08037-7
    I. Title.
PS3565.S813F59   1992
813'.54—dc20   91-36156
                                                                    CIP

PUBLISHED SIMULTANEOUSLY IN THE UNITED STATES AND CANADA

PRINTED IN THE UNITED STATES OF AMERICA

BVG   0 9 8 7 6 5 4 3 2 1

for Trisha Lester

FIXIN' TO DIE

Jenny Swale played Eurythmics' cover of "Winter Wonderland" twice in a row, and pressed the rewind button on the dashboard tapedeck to play it again. She knew just how long it took (*six Mississippi*) to get back to the beginning of the cut. When Jenny sat back to enjoy the third time, Elvis Polk shot her in the brainpan.

Elvis had never heard this version of "Winter Wonderland" before in his life, but it was growing on him, so that wasn't why he popped Jenny. A lot of home boys thought Christmas was a hunkie holiday, worth two snaps, but Elvis kind of liked it, liked the cold and the early dark and the trees and ornaments and lights and shit, they reminded him of old movies, TV shows, stuff he watched so he didn't have to think about its being cold and dark early and about never having had the trees and ornaments and lights and shit, so that wasn't why he popped Jenny either.

And word up Elvis liked Jenny: she'd recuffed him in front as soon as they'd left the J so he wouldn't have to sit on his hands for two mothering hours on the drive down; she'd bought him lunch, a ham and Swiss on rye and a Coke; she'd let him stay cuffed in front all afternoon and starting out on the drive back. It was time, that's all, and as good a place as any, so Elvis blew a hole in the back of Jenny's head, then shot Luther Todd in the forehead as Luther jerked around toward the crack of the handy little .22.

"Awright, Luther," Elvis said. "Awright, Jenny."

Elvis tucked the .22 back inside his Triple Fat Goose and slid along the back seat. He got his arms over Luther's head despite the handcuffs and got hold of the wheel just in time to miss sideswiping the guardrail. Luther's big foot, even bigger in a Reebok Twilight Zone Pump, was still on the gas and the weight of his big body was making the Volare go faster. Wouldn't you know it: alive, Luther hugged the speed limit like a grandma with a learner's permit; dead, he had the pedal to the mothering metal.

Elvis waggled Luther from side to side, and Luther's Reebok came off the gas. The Volare slowed down and down. Elvis steered to a stop on the verge. He lifted his arms off Luther and slid back along the seat toward Jenny, who had the key to the cuffs.

Luther pitched forward on the horn button, scaring the shit out of Elvis.

There wasn't much traffic and what there was was people hauling ass to get home before the snow hit—eight inches to a foot was the last forecast they'd heard before Jenny axed if either of them minded if she turned off WINS and put on the Christmas tape, but with Elvis Polk's born-under-a-bad-sign-if-it-weren't-for-bad-luck-he'd-have-no-luck-at-all-luck, some good mothering Sumerian would think he was honking for help and pull over, and he'd have to pop him too.

Elvis got Luther by the collar of his Ice-T jacket and pulled him off the horn and propped him up. He got the key from the side pocket of Jenny's leather jacket and unlocked the cuffs.

When he'd rubbed the tingle out of his wrists, when he'd reached over the seat to the dash and turned off the key, killing the lights and the engine and the tape that was starting to wear him out, when he was breathing regular, Elvis thought about pulling off the road somewhere and turning Jenny Swale, dead or not. Jenny wasn't Elvis's type of she-ra—she had little tiny tits and scrawny bowlegs; Elvis liked serious hooters and a wide load—but she was the only she-ra on hand. And Elvis hadn't turned a she-ra, his type or not his type, he'd just been turning Japanese or getting lips or hips from some rookie in the J since the last time he was on the street, after he did points for what he didn't even remember, a summer when miniskirts were supposed to be making a comeback, the hooker he picked up on Forty-deuce and turned at a motel on Twelfth Avenue was wearing one up to her love slit, and now minis were gone again, so he'd heard, she-ras were wearing dresses down to the floor practically, and with Elvis Polk's born-under-a-bad-sign-if-it-weren't-for-bad-luck-he'd-have-no-luck-at-all-luck, he'd missed the whole mothering thing.

Trouble was, Elvis knew he wouldn't be able to turn Jenny with Luther sitting there, dead or not. It would be dissing Luther, as much as it would be dissing Luther to dump Luther out on the cold ground while Elvis turned Jenny. Elvis supposed dumping *Jenny* out on the cold ground and turning her wouldn't be dissing Luther quite as much, but it would word up be a way to freeze his Louisville Slugger off.

Elvis hardly knew Luther, but Luther was special to him: He wanted to *be* Luther. A blond-haired, blue-eyed hunkie, bearing (burdened with, was his view of it) the name of the most famous hunkie of all time, just about, a man whose fans wouldn't let him die in spite of the photographic evidence (pictures don't mothering lie) of him lying there dead, wrapped around his mothering commode, Elvis Polk had run most of his life with home boys (and *from* hunkie five-ohs), in the J and on the street. Elvis walked home boy, talked home boy, thought home boy, felt home boy. Trouble was, in the J and on the street, Elvis had been short of decent home-boy role models—with the result that he had spent as much time as he had in the J and on those particularly mean streets.

Elvis hardly knew Luther, but Luther was a home boy Elvis could model himself after; Luther was a home boy Elvis could admire; Luther was a home boy Elvis could just about love.

Riding down from the J, Elvis had grooved on hearing Luther talk about growing up in East New York, running with a posse (only they didn't call them posses then, Luther said, they called them just plain gangs), rumbling over turf with other gangs, roughing Jews and wops and micks, copping forty-five records and comics and sodas and Twinkies and Kools, then one day seeing the light when a toy five-oh from Narcotics gave a talk at Luther's school and housed Luther by saying how having a number on a badge was a sight better than holding one up in front of you for a mug shot or having one on a tag on your toe in the morgue. Maybe if Elvis had met Luther a little sooner in his life, if he hadn't been born under a bad sign, if he had some luck at all besides bad luck, maybe Elvis would've turned out to be a five-oh too. He hoped it wouldn't be dissing Luther, he hoped it would be a kind of r-e-s-p-e-c-t that Luther might could even understand and appreciate, if Elvis slipped out of the skiffs he was wearing and into Luther's toy Reebok Twilight Zone Pumps, something to remember Luther by.

And anyway, Elvis wouldn't feel right turning Jenny Swale after how nice she'd been to him, recuffing him, buying him lunch, letting him stay recuffed for the drive back, axing Luther *and* axing him if they minded if she turned off WINS and put on the Christmas tape. Elvis had trouble turning she-ras who were nice to him: He couldn't get hard, he stayed all soft and shriveled up. She-ras who treated him like shit he could turn till they were sore and so was he, he could turn them till his Louisville Slugger fell off.

So Elvis got out and stretched and walked around the back of the Volare and got in the driver's door. He heaved at Luther with his hip till there was room to work the old-time steering-column shift lever. He turned the key and the lights went on and the engine started up and Eurythmics started singing all over about sleigh bells ringing and snow glistening and shit. Elvis never wanted to hear the mothering song again and he switched over to the radio just in time for the WINS five o'clock news.

The usual shit: some plane crashed somewhere; somewhere else an earthquake; some coffee company said it was a mothering lie that there was scutter in their Colombian coffee; the mayor said he hadn't meant to say the governor was a wimp; the governor said she hadn't meant to say the mayor was an asshole.

Elvis didn't need to lobe this shit. What he needed was some Frankie Crocker on the radio. Like Frankie liked to say, Whenever Frankie Crocker isn't on your radio, your radio isn't really on. Elvis switched to 107.5, but there was news on there too, some she-ra announcer saying a former hero cop was hoping the New Year would be an unhappy, unhealthy one for cop killers in the Empire State.

"State Senator Steven Jay Poole of Manhattan," the she-ra announcer said, *"a New York Police Department undercover officer paralyzed from the waist down in a 1978 drug shootout, is optimistic about chances for reinstatement of the death penalty in New York State, which hasn't had an execution since 1963. Speaking at a news conference on the steps of police headquarters, Poole sounded a warning to anyone who turns a gun on a law-enforcement officer. . . ."*

Then a man's voice, smooth. Not Frankie Crocker–smooth. When Frankie Crocker said something like, well, when he signed off the same way night after night after night—*"It's been real and you've been regular. May each of you live to one hundred and me to one hundred minus a day, so I'll never know nice people like you have passed away"*—just before he played "Moody's Mood," you knew he knew it was smoke, some of it, anyway. This wack Poole motherfucker was just ice, that's all, just ice, smooth and at the same time jagged and sharp and cold and killing.

". . . Life in jail for an animal who kills a cop, a sheriff, a deputy, a prison guard, a state trooper, any guardian of law and order, is a strangely luxurious punishment for murder. How do we explain to the loved ones left behind by the murder of a cop, a sheriff, a deputy, a prison guard, a state trooper, any guar—"

Elvis didn't need to lobe this shit. He switched off the radio. First off, any time anybody called New York the Empire State it made Elvis think of his moms, who when Elvis was a kid and thought people were saying New York was the Vampire State thought it was so mothering cute she made him say it all the mothering time; she'd point to the Empire State Building, which they could see from where they lived in mothering Corona, and say, "Now what's that *big* building called, Elvis?" and he'd say, "The Vampire State Building, Moms," even after he knew it *wasn't* the Vampire State Building. Thinking of his moms was worse, just about, than lobing wack motherfuckers wishing cop killers an unhappy, unhealthy New Year.

Elvis did some calculating. Not quite an hour before they were supposed to be back at the J, before they'd try to clear the count and come up one short. He could go fifty miles in not quite an hour, easy; without riling a Smoky, he could be in another state. So maybe his born-under-a-bad-sign-if-it-weren't-for-bad-luck-he'd-have-no-luck-at-all-luck *was* changing. Maybe *this* was Elvis Polk's luck.

He switched the radio back on in time to miss the rest of the news and in time to hear Frankie Crocker say another thing he liked to say, "There ain't no other like this brother," and give the call letters —"WBL *Kicking* S." Then Frankie kicked back Foxy Brown's cover of Tracy Chapman's "Baby Can I Hold You."

Elvis sang along,

> "Sorry, is all that you can't say.
> Years gone by and still words don't come easily.
> Like sorry, like sorry.
> Forgive me, is all that you can't say.
> Years gone by and still words don't come easily.
> Like forgive me, forgive me,"

the first flurries of snow swirling in the headlight cones, on the seat beside him, their blood and their brains on the dash, on the seat, on the windshield, two dead guardians of law and order.

2

"Could you please ask the deejay to play a slow, humping song?" Ann Jones said.

Joe Cullen concentrated on keeping what he thought was time to Kyze, "Stomp (Jump Jack Your Body)."

"Feeling old?"

"Old-*fash*ioned. I like to make contact with my partner every forty or fifty tunes. Ask him to play 'As Time Goes By.' "

"I don't think this kind of deejay plays requests. He's an artist on a roll."

"Is that like a ham on rye? Maria said Quincy tried to get Frankie Crocker to deejay."

"Frankie'd be great," Cullen said.

Ann rolled her eyes and walked off the ballroom floor, leaving Cullen in mid-shimmy. He pretended for a while that he'd rather dance alone than quit before he'd had enough, then followed after her. He pressed the heel of his hand into his left hip, which truly ached from the uncustomary gyrating.

Ann was leaning on the banister of the staircase spiraling down to the main floor. She turned sharply as Cullen got close. "Jesus, it happened again. I thought you were coming from in *front* of me, not behind. This is a strange place."

Among the strangest: Out somewhere near where Queens and Nassau counties blur together, looking like a vast bowling alley or maybe a discount appliance dealership. On the outside, a thousand cement mixers' worth of reinforced concrete, the crude angles only somewhat softened by the half-foot of snow that had fallen over-night and that traffic had already transformed from virginal to slat-ternly; and on the inside, a fragile fist in a rough-tough glove, miles and miles of mirrors. Walls, ceilings, doors, halls—anything that wasn't carpeted was mirrored. All of the mirrors reflected all of the others—*and* reflected everyone and everything reflected in them. And had them reflected back, and reflected them back again, on and on, in and in. That man coming toward you (or was he going away from you?)—was that you, or was it someone else? That co-quette—was she smiling at you, or at someone else, or at herself? In certain narrow corridors, a rank of oneself receded forever on one's right, back into history, while on one's left another rank advanced into the future. Or was it the other way around?

Alone (he had thought) in a men's room, Cullen had sung softly but out loud Tracy Chapman's "Baby Can I Hold You." Coming out of the stall, fussing with his breast-pocket square, he had blushed to find himself surrounded by a dozen men fussing with theirs, then had snorted when he realized they were he and he was they.

The place had a name, Boulevard Manor, but might as well have had none, for Boulevard Manor gave no hint of the place's raison d'être: weddings. Industrial-strength weddings with bridesmaids and groomsmen and ring bearers and flower girls; with the bride's cousin (or was it the groom's aunt?), who once auditioned for *Star Search,* singing, a capella, "Both Sides Now" or "The First Time Ever I Saw Your Face"; with royal-blue (in this case) plastic swizzle sticks—MARIA & QUINCY 14 DEC. 1991—topped by figures of a generic Caucasian bride in veil and train and, half a head taller, in a morn-ing coat, a generic Caucasian groom—never mind that the flesh-

and-blood bride was Hispanic, wore a strapless minidress, and was the same height as the African-American groom, in a powder-blue tuxedo, only because he had a four-inch-high fade haircut.

The wedding, in the Tristan~Isolde Room, of Maria Esperanza, a detective second-grade in the Internal Affairs Unit of the New York City Police Department, and Stacy Ladislaw, a bailiff in the Bronx County Criminal Court, was one of a bunch in progress that afternoon. Down a hall of mirrors to the left, in Dante~Beatrice, Tamara was marrying Nathan. (Cullen, also a cop, Maria Esperanza's partner, hip to clues, had learned as much from a swizzle stick dropped by one of several young ushers who had escaped the celebration for a while and were dueling in the hallway, stirrers simulating rapiers.) To the right, in Romeo~Juliet, Lourdes was marrying Jaime. In Hero~Leander, on the other side of the second-floor lobby, Antonia was marrying Antonio ("Sounds like Shakespeare," Ann had said as she and Cullen studied the notice board in the lobby). In Orpheus~Eurydice, Poppy was marrying Barry.

And those were just the matinees. Lourdes and Jaime's maître d' was checking his watch and twisting his forelock because the wedding was running on Latin time—running two hours late—and the maître d' (a gringo) had Amy and Nguyen booked in R~J at six. Sharon and Neil, Melanie and Don (emphatically *not* Griffith and Johnson), Latifa and Sharif, Ye-Mei and Shi Jei, had scheduled their leaps to matrimony that evening in, respectively, Pygmalion~Galatea, Cupid~Psyche, Apollo~Daphne, Echo~Narcissus. ("A lot of these couples didn't make it," Ann had said. "Do you think they know that?" And: "They forgot a room for Bonnie and Clyde.")

Ann sat sidesaddle on the banister, making Cullen, a mild acrophobe, nervous, and watched Antonia and Antonio posing on a banquette for a photographer with a Hasselblad and an unshakable sense of which stances connoted bliss and which didn't. The black-eyed Antonia's rigid lips and askew elbows said she thought the photographer was full of shit; Antonio, getting razzed by groomsmen and ushers on the sidelines and fearful of Antonia's black-mustached mother, who stood hip-to-hip with the photographer, trying to muscle a peek in the viewfinder, grinned goofily and did as he was told.

"I've decided," Ann said, "to become a vegetarian."

Cullen smiled—with relief. He'd been pretty sure she was going to say something about weddings, especially about their having been together four and a half years without having one. "That roast beef was pretty grim."

"It was calamari that did it," Ann said. "I like calamari in restaurants, but I've never thought to make it at home. The other night I stopped after work at the twenty-four-hour fish store on Broadway. I was thinking shrimp—it was cocktail sauce I really wanted—but the calamari was on sale, so I got some. I figured I'd shake it up in bread crumbs and fry it, but for the hell of it I looked in the *Joy of Cooking.* It said—I'll never forget this as long as I live—it said: before cooking squid or octopus, make sure it's dead.

"There was more: something about 'a conclusive blow,' but I only skimmed it. A conclusive blow, salt to taste, sauté in super-unleaded olive oil."

Cullen laughed.

Ann got off the banister. "What about it? *Is* Maria an extra virgin?"

He took a step away—to get a better look at her and just in case. Sometimes like an errant Ping-Pong ball, sometimes like a ricocheting bullet, her mind worked mysteriously. "You okay?"

"Come on—you must've talked about things like that, riding around in the old whitetop, when you weren't nabbing perps and getting little old ladies' cats out of trees and giving tickets to double-parked stretch limos and adding Pakistani news vendors to the pad: where you lost your virginity, and if not, why not? Is Maria an extra virgin or an extro*vert*?"

Cullen was about to quibble—that they drove their own cars, his Valiant, Maria's Taurus, not squad cars; that they didn't do felonies or pets in jeopardy or traffic; that the pad was ancient history, modern cops put the arm on criminals with lots of ready cash and an inability and reluctance both to holler cop—to quibble and to wonder what the hell was bothering Ann. Maria Esperanza reprieved him by walking up to them just then, a lodestone with her spectacular figure for the eyes of Antonio's groomsmen—and for Antonio, a popinjay for darts fired by the black-eyed Antonia and her black-mustached mother. "Hi, guys."

"Hi, yourself," Ann said. "You look like a goddamn goddess. I was just getting on Joe for having a goddamn goddess for a partner."

Was that what she'd been doing? Cullen didn't think so.

Maria smiled, but her face was cloudy. "Maslosky called the banquet office for you, Joe. They couldn't find you, so I took it. He apologized—Maslosky—he was about as civil as it's possible for him to be, he really was."

"As civil as a boa constrictor?"

"He really was. He wouldn't tell me what it's about, he just said you should call A.S.A.P."

Cullen's hip began to throb all over again. He touched Ann's elbow in an attempt to seem unconcerned, an attempt to get her to *be* unconcerned at yet another inconvenient call from duty. "Maslosky won't learn the computer; he always needs help finding things. That's probably it."

Ann's elbow was icy and hard. His *probably* was transparent; it didn't show up in any of the many available mirrors, like a vampire's. *"I sometimes think,"* Ann had said the last time a telephone had tolled for him in the middle of some fun, or maybe the time before, *"that you like being a public servant because it so often gets you off the hook of your private responsibilities."* "We came in your car, don't forget. I don't want to be stuck out here in the middle of nowhere in all this snow. I'm sorry, Maria. It's not the middle of nowhere, I just don't want to be stuck out here."

Maria touched Ann's hand. *"I* couldn't find my way home." In a gravelly voice she added, "Fuckin' Maslosky."

Ann echoed her. "Fuckin' Maslosky."

"I'll be back," Cullen said, and went downstairs, limping a little.

"He'll be back," Ann said.

"He *will* be back," Maria said. "They always come back. . . . So what is it, Annie? Do you always get edgy when another one bites the dust?"

"That's what men say, isn't it—*guys* say—when one of the *guys* gets married."

"What do you say, when a sister gets married?"

"*Mazel tov.* How do you say it in Spanish?"

"*Felicidades.*"

"*Felicidades.*"

"Is that really what you say? *¿De veras?*"

Ann shrugged. "Whatever I say, I sometimes think, 'Fuck you. I don't want to get married anyway, so fuck you.' Joe's made this . . . stipulation. He wants to wait to marry until both his kids are in college. James started at Rutgers this year, Tenny has two more years of high school. I'm afraid when she starts college he'll say he wants to wait till they both graduate, then till they get Ph.D.s, then till they get jobs, then till *they* marry."

"Quincy had a stipulation," Maria said. "He stipulated we wait till he was making as much money as me. I told him 'Stipulate this.' Men are undependable wimps. It's up to us to take them down the road to new experiences, leading them by the hand and kicking them in the ass at the same time."

"They act so smart," Ann said, "so able. They act like they know everything about us, and they don't know shit. That's what I hate about Frankie Crocker."

Maria laughed. "You do hate Frankie Crocker."

"Not his ain't-no-other-like-this-brother attitude. I can live with that, it's colorful, it's harmless. I hate his condescension. The Evening Bath. Do you know about the Evening Bath?"

Maria made her voice Frankie Crocker–smooth and sable. "Tension-busters. A chance for working women everywhere to relax and let the cares of the day slip away. . . . Quincy's usually home in time for the bath," she went on in her own voice. "Sometimes, when I'd be coming over after work, he'd tape it for me to listen to when I got there. The music's toy, Annie, you can't deny that. Frankie has dope taste."

"It's his arrogance. Imagining himself getting into the tub, scrubbing our backs, rubbing our necks, drying us off, putting on creams and powders. Waving his dick in our faces is what he's saying, he just doesn't say it."

Maria heard her name being called and gestured that she'd be right there. "My mother's probably afraid Quincy and I've already had a fight. Don't get so worked up about Frankie Crocker; he's just another dude. I'm rooting for you and Joe. He's a very decent man. And *muy guapo*."

"Joe calls me *guapa*—he learned it from you—when things're a little tense. He thinks talking like a mambo king will soften me up."

Maria started moving away but took Ann's hands and squeezed. "I want to spend time with you, Annie—just us two—when we get back from the islands. But I want to say to you now that I really like what you're doing in your new job. I know you were ambivalent about working in television. I know it must be hard working with Samantha Cox—"

Ann laughed. "Hard? Samantha?"

"—but I think what you're doing is a lot more immediate than your magazine stuff. More important to more people. I especially like your Quintana Davidoff stuff. It's very powerful."

"Quintana Davidoff. Everybody's favorite victim. Do you think it's because of her name?"

"It's because of her promise."

Ann nodded. She kissed the bride's cheek. "Thanks for saying all that. It's nice to hear. *Felicidades.* Now get back in there."

"Hi."

Ann looked at Cullen's reflection in a mirror but didn't face him. "Computer anxiety?"

"Two detectives got killed. Luther Todd and Jenny Swale, Air Cargo Hijacking. A con named Elvis Polk. A job at Kennedy last month had the same MO as one a couple of years ago. Polk was doing points for fencing goods from that job. The Ds brought him down from Wallkill to see if he'd serenade them with some names."

Cop talk. He didn't usually talk cop talk off-duty. Cop shooters hit each and every cop. "I'm sorry. Did you know them?"

"No."

"Do you have to go?"

"Not right away. I'm in on a meeting at five."

"Were they dirty?"

"Not that I know of. But it's SOP to check them out."

"That can't be fun." He was *guapo,* damn it. There was plenty of time between now and five to take him home and fuck his brains out, and that was what she wanted to do. But she knew that wasn't going to happen. His left hand was a fist and it was grinding into his left hip. That meant his hip hurt and the reason it hurt was that one hundred forty-three days ago (but who was counting?), he'd been winged in that hip. His hip hurt all the time as it was; it was so often the reason he couldn't get it up and keep it up; now he would be all pain, all hard except where she wanted him hard. "Where did Elvis Polk get the gun?"

"It wasn't Todd's or Swale's. Polk dumped them on a back road in Rockland County; their pieces were on them. He took Swale's car and Luther's shoes."

"His shoes?"

"You know—his power sneakers."

Ann took his arm and hugged it in both of hers. "I'm sorry. And I'm sorry I was cranky before."

"Weddings."

"Work. This isn't the time to talk about it."

"Talk about it. I'd rather not talk about dead cops."

Ann faced him, so she couldn't see herself in any mirror. "People think working with Samantha is what's wearing me out. Samantha's fine, she's who she is; she's a star and I'm a bit player and that's fine. What's wearing me out is going into people's homes night after night. You have to dress for it, you have to be *on.* It's not like at the magazine: No more blue jeans, T-shirts, sneakers; no more feet up on the desk, laptop on my lap, a bag of Fritos in the drawer, picking my nose if I felt like it, plucking at my panties if they got all in a bunch, taking all afternoon, all day, several days, to come up with a lead, a word. I'd come up with a lead and I'd take the rest of the day off—go to a movie at the Thalia, when there was a Thalia, or Theatre 80. Now I have to go on the air and share my lead with millions of strangers.

"I never wrote anything that was so immediate to so many as the stuff I've done on Quintana Davidoff. An old-timer at the *News* when I was starting out said once if I ever got two letters about a piece I'd written I'd be entitled to say I'd gotten a 'flood of mail.' And he was right. But the television audience is connected to you; you can feel the tingle. Most nights we're not even off the air yet and the phones light up. People want to tell you what they feel about what you just said; they want to talk back, argue, correct, agree. It's tiring." Ann looked at her watch. "Can we dance a little more before you go? Or would that be ghoulish?"

"I haven't had a chance to talk to Quincy," Cullen said. "I should do that. Is there something new on Quintana?"

Ann shook her head. "No. Quintana's still dead."

3

"When I'm president, once a year people will have to go to work in their bathing suits. Everyone: the boss and the kid in the mailroom, the principal and the custodian, the mayor and the metermaid. Not to be provocative, not to make fun; to humble, to equalize. Everyone will see everyone else's imperfections, *and* their own. Everyone will be nicer, the rest of the year, nicer to each other."

So said Connie Carrera, lying on her back on a Snoopy towel at Jones Beach, June 1972, her hands behind her head, a crop of stubble in her armpits, to Joe Cullen, propped on an elbow beside her. Cullen knew he loved her because he didn't mind the stubble, the stubble wasn't putting a dent in the erection he'd had for some time now, ever since Connie sat up to reach for her Coppertone; she had come to a stop at the top of her sit-up, but her bikini top, whose straps she had untied for even tanning, kept on going—a body in motion tending to remain in motion. They would laugh about it in years to come, but at the moment they were pretending it hadn't happened. They had known each other just two months tomorrow (she taught at a nursery school that had its outdoor playtime in Washington Square Park, where he, a uniform in the Six in those days, walked a beat) and had done only some light fumbling, so her words on the abasing effects of near-nakedness were admonitory: He still hadn't seen everything, and he had shown her no more than had the guy on the next blanket, or the next or the next.

Two hundred million years later, having married, bred with, divorced, and seen everything of Connie Carrera, Cullen remembered her campaign promise as he sat at a long, long table in a police headquarters conference room, listening to men deficient in humility be everything but nice to one another or to anyone else. They were fully dressed, mostly for the weekend (Cullen had come straight from dropping off Ann and still had on his only dress suit, blue), and getting them less dressed would have been prodigious; a world in which fifth-rate asshole scumbag dipshit punks blew away cops two at a time was not a world in which they intended to walk around in their jocks.

The epithets had been heaped on Elvis Polk by Police Commissioner Phil Hriniak, who was wearing a suit too, the black that befit condolence visits. As others around the table had put on the table what few facts they had in hand, Hriniak had sunk lower and lower in his leather armchair, until he appeared to Cullen, nearly facing him, like a sixty-year-old child who had crashed a meeting of grownups. Finally, having been debriefed all he cared to be, thank you, Hriniak had winched himself up straight, struggled out of his coat, yanked at his tie. He centered the yellow legal pad on which he had made a few notes, abused Elvis Polk, and began the summing up that was his perquisite—and was also his way of letting you know how *he* would have put it.

"So . . . the Mercury Freight Thanksgiving Day heist and the SpeedAir heist, May '88, had the same handwriting. Detectives Luther Todd and Jennifer Swale, Air Cargo Hijacking, noticed the similarities, similarities Captain Conigliaro has made intelligible to those of us without experience in this area."

Conigliaro, commander of Air Cargo Hijacking (royal-blue velour polo shirt, acid-washed jeans, navy Adidas), pinched the sides of his mouth, lest he smile. With two detectives hammered, even if the PC stroked you, you didn't strut.

"Todd and Swale," Hriniak continued, and interjected, "—Todd was thirty-four, twelve years in the Department, married but separated, no kids, lived with his parents; Swale, twenty-seven, five years, single, lived with a roommate, female—Todd and Swale got word Elvis Polk was proposing a serenade. Polk was popped in August '88 attempting to sell items from the SpeedAir job to a fence, a Department sting. He denied involvement in the heist and copped to possession of stolen property. He's doing two to six, and blew a parole opportunity last month when he stabbed another con with a screwdriver—an argument over what radio station to play in a day room. There's an interesting document here"—Hriniak slid a bureaucratic flimsy out from under his pad and held it up by a corner between thumb and forefinger—"a psychiatric evaluation that says Polk suffers from the delusion—did I say he's blond and blue?—that he's an African-American. Probably wanted to hear WBLS."

The room's only, and the Department's highest-ranking, African-American, Chief of Department Powell Ruth (gray flannel slacks, maroon cashmere turtleneck, double-breasted blue blazer, Gucci loafers—Ruth dressed down looked more dressed up than most cops dressed up), laughed. "That's WBL *Kicking* S, Commissioner."

Hriniak's eyes lost their focus for just a moment while he wondered if he'd heard what he thought he'd heard and what it meant if he had heard it. Then he said, "Is it?" and laughed too, so anyone who wanted to could.

Cullen only smiled. You could divvy up the world, he believed, according to tastes in radio stations: Over here were the National Public Radio types, over here the Soft Rock/Lite FMers, over here Classical, over here Jazz. MOR, AOR, Classic Rock, Oldies, Country, All-News, All-Sinatra, All-Elvis, Talk, Soul, Salsa, Hip-Hop, Metal, Zydeco, Religion, Sports—you were one or you were another; you were rarely more than two, almost never more than that. Cullen was suddenly interested in Ruth, who he would have said was too exalted to listen to anything everyone could tune in on. The next time Frankie Crocker (There ain't no other like this brother) came back on the air after the news and the weather and the traffic and did a *box check*—"Check the treble, check the high hat, check the bass. Yo, 'cross the street there, crank it *up,* home boy: Mantronix featuring Wondress, 'Got to Have Your Love' "—Cullen would try to imagine Powell Ruth, up in his brownstone on Hamilton Terrace, pinning the needles on his rig.

"Elvis Polk"—Hriniak tipped back in his chair and through the half-glasses on the end of his nose read from the pad he'd scribbled on; his right arm was up and crooked and the middle finger of his right hand traced the perimeter of the widening bald spot on the back of his head, a sentry guarding against further defections—"like I said, Caucasian, thirty-one, five-eight, one-fifty, blond and blue, gold-capped front teeth, like a home boy, pair of dice on one cap— two threes, six the hard way—a crown on the other, five tattooed teardrops on his left cheek, a tattooed heart on his left bicep with the words 'Undertaker, Undertaker,' a tatooed coffin on his right bicep with the words 'Fixin' to Die.' The teardrops mean tours in the J; I don't know what the 'undertakers' mean." Hriniak looked over the top of his glasses. "Anybody?"

Cullen waited. He figured it was Ruth's to answer if he wanted to, if he could. Finally he said, "It's from a gospel song, 'Will the Circle Be Unbroken.' 'Undertaker, undertaker, won't you please drive real slow. That's dear sweet old so-and-so. I hate to see him go.' 'Fixin' to Die' is a Bukka White song. Dylan covered it."

Legs were uncrossed and recrossed, crotches eased, throats cleared; sidelong looks crept around the table; water was poured, coffee sipped from Dunkin' Donuts containers. That Cullen, subordinate to everyone there (except Patrolman Sid Braverman, Hriniak's driver-bodyguard, seated like a Semitic Buddha by the door), went back a long way with Hriniak, superior to them all, was well known. (Back to the days B.C.—Before Connie—when Cullen, a City College student, worked nights in a Duffy Square record store that was on the beat of Hriniak, in uniform in Midtown South and a jazz collector; they got to talking over the Getz–Gilberto bin the way he and Connie would one day get to talking over the sandbox.) What wasn't known, least of all by Cullen and Hriniak, was what to do about the friendship, especially since, as Hriniak had moved first indoors, then downtown, then upstairs, it had come to consist mainly of chance meetings at which they shrugged and shucked in semi-mock dismay at how long it had been since they had gotten together socially. (At the last dinner *chez* either of them—Christmas 1979—Cullen was a detective two and still married to Connie Carrera; Hriniak was a deputy chief inspector with all his hair, Beryl Hriniak was still a blonde.)

Then there was the Department-wide bewilderment at Cullen's store of music trivia. He had won the Detectives Endowment Association's *Jeopardy!* Night with a run of correct answers—correct questions—in the category Pop & Rock Music (A: Gordon Sumner, Robby Van Winkle, and Dave Evans. Q: Who are Sting, Vanilla Ice, and The Edge? A: British rock bands that suffered the tragic deaths of their original drummers. Q: Who are Led Zeppelin and The Who? A: The setting of a Bruce Springsteen song about the doomed love affair between Spanish Johnny and Puerto Rican Jane. Q: What is Fifty-seventh Street? A: He was caught in the rain with his friend Billy half a mile from the county fair. Q: Who is Van Morrison?) and was favored against the champs of the Patrolmen's Benevolent Association and the Sergeants Benevolent Association in an impending *Jeopardy!*-Off for the benefit of the Police and Fire Widows' and Children's Fund right after the New Year.

Looking sorry he'd asked, for word that he'd been mining Cullen's musical lode was sure to get out, and, bingo, charges of nepotism, Hriniak went on: "Todd and Swale, like I said, got word from Polk's lawyer, Margaret Morris, Legal Services, that her client was more interested in singing a SpeedAir serenade than in the past, seeing as how, thanks to his handiwork with the screwdriver, he was a little farther than he had been from the mouth of shit's creek. They took custody at Wallkill at ten A.M. yesterday and drove to Cargo Hijacking at Kennedy, arriving about twelve-thirty. At approximately one-fifteen they were joined by Margaret Morris and Queens County ADA Carlton Woods. They talked about an hour, no deals were cut, but there was a, uh, understanding, Captain Conigliaro tells us, that further discussions could be profitable to both sides.

"Todd and Swale left with the prisoner at approximately four P.M. It was Swale's car, but Todd was driving, Swale riding shotgun, Polk in the back seat. It's a two-hour drive with traffic. The warden got on to the Troopers about six-thirty when they couldn't clear the count, the Troopers got on to us. By the time I was notified by the first dep it was eight-thirty. Some kids out sledding found the bodies this morning, in a culvert near Nanuet. Why is it always kids—kids having fun?"

And where was the first dep, Cullen wondered, First Deputy Commissioner Susan Price, Hriniak's second-in-command, the Department's highest-ranking woman? Were they going to strip down, after all, and were they more afraid of her showing them hers or of showing her theirs?

Hriniak drank some coffee and grimaced it down. "Near as we know—Rockland County's in on this and we've got to do some stuff twice—they were hammered around five, five-thirty, at extreme close range, Swale in the back of the head, Todd in the forehead. They were not hammered in the culvert, they were hammered somewhere else and dumped there. Polk is *sayonara*, Swale's car, an '86 Volare, is missing. Smart money says Polk has different wheels by now. He also appears to have Detective Todd's shoes, Reebok basketball sneakers, the kind you pump full of air to make them fit better. He'll need a lot of air, Polk; he's a size nine, Detective Todd was a twelve.

"The piece was a small-caliber handgun, a twenty-two or a twenty-five. I figured, I guess everybody figured, it was somebody's off-duty piece, Polk got it from a locker somehow at Air Cargo. But preliminarily all the off-duty pieces are accounted for, none of the lockers were broken into. That's not to say Polk couldn't've opened a locker and relocked it, that somebody's short a piece and not telling. He was cuffed in front, Polk."

Hriniak sat forward, took off his glasses, put aside his pad. "A violation of procedure, against the regs, not repeat not SOP—we all know that and we all know it's not the first time and it won't be the last. Polk ate a sandwich, he had coffee, he went to the can, he took some notes on a pad his lawyer gave him." Hriniak flicked his fingers across his pad. "Hard to do with your hands behind your back and hard to get a man with his hands behind his back to roll over for you. You can break him down, sure, make him tell you he killed *Lin*coln just to get you out of his face, but not easy to get him to roll over on somebody. Anybody says otherwise has never had to do it. Plus, it's Christmastime, for Christ's sake.

"Polk was by himself more than once. He was by himself in Todd and Swale's office, cuffed to a radiator, according to Captain Conigliaro, but only by one hand because that's when he was eating lunch. He was by himself in an interrogation room, cuffed but not *to* anything because the door locks from the outside only and everything inside is bolted down. He was not by himself, exactly, but alone in a hallway with his attorney, both hands cuffed, plus she was his bond. Leaving him by himself all those times would be a major fuck-up if Polk were a violent felon, but aside from poking this con with a screwdriver—it barely broke the skin, the warden tells me; the guy was out of the hospital the next day—he has no record of violent felonies."

Hriniak put his glasses back on and pulled his pad close. With a pencil point he ticked off Elvis's blemishes: "He's been doing this seventeen years, since he was fourteen: truancy, possession of a gravity knife, petty larceny, truancy and escape, possession of burglary tools, grand theft auto. Like I said, he's a fifth-rate asshole scumbag dipshit punk, but does he sound to *any*body like a cop killer?"

He sounded to Cullen restless and ornery, a *Jeopardy!* answer to the question: Who is Merle Haggard?

"The *me*dia," Hriniak said, "—when did the press become the *me*dia? Did they take a vote on it or what, or did somebody just decide?—the *me*dia is dancing all over the graves of these poor fucking cops. They're lining up outside, snow or no snow, to point fingers. You saw, you who were at the press conference, you saw them put Suzie Price through the wringer, she was so wrung out I told her to go down to the gym for a half hour, slam the shit out of a heavy bag. Samantha Cox, shit. Samantha Cock*sucker.*"

4

This time, everyone looked right *at* Cullen—Ruth and Conigliaro, Hriniak and Braverman; Chief of Detectives Paolo Abruzzi (lamb's wool polo shirt, sharkskin slacks, Guccis too; the joke was that if Abruzzi and Ruth couldn't outsmart John Gotti, they could at least try to outdress him); Captains Richie Maslosky of Internal Affairs (red Gore-Tex running suit; he'd switched addictions from smoking to jogging after a mild stroke) and Elihu I. Novak of Homicide (wash-and-wear shirt, the pants to an old suit, Hush Puppies—Novak might take a day off, but he wouldn't enjoy it); Detectives Mike Radnor of IAU and Donnie Drago and Tim McIver of Homicide (all in baseball caps, ski jackets, blue jeans, black leather training shoes—to anyone but a blind man, cops). So this was why he'd been summoned here this late afternoon—because they thought him in cahoots with Samantha Cox.

Some collaboration. Samantha was the first-magnitude star of Channel 14's six and eleven o'clock newscasts, on which Ann was—Ann's phrase—a forty-watt bulb. Ann, not he. His . . . his girlfriend, not he. *He* had been in Samantha's gravitational field just once. She had touched him once, taking his hand in her cool, hard hands; she had commanded in her cool, hard voice that he call her Sam; she had concluded that they must do lunch and do it soon; she had conveyed unmistakably the impression that she had been motivated since getting out of bed that morning by the prospect of finally meeting him—and yet had all the while looked with her cool, hard eyes right past him, right through him, at someone else, someone more interesting to her than he, who, having been met, netted, pinned up, mounted, labeled, catalogued, was now of no interest whatsoever. With a crisp move of her slim wrist, she had propelled herself around him (his memory had offered up an image from his misspent youth: a roller-derby queen, tousled and tough, cracking the whip), around him and past him and across the room, where she had extended her cool, hard hand at her quarry and commanded that *he* call her Sam.

A few more times that night—Channel 14's annual Midsummer Night's Ball, a ticket so hot people forsook the Hamptons, the Cape, the Vineyard, to attend—Cullen's eyes had encountered Samantha —er, sorry—*Sam* Cox's, and had been brushed off. The only indication that he was even a smudge on her memory had been Ann's report, just before Thanksgiving, that Sam had asked if she were spending the holiday with him—"with Jim."

Hriniak: "Samantha Cox and a crew were out at Kennedy this morning, doing a story on air-traffic controllers. Some whistle-blower talking about drug abuse. When they heard about the hammer, they came down on Air Cargo like vultures. Conigliaro was in Nanuet, there were only junior people on hand, Cox chewed them up and spit them out. They didn't know what hit them." Hriniak tipped his head at Braverman, who got up out of his chair and went around to a television and a VCR on a rolling table in a corner. "This was on at six; there'll be more at eleven."

Braverman switched on the TV and the VCR. *Clicks, whirrs,* then Samantha Cox in a trademark red outfit, a suit this time, with a short, tight skirt that ended above her knees and a jacket with *Star*

Trek shoulder pads, offensive-lineman shoulder pads. Her hair was ultrablond, ultracoiffed; her lips were ultrared, ultrasucculent; her teeth ultraperfect, ultraivory; her skin ultralucid, her figure ultralithe, her carriage ultrasovereign. If Samantha Cox were to go to work in a bathing suit, if she were to go to work in a gunnysack, the effect would be like that of a neutron bomb. (In fact, Samantha fully clothed had been pretty decimating: Channels 2, 4, 5, 7, 9, and 11 obstinately continued to broadcast local news shows after Samantha's arrival from Los Angeles a little over two years ago, but from the ratings books it appeared that only a few friends and relatives of the principals were watching anything but NewsFocus 14. And who knew that those friends and family weren't participants in the ritual conducted by hundreds of thousands who weren't home at six P.M. or still up at eleven of—as *New York* magazine put it in a cover story on the practice—"Videotaping Samantha: The Town's Latest Guilty Pleasure—Using the VCR to Trap Cox the Fox"?)

A sorceress when it came to telling a story with images and sounds, Samantha began beguiling her audience this time with a tracking shot through Air Cargo Hijacking's squalid Quonset in a patch of Kennedy airport that in the snow looked more like the South Pole than south Queens. The moving camera on the cameraman's lurching shoulder represented the edgy eye of the sociopathic prisoner, looking here, there, everywhere for a way out, a weapon, a chink.

Down a hall, through a door, through another, into a room with a thick metal door that slammed shut behind "the prisoner." Where there had been noise—raised voices, ringing phones, the bang of a drawer of a cheap metal desk, typewriters, jetliners laboring aloft—there was now (nice touch) suffocating silence broken only (brilliant touch, award-winning touch) by nervous nasal breathing. Sociopathic breathing.

Two metal chairs and an old metal desk were the room's only furniture, and after enduring the awful silence for a moment, "the prisoner" swiftly opened and shut the desk's six drawers. Empty. Shit.

The door was opened then and "the prisoner" was escorted down the (noisy) hall to another room, an office, clearly less secure, less intimidating than the first room. There were two newish metal and laminate desks in the office and on them and on the bulletin boards over them were photographs, cartoons, funny greeting cards (the reigning Peanuts gang and the pretender Garfield), Post-it notes, while-you-were-out telephone messages, coupons, clippings, pennants, lapel buttons, train schedules.

Left alone again, "the prisoner" rifled the desk drawers, three in each desk. Envelopes, paper, Post-it pads, note pads, legal pads, steno pads, rubber bands, paper clips, staplers and staples, pens, pencils, rulers.

(No scissors, Cullen noticed. He had scissors in his desk, which probably wasn't very smart, was it? He had used them just yesterday to cut from the *Times* an ad for a watch he liked, a "faux classic with yesterday's style and today's accuracy." He had given the ad to Ann that morning on the way to the wedding in response to her ultimatum that he tell her what he wanted for Christmas or he would get ankle socks and boxer shorts. She had looked at the ad, rolled her eyes—at the "faux," he knew—and put it in her handbag.

(Cullen noticed too that "the prisoner's" hands, which appeared in the frame from time to time, were manacled with what looked like Department-issue handcuffs. [Maybe *that* was why he was here—to roll the head of whatever cop had lent his cuffs to the simulation.] But how did the cameraman, if those were his hands, get them in the frame and still operate the camera? He would have to ask Ann. And would Ann tell him, or were TV journalists like magicians, sworn not to tip the gaff?)

Finding nothing in the desks to use as a weapon, "the prisoner" then turned to two decrepit lockers, propped side by side in a corner of the office like a couple of drunks awaiting booking, their battered, warped doors held shut by combination locks that every viewer who remembered his schooldays knew had been set to open with a single final spin to the right. (So as to save time that would be spent . . . how? Or would it be squandered?) Even if they hadn't been two-thirds opened, the locks could still have been freed, they looked, with a good hard tug.

"The prisoner" didn't tug the locks or spin them; instead, the camera panned cleverly around to reveal Samantha, sitting legs crossed on one of the desks, a blaze of thigh exposed, a microphone close to her lips, looking more like a torch singer on a piano than a reporter on a story. "Investigators don't know yet where Elvis Polk got the gun that killed Luther Todd and Jennifer Swale," Samantha said in her cool, hard voice. "But they can't discount the grim possibility that the weapon belonged to one of the victims and was carelessly stored in one of these flimsy lockers. . . . Another disturbing question—"

"Enough of this shit." Hriniak launched himself up out of his chair and extinguished picture and sound with a couple of jabs of his fingers. He turned on them, as big as a bear, and mean. "At eleven o'clock Miz Cock*sucker*'s going to have a guest—Steven *Jay* Poole. When did Steven *Jay* Poole become Steven *Jay* Poole? Didn't he used to be *Steve* Poole, *Stev*ie Poole, Everybody *Out* of the Poole some guys used to call him? Brooklyn Vice, Brooklyn Homicide, Brooklyn Major Cases, a good cop, not a great cop, an okay cop. Now he's Steven *Jay* Poole, State Senator Poole, *hero* cop, wheelchair jock, Mister Punishment with a capital *P* and it rhymes with *C* and it stands for Chair, Mister Throw-the-Switch-and-Watch-'Em-Twitch.

"Hey, I think cop killers should die. I think *any* scumbag who kills somebody should die. I think the chair's too good for such scumbags; they should chain such scumbags to a tree in Central Park and sell rocks. What I also think, however, is people like Steven *Jay* Poole should take a big deep breath, sit back, let the bodies cool off a little, let the families bury their dead, instead of driving his wheelchair like Mario fucking Andretti to get to every TV studio in town to make a pitch for capital punishment."

He'd been pacing. He stopped. He got smaller. "Anyway, that's not the point. The point is, the other disturbing question Samantha Cox asks besides 'Where Did Polk Get the Piece?' is the one I'm asking too: The other disturbing question is 'Why?' What we have here is an escape by someone who wasn't an escape risk, who'd done enough time, and not real hard time, that he could've done more time easy, doing time was what he did, it was who he was. So why? Why'd he risk everything, why'd he hammer two cops who probably cared a little bit about him, who probably thought he was an okay guy as fifth-rate asshole scumbag dipshit punks go? Why did he hammer two such cops when it meant winding up with twenty thousand more cops wanting to ream his ass and hang him by the balls from the flagpole in the plaza downstairs?

"Anybody? . . .

"*Nobody?* . . .

"Right.

"Yes, Sergeant? Going somewhere? What? What is it?"

Oh, nothing. Cullen waved a hand backhandedly and tried to say "Oh, nothing," but nothing would come out. It was like that sometimes, since the day one hundred forty-three days ago (but who was counting?) when he got winged. That same day, one hundred forty-three days ago, his partner, Neil Zimmerman, got winged too—an hour or so before Cullen but, unlike Cullen, who was winged near but not in the spine, who thought for a while he might not walk again but who walked just fine except that his hip hurt all the time —winged too and, unlike Cullen, decked, taken out, whacked, polished (the slang changed with the times), done, Z'd, K'd, whelmed, wasted, downed, berked, blacked, zeroed, savaged.

Hammered.

Killed.

Sometimes, thinking back to that day one hundred forty-three days ago (or sometimes *not* thinking about it, thinking about George Steinbrenner, about pizza with anchovies; thinking about Anne Archer; thinking about whether to rent *Turner and Hooch;* thinking about Dan Quayle or Quincy Jones or *Sexing the Cherry,* about Lip Trip SPF 15 sunscreen or Pilot #2 automatic pencils or Irish breakfast tea), Cullen would lose it, he would burst, he would dip and wobble and trip. White-hot flashes would sear his eyes and white-hot bile would erupt in his gut; he would weep white-hot tears, shaking all over all the while as if he were not white-hot but blue-cold. If thinking about Anne Archer, if thinking about lip balm, could push him over the edge, imagine what thinking about and talking about hammered cops could do. And at Christmastime, for Christ's sake.

"I'll be all right," Cullen managed to say, or tried to. But he knew he wouldn't be all right, so he got up and walked out.

He went to a men's room and splashed cold water on his face and rubbed his cheeks with his palms. He splashed and rubbed, splashed and rubbed, splashed and rubbed, splashed and rubbed. He dried his face with scratchy paper towels and balled them up and fired them all over the men's room. The wettest ones clung where they struck. He collected the balled-up towels and dropped them in a wastebasket and went out in the hall and sat on a bench, a faux Shaker bench, near Hriniak's office. He hugged himself and rocked and hummed:

> *Undertaker, undertaker, won't you please drive real*
> *slow.*
> *That's my dear sweet old partner. Lord I sure hate*
> *to see him go.*

After a while Hriniak came out and sat on the faux Shaker bench too. He passed his hand over his bald spot, but there had been no improvement. "I had an *ex*-partner hammered once. Remember?"

"Cassidy?"

"Casey."

"Casey."

"He went into undercover narcotics. Talk about a death wish."

Cullen hugged himself tighter. He felt something in an inside pocket and fished it out: the swizzle stick—MARIA & QUINCY 14 DEC. 1991.

Hriniak took the stick from Cullen and studied it. "How're you and Esperanza working out?"

"Good. She's good. She's emotional, but she knows how to use it, use her feelings."

"I guess I meant"—Hriniak tried to flip the stick end over end, knocked it away, leaned way over to retrieve it—"well, she's, uh . . ."

"*Guapa?*" Cullen said.

"Come again."

"Beautiful. And a piece of ass."

Hriniak nodded, glad he hadn't had to say it. "That ever a problem for you?"

"Hey."

"I'm sorry. I know you're a pro. It's just . . . Well, when you work in the same small office, when you drive around in the same small car—"

"We put in for a bigger office, one with a window, and for a limo. We're on the waiting list. In the meantime we take lots of cold showers."

Hriniak sighed. "I said I was sorry. What I'm trying to say is this. Jenny Swale . . ."

Cullen waited and waited, but the name just dangled there.

Hriniak tried another route. "We wrapped things up inside. Novak, McIver, Drago, Radnor, Conigliaro—they all took off. Ruth, Abruzzi, Maslosky—they stuck around a minute. Suzie Price came back; she knows about it too. You'll be working just on this part of it—everybody's clear on that. Your partner's on her honeymoon, it's convenient. If you overlap with the Homicide Ds, with Radnor's people, just say you're clearing up some administrative things, some loose ends. Jenny Swale had a roommate, a woman named Jo Dante, works at a sound studio, which I'm not exactly sure what it is, something to do with movies, TV. It's in the West Fifties somewhere, Maslosky has the address if you can't find her at home. You should probably talk to her." Hriniak's shoulders were slumped, his elbows were down between his knees, his hands wrung each other.

"Phil?" Cullen said.

Hriniak glanced up momentarily. "Fuck'm I talking about? That what you want to know?"

"Okay."

Hriniak sat up straighter. He touched his bald spot. "Jenny Swale worked down the hall a while last spring. Admin. She did some investigative stuff—background checks, things like that. You know that?"

"I'm not up on this floor much."

"Anyway, she had a bid in for a long time to work on the street. Air Cargo opened up, it wasn't what she wanted, but she settled for it. She wanted to get out of here, off this floor, on account of she'd filed a grievance. A har*ass*ment thing. Or is it *har*assment? You're a college guy—how do you pronounce it?"

That wasn't the kind of thing Cullen had learned in college. In college he'd learned: how to spirit noncirculating books out of the library overnight; how to second-act Broadway plays; how to tie a bow tie; how to unhook a bra one-handed; how to use chopsticks. "Ann's friend, Mabel Parker? Used to be an ADA? She's in private practice now. She handles a lot of sexual *har*assment cases, and that's how she pronounces it."

Hriniak drifted off somewhere for a moment, then came back. "Funny you should mention Mabel Parker. She handled the New York County end of the SpeedAir job. She didn't put Elvis Polk away, exactly, but she helped."

"What did you always used to say? It's a one-horse world."

Again Hriniak drifted, again he returned. "Sexual *har*assment— that's what Jenny Swale's grievance was about." Hriniak pointed to his bald spot this time, as if it were evidence of his innocence. "She named me."

At home, half standing, half propped against the kitchen counter (after a day of standing, dancing, driving, sitting, his hip hurt whether he sat or lay down or stood, but least if he stood), drinking a Corona, Cullen played the two messages on the answering machine on the wall.

One was from his son, James, and his daughter, Tenny.

"Hi, Dad."

"Hi, Dad. I'm on the phone upstairs. Ten's in the kitchen."

"Oh, right. Where I belong, right?"

"Hey, don't have a cow, babe. I didn't say that."

"Don't call me 'babe,' teed."

"Oh, this is great. This is a great message for Dad to get. Let's call back."

"He'll get this anyway. *It doesn't matter. Let's just go ahead. . . . We're calling, Dad, 'cause we want to know what you want for Christmas. Mom said you said something about a watch—"*

"And Tenny freaked out 'cause she got you a watch last Christmas, and you never wear it."

"I didn't freak *out, and it wasn't last Christmas, it was the year before."*

"He never wears it."

"I didn't freak *out."*

"Don't have a cow. Dad, there're these hockey gloves. CCM's—"

"Ja-ames."

"What?"

"We're calling to find out what Dad *wants, not to tell him what teed gloves* you *need for that teed game you play."*

"Well . . ."

"Dad? Call us back, okay?"

"Bye, Dad."

"Bye, Dad."

"Get off the phone now, Tenny. I want to make a call."

"Who to, lover boy?"

"Just get off, okay?"

"Kathy?"

"Just get off, Tenny, God damn it."

"Don't have a cow, man."

"Tenny, I'm coming down there."

"*To the kitchen? Right. The only place safer than the kitchen is the shower. You never go in either one.*"

"*Listen, lint-for-brains.*"

"*Joe?*"

"*Oh, uh . . . Mom? Dad wasn't home. We left a message.*"

"*Then who're you talking to?*"

"*We're just, uh, you know . . .*"

"*Hang up, James.*"

"*I am. I already was. I was going to. Tenny—*"

"*Hang. Up. Stephanie . . .*"

"*I hung up. James didn't—*"

"*Stephanie . . .*"

"*Bye, Dad.*"

"*Bye, Dad.*"

"Hi, Joe," Connie said. "*Bye, Joe.*"

The second message was from Ann, without preamble, the message of a professional message-leaver: "*How'd it go? Okay, I hope. Call me when you get in. I'll be up late. . . . Bye. I didn't catch the bouquet. Oh, you know that. You were still there, I forgot. . . . Bye.*"

Late. Late was relative. Late was ambiguous. For some, midnight was late, for some, ten-thirty. On a Saturday, when you'd been all the way out to ultima Queens to go to a wedding, who knew what late was? He would call Ann tomorrow, and if she complained, he would say he'd thought she said not to call *too* late. So she couldn't prove that she hadn't said that, he erased the message.

He thought about watching television, but that would mean moving. He thought about turning on the radio on top of the refrigerator, but Frankie Crocker wouldn't be on, and when Frankie Crocker wasn't on your radio, your radio wasn't really on.

So he drank another Corona, and another and another. He drank all six, and was able, when he lay down on his bed, still wearing his shirt and tie and the pants to his only dress suit, blue, to sleep.

5

Elvis Polk turned Jenny Swale, hammered or not, and made her feel so fine she came back to life. Her brains and blood and shit got sucked back inside the hole in her head and the hole closed up and healed and her eyes popped open. She grabbed Elvis's head in both hands and stuck her tongue way down deep inside his mouth, like she wanted to kiss his heart.

When Elvis stuck his tongue way down deep inside Jenny's mouth, trying to kiss her heart, she bit his tongue off and spit the bloody chunk at him.

The dreamed pain was so sharp, the dreamed turnabout so unexpected, Elvis sat straight up out of the dream. He clapped his hands over his mouth to stanch the dreamed gush pump fountain of gagging, drowning blood.

Frightened, ever frightened, of sleeping in a strange bed, Elvis had left the bathroom light on and could see himself reflected in the mirror of the dressing table facing the foot of the bed. Hands to mouth, shoulders scrunched, legs yogi-crossed, he looked like the mothering ceramic speak-no-evil monkey that had squatted alongside the see-no-evil monkey and the hear-no-evil monkey on top of the chiffonier in his moms's living room.

An abiding regret of Elvis Polk's was that he hadn't, while his moms was still alive to appreciate it, picked up those mothering monkeys and one at a time Doc Gooden–fastballed them into the fireplace—one, two, three strikes you're out—by way of letting the whining old fool know what he thought of her holding mothering monkeys—mothering cer*a*mic monkeys—up to him as models of behavior.

Elvis flopped back down on the bed and tried to go back to sleep, but his moms was loose now inside his head, scrabbling around like some kind of half-bug, half-rat, half–mangy old dog, yapping at him, mewling, nipping. Elvis squeezed his eyes tight, trying to crush his moms between his eyelids, but she kept wriggling free, sweating and wheezing from the effort. He finally drove her off by projecting on the insides of his eyelids a slow-motion instant replay of her death that he knew she wouldn't be able to watch, Summerall and Madden doing the play-by-play, the sell-out crowd at the Meadowlands standing and whooping and screaming.

There she was, kind of like Elvis, come to think of it (Elvis *Presley*, that is), wavering, toppling, tipping, crashing down on the kitchen floor (Elvis Presley went down on his bathroom floor, but try to tell that to his dog-ass fans, who kept thinking they saw him in K marts or Piggly Wigglies), landing all splayed out this way and that, her housedress up to her thighs, one knee-high in a clump down around one ankle, her tongue lolling out of the corner of her mouth, her eyes rolled back in her head so all you saw was mostly bloodshot white. The dish towel she always hung over her shoulder so she could mop up spills or wipe sweat off her face or harvest some snot or grab a hot pan handle or flick Elvis's butt (Elvis *Polk*'s, that is) to get him to get a move on, the dish towel was lying on the floor beside her like a pet or something, like her mangy old dog waiting to see if she was ever going to move again or what, wondering if it licked her face if she'd reach out and pat it and heave up off the floor and feed it, or, more likely, if she'd reach out and twist its ear and heave up off the floor and haul off and kick it in the ribs, which was how she usually treated the mangy old dog but which would mean she was alive at least.

A pot of so-called stew was boiling over on the stove and sticking and burning (which meant it had a shot at tasting better than usual); on the little TV on the counter, some she-ra was begging some guy not to leave her for some other she-ra; the phone was ringing and ringing and ringing—one of his moms's pit-bitch friends probably, calling to yak about how in the *last* hour's soap some she-ra begged some guy not to leave her for some other *guy*—ringing and ringing and ringing, the pit bitch not having the brains of a drill press to figure that maybe Miriam Polk wasn't answering the phone because she'd bought the farm.

In fact, Miriam Polk had died in a hospital while Elvis was doing points for what he couldn't remember, died in a clean white bed probably, her life leaving her like a little burp, a little fart. But Elvis liked to think of her dying on the kitchen floor like that, dying with her ratty corduroy slippers on, dying as she lived—gray and damp smelling and covered with stains and sores and bruises. She deserved that kind of death, Elvis firmly believed, because of the life she'd led: because she'd started running around with home boys while still in junior high school; because she'd turned a bunch of them and gotten knocked up by one of them; because she'd been such an uptight tight-ass tight-twat hunkie bitch that she'd let the home boy that knocked her up ram his Louisville Slugger inside her love slit and shoot his wad but had somehow stomped on all the home boy's genes, mopped up all the home boy's blood, rejected all the home boy's tissues and muscles and tendons and bones, had cleaned mothering *up* after the home boy so it was like he'd never been in her love slit at all.

And instead of having a home-boy baby with crinkly home-boy hair and home-boy lips and nose and skin, she had a hot wet pink blond baby that she named Elvis, after the most famous hunkie of all time, whose every single record he ever made she had in the cabinet next to the chiffonier with the mothering see-no-evil, hear-no-evil, speak-no-evil monkeys on it, and she would sing to *her* Elvis the mothering words of every song on every one of those records, 'cause she knew every mothering word of them, scrunching up her eyes and groaning along with "Love Me Hound Dog Don't Be Blue Suede Heartbreak Christmas Without You."

Another abiding regret of Elvis's was that he hadn't, while his moms was still alive to appreciate it, Doc Gooden–fastballed those mothering records into the fireplace, by way of letting his moms know what he thought of her dissing his home-boy old man, whose name was Vurnell probably, or Jesse or Lamont or Roland or Jamal, by having a hot wet pink blond baby named Elvis. He couldn't even go to his moms's now and fastball those mothering records, to let her know posthumously what he thought of her dissing his old man: His moms's sleazeball brother had sold the house and everything in it, the Elvis records and the mothering monkeys and the mangy old dog, and moved to Florida. Pensamotheringcola.

Elvis rolled off the bed and went to the window. Slipping the back of his hand in under the shade, he lifted it a tad and saw what there was to see. Nothing. Cement and tarmac and mud. No snow—the snow had run out twenty miles back east. Not much day left. He'd been in Js that had more going for them than this nothing motel outside a nothing town off some nothing road in the middle of Nothing, Pennsylvania, maybe, or maybe it was Nothing, New York, the Vampire State. Wherever it was they had never seen tattooed teardrops before and didn't know what they meant if they had.

"Got a smudge on your face there, friend," the she-ra in the office had said to Elvis as he signed the motel register, signed it *Michael Gooden,* a combo, one from Column A, one from Column B, of his two favorite home boys, slamdunking downtown Michael Jordan and flamethrowing downtown Dwight Gooden, Air Jordan and Doctor K. And the she-ra had taken a Kleenex box from under the counter, a box Elvis already knew was there because he'd hauled himself up on his elbows to take a look when the she-ra's back was to him, to see if there was maybe a piece behind the counter, a shotgun, an old Colt or something, he didn't give a shit, he'd just feel better strapped with something with more pop than the mothering little .22.

Elvis didn't take a Kleenex, he just stood there looking at the she-ra, noticing the little new moon indent in her forehead over her right eyebrow, wondering what made it, was she born with it, or did somebody whack her with something when she was a kid, Doc Gooden–fastball something at her? Or did she just make the indent herself a minute before he drove up, sitting there digging a fingernail into her forehead to keep from going crazy at the thought that what she was doing with her life was working in a nothing motel in a nothing town off some nothing road in the middle of nothing?

Elvis didn't take a Kleenex, so the she-ra pulled one out of the box and wrapped it around her pointer finger and licked it and reached across the counter and gently, gently, rubbed at Elvis's cheekbone under his left eye. "Hunh."

Elvis knew what she was hunh-ing about, but he said, "What?"

The she-ra rubbed once more, hard, then pulled her hand away real quick, like she knew she shouldn't have. "I thought it was dirt, but it's not. It's like a birthmark."

" 'S a tattoo," Elvis said.

"A tattoo?"

"Word up."

"What?"

" 'S really a tattoo. Word up."

The she-ra scrunched her eyes and looked at him along her nose. "You from Pittsburgh?" Then real quick again, like she knew she shouldn't have asked, "How long you staying, uh"—she stuck her chin out to read the register upside down—"uh, Mike? How long you staying, Mike?"

Did the she-ra know his name wasn't Mike and as soon as she could, would she call the five-ohs and tell them a motherfucker in a pair of loose Reebok Twilight Zone Pumps had just checked in using an alias? Or did the she-ra know his name wasn't Mike and what else was new, if she had a spoonful of booshit for everyone who signed in using an alias she'd be Manure Queen of the Western Hemisphere? "Couple nights."

The she-ra swung the register around and wrote some numbers next to his name. "Like I said, twenty-five a night, cash in advance. Two nights in advance, you get a fifteen percent discount. Comes to forty-two fifty. They're tears, aren't they?"

Elvis knew what the she-ra was talking about, but he said, "What's tears?"

The she-ra reached out her hand again but stopped short of his face and kept it hanging there pointing, like a dancer or something, like she knew she shouldn't touch him again. "Five little teardrops running down your cheek. Did it hurt? Did it hurt when they tattooed right close to your eye like that?"

Elvis shrugged. It would've word up certain hurt if he hadn't blown a flute of ice before letting Tommy Needles do his thing. "Didn't have them done all at once. Had them done like over time, like."

The she-ra let her hand fall slowly, slowly. "What do they mean? I mean . . . are they . . . did they . . . Did someone *die,* did your friends, did your family *die?* I know, I know, it's none of my business." Real quick, the she-ra held her hand out to shake, like she couldn't go a minute longer without introducing herself. "Renata. Renata Kazmeyer."

The she-ra was short and had to go up on tiptoe to get clearance for her elbow over the counter. Her hand was small but strong. " 'S up?"

"Is it Mike or Michael?" Renata Kazmeyer said. "Some Michaels like Michael and some like Mike."

Slamdunking downtown Michael Jordan was always Michael, 'cept when he was Air, never Mike. "Michael."

"Pleased to meet you, Michael."

" 'Eased to meet you."

"And I love those teardrops, I really do. They're sad, and, well, I shouldn't say this, I know, but I will, they're *very* sexy."

Little tiny tits, scrawny bowlegs—Renata Kazmeyer looked a lot like Jenny Swale: not Elvis's type of she-ra. She wore jeans and a plaid shirt with the shoulder strap of a man's undershirt peeking out up beside her collar, which he knew got some guys worked up but which didn't hold a candle as far as he was concerned to a short, shiny red or gold or silver dress, cut down to the nipples practically in front and so tight over the ass you could play snare drums on it. But something about the way she said *sexy*, and her saying it at all, made Elvis's Louisville Slugger try to stand up and holler in spite of his tight 501s.

And thinking back now on Renata Kazmeyer's saying *sexy*, Elvis's Louisville Slugger stood just about straight up and hollered under his Fruit of the Loom.

So Elvis got back in bed and turned Japanese until his Louisville Slugger stopped shouting. He started out with a picture of Renata Kazmeyer on the inside of his eyelids, but she kept changing into Jenny Swale, and Jenny kept biting off his tongue and spitting it at him, so he switched to a picture of Lux Two-Oh from the J. Lux was short for Electrolux, like the vacuum cleaner, because he could clean anyone's Louisville Slugger, and two-oh was the number of Louisville Sluggers he'd cleaned in a row in the weight room one time before the bulls wondered how come it was so quiet in there, no clanking and grunting and shit, and took a look and found out why and put a stop to it just as Lux was about to make it two-one. Give Elvis a she-ra anytime when it came to doing the nasty, but when it came to getting his Louisville Slugger cleaned, Lux Two-Oh was the finest he had ever run across.

Elvis was sure he'd go back to sleep now, but he still couldn't, so he got up and put on his 501s and a T-shirt and Luther Todd's Reebok Twilight Zone Pumps and went out and started the Delta 88 he'd found sitting all by its lonesome in a strip mall on some highway somemotheringwhere and boosted it to put it out of its misery. It was colder than the mother bing, and Elvis didn't want to sit in a cold car while it warmed up.

Back inside, Elvis turned on the radio and tried to pick up WBL Kicking S, but all he got was fuzz. He found some station that was playing Barry White, "I Wanna Do It Good to Ya," and probably thought it was the jam. Shit. Not even twenty-four hours away from him, and Elvis missed the shit out of Frankie Crocker. There wasn't no other like that brother—word mothering up. When Frankie Crocker wasn't on your radio, your radio wasn't really on—word mothering up. And it was going to get worse, 'cause the farther away he went, the farther away Frankie'd be.

Elvis took his gold tooth caps out of an ashtray on the dresser and slipped them over his front teeth. He had them flipped around—he liked the etched pair of dice (six the hard way) on the left and the etched crown on the right—but he wasn't going to be wearing them out, so he just left them. He grinned at himself for a while in the dresser mirror, then went into the bathroom and grinned at himself a while longer. Then he took the caps off and wrapped them in a piece of toilet paper and put them in the money pocket of his 501s.

Elvis gave the radio one more try, and tripped over a she-ra news broadcaster telling him what he didn't need a she-ra news broadcaster to tell him, that five-ohs from "throughout the tri-state area and beyond" were "scouring the Eastern seaboard in search of clues" to his "whereabouts."

"Meanwhile," the she-ra announcer said, *"the brutal slayings have fueled the debate over the death penalty in New York State. State Senate leaders met in Albany this morning to consider scheduling a vote to override Governor Margaret O'Keefe's veto of capital punishment. State Senator Steven Jay Poole of Manhattan, a former New York City police officer disabled in a drug shootout, says the governor is soft on crime. . . ."*

Poole's voice again—smooth, jagged, sharp, cold, killing: *"The governor accuses us of standing in the way of her 'solution' to this kind of bestiality. Her 'solution' is a bill that would make this kind of bestiality punishable by life in jail. No parole. She says the electric chair is not a deterrent. And maybe it's not. But what kind of deterrent would a life sentence be, and the hell with deterrence, anyway. What about punishment? I say no more slaps on the wrist for people like Elvis Polk. I say the electric chair's too good for people like Elvis Polk. I say off with the heads of people like Elvis Polk."*

Cheers in the background. Shouts of *"Yeah, yeah! Off with their heads!"* Then the she-ra announcer again. *"Governor O'Keefe expressed her condolences to the families and friends of the slain detectives. But, as she has in the past, O'Keefe charged that the Republicans value the death penalty as a political issue and don't really want a change in the law. . . .*

"Also in Albany—"

Elvis flicked off the radio. He put on his Triple Fat Goose and went out the door. Renata Kazmeyer was sitting on the hood of the 88, straddling the slim chrome hood ornament. "This your father's Oldsmobile?"

Elvis didn't scope much tube in the J, but he knew Elvis's ex–old lady and daughter (Elvis Presley's) one time did an Oldsmobile commercial. That normally would've been reason enough for him to pass up boosting the 88, but boosters can't always be choosers. "Friend's," Elvis said, knowing Renata Kazmeyer's next question would be if his *friend* lived in Scranton, since the license-plate frame had the name of a dealer in Scranton, did *he* live in Scranton too?

Renata Kazmeyer didn't ask her next question right away though. She just looked at Elvis for a while, her hands in the pockets of a red down ski jacket that was leaking feathers out of a bunch of seams, her shoulders hunched so the collar was up around her ears, her knees jiggling to speed up the circulation, or maybe because she'd had too much coffee and had to pee, or maybe she was on something. Her hair, dark brown indoors, a lot of red in it outside like this, was pushed back over her ears; she had a diamond stud in one earlobe, in the other just an empty hole. Her eyes were wide apart and spooky pale, not like an albino's, like Pink Jeff's from the J, but close.

"You want to hear my life story, Michael?" Renata Kazmeyer finally said. "The short version or the long version—take your pick."

Shit. She was never going to forget him, which meant he was going to have to pop her.

6

"Ask *Jim*."

"Who?"

In what Bill Ellis, NewsFocus 14's executive producer, called (out of her hearing) her Humor the Handicapped voice, Samantha Cox said, "Your *boyfriend*."

All of a sudden Ann Jones felt very tired for ten in the morning and very old for thirty-five. "*Joe* Cullen isn't . . ." *Isn't my boyfriend,* she started to say. *Boyfriends I had in high school, in college, in the days when I lived with two roommates, one's cat, the other's stuffed animals, all our bicycles, in a one-bedroom apartment at Seventy-second and York, a scarf on the doorknob meant* Go see a movie; *now that I'm thirty-five going on ninety-five, now that I live in a garden apartment on Riverside Drive (oh, all right—it's a cement backyard), I have a lover, a paramour, a . . . suitor, a . . . a . . .* But she let it slide. "He isn't a source. I have police sources, but it's been understood on both sides of the fence for a long time that he's not one of them. We couldn't function, either of us, if—"

"Then *I'll* ask him," Samantha said, and flipped open her Filofax as if Cullen's number had been written down there all along. "Were either of these cops ever the target of an Internal Affairs investigation? It's a simple question. He doesn't have to go on the record."

"Oh, I don't—"

Ellis butted in protectively. "Sam, I think we have to respect the arrangements Ann has in place, not only with her sources, but with those who, for whatever reason, aren't her sources."

Samantha's long neck got even longer; her tongue flicked and flashed. "Of course you think that, Bill. No surprise there. Anybody surprised? Of course not." She snapped her Filofax shut and rose up and up from the sofa on which she presided over morning staff meetings, a cobra in a red knit surplice dress. "You've never been ambiguous, Bill, from the moment Ann joined our happy family, about your respect for her ar*range*ments." And Samantha sashayed out the door, hooking one finger over her shoulder to summon after her her assistant—her momentary assistant, a young woman whose name no one had bothered to learn, for she would be gone in a few weeks, her ego limp and flat, her spine warped into a perpetual kowtow, to be succeeded by another young woman whose name no one would bother to learn.

Ann made a move to follow Samantha, but Ellis waved her back in her chair. "Comes with the territory. I'm surprised we haven't had a walkout since you came aboard. Once upon a time—remember, Terry? Chris?—we had two or three a week."

Terry Tubbs, the sports guy, and Christine Rucker, the consumer reporter, the show's senior talent, smiled thinly; their nostalgia had a bitter aftertaste. Webb Crutchfield, the weatherman; Nola Moskowitz, legal affairs; Charlie Peck, the movie and theater critic; Roz Imberman, gossip, looked forlorn. They were newer kids on the block, and had only *heard* of Samantha's legendary serial eruptions.

Ann felt a longing too—for blue jeans, T-shirts, sneakers, feet up on her desk, laptop on her lap, Fritos in a drawer, picking her nose if she felt like it, plucking at her panties if they got all in a bunch, taking all afternoon, all day, several days, to come up with a lead, a word, coming up with a lead and taking the rest of the day off, going to a movie at the Thalia, when there was a Thalia, or Theatre 80: longing for good old *City* magazine.

Ann had gone from the University of Michigan *Daily* to the *Daily News,* and, after eighteen months, from the *Daily News* to *City,* where she had imagined she would work until she dropped—it was that *gemütlich.* Then, in what to Ann had been an instance of life imitating *Falcon Crest,* her rich millionaire boss had gotten all tangled up in a sex and murder scandal so messy it had nearly ensnared her too; it was terribly complicated. Another rich millionaire had bought *City*'s offices and plant, changed the magazine's name for form's sake to *Metro,* and offered Ann a job. She had declined, for the place's vibes were beyond bad, *and* she couldn't work for a magazine called *Metro. Metro* was a word that was thrown around in Sun Belt cities, renascent Rust Belt cities, cities that were in no way at all metropolises (*mother cities,* in the Greek); they were bimbos or spinsters.

The tense equality that had prevailed at *City* was what Ann missed most. There had been stars on the book—she had been one of them—but they had shone one at a time, when one of them had something to say that was sexier than what the others had. The staff hadn't all been happy all of the time about the arrangement, but neither had they been stupid: There could be *only* one cover story, and sooner rather than later, usually, your turn would come around.

Here at 14 it was all Samantha. Queen bee and drones, drill instructor and grunts, high priestess and disciples, shark and pilot fish—the talent sometimes had metaphor contests to define their relationship to her. Whatever Samantha was and whatever they were, she was large and they were minuscule. Even when she wasn't around, on assignment or on vacation or off for the weekend, Samantha still got top billing over Nola or Nancy Albright (on vacation herself this week—"somewhere they've never heard of the cunt" was all the destination Nancy would tell Ann), who would intro and outtro themselves by saying, "Sitting in for Samantha Cox, I'm . . ."

Old times be damned, never mind Samantha, the money was better here, a whole hell of a lot better. The money made do-able what Ann had always denigrated doing—sitting with her elbows on a piece of hypermodern furniture, her fingertips on a script she wasn't reading from, peering at a prompter she *was* reading from but was pretending she wasn't, explaining to viewers who had tuned in mostly to hear tomorrow's weather forecast the events they could figure out for themselves if they just looked at the newsfilm, whose existence was the reason the report was on in the first place: No pictures, No Story (oh, maybe a headline)—that was the rule, the (naturally) unwritten rule.

Cappy and Tippy and Mopsy and Suzie, the yuppie newshounds —newsbitches: That was how Ann Jones of *City* magazine used to characterize female television-news reporters—interchangeable, immaculate, incurious, inconsequential. And now she was one of them, spiffy and spangled. She had her dresses made (Look, Ma— *dresses*) in East Side boutiques that had her measurements on file and FedExed her swatches and patterns so she didn't have to *shop*. She spent for shoes what she would have once balked at spending for a coat. She got her hair done once a week, instead of once in a while (by a coiffeur who shuttled from busy client's office to busy client's showroom to busy client's studio in a stretch limo driven by a blonde in skimpy leather livery), and had traded in a collegiate French braid for a power twist. In restaurants where she would have once been shown the door she was shown to advantageous banquettes by headwaiters who knew her on sight and knew her usual. In the old days she had sometimes undressed for bed and been unable to remember how that rubber band got around her wrist; nowadays she wouldn't recall having put on that Tridor Oyster Perpetual Lady Datejust Rolex.

Bedtime, nowadays, was closer to the bedtime of club kids than of thirty-five-year-olds with garden apartments on Riverside Drive. On her first day on the job, following a couple of weeks of contract negotiations, business lunches, informal orientation, some light coaching, facing the reality that that first day wasn't going to end until nearly the next day, Ann remembered a television interview with Katharine Hepburn, who recalled her joy at getting her first part in a play and her simultaneous horror on realizing, after years of early to bed and early to rise, studying acting, voice, dance, that she'd been training to work at night, when she was no good for anything. Ann was getting only a little better: night work was not restful, and what a mess it made of your friendships, your . . . (why was there no good word for this in a language with nearly a half million words?) your . . . association with your lover, your paramour, your . . . your suitor, your . . . your . . .

"Annie?"

Ellis, wanting the only thing he ever wanted—more more more on Quintana Davidoff. Quintana Davidoff *was* still dead, though there were heelmarks from here to Montauk that testified to News-Focus 14's struggle to keep her from crossing the bar. There might not be life after death for Quintana, but there sure as hell was videotape. "Nothing airable. Mark Gunther, the dean at Mid-dlebrooks, is trying to reach Yo Yo Ma. He's on tour in the Far East. Quintana took his master class. Gunther's not sure, though, that he'll go so far as to say Quintana was the next Casals."

A former three-pack-a-day smoker (Chesterfield) who now chewed sixty sticks of Nicorette, Ellis shifted his gum around. He hadn't traveled all these miles, from morning man slash news direc-tor slash weatherman slash sales manager slash janitor of a windmill-powered (practically) AM radio station in Feedbag, Iowa, to commander in chief of a local news show with a ten share of television's cruelest market, by letting pansy deans of music schools tell him how far someone would go in front of a camera. The disfig-uring, dispiriting, career-vaporizing crucible of experience had given him not only his snow-white hair, his palsy that spilled the drinks he poured to still it, his habit of reaching around behind him to feel for a dagger between his shoulder blades; it had also given him the certainty that people would walk right up to the brink of self-destruction at the sight of a camera, would go over the edge at the merest encouragement, and sometimes all on their own. Everyone wanted to be on television, it was as simple as that, *and* everyone knew that everyone else was competing with them for airtime. By their lonesome, they came up with their own gimmicks, their own hooks; invited, encouraged, they trampled you in their rush to hit their marks.

And that was just on run-of-the-mill stories. On *good* stories, world-class tragedies like Quintana Davidoff's, they lined up around the block. Yo Yo Ma would *pay* to be bumped to the head of the queue. Casals would pay. *Bach* would fucking pay. So don't tell Billy Ellis, Mister Pansy Music School Dean.

Fourteen years old, a Middlebrooks freshman, first cello in the *senior* orchestra, right wing on the coed junior-varsity field-hockey team, third board on the girls' chess team, French, Math, and Biology clubs, rehearsing the part of Esther in *Meet Me in St. Louis*, B'nai B'rith Girls, straight As, Meryl Streep look-alike, daughter of a controversial economist and a writer-illustrator of children's books (mother and father, respectively, a reversal of stereotypes and expectations), Quintana Davidoff had been walking, late in the afternoon of the Saturday after Thanksgiving, from a bus stop on Riverside Drive to her brownstone near West End Avenue, when she was struck on the head by a bottle that plummeted from the roof or an upper floor of one or the other of two contiguous fifteen-story apartment houses. She died in that twilight instant.

The afternoon, the day, the several days before, had been unseasonably clement, and Quintana, wearing jeans, a Middlebrooks sweatshirt, a blue jean jacket with a portrait of Roland Gift hand-painted on the back, had been dawdling, according to witnesses, perhaps enjoying the setting sun's lurid skypainting over the Palisades. She had been at a friend's, a clarinetist's, playing Mozart (or, as Quintana liked to say, to get a rise out of her teachers, jamming the Wolfman), and was carrying her cello on her hip; she had stopped at one point to shift the case from one hip to the other. The speculation wouldn't end: What if she hadn't . . . If only she had . . .

The bottle was a liter of eighty-proof Stolichnaya vodka, purchased, according to its price sticker, at a busy discount liquor store on Broadway, God knew when and by whom. The seal had been broken and Quintana's hair and clothes dampened with alcohol, meaning the bottle had been partly full (or partly empty; different observers put it differently) when it struck her and broke into several large shards.

Fingerprints, cried armchair detectives from the Battery to the Bronx, and, sure enough, there were dozens of partials. But what to compare them with, when dozens of innocent fingers would have touched that bottle from the distillery to the retailer? *To the prints of the tenants in the two buildings,* the armchair sleuths answered. Impractical, maybe even unconstitutional, especially since a look at the roster of those tenants would make any investigator careful where he stuck his nose: an executive of the American Civil Liberties Union, a best-selling gadfly novelist, a feminist crusader against pornography, an actor-environmentalist, a psychologist-author on parent abuse, a Nobel laureate physicist, a city councilman, a congressman's legislative affairs director, a state senator (the very Steven Jay Poole who was calling for the heads of cop killers)—individuals unaccustomed to being pushed around. The rest of the iceberg: a retired premier danseur, a folk singer, a biographer of movie stars, a playwright, doctors, dentists, lawyers, bankers, brokers, psychiatrists, professors, a composer, a radio talk-show host, a convicted cocaine smuggler turned restaurateur—typical inhabitants of typical Upper West Side buildings (buildings on the north-south thoroughfares, at any rate), what one newspaper columnist (who lived in the Village) called "liberal luxury liners steaming serenely across a sea of crime, degradation, violence, and corruption." Notwithstanding the foul weather, the passengers were up on deck, hoping to be interviewed by boarding party after boarding party of reporters.

So who the hell was some pansy music-school dean to tell Billy Ellis *any*thing? "Well, it's your story, Annie, and if you say there's nothing airable . . ."

It was Ann's story because Ann had gotten there first. She had been out running in Riverside Park in that same balmy twilight and was on her way back to her garden apartment. She had called for a crew from a pay phone on the corner, spruced up with a hairbrush borrowed from a woman cop who recognized her and said she was a fan, and went on the air live just after six, wearing her Hind Night Blade tights, her Russell Athletic sweatshirt, her New Balance 495s, the bar flashers and alley lights and beacons of whitetops and EMS ambulances gyrating behind her, before the yuppie newsbitches— the other yuppie newsbitches—even knew what hit them. She had found some new angle on the story nearly every weekday since, and she knew that to say she was out of angles was to say that she had slowed to where the newsbitch pack might not only catch up to her but overtake her and devour her.

"Well . . ." Ellis waited a while longer, for more more more on Quintana Davidoff wasn't all he wanted (Samantha had been right). He wanted to sweep clean the top of his rosewood desk, sweep away the Emmy, the ashtray he now used for gum wrappers, the photograph of his ridiculous wife and their preposterous sons, bend Ann over facedown and fuck her cunt and her ass; he wanted to lie on the sisal rug and sit Ann down on his face; he wanted to perch up on the windowsill, with its views of 30 Rock, Black Rock, the old ABC building—who the hell owned it now? some Japanese, probably —his own apartment building on Central Park South (though not of his apartment, where his ridiculous wife was surely salivating for her first martini of the day; his apartment faced the fucking park), while Ann sucked him off and sucked him off again. Until that happened—or until it didn't—he would endure her reluctance, acquired on that candyass magazine, that candyass newspaper before that, to go public with the insubstantial and the unsubstantiated.

"Well . . ." Ann waited right back at Ellis. She knew what he wanted—everything he wanted—and she wasn't going to give him any of it. Her body she wasn't going to give him because she didn't sleep with men she worked with—not bosses, not copy boys—and because she had . . . an association with Joe Cullen, her lover, her paramour, her . . . her suitor, her . . . her . . . Her story she wasn't going to give him because there was really only one thing more *to* give: the answer to the question, Who dropped the bottle on Quintana Davidoff's head?

Ann knew the answer. She had known it since early on the morning after the Saturday after Thanksgiving. Nobody knew that Ann knew. Joe Cullen, her lover, her paramour, her . . . her suitor, her . . . her . . . , with whom she had had a drink at Docks just after midnight on the Saturday after Thanksgiving, didn't know she knew. Her best friend, Mabel Parker, with whom she talked on the phone every day and had breakfast every Saturday, didn't know she knew. Her mother, back in Michigan (where she'd been born and raised, as well as gone to college), and her brother, out in California, whom she phoned weekly, didn't know she knew. Elfriede Milford, her therapist, whom she saw Wednesday mornings at eight, didn't know she knew. Someday, maybe, they'd all know; right now, well . . . That was all: Well . . .

Ellis breathed in and out through his nose, wanting a cigarette, a pack, a carton. "Well . . ."

"Well," Ann agreed. "Un*less* . . ."

Ellis sat up straighter. "What?"

"You've got to give this to someone else, give it to Nola, you didn't hear it from me, I wasn't at this meeting, I didn't bring it up."

"And what *is* it—this *it*?"

"Poole. Steve Poole. He's looking for ways to take the heat off him and his neighbors. He wants to fly the Davidoffs up to Albany for the opening of the death-penalty debate."

Ellis smiled. Debates on anything were deadly stories. This would be a story with pictures, pictures, pictures. "*Is* he?"

Nola—Nola Moskowitz, Esq., LL.B. NYU Law—sat forward. "I

don't get it. Even if someone deliberately dropped that bottle— threw it, even *aimed* it—they'd never be able to prove premeditation. They might find who killed Quintana, but the killer won't get the chair. The Davidoffs'll be a distraction; Poole's credibility'll be damaged."

"Nola?" Ellis said.

"I know." Nola got her stuff together. "Get thee to Albany."

"Sorry, Nole," Ann said. *"Al*bany."

Nola patted Ann's head as she went to the door. "I'll get even. I have sources in Hartford, Trenton. *Harr*isburg."

7

"Name?" *Crack.*

"Cullen."

"With?" *Crack.*

"Uh, I'm alone."

Crack. "What *com*pany?"

"Oh. Uh, the police."

Crack. "You're *kid*ding! They're back to*geth*er? Sting? Stewart Copeland? *All* of them?" *Crack.*

Cullen flashed his shield. "Sergeant Joseph Cullen, New York City Police Department, Internal Affairs Unit, to see Jo Dante. Yes, I will have a seat. Thank you."

The receptionist's name, Cullen with the Police, hip to clues, deduced from a monogrammed Mickey Mouse hat pinned up on a bulletin board behind her, was Mystee. Mystee's Fashion Tech eyes performed laser surgery on Cullen's balls as he went to sit in an entomic leather-and-steel chair on the other side of VU Sound Magic's foyer. The chair was tipped back as if ready for lift-off, the carpet was deep enough to wade in, the walls were covered with some fabric thicker than most carpets, the lighting was indirect, the air smelled and tasted synthetic. The only clue that there was a world outside, a world with seasons and ceremonies, was a foot-high artificial Christmas tree on a table that looked like a meteorite that had recently landed next to the chair. The tree was decorated, Cullen saw on leaning very close through the gloom, with microcassettes, and he now understood that those plastic rectangles Mystee was wearing for earrings were microcassettes too. When in Rome . . . When in the Brill Building.

Mystee cracked one more crack, then herded her gum into her cheek. She picked up the phone and called an extension, using a pencil to push the buttons, for her fingernails were mandarin. While she waited for someone to pick up, she checked her hairdo in the glass of a heavy door off to her right that seemed to lead back into VU's bowels, jabbing with her nails at her wild orange tangle, doing nothing apparent to Cullen with the Police to alter it, but apparently satisfying herself, for she swiveled away from her reflection, giving a last good-bye look over her shoulder, to rummage in a vast shoulderbag for something.

An emery board. Scratch, scratch, scratch.

Finally: "Jo? . . . Mystee." She whispered, but so fiercely she might as well have shouted. "There's a *cop* here. . . . I swear to *God* . . . Yeah, a guy. An *old* guy . . . Yeah . . . Yeah . . . 'Kay." Mystee hung up and lifted herself up on her elbows to see over the rim of whatever the furniture is called that receptionists sit behind. "Sir?"

Cullen tried to raise his eyebrows—his old eyebrows—as high as she had raised hers. "Yes?"

"Jo'll be right out."

"Thank you."

Crack. "Kinaxya sumthin?"

"Sorry?"

"Can I *ax* you sumthin?"

Had he ever killed anybody? "Sure."

"Jeverkill anybody?" *Crack.*

"No."

Her elbows slid apart and her eyebrows slumped disappointedly. "*Nev*uh?"

"I'd remember."

She continued descending, then had an idea, and propelled herself partway back up. "Jever—"

"Yes, I have seen people killed, and I don't want to talk about it."

"*Okay. Jes*us. Chill *out.*" *Crack.*

Cullen ground his teeth for a while, and was still grinding them when Jo Dante pushed through the heavy door and walked up to where he sat, hand extended. "Sorry you had to wait. I'm Jo. You're not so old. I know—you expected someone small and dark. My mother's Finnish—I got her hair and skin and eyes; my father's Italian—I got his name. There's nothing I can do about it. Something wrong?"

Nothing much. Just that there was a school of thought that held that an important catalyst in the chain of events that culminated, one hundred forty-five days ago (but who was counting?), with Cullen winged and his dear sweet old partner, Neil Zimmerman, hammered, had been Cullen's tumbling irresponsibly for an exotic principal in an exotic murder investigation, a woman with olive skin (Jo Dante's was arctic-white), with dark dark hair cut in a ducktail and pompadour (Jo Dante's was pale and straight as straw and framed her face like a helmet of white-gold mail), a woman whose accessories included black French-maid French-whore garterless stockings and glen-plaid Bruno Magli pumps. (Jo Dante's footgear was gray ragg wool socks and Timberland moccasins, the laces untied, the lace ends fashioned, à la mode, into hangman's nooses.)

So although he struggled up out of the leather-and-steel chair and took her hand and appreciated the strength of her grip, appreciated that she didn't back away, that she stood her ground, hands in the hip pockets of her faded blue jeans now, flat chest right out there for him to see that it wasn't that flat, that there were strong surges against the plain white cotton camisole she wore under a man's faded blue work shirt, somewhat unbuttoned; although he looked right into her eyes and appreciated that she looked right back into his, appreciated that she was so tall that they were right there, her eyes, that they were sky-blue, her eyes; although he smelled her and appreciated the blend of tobacco and coffee and nameless new scents and her, Cullen wasn't going to tumble irresponsibly for Jo Dante. He was sure of that; he knew it like he knew the back of his hand.

For one thing, she wasn't his type. She wasn't tall enough, she wasn't flat-chested enough, her eyes weren't blue enough, her work shirt and blue jeans weren't faded enough, her camisole wasn't plain white enough, there wasn't enough tobacco in her blend, not enough coffee, not enough nameless new scents, not enough her. Her skin wasn't arctic-white enough, her hair wasn't pale and straight enough, not enough like a helmet of white-gold mail.

"No. Nothing wrong. I'm Joe too. Joe Cullen."

They looked right at each other for a moment more and thought about what it would be like if they married: Joe and Jo Cullen, Jo and Joe Cullen. Joe and Jo too, Jo and Joe too. Joe I and Jo II, Jo I and Joe II. By Doctor Seuss.

She spoke first. She spoke at all. "I'm on a deadline. If we could go inside, it'd be helpful. You're wondering what I'm doing at work when my roommate just got murdered. It keeps me from thinking about it. Did they catch him? They didn't catch him yet, did they?"

They meaning the police, whom he was with. "No."

"In show biz, they catch them in an hour—on TV; or two—in the movies. It must make your job harder. People get their hopes up."

They were already halfway down a long, narrow hallway, having gone through the heavy door and walked along two shorter narrow hallways. There were more heavy doors along the way, and through some that were ajar Cullen got glimpses of dim-lit rooms, consoles, reels, tresses of film and tape. "This is my first time in the Brill Building. It's not what I expected. What goes on here exactly?"

"You expected Carole King and Gerry Goffin, Leiber and Stoller, people trying out lyrics on one another? We do sound re-creation. We're foley artists. We never see the light of day. Jenny used to say I was genetically suited to be one. I'm like an albino fish in a cave."

Cullen said, "Foley?"

Jo Dante opened a heavy door at the end of the narrow hall and held it for Cullen. "Did you know Jenny?"

Cullen stopped on the brink of the room's blackness. He wouldn't have wanted to enter it alone; he appreciated that she was going to go in with him. And he appreciated that all of the questions they were asking each other weren't getting answered, that there were gaps and overlaps, loose ends—as in real life, not as in show biz. He wasn't going to tumble irresponsibly for her, he knew that like he knew the back of his hand, but he could appreciate things about her.

He wasn't going to tumble irresponsibly for her, above all, because he was a pro. The PC himself had said so, sitting on the faux Shaker bench in the hall outside his office just the other evening, telling Cullen about the allegation of an officer who hadn't been born when *he* became a pro that he had *har*assed her sexually.

"You're a pro. Treat it like any other investigation. *Any* other."

"Difficult," Cullen had said. "She's dead, you're the PC, we're old friends. Maybe impossible."

They were all alone in the hall, but Hriniak lowered his voice. "Don't talk this up, but over the past year we've been ranking Ds according to their IR—their Integrity Rating. You're in the ninety-ninth percentile."

"IR."

"I know, it's bullshit, but it's something to go on. People trust you is what I'm saying. Plus, realistically, how long has it been since you and I were really close? I'm busy, you're busy. I'm on this floor, you're downstairs or out in the street. Our paths cross every couple of months, getting in or out of an elevator usually, you usually with a buddy or your partner, which makes it hard for me to just stop and breeze with you 'cause they get nervous, I *am* the PC, me with Marie or Eleanor running after me yelling what I forgot to do 'cause I'm hurrying to what I'm already late for. Yeah, we used to talk on the phone, but I don't remember the last time. There were some dinners, the wives included, but—no offense, Joe—I'm kind of vague on when they were."

"The last one," Cullen said, "was at your house, Christmas, 1979. I was a detective two and still married to Connie. You were a DCI with all your hair, Beryl was still a blonde."

Hriniak laughed, rocking back on his buttocks on the faux Shaker bench till his feet were off the floor, punching a thigh with a fist. "A DCI with all my hair. Beryl still a blonde." He laughed and rocked and punched again.

It hadn't been that funny; it had been very nearly insubordinate. "Things all right with Beryl, Phil?"

Hriniak stared, then remembered that this was an investigation like any other and that it was *sex*ual harassment they were talking about. He composed himself, shot his cuffs, whisked his lapel with his fingertips—like a wise guy, Cullen couldn't help thinking, a wise guy buying time. What had Ann called Hriniak a couple of weeks ago, making Cullen laugh? The *capo di tutti* cops. "Look. Jenny Swale. You know Bernstein, don't you? The Department head-shrinker?"

Cullen got wary. Bernstein (precisely, the Department psychologist) had been leaving messages suggesting Cullen come and see him ever since he came back on duty after he was winged and his dear sweet old partner, Neil Zimmerman, was hammered one hundred forty-five days ago (but who was counting?). Cullen hadn't returned the calls: He was busy, Bernstein was busy; Bernstein was on his floor, Cullen on his, or out in the street. Their paths crossed every couple of months, getting in or out of an elevator usually, Cullen usually with a buddy or his partner, which made it hard for him to just stop and breeze with Bernstein because they got nervous, Bernstein *was* the Department headshrinker, Bernstein with his secretary running after him yelling what he'd forgotten to do because he was hurrying to what he was already late for. "I know of him."

"I talked to him doctor-patient. I'm telling you what we talked about, so you can ask him about it. I'm suspending the privilege is what I'm saying."

Talked to him doctor-patient. Cullen had wished he had thought to look at it that way. He had been reluctant—understandably reluctant, he thought, given his age, his old-fashioned upbringing, which had inculcated him that only the daffy and deranged needed mental-health professionals—to have *a therapy session with a headshrinker;* but it would have been a piece of cake, no sweat, hey, no problemo, to *talk* to Bernstein *doctor-patient.* If Hriniak could do it, being older, far and far more old-fashioned, less in touch with his emotions and more frightened of becoming familiar with them, Cullen could do it. He would call Bernstein in the morning. Rats— tomorrow was Sunday. Well, then, he'd call him Monday. Or maybe next Monday; he had some things to clear up. Or next month. Next month might be better, next month looked pretty wide open. As of now. You never knew what might come up. You couldn't know, there was no way to tell in advance.

"He said, Bernstein said, that, uh, that Jenny Swale was a, that she had a, that she was a . . . I mean, the way I understood it, Joe, there're women who get this idea that a man, it could be any man or a particular man—"

"Phil? Hang on a sec, okay? Please. You said treat it like any investigation. Any investigation that had a jacket, I'd start by reading the jacket. So why don't I do that? I'll do it tonight, I'll do it right now."

"Yeah, well," Hriniak said, "the jacket was disappeared."

"Oh fuck."

"Yeah."

"What about the backup? What about RR?" RR (not to be confused with IR) was Chief of Detectives Abruzzi's stepchild, brought to him for adoption by a prospective son-in-law, a data-processing entrepreneur: Redundant Record-keeping, a means of bringing the Department's filing system into the twentieth century just in time for the arrival of the twenty-first. "Where're the computer disks? The backup tapes?"

Hriniak tried not to smile. "Shows you whoever disappeared the jacket knew what he was doing. The backup's been erased or deleted."

"Shows you whoever disappeared it wasn't you."

Hriniak had to smile. " 'Cause I don't know a backup disk from a slipped disk? You're right, I don't. Suzie Price, Ruth, Abruzzi— they're all up on this high-tech crap. I'm just sitting on my duff watching it whiz by, thinking, So what if I don't pick it up? I'm looking at retirement in a couple of years, anyway, in less than that it might all be done by robots. You know, when I was starting out . . ."

Cullen didn't want to hear about it, to hear about the days when paperwork was done on stone tablets; when men were men, and women, except for a few bulldykes, maneaters, and congenital spinsters, knew better than to join the PD; when sexual harassment meant leaving the seat up on a station house's only toilet. "What was *in* the jacket, Phil?"

Hriniak looked startled to find himself back in the present so soon after stepping into the past. He jammed his fingers together, like a confessant. "Memorial Day weekend. I was going down to Washington in the middle of June for House Judiciary Committee hearings on street crime, Beryl's sister was in town with her dipshit husband, I came in here to work on my statement. It was nice and dead. An hour after I got here maybe, I heard the elevator. Somebody from Headquarters detail on his rounds, I figured, or maybe Braverman coming back upstairs from the canteen. He went down to watch the Indy 500; I can't tell first place from last place, but he likes that shit. Then I heard this radio, playing loud, real loud, louder even than you'd play it if you were all by yourself, listening to a big band or something—Goodman, Bird, Dexter Gordon—like you'd play it if you were drunk or stoned, or wanted to really piss somebody off.

"I think it's on the street. I go to the window to see where it's coming from, wishing I had SWAT training and one of those Luger caliber carbines, so there'd be one less boom box in the world. Then I zero in on it—it's inside, down the hall, in Admin. I dial Admin, no answer. I go down the hall, knock on the door, which is always locked, it's set on a buzzer, no answer. I try the door, it's not locked, I go in.

"There's Jenny Swale, up on a desk, dancing to the music. She has her back to me and I don't recognize her at first, I think she's someone else. She's got her hair piled up on her head in a way she doesn't usually wear it, she usually wears it down or in a ponytail, she's wearing a miniskirt like they used to wear in the sixties, I mean *real* short, a pair of cowboy boots, a kind of cowboy string necktie, big hoop earrings, and a smile. No shirt, no bra, no nothing upstairs.

"You said you're not up on this floor much, Joe, you don't remember Jenny. She was cute, not a beauty, she was thin, she never wore clothes like that, she wore regular skirts and dresses, but mostly pants, not tight pants, and I don't even remember what kind of tops, but whatever kind of tops they didn't get the troops riled up, which doesn't take a whole hell of a lot, frankly, Marie and Eleanor get them riled up sometimes, and they're both ex-nuns. She was somebody, Jenny, who a lot of guys would be comfortable taking home to meet their folks, but I can't see a lot of them saying, 'Hey, Jen, why don't you take your shirt off and dance on a desk?'

"Anyway . . . I start to shut the door, go back to my office, work on my goddamn statement. Hey, I can live with the radio on, you want to play the radio, you're working on a holiday, play the radio, no problem, go ahead, don't mind me, sorry I interrupted. I feel somebody behind me, I feel the way I felt the only time a bad guy ever threw down on me, Washington Heights, October '62, Dee Dee Estefan, a pimp, he was hammering other pimps' girls. He pulled the trigger, Dee Dee, his piece jammed, Teddy Brock shot it out of his hand, broke his wrist, like he was Tom Mix or something. Teddy Brock . . ."

Cullen let Hriniak slog through his memories this time; it wasn't the time, this time, to harness him to the present.

Hriniak didn't stay away long. ". . . Anyway, I feel somebody behind me, I turn around, it's Braverman, a Twinkie in one hand, a diet Coke in the other, a look on his face like 'I'll drive you around and get you coffee and watch your ass 'cause that's what I'm paid to do, but don't rub my nose in your shit.' "

"A setup, Phil?" Cullen said. "Is that what you think?"

Hriniak twitched, not wanting to be rushed but knowing too that he was running out of facts, it was time for some conjecture. "The next working day, Jenny filed a grievance, said I promised her a promotion if she stripped for me, danced around while I jerked off, blew me. She listed Braverman as a witness.

"Maslosky came straight to me, said, 'What the fuck?' I said, 'She set me up.' He said, 'Along with *Braverman*?' I said, 'Shit, no.' He said, 'So she's doing this *solo*?' I said, '*Some*body told her I came in on a holiday, *some*body told her I was in the building, *some*body probably even told her Braverman was tired of watching race cars make left turns and now he was on his way back upstairs."

"Why not Braverman?" Cullen said.

" 'Cause he looked sick," Hriniak said. "If he'd set me up, he'd've looked nervous, he'd've looked edgy, he'd've looked wired, but he also would've just pulled it off, so he wouldn't've looked sick."

Cullen didn't follow exactly, but it was that kind of call—a judgment call, a seat-of-the-pants call. "Who knew you came downtown, besides Braverman?"

"Beryl, her sister, her sister's dipshit husband. Braverman's wife. And his kid, I guess. His kid's six. Do six-year-olds know things? I don't remember."

When Cullen's daughter, Tenny, was six (five and ten months, precisely), she had written a poem called "Know":

by Stephanie Cullen

(KNOW)

(a poem)

Who lights the moon?
Who makes the stars?
Who does the sun?
Who does it all?
Why are there mice?
Why are there cows?
I want to know!
I want to I want to I want to know now!
How I wish you would tell me.
I wish you would so.
Oh oh oh oh oh.
Why don't you tell me?
Oh tell me right now!

"When you got here," Cullen said, "who knew you had?"

"You know, there were guys around. I didn't pay attention."

"A holiday, guys're supposed to log in."

" 'Supposed to.' You know how it is, guys double-park, say they're staying five minutes, they don't log in. Other guys don't log in 'cause they think they're too important to log in. You know how it is."

"Who was on the door?"

"Messina. Paul, I think, Messina. HQ detail."

Cullen got up off the faux Shaker bench, suddenly crowded with coincidences.

"What?" Hriniak said.

Cullen could dole this out, troll with it, or just dump it in Hriniak's lap. It was late and he was tired, so he dumped it. "We vetted Paul Messina for a while, Zimmerman and I, three years ago. He was in the Two-Four at the time. He came up clean, but he has a cousin, Nick Messina, who'd just taken a tumble on the SpeedAir job."

"Jesus, Mary, and Joseph," Hriniak said.

"The disappeared jacket," Cullen said, "it's part of the setup, isn't it? It was disappeared to make it look like you tried to cover up, right?"

Hriniak shrugged. "I guess. I don't know. *Speed*Air? Messina and SpeedAir, Elvis Polk and SpeedAir. Polk and Jenny Swale, Jenny Swale and Messina. What's the connection? What is the fucking connection?"

Cullen wondered just how late it was. He wondered if Ann would get him that faux classic watch with yesterday's style and today's accuracy.

"What?" Hriniak said. "Say it."

Cullen said, "Well, *you're* the connection."

8

"Preposterous."

That was Jo Dante's review of Joe Cullen's tale of the talk on the faux Shaker bench.

"Which part of it?"

She looked disappointed; she had known him only a few minutes and already he was patronizing her. "Jenny wasn't very sophisticated. That was one reason I liked living with her. I've been known to be a little too sophisticated."

That was it. That was why Cullen wasn't going to tumble irresponsibly for Jo Dante: She was a little too sophisticated. Although, of course, now that she'd said that, he wanted to know just what she meant by it, just how sophisticated was she? And, of course, he *didn't* want to know what she meant by it, he didn't want to know just how sophisticated she was, he didn't want to hear about it, he wished she hadn't said it. "So you're saying what—that Jenny was too naïve to do a strip-tease for a man? That she was too naïve to entrap the police commissioner? What?"

Jo Dante came up out of what Cullen now knew—was now so-phisticated enough to know—was called a foley pit, a sandbox-size depression in the floor of what he now knew was called a foley stage. She sat on a wooden bench at the edge of the pit and wrestled off the Wellingtons in which she had been sloshing around in the half-foot of mud the consistency of tomato paste that half filled the pit. While Jo Dante had sloshed, she had watched a movie screen above the pit on which had been projected a film clip of a blonde who looked like a faux Kim Basinger, fleeing in what was left of a wet, rent cotton dress through a creepy swamp, looking back with terror-ized eyes over one naked shoulder. Her nipples were long and thin and hard.

Bayou Regrette was the title of the low-budget indie prod (Cullen had glanced at a *Variety* at one point while Jo Dante took a phone call and had swiftly become sophisticated in show-biz lingo) of which this scene was one small piece, and it was Jo Dante's job to match her sloshes with the footfalls of the faux Kim Basinger. Mi-crophones recorded the sounds of the sloshes on reel-to-reel tape (VU meters on the engineer's console registered volume units—Cullen was *so* sophisticated, and in such a short time); the tape would be transferred to film and editors would synch the sounds up with the picture. ("You can't get good live sound on a shot like this," Jo Dante had explained. "The camera dolly, the crew, the ambient sounds—there might be a highway right close by, or an airport—it's all too noisy. You have to lay in the sound.") Other people's shop talk was always interesting.

Jo Dante put her hands inside the Wellingtons and clapped them together over the pit to knock off some of the mud. "Is naïve the opposite of sophisticated? Jenny wasn't naïve. How could she be and be a cop? Mystee, at the desk, said you were old. To her you are, I guess. How long've you been a cop—twenty years?"

"A little more." But who was counting? "Do you think someone put Jenny up to it?"

Jo Dante used her forefingers to shoehorn her Timberlands back on. She had difficulty. When they were finally on, she tugged the discomfort out of her forefingers. "My feet always swell in the mud pit. Must be the boots. She's barefooted, but I find bare feet sound like armpit noises, so I wear the boots. I guess I need different boots."

Different boots were abundant on metal shelves along one wall of the foley stage: motorcycle boots, hiking boots, cowboy boots (two pairs, one with spurs), paratrooper boots, Maine Hunting Shoes, fisherman's waders, fireman's boots, construction-worker boots, jack boots, dominatrix boots, galoshes, ski boots (cross-country and downhill), riding boots (dress, hunt, polo), hobnail boots.

Not only boots: stacked heels, stiletto heels, platform heels, fuck-me pumps, spectator pumps, flats, espadrilles, sandals, loafers, brogues, wingtips, bike shoes (with and without cleats), baseball spikes, football and soccer cleats, hockey skates with rubber guards on the blades, sprinter's spikes, huaraches, clogs, Reef Runners, high-top sneakers, low-cut sneakers, Top-siders, toe shoes, tap shoes, flip-flops, Hush Puppies, shoes with no laces, shoes with loose heels, shoes whose soles drooped like the tongues of tired dogs.

"My tools," Jo Dante had called them, and had explained that she picked the pair that most closely approximated the footwear of the actor or actress the sound of whose gait she was trying to fabricate. (Though not always: Sometimes something altogether unlike the appropriate footwear made the most appropriate sound. "The skates, with the guards on, squeak better than the huaraches," Jo Dante had said. "They sound more . . . tropical, more *mañana*.")

Depending on the surface over which the actor or actress walked or ran or stumbled or skipped or danced or hopped or cartwheeled or limped or crawled or was dragged or shoved, Jo Dante walked or ran or stumbled or skipped or danced or hopped or cartwheeled or limped or crawled or had herself dragged or shoved across the appropriate foley pit. Besides the pit that was now half filled with mud, there was a pit half filled with leaves and twigs and another half filled with sand and gravel; there was a concrete pit, a marble pit, a pit of carpeted parquet; any of the pits could be covered with lids made of wood, linoleum, rubber, steel plate, or metal grating.

Crutches, canes, walking sticks, walkers, umbrellas; an acoustic guitar, a violin, a banjo, a mandolin ("I don't play them; I hold them. Each one makes a different sound when you handle it, when you take it out of its case"); balls, gloves, mitts, bats (aluminum and wood), a hockey stick and puck; bottles of many sizes and shapes, some with liquids in them, some empty; a window frame fitted with blinds, curtains, and drapes; a shopping cart, a kid's wagon, an adze, an axe, a ball-peen hammer, a hacksaw, a ripsaw, a chain saw ("I don't do slice-and-dice, but this works for motorboats, for lawn mowers, for certain old airplanes"), cymbals, a tray of teacups and saucers, another of coffee mugs ("It's just *not* the same sound: Mel's Diner is *not* the Palm Court"); a bomber jacket, a motorcycle jacket, a kid-leather jacket ("Try them on; you'll hear the difference"); a quirt, a yardstick, a riding crop, an authentic vaudeville slapstick; zippers of various sizes sewn into a piece of canvas mounted in a frame ("This is my invention. Other artists make their own and sometimes they call them Dantes. Foley was a Hollywood techie in the thirties—you asked me before").

Still kneading her forefingers, Jo Dante said, "Put her up to it? I don't know what you mean."

The attention she was paying to her hands made Cullen notice the back of his hand: Distended veins (or were they arteries?), birthmarks, snarls, cuts—he didn't recognize it, he didn't know it at all, it was an *old* guy's hand. An old guy who was losing the thread he'd trailed along behind him, who needed to go back to the beginning. "Jenny never said *any*thing to you about filing a grievance?"

Jo Dante just shook her head. She didn't look at him; she kept on stroking her fingers, mesmerizing herself.

"*Noth*ing?"

She focused sharply on Cullen now. "I just said no."

"I know you did. I find that incredible, I'm afraid, that a roommate wouldn't confide something like that. Did she have other close friends she might've told? Less sophisticated friends, maybe?"

Jo Dante finally let go of her fingers and hugged her stomach as though he had jabbed her there. "That wasn't necessary. Did you think I was being provocative? Did you think I wanted you to ask just how sophisticated I was?"

With what he hoped was sophistication, Cullen said, "No."

"I'll tell you. Then you won't have to wonder."

No, hey, wait. He liked wondering. Wondering was what he did for a living. To wonder was his civil right, an inalienable right. There was a song about him, "The Happy Wonderer."

Jo Dante searched among the boots and the shoes and the other foley art supplies and came up with a box of foreign cigarettes. "How's your Yiddish?"

Cullen had to laugh.

"My sister once went out with a guy who'd studied to be a rabbi. It didn't work out, but she knows a lot of Yiddish. *Farblondjet* means lost—really pathetically hopelessly lost. That's how sophisticated I was."

The cigarettes were Silk Cut, arguably a sophisticated brand. That Cullen recognized them by sight came about this way: He had read a piece in *Rolling Stone* about Sinéad O'Connor, who, the author observed, smoked Silk Cut cigarettes, which Cullen had never heard of. A few days later, stopping at Village Cigars for some Trident, and, knowing the store carried lots of foreign cigarettes, he had asked the clerk to point out Silk Cuts, just to know how they were packaged. Now, did that mean Cullen was a sophisticate, or merely a trivialist? (A: Sinéad O'Connor. Q: Who smokes Silk Cut cigarettes?) Cullen couldn't help it, he said, "And now you're found?"

Jo Dante shook loose a cigarette and broke off a match from a matchbook and lighted it and lighted up. She exhaled out of the side of her mouth. "What's with you, Joe Cullen? Why're you so hostile?"

"Because I feel kind of *farblondjet* myself. Is that how you pronounce it? Think about it: Police officers don't allege that police commissioners try to coerce a blow job out of them and not tell their roommates. They just don't. You say Jenny didn't, I say you're lying. You're probably lying because she not only told you, she told you who put her up to it. You're possibly lying because *you* put her up to it—why, I have no idea, but anything's possible. I'm an old guy— *any*thing's possible. Either way, you're lying. I just met you, I'm not out to get you, and you're lying to me. So I feel *farblondjet,* and when I feel *farblondjet,* I get hostile."

The projectionist in the booth looking down on the foley stage got on the intercom just then and told Jo Dante that another reel of film, the faux Kim Basinger on dry land now, still running from whomever or whatever was chasing her, was racked up and ready to roll.

She told the projectionist to wait one more minute. To Cullen she said, "Jenny's funeral's tomorrow. Are you going?"

"Sure. Why not? I hardly knew her."

She reached across the not very great distance between them but couldn't quite touch him. "Please don't. It hurts."

"Maybe it won't hurt so much if you just tell me."

She watched her Silk Cut burn. "Tomorrow."

"It'll hurt all night if you wait till tomorrow. Tell me now."

Jo Dante made a sudden move; Cullen thought she was losing her balance, fainting, and he dipped to catch her. But she had only bent to pull off a Timberland. She pulled off the other too, then pulled off her socks, her Silk Cut stuck in the corner of her mouth as she did, one eye shut against the Silk Cut's smoke. Was she going to take off her work shirt, her blue jeans, her camisole, and dance on a desk? Would she tell her roommate about it, if she had a roommate?

Jo Dante stepped down into the foley pit filled with sand and gravel. Bare feet on dry earth didn't make armpit noises, Cullen with the Police guessed. "There's a man . . ."

"Yes?"

"He'll be there tomorrow."

"Oh?"

"If I can see him, point to him, I'll feel better about it than if I just tell you his name."

"Why?"

Jo Dante took a last puff of the Silk Cut and suffocated it in the sand. She put the butt in half an aluminum film can brimming with butts, all of them suffocated or drowned, none of them ground out, Cullen with the Police noticed—her MO. "Indulge me," Jo Dante said.

"I'm not in the indulgence business," Cullen said. "That's a sophisticated business. I'm with the Police. In my business we ask questions, we don't get answers, we put people in jail sometimes, or suggest that they get a lawyer. It's an unsophisticated business."

Once more Jo Dante hugged herself. "You're doing it again."

Cullen went right up to the edge of the foley pit. Why did this feel like a scene out of show biz, not like real life? "If you're in danger, Jo, I can help you, I can make you safe. If the only danger you're in is from me asking you questions, if this is just smoke, if you're just buying time, if you're going to disappear on me, I assure you I won't rest till I find you." That was hyperbole: He would rest often, he would need to rest, on the subtle spoor of such sophisticated prey. But this was show biz.

Jo Dante shook her head. "It's not smoke. Tomorrow. Please." She backed away a step, then another, till she was in the middle of the foley pit of sand and gravel. The pit wasn't very big at all, but she looked very, very far away. She looked as though she were in the middle of the Nafud Desert. She looked *farblondjet*.

The lights went down. After a countdown of academy leader, the faux Kim Basinger appeared on the screen, running down a road through a menacing landscape that anyone who had ever seen a movie could have told her she had no business in alone, not in that dress, what was left of it. What was left of the dress was wet, and so was the faux Kim Basinger's hair, and Cullen guessed that meant that when he finally paid his seven-fifty to see *Bayou Regrette,* this sequence would come after the sloshing-through-the-swamp sequence, although Jo Dante had given him some sophisticated inside information—that *Bayou Regrette* had continuity problems, that its actors were sometimes wet in one angle and dry in the next, that their cigarettes grew and shrunk from shot to shot, that the time on clocks on walls behind them jumped around. Cullen with the Police noticed that the faux Kim Basinger's nipples were no longer long and thin and hard; they were scarcely noticeable. Nipples must drive the people charged with continuity nuts.

Or maybe Cullen wouldn't pay seven-fifty to see *Bayou Regrette.* Maybe Jo Dante would invite him to a private screening, cast and crew and close friends. Maybe she would sit next to him and move closer to him when the lights went out and put an elbow up on the armrest next to his elbow. (It would be too dark to see the back of his hand.) And maybe when the faux Kim Basinger appeared on the screen, running through the landscape she had no business in in that dress, maybe Jo Dante would find his hand in the dark and hold it between both of her hands and they would remember how Cullen had stood there in the dark of the foley stage and watched Jo Dante in the foley pit full of sand and gravel, barefoot, running in place, timing her footfalls to the footfalls of the faux Kim Basinger, running in place with great grace, her arctic-white skin shining ghostly in the dim light, her pale yellow hair like a banner behind her, as if she truly were moving swiftly, so swiftly that his heart hurt, and he had to walk out of the foley stage, through the door, into the long, narrow hallway, down the hall, down the two shorter narrow hallways, through the heavy door, past whatever it is called that receptionists sit behind, where Mystee cracked her gum and waved good-bye.

"*Ciao,* awfissuh," Mystee said.

9

If VU Sound Magic had been miserly with Christmas spirit, O'Boyle's Tap House on Queens Boulevard across from Borough Hall was spendthrift. A real-live tree (or, at any rate, one recently executed) listed like a regular customer in a corner back of the jukebox. Absent a traditional stand (when in a courthouse bar, one thinks in legalese), it was merely propped in a fire bucket full of water; the tree sprouted traditional ornaments though—balls and bells and candy canes—and was topped by a synthetic supernova. Santa Claus faces, cheaper by the dozen, hung everywhere there was something to hang from; tinsel and streamers draped and looped; mistletoe hovered. Seasonal music played on a cassette deck on a shelf above the bar (played *larghetto;* the deck was in need of a tune-up)—right this minute, Eurythmics' cover of "Winter Wonderland."

The yuletide cheer was underappreciated, for the only customers were Assistant Queens County District Attorney Carlton Woods and public defender Margaret Morris—and now Sergeant Joe Cullen, with the Police, forty-five minutes late because he didn't have a watch with any day's style or any day's accuracy, and because he hadn't expected to find motion-picture sound re-creation so absorbing.

Talk about absorption, Carlton Woods and Margaret Morris didn't seem to mind that Cullen was late, didn't seem to have noticed. They were in a booth in the back, sitting closer together than either one's boss surely would have liked. Shop talk, Cullen figured. Carlton Woods had prosecuted and Margaret Morris had defended Elvis Polk three and a half years ago after Polk tried to negotiate the sale of stolen computer hardware to a fence who was not a fence, *he* was with the police; they had both been in attendance more recently when Polk had been asked by Detectives Luther Todd and Jenny Swale if he had any insight into similarities between the Mercury Freight Thanksgiving Day cargo heist and the SpeedAir job, whence that stolen hardware had come. Elvis Polk having hammered Detectives Todd and Swale, Carlton Woods and Margaret Morris had a lot of shop to talk.

But they hadn't been talking shop, it turned out, they'd been talking motion pictures—not their sound re-creation, the finished product.

"We can't decide," Margaret Morris said when Cullen sat, "maybe you can help us: When a movie ad says 'Two thumbs up, Siskel and Ebert,' does that mean both Siskel *and* Ebert liked it and gave it a thumb-up apiece? Or could it possibly mean only one of them liked it, but liked it a lot—"

"What Margaret's saying is"—Woods plucked the baton from out of Margaret Morris's hand, ready or not, and sprinted past her—"shouldn't a movie both Siskel *and* Ebert really like get *four* thumbs up, and doesn't that mean that a two-thumbs-up-Siskel-and-Ebert movie could actually be—"

"Two thumbs up, Siskel *or* Ebert?" Cullen hated punchline thieves, but Carlton Woods was pumped up and he wanted to bring him down a little, for efficiency's sake.

Margaret Morris laughed and said, "Ex*act*ly."

The waiter, who notwithstanding the music had been watching

Oprah Winfrey on the TV behind the bar, came over to take Cullen's order. He looked like a biker—tattoos, ponytail, potbelly, a T-shirt with what from a distance looked like a hot dog with a smiling face but that turned out to be a condom, ditto, over the slogan *Poking Fun*—but he had gentle eyes and a gentle voice. A recovering biker? A born-again biker? A Krishna biker? "What can I get you, sir?"

"Coffee," Cullen said. "Please. Black, no sugar."

"Only way to drink it. How about you, folks? Ready for another?"

Margaret Morris emptied her highball glass and pushed it forward with her fingertips, like a tentative chess player. "A tonic and Coke."

"Tonic and Coke." The waiter reached for her glass and Margaret Morris jerked out a hand as if it had all been a trap to see if he would take such an order. "No! A tonic and *Tab*."

The waiter, who had heard everything, sneaked Cullen a smile. *We know the type, don't we, hoss?* the smile said. *A closet fatty who orders a cheeseburger, double fries, onion rings, and a* diet *soda. Or a sundae, three scoops, extra hot fudge, but* no *whipped cream. Who's zooming who, hey, hoss?* "Another Tanqueray and grapefruit juice for you, sir?"

Carlton Woods just nodded. The swizzle sticks lined up in front of him told Cullen from the Police that it would be his fourth. "We've done little else for several days, Sergeant, but answer your colleagues' questions, and I'm offended at the implication that Miss Morris and I have some culpability in these officers' deaths. I won't insult you by adding how sorry I am that they died so brutally." Woods had the looks to play on television, say, just what he was—a hip smart svelte young African-American: American enough to have the respect of whites, to get their dinner invitations, their job offers, to be tapped to join some of their organizations (the ones whose memberships were overt); African enough to be able to go home on Sunday to see his dear sweet old moms without being dissed by the 'hood home boys. The hyphen would never be an equal sign, it would always be a barricade over which he had to clamber, commando-quiet, stoic about the spikes and the broken glass, from one aspect of his personality to the other.

Margaret Morris put a hand on Woods's arm. "Now, Carl . . . Sergeant Cullen said on the phone he's not investigating the homicide per se. He's checking into the officers' backgrounds."

Woods looked at Cullen sideways, trying to find a loophole through which to see into *his* background. "Aren't you friends with Hriniak?"

Tom Glazer sang, *larghetto,* "Jesus, Jesus, Rest Your Head."

Cullen nodded thanks to the waiter for his coffee and made a big deal out of stirring it—he never stirred his coffee—until the waiter had left the tonic and Tab for Margaret Morris and the Tanqueray and grapefruit juice for Carlton Woods and had gone back to the bar.

Woods drank off half his drink in a swallow. "He *is* friends with Hriniak. I heard about him when Charles Story bought it. Remember? He was friends with Story. He was friends with the guy accused of killing Story—Valentine, Tom Valentine. He was friends with Hriniak, Story's successor. It was weird: a mid-level IAU detective—everybody's friend. And he's friends with that reporter, she used to be at *City,* now she's on the tube, Ann Jones. He's *that* Cullen. *E*verybody's friend." Woods drank off half of what was left.

"Carl," Margaret Morris said.

That Cullen, no friends in sight, got out his notebook and opened it to a clean page. "Don't talk about me like I'm not here, Carl."

Woods killed his drink. "Don't call me Carl."

"He's right, Carl," Margaret Morris said. To Cullen she said, "He's sorry."

Woods swiveled toward her as best he could, being so close already, being so drunk. "Don't talk about *me* like I'm not—Ow!" Before he could smack her, his head had smacked the back of the booth. He grabbed at his head with both hands, as if he could remove it and repair it. "Ow, ow, *ow!*"

The waiter was up off his barstool and halfway to the booth. He raised his eyebrows at Cullen: *Need help, hoss?*

Cullen showed the waiter the palm of his hand. He hooked an ice cube out of Woods's glass and wrapped it in a paper cocktail napkin. He pressed the napkin on Margaret Morris.

Margaret Morris stared at the cold, wet clump for a moment, then got the point and took it. She reached out to hold the napkin to Woods's head.

Woods took a swipe at her hand and knocked the napkin one way and the ice cube another.

Madonna, *larghetto,* sang "Santa Baby."

Woods wept.

When he had stopped weeping, Cullen said, "What haven't you been asked? You're both trained interrogators. Sometimes the really important questions don't get asked." They were both trained interrogators, so he didn't say, as he would have said to someone untrained, that the really important questions didn't get asked deliberately or incompetently, but because people get on a track, get going forward, and they can't stop, they can't back up. The track doesn't double back.

After a moment Woods burbled, "Wide day zwidge gars?"

Cullen looked at Margaret Morris for a translation, but she was dabbing at Woods's cheeks with another, drier cocktail napkin. It appeared to be her life's work, her destiny.

Woods brushed away Margaret Morris's hand. "Why," he said, "did they switch fucking cars?"

Cullen could hear Hriniak, at the head of the long, long table in the police headquarters conference room: *"Todd and Swale left with the prisoner at approximately four P.M. It was Swale's car, but Todd was driving, Swale riding shotgun, Polk in the back seat."* "The detectives drove down from Wallkill in Todd's car?"

"A Geo," Woods said. "Swale's was a Volare."

"And you think . . . what?"

"*I* didn't slip Polk the fucking gun, if that's what you're saying, Cullen. And neither did Maggie."

Maggie. "You didn't slip Polk the fucking gun, which means maybe the gun was planted in the Volare. Did Todd's car break down that you know of? Did they routinely alternate cars? How did whoever planted the gun ensure that they took that car?"

Woods waved a hand like a schoolboy wanting the bathroom pass, trying to get the waiter's attention. *Oprah Winfrey* was over now and the waiter was watching the news—a commercial loft building on fire. "How the hell would I know?"

Cullen contemplated driving his foot into Woods's crotch under the table. He contemplated reaching across the table and taking Woods by the ears and slamming his forehead down onto the table. He had a better idea: He would treat Woods as if he weren't there. "Miss Morris. Maggie. The time to clear all this up is now, not later. It doesn't look terrific, right now, that a PD and an ADA on the same case have a thing for each other; it's going to look terrible later. If you have any idea how Polk got that gun, it—"

"Ax her!" Woods thrust an arm out toward the TV, kept on thrusting it, lapsing into hip-hop. "Ax the bitch what went down. Fuck's she so stupid hip 'bout what went down? You scope the shit she's been jamming? Who the bitch housing, man? 'S like she was *there*, homes, like she was *in* the fucking room. Fuck don't you ax her? Waiter! *Waiter*, goddamn it, can I get another fucking drink?"

Her and *she*—and *the bitch*—referred to Samantha Cox, in another trademark red outfit, a wool jersey chemise with mock turtleneck and padded drop shoulders, her ultrablond hair worn up this evening in an elaborate swirl. Big gold hoop earrings, no microcassettes for Sam. What she was talking about now Cullen couldn't make out—Bing Crosby was singing, *larghetto,* "God Rest Ye Merry, Gentlemen"—but projected behind her (by means of a Chyron? a Dubner? Ann had told him what the technique was called and he had forgotten, which was unusual, because other people's shop talk was always interesting, because he had shown promise of becoming a television news production sophisticate) was a picture of the mayor, so the mayor was probably what she was talking about. Whatever she was talking about, the waiter was attending to it as if it were a tip on a sure thing. Woods, for the waiter, wasn't there.

"Sergeant . . ." Margaret Morris put a hand out close to Cullen's hand. "I think Carl and I better go. I suggest we meet again some-where less public and less full of temptations. Can I call you first thing tomorrow to set up a time?"

Cullen wasn't all there either. He was up by the waiter, watching Ann Jones on the TV now, trying to read her lips. Shouldn't it be easy for him, he who had watched those lips say *I love you* and *Be in me from behind*? Shouldn't he, who could get hard just like that at the thought of the way they attenuated when she sucked on him, be fluent in those lips? Apparently not. The logo projected behind Ann meant nothing to him; the film clip she introduced—any people in any room anywhere, cutaways to head shots of a few of them, then the room again—meant nothing; Ann again (in her outtro, he was sophisticated enough to know it was called; the opposite of intro) moved her lips and meant nothing.

"Sergeant? . . . Joe?" Margaret Morris leaned way over, trying to intersect with Cullen's concentration.

"Uh. Oh. Sure. Sorry. Tomorrow? Sure. I've got some funerals tomorrow, so call me at home as early as you want or downtown in late afternoon. You have my home number, right? You going to be all right, Carlton?"

Woods, who had made a tower of his fists and had been resting his forehead on it, looked up suddenly, startled to be talked to as if he were there. The move was a mistake, for it upset things precari-ously balanced. Woods lurched up suddenly and quickstepped to-ward the men's room, his neck stuck out, a hand over his mouth.

Margaret Morris went after Woods.

John Cougar Mellencamp sang "I Saw Mommy Kissing Santa Claus," *larghetto,* then the Pointer Sisters sang, "Santa Claus Is Coming to Town," *larghetto.*

Margaret Morris came back and sat down just as some choral group began singing, *larghetto,* "Angels We Have Heard on High."

"There's one other thing we haven't been asked, Joe. Elvis Polk called me and asked if I was interested in similarities between the Mercury and SpeedAir jobs."

"Yes?"

"He'd copped to possession of stolen property traced to SpeedAir."

"Right."

"Elvis didn't know anything about SpeedAir," Margaret Morris said. "He didn't know squat. He ended up with some hot computers, period. How they got hot he had not a clue."

"And you think . . . ?"

"I'd be speculating."

"And you speculate . . . ?"

Margaret Morris shrugged. "It feels like a contract hit. Someone wanted Todd and Swale taken out. It was someone who knew they caught the Mercury job. The someone got Polk to call me, to pretend to know about a SpeedAir-Mercury connection, to have me arrange a meet with Todd and Swale, and with Carl." She glanced over her shoulder toward the men's room, getting conspiratorial. "*I* think, by the way, pieces were planted in both cars, so the switch isn't significant."

An orchestra, heavy on the strings, *larghetto,* played "Away in a Manger." Cullen stared into his coffee. His reflected forehead looked high and wise; his actual forehead felt cramped and stupid. "Can you do me a favor, Maggie?"

Margaret Morris smiled. "I like that you call me Maggie."

Don't. Don't tumble irresponsibly for me. It's bad enough that you've tumbled for Carl—Carlton. "I'm working without a partner at the moment. I don't have a contact at Wallkill. Can you find out who Polk's visitors were, who called him? Since Thanksgiving, say. Since the Mercury job."

She smiled more. "I can already tell you the answer. As long as I've represented Elvis Polk, I've been his only visitor, his only caller. He's a loner—no family, no friends. Maybe you heard—he's a Caucasian who wishes he were black. He makes everybody nervous."

"So someone inside made the contact."

"I'd be speculating . . . But there is Roy Reagan. No one ever asked us about Roy Reagan either."

Cullen's stomach didn't feel so good either all of a sudden. There were really important questions that sometimes didn't get asked, not deliberately, not incompetently, but because people got on a track, got going forward, and couldn't stop, couldn't back up, couldn't double back. And then there were questions that didn't get asked, period. "Okay. Who's Roy Reagan?"

"Elvis was up for parole last summer," Margaret Morris said, "but he blew it in May when he and a con named Roy Reagan got in a fight in a day room over what radio station to play—or so it seemed. Elvis stabbed Reagan with a screwdriver; the wound was superficial. Reagan was doing points for running a chop shop in Ozone Park. You live in Queens, so you know Ozone Park's right next to Howard Beach, and you know who lives there. Reagan's chop shop was too close for optimum competitive business comfort to a Howard Beach chop shop run by a couple of brothers with *links,* as they always say in the tabloids, whatever *links* are, with *links* to organized crime. Competition was not the brothers' idea of a good time, they dropped a dime on Roy Reagan. You probably don't talk to as many bad guys as I do, you probably haven't noticed that 'dropped a quarter' never had any currency, so to speak, when the pay-phone rates went up, cons still say 'dropped a dime.' "

Other people's shop talk was interesting *and* useful. (A: Sing, squeal, rat out. Q: What do you do when you drop a dime?)

"The fight felt like a setup," Margaret Morris said, "a provocation. I met with Reagan's lawyer and encountered a much more formidable stonewall than such a petty incident would produce. I can't prove it, but I think it worked this way: Someone wanted Todd and Swale taken out. They wanted the job done by a con without a violent record. They got Reagan to provoke the fight—the price for getting the wise guys off his back once and for all, Elvis's parole was canceled, Elvis was vulnerable to an approach."

Cullen thought about it. "Why a con without a violent record?"

"Their guard'd be down. Todd and Swale's guard."

"Who's the someone?"

"Beats me."

"Answer: 'Beats me.' Question: 'Who's the someone?' "

Margaret Morris frowned. "Sorry?"

Cullen shook his head. "Nothing."

Margaret Morris clicked open her handbag. "I'm sorry, Joe, about those cops." She tipped her head toward the back, where Woods had run. "He's sorry too." She took out her wallet. "Let me get it."

"I'll get it," Cullen said. "You take care of Carl."

"He'll be better tomorrow, Joe. I promise."

"Call me." Cullen got up and got away before she could lean across and kiss his cheek, which was the inevitable outcome of all this Maggie and Joe–ing. He went to the bar to pay the tab.

"How's your friend feeling?" the waiter said.

Cullen said, "You Borough Ds or Queens DA?"

The waiter blurted a laugh. "Takes one to make one, I guess. Amazing, though, how many guys who ought to make one come in here and don't. Albert, Nick Albert. Safe and Loft, temped over to Queens DA. We're after some dirty court personnel, that's all I can say. You're Cullen, right?"

That Cullen.

"I met Zimmerman once. An investment seminar."

Cullen smiled. "That would've been where to find him."

"Tough break. You doing okay?"

"Yeah. You know."

Nick Albert put Cullen's change on a cork-lined tray. "Your friend Woods? That's his name, right—the brother?"

"Yeah."

"There's another bar down the boulevard a ways. The Everglade. Forest Hills, I guess it is, or maybe it's still Kew Gardens. Anyway, this place here, O'Boyle's, you come to be seen; the 'Glade, the understanding is, everybody respects it, you go so you can say you weren't there and everyone'll swear to it. Lawyers take their secretaries, Ds take their snitches, judges get drunk, one of the waitresses is a guy, he gives hand jobs in the pantry. I go there on my lunch hour sometimes, for a change of scenery, for some pretty good pastrami." Albert slapped his belly as testimony to Everglade pastrami.

"Right after Thanksgiving—I remember 'cause they were pushing turkey instead of pastrami—I saw your friend Woods in the 'Glade with Paulie Messina. I went through the Academy with Paulie; I was afraid he'd make me, but he didn't, maybe because he's a scumbag, maybe because I had short hair back then, didn't have this gut, dressed straighter. With one thing and another, I missed the sixties, so I thought I'd do them now, while nobody else was using them.

"It was strange seeing Paulie out here, talking to an ADA. I mean, Paulie's on our side, but sometimes you got to wonder. Paulie's from Howard Beach; he's got wise-guy relatives—a cousin or something did points for a Kennedy heist a few years ago; he drives a Miata, which I'll be able to afford right after the Rockefellers say the hell with it, we're signing everything over to Nick Albert. Just as I was leaving, a guy came in I couldn't place, but I remembered later he works for Steve Poole. Remember Steve? Big guy, bald as a cue ball, one of those big mustaches. Drives Poole around, handles his chair and all. Larry or Harry or something like that. He went over to your friend Woods and to Paulie. I don't know if he sat down, but he said hello."

Albert shrugged at the quality of his own information. "Don't know what it means, don't know if it means, just thought you ought to know . . . This my tip?"

Cullen heard Hriniak, on the faux Shaker bench, saying, *"Messina and SpeedAir, Elvis Polk and SpeedAir. Polk and Jenny Swale, Jenny Swale and Messina. What's the connection? What is the fucking connection?"* "That's your tip. Thanks. Good hunting."

"Hey, Merry Christmas," Nick Albert said.

Stevie Nicks sang "Silent Night"—*larghetto.*

10

Of all Ann's shop talk, Cullen's favorite was from her days at the *Daily News*, her first job in New York, back when she lived with two roommates, one's cat, the other's stuffed animals, all of their bicycles, in a one-bedroom apartment at Seventy-second and York, a scarf on the doorknob meant *Go see a movie*, back before she knew Cullen, a detective two then and married to Connie Carrera.

At the *Daily News* in those days it had been the custom, current events permitting, to dismiss the troops half an hour before the ends of their shifts. *Taking a slide,* the ritual was called. "Take a slide," the night city editor would say to the dayside reporters sitting around with their feet upon their desks, the one-star having been put to bed, the picture assignment editor would say to the photographers slouching around the city room flirting with the copy girls, with the editors' secretaries. Throughout the night, after the two-star, after the four-star, after the four-star Final, the slotmen on the national desk, the copy desk, would tell the rewritemen, the copy editors on the rim, to "slide on out of here."

Stepping out of O'Boyle's into mid-December's sorry impersonation of an early evening, Cullen thought about bucking the traffic back to Manhattan and shoving a few papers around for a while, mostly to appease Maslosky, who was always complaining that Cullen made only cameo appearances in the shop, did some phantom paperwork, vanished without a trace. Maslosky would be impressed at his coming back downtown so late after having been all the way out in Queens, just a few blocks from his apartment building no less, after not just bucking the traffic, after getting stuck in it. Maybe he would put Cullen in for some award.

Or Cullen could take a slide.

There had been a very recent time when Cullen, by then a detective sergeant, would have seized an opportunity like this to call Ann Jones, by then at *City* magazine, and suggest that she slide on out of her office too, that she meet him at his place, or he could come to hers. ("So you can slide in me?" "Sure." "I'm out of here.")

But Ann wasn't at *City* anymore. *City* was *Metro* now, and Ann, who could go on about why *metro* was a four-letter word, was in TV. In TV, on TV, of and by TV, the forty-watt bulb, maybe (as Ann put it when going on about her career change), of the newscasts of which Samantha Cox was the first-magnitude star, but incandescent nonetheless, brighter than anybody around here, brighter than he.

And busy? Busy, busy, busy. Up and out at dawn, sometimes, to hear her tell it (hear her on the telephone, if he could get her on the telephone, if she wasn't out on assignment or in a production meeting or an editorial meeting or in the cutting room or on the phone or on the air), work, work, and more work, crawling home well after midnight, up and out at dawn all over again, hickory dickory dock, all around the clock, all over town, riverrun past the greater tristate *metro* area, all around the world.

How busy was she? Not busy enough, apparently, for she had even started talking about doing the occasional weekend stint—updates, teases, pinch-hit anchoring. Overdressed, overcoiffed, over-serious intruders into people's leisure time, Cullen often thought of the other forty-watt bulbs he saw doing such stints, often wanted to call in and ask the pinch-hitters when occasional had become frequent had become regular for them, often wanted to call the pinch-hitters' loved ones and ask whether they had found someone to pinch-hit for the pinch-hitters at home.

"They want your body all *the time. They want you out on the street for a standup at seven in the morning. They want you in the studio that night to intro that standup on the six; they want you back to intro it again on the eleven. They want you out at seven again, getting reaction people haven't even had time to have."* That was Ann on the damnableness of her job, dismay upping the pitch of her voice, widening her eyes, causing her head to turn from side to side. Now and then she would waggle a thumb in the direction of the Devil, making sure you saw him standing by her side, a finger on the trigger of the gun he was holding to her head, making her do it. Now and then she would confess that it wasn't the Devil making her do it, it was those paychecks.

Ann had never flaunted them, but neither had she concealed her pleasure that they were substantial, and Cullen hadn't been able to resist looking at one that peeked provocatively, like a bare shoulder, from a ripped-open envelope lying in plain sight, not in a cubbyhole or anything, on the rolltop desk in her apartment: She had been paid for one week what he was paid for four (working a fucking lot of overtime and at one point—but hey, who remembered exactly when?—getting winged).

He wanted her body—what about that? He wanted her in his bed at seven in the morning, doing standups, sitdowns, spinarounds, gimme a bale of hay; he wanted her in his bed at six that night, doing them again; he wanted her back at eleven, doing them again and again and again.

But yes, Virginia, there is no Santa Claus, not this Christmas, so Cullen didn't bother to call Ann, he just slid on home. He half stood, half propped himself against the kitchen counter, drank a

Corona, and listened to WBL Kicking S. The Evening Bath was running late, for some reason, and Frankie Crocker (There ain't no other like this brother) was playing hip-hop: Heavy D & the Boyz, "Gyrlz, They Love Me."

Cullen drank another Corona. Frankie played MC Lyte & DJ K Rock, "Stop, Look, Listen." Cullen drank another Corona. Frankie played Mr. Lee, "Get Busy," and Digital Underground, "The Humpty Dance." Cullen drank another Corona. Frankie started the bath, with something by Coleman Hawkins. Cullen had finished the six-pack, but he thought there was another on the floor of the kitchen closet.

He looked.

There was.

Cullen put five Coronas in the freezer, opened the sixth, and drank it warm. Frankie played Smokey Robinson, "Everything You Touch."

In the kitchen closet, Cullen had noticed, was a Manhattan white pages. He hadn't used it in a while. It seemed a shame to let such a valuable reference tool sit idle. He got it out and looked up the number for VU Sound Magic. When Mystee answered, he would say he'd lied, he'd killed several men and a couple of dogs.

A man answered. " 'Lo."

"Uh, Jo Dante, please."

"Who?"

"Jo. Dante."

"He work here?"

"She. Yes."

"Uh, everybody's gone. Nobody's here. Just me. Security. Who's this?"

"Never mind. Thanks."

"Yo! Brother!"

Cullen had nearly hung up, and he lifted the phone back to his ear. His heart went flip-flop-flip. "She *is* there?"

"You're listening to Kicking S. I can hear your radio. I'm listening too, on my Walkman. Smokey Robinson. Ain't no other brother like Frankie Crocker."

"No," Cullen said. "There ain't."

Cullen looked up Jo Dante's home number. Not listed. He looked up Jenny Swale's. Not listed. He went to the coatrack in the front hallway and got his notebook out of a pocket of his overcoat. From the papers stuck under a rubber band around one cover he extracted a copy of Jenny Swale's personnel record and found her home number. Back in the kitchen, he dialed it. The phone rang and rang and rang. Eleven times. Cullen hung up.

Frankie Crocker played Michael Jackson and Paul McCartney, "The Girl Is Mine."

Cullen drank another Corona.

Ann usually took cabs home, but tonight—this morning—she ordered up one of the station's cars. She had to be up and out by eight to do a puff piece—an Olympic-medalist figure skater introducing his line of skin-care products with a few triple toe-loops at Wollman Rink—and she didn't want to show up looking like the skater's mother. Bill Ellis had said after the six that in the piece she had done on a family learning to cope with a mother's Alzheimer's he hadn't, from a distance, been able to tell Ann from the mother. Bitchy hyperbole born of Ann's not going to bed with Ellis and not telling him Who Dropped the Vodka on Quintana Davidoff, but still . . . He *was* the boss and she respected his instinct for what turned viewers off and made them tune out.

The driver's name was Bobby and he looked like young Martin Sheen—the Martin Sheen of *Badlands,* who, people had said (not her, just people) looked like James Dean. He hadn't really, no more than he had later looked like JFK (as people had later said). Bobby didn't look like JFK or James Dean. He didn't look like Charlie Sheen or Emilio Estevez. He looked like young Martin Sheen. He looked good and he knew it.

Bobby had pulled up outside 14's front door blasting a tape Ann didn't know. He'd turned the volume down when she got in and kept it down pulling out of the driveway. At the first light Ann said the music had sounded good and to please crank it up.

"Animal Logic," Bobby said. "Some ex-cops."

"*No.*" She said it so sharply it startled both of them.

"Hey, joke," Bobby said. "Stewart Copeland. He was with the Police."

Ann used to be with the Police too. What the fuck was happening? Or had it happened? Was it over? And so suddenly? Or had it been gradual? Had it been unraveling from the moment she and Joe Cullen met, May 21, 1988 (three years, five months, three weeks, five days ago—but who was counting?)?

Joe Cullen had caught the Harris Schwartz job, and Ann had gotten a tip from a cop she'd met on the Howard Beach thing and who wanted to get in her pants that a story worth writing was the unwritten one of a decorated cop who spent one night a week playing rubboard in a zydeco band at a faux Cajun joint in Chelsea, one night in a bunny outfit at a cocktail lounge at Newark Airport, answering to Roxanne, the rest at home with his two kids and his wife, who was sometimes mistaken for Valerie Bertinelli.

Ann had called Joe, and called and called, but he hadn't returned her calls, so she had staked out headquarters and, on a limpid spring Saturday morning (the hot-to-trot cop told her Joe worked Saturdays and took Mondays off), confronted him in the plaza outside.

"Sergeant Cullen?"

"Ann Jones." It wasn't a question; he was sure.

Off balance—because he was sure he'd made her and because he was *guapo*—she'd decided on belligerence. "What the fuck? You can't return a phone call?"

"I passed your messages on to Public Information. They're authorized to talk to the press."

"I want what they don't know, what only you know. Let me buy you breakfast."

"How about dinner?"

"Okay, dinner. When is good for you? Can I bring a tape recorder?"

"If you like, but I won't say anything into it about Harris Schwartz. We'll talk about the weather, about where we're from, where we're going, about our favorite female vocalists, our favorite foreign films."

"You mean . . . like a date?"

"Sure. Okay. Good. I've been divorced eight years, I have two kids, a girl eleven, a boy fourteen. The proximate cause of the divorce was the discovery that I'd had an affair with the midwife who delivered my daughter, but that was acting out. I've had three or four relationships since the divorce. I like being by myself, I like spending time with my kids. The women I've seen have wanted more of me than I've wanted to give. I live in Queens, Kew Gardens, which to some women makes me geographically undesirable."

Ann had dragged men she was seeing kicking and screaming to double sessions with her therapist and listened to them be less . . . less . . . Well, what exactly was it that he was being? Before she had been able to decide, she had had to take her turn:

"You must be forty-four or -five. I'm thirty-three. I don't know how many relationships I've had. Not an uncountable number, but not worth the trouble of counting. My mother was a virgin when she married and has been with only one man ever since; in many respects, I'm my mother's daughter. Yes, there's a contradiction there. I want to be a mother; I also want to be a star. My favorite female vocalist is Kim Carnes, but that'll pass. My favorite movie, foreign or domestic, is *I Know Where I'm Going;* most people've never heard of it—"

"Michael Powell. Wendy Hiller, Roger Livesey."

Surprise me. Ann had never said it out loud, but she had always said it silently to the men she went out with—all twenty-seven of them; she *had* counted. *Surprise me. Say something I've never heard said, do something I've never seen done, show me something magical, tell me something tragical, make me giggle, make me wiggle. Fucking* move *me!* And here was this . . . this *cop.* "The midwife who delivered your daughter . . . So you stood there by the examination table, being an involved father and all, and watched this woman put her hand up inside your wife, and it turned you on. Do you like the girl-girl spreads in *Penthouse,* or are you into really sick stuff—enemas and all that? How's Monday night? Eight o'clock. The Blue Mill."

"How about tomorrow night?"

"I can't tomorrow. Monday."

"Monday's good."

"I'll meet you there."

"I look forward to it. . . . Since the midwife, I've been faithful to the women I've been with."

"Yeah? I haven't. Been faithful to men."

"That doesn't change what I said."

"No. It doesn't."

"See you Monday night."

"See you Monday night."

"Bye."

"Bye."

"Bye."

And so on, till right now, right this minute, and they weren't really much closer now than they had been then—closer to being a couple. They knew it, they admitted it, they were almost, she sometimes thought, proud of it. Ann Jones of NewsFocus 14 and Joe Cullen with the Police were going to be the last loners on earth, a forever wild, forever crazy gal and guy. The logical, the animal logical, thing for them to do would be to be alone together. But not them—oh, no, not them; they were going to be together alone.

Here it was Monday night turning Tuesday morning, and Ann Jones of NewsFocus 14 hadn't talked to Joe Cullen with the Police, her so-called lover, paramour, suitor, her so-called . . . , since Saturday afternoon, driving back to Manhattan from the wedding in the middle of nowhere. They had talked small talk:

He: So what was the argument about?

She: You mean with the guy in the piqué suit?

He: Is that what that's called?

She: We were standing near the piano. He asked if I knew how to "tickle the ivories, metaphorically speaking." I said I didn't *and* I didn't think that was a metaphor. "Long arm of the law" is a metaphor, "dawn of the age of Aquarius" is a metaphor, "still unravish'd bride of quietness . . . foster-child of silence and slow time" is a metaphor. "Ivories" is synecdoche—the part for the whole, the material for the thing made: pigskin for football, threads for clothes. He turned out to be a smart son of a bitch; he teaches somewhere. He said "the law" was metonymy, wasn't it, and speaking of their long arms, what kind of lovers did cops make?

I changed the subject to sheepdogs. I saw an old *Nova* at three o'clock the other morning about sheepdogs: Some are trained to work a pack from the rear, nipping at the sheep's hindquarters, yapping at them; some are trained to work from in front, staring the sheep down, intimidating them. He asked which way I liked it. He was one of those guys: You say it, he finds the innuendo. Then he asked me to marry him.

He: So it *wasn't* an argument.

She: I didn't say "argument"; *you* said "argument."

He: Are we about to have one now—an argument?

She could easily have had one. She was pissed off: She hadn't caught the bridal bouquet; she had been sure she would. She had even rummaged in a drawer of old stuff for a famous photograph taken three and a half years ago (the day after she met Joe; the reason she couldn't have dinner with him until the next night though she wanted to make a dinner of him right then and there), taken at the wedding of Polly Craven, Ann's roommate in her senior year at Ann Arbor, to Parke Avenel (Park Avenue, Ann called him— because that's where his family would have lived if they hadn't lived in Lloyd Harbor, because he was a rich spoiled brat, and because Ann had wanted Polly to marry Don Coward, a college boyfriend of Ann's [No. 4], even though he was a known scumbag, so that her name would be Polly Craven Coward).

The photograph was an accidental triptych: On the left was Polly, who had just thrown the bouquet—overhand, a high, hard fastball; on the right was a group of bridesmaids, friends, relations—nubile women all and all determined *not* to catch any stupid flowers, thank you, not just yet, not until they made partner or got a corner office or a name on the door; in the center, giggling, shrieking, in the proper spirit of the moment, was a band of girls aged twenty months to thirteen years, reaching up vainly as the bouquet passed over their heads. Rising out of the group on the right (this was the famous-making, funny part), elbowing, pushing off, slashing, face-masking, high-sticking, committing every personal foul in the book, every game misconduct, snatching the bundled white roses and ivy out of the hands of the maid of fucking honor, snatching victory from the jaws of defeat, was yours truly, Ann J. (for Judith) Jones.

Ann had found the famous photograph in the drawer of stuff (for a long time a magnet had held it up on her refrigerator, but it had made Joe nervous, he stopped snacking, he was wasting away, she couldn't have that), had rubbed it for luck, and had taken her place among the marriageable women that afternoon confident of another win, not taking into account that the fix was in, that Maria Esperanza, a cop no less, sworn to uphold law and order, had a sister to whom she practically *handed* the goddamn flowers before everyone was even *ready,* while some of those who would have liked to take part were even aware that the stupid fucking ritual was taking place.

They didn't have an argument, they barely spoke the rest of the way, and here it was Monday night turning Tuesday morning, and the last communication Ann Jones of NewsFocus 14 had had with Joe Cullen with the Police, her lover, her paramour, her . . . her suitor, her . . . her . . . , had been the message she'd left on his answering machine around ten o'clock Saturday night: "How'd it go? Okay, I hope. Call me when you get in. I'll be up late. . . . Bye. I didn't catch the bouquet. Oh, you know that. You were still there, I forgot. . . . Bye."

Joe hadn't called her back. What did that mean? It meant he hadn't called her back, that's what it meant. You didn't have to be

Freud to figure out what *that* meant. A dog could figure it out, using a little animal logic.

Animal Logic reminded Ann of Fleetwood Mac and 10,000 Maniacs: great beginnings, but halfway through the song and your mind was somewhere else.

The side ended just at Ann's door and she lied to Bobby and said she really liked Animal Logic. Bobby took the cassette out of the deck and put it in its case and gave it to her.

"Oh, really, I can't—"

"Hey, it's cool. Want me to carry that stuff?"

Ann was lugging home a net newsfilm bag full of cassettes of old shows picked at random from the archive to study in the hope she could get a handle on this godawful business that paid its practitioners so much and gave its audience so little.

What Ann wanted was for Bobby to carry *her,* to grab her up in his arms fifties-style and kick in the front door and the door to her apartment and toss her on the bed and rip off his jean jacket and white T-shirt, unzip his jeans (he was wearing a suit and tie, but, hell, this was a fantasy), flip up her skirt, pull down her L'eggs, slam-bam fifties-style thank-you-ma'am, roll off her, comb his D.A., light a Lucky, peel rubber in his '55 Chevy. It would be a nice change from the usual: heating up some Progresso soup, watching Letterman, masturbating to pictures from *Triathlete* magazine. Night work wasn't restful, and what a mess it made of your friendships, your . . . association, your sex life.

But Bobby was a nice kid, he didn't hit on the talent. He took the net bag and Ann's briefcase and her keys. He unlocked the door and held it for her. He found her mailbox all by himself and unlocked it and held the lid up so she could pry out the contents. While she winnowed junk into the wastebasket by the mailboxes, Bobby went where she pointed him, down the hall and around the corner to the front door of her (ahem) garden apartment.

All that was worth saving was a letter from her brother and a

Tweeds catalog. When it came to pretentious text, Tweeds was hands down her favorite, so much so that she couldn't resist flipping pages to read some of the names for colors the euphemism department had come up with: Halloween, Hide, Thunder, Breen, Mongoose, Raisin, Deer, Sanguine, Alaska. Perfect.

Bobby put the net bag down and opened the top lock. He opened the top lock and the door blew up in his pretty face and his pretty face blew all over the hall.

11

An inspector's funeral—that was a cop's compensation for getting hammered on duty. For oozing to death gut-shot or going out in a blaze of pain with a bullet hole where an eye had been, for getting studded by a sawed-off shotgun or made bloody lace by a MAC-11, like Cullen's dear sweet old partner, Neil Zimmerman, the Department gave you a firing squad, muffled drums, bagpipes.

Inspector's funerals were always in Queens somewhere, or out on the island. Unless they were on Staten Island, or in Westchester or Rockland or Brooklyn or the Bronx. (They were never in Manhattan because cops don't live in Manhattan, because, any cop would tell you, zookeepers don't live in the zoo.) There were always low buildings, always lots of sky, always ranks of cops with black ribbon on their badges. Cub reporters covering their first inspector's funeral surveyed those ranks and, clever as clever, made notes to write about *a sea of blue*. Veterans of a score of inspector's funerals wondered where the nearest bar was and would it be open, and hoped that for a twenty-first time they'd be able to get away with writing about *a sea of blue*. The sea of blue was always scudded with the colors of uniforms of cops from other towns, other states, once in a while other countries: the fraternity of grief.

It was always cold at inspector's funerals, unless it was raining, unless it was hot. The funeral parlor was always next to a candy store, in its grimy windows grimy boxes of plastic model ships and planes whose assembly hadn't been anyone's hobby in thirty years. Forty years. A gray-haired, gray-faced woman, the owner's wife or mother or grandmother, always watched from a window above the store, a gray cardigan sweater clutched close if the weather was cold, if it was warm her bare gray wattled elbows on a pillow on the sill. A mutt always wandered loose, dog-paddling through the sea of blue; a baby always bawled; a child always giggled spontaneously, and was sharply shushed.

The cemetery was always vast as Kansas, chock-full of gravestones, buzzed by tumultuous jets, ringed round by mysterious inaccessible highways. Killer mud always sucked at the mourners' shoes. The priest always strived to be heard over a snapping wind and always lost—except when he was a rabbi or a minister and then he still lost. The widows always jerked convulsively at the rifle salute. Their dead husbands were never inspectors; inspectors died in their beds.

Cops' widows: now there was a group worth some study. Mourning was their second skin, bereavement was their destiny, a dirge their anthem. Look at Anita Todd, Mrs. Luther Todd on paper still, on the books, but separated from her husband for two and a half years and well down the road to a new life, her own life; bound to Luther still only by inertia, convenience, and necessity—taxes, insurance policies, shared assets and liabilities; by paperwork. See Anita Todd being the perfect cop's widow; see her flinch from the *karack-rack* of gunfire; see her veil filling like a spinnaker in the snapping wind; see her quiver, her shoulders quake, her knees; see her slump into the arms of sister cop widows, widows in black, black widows. See them suck out of her the last of her singularity, inoculating her with desolation, spinning her up in their web of—

"Jesus. Connie." Standing in the paltry lee of a thin tree on a cemetery hill in outermost Brooklyn (*was* it Brooklyn? Yes, it was Brooklyn), up to the uppers of his dress shoes, doubling as his funeral shoes, in the hilltop's caul of snow, Cullen was startled out of his chilly reverie, blurted in his surprise at the sight, down there among the widows, of that advocate of an annual day of near nudity, Connie Carrera Aiello, his ex-wife. He moved out into the wind and down the hill, and by the time he got near the grave, Anita Todd had been borne off to one of the widowmobiles. He touched Connie's elbow and she whirled, her eyes full of fright, as if he might be Death confirming her reservation, since he happened to be in the neighborhood, to Samara.

"Hi. Sorry."

"I saw you before, walking down the hill." Connie kept a shoulder turned toward him, looked into the distance, talked out of the side of her mouth, like a snitch on a street corner, not wanting to be made and looking altogether conspicuous and suspicious. "You were limping."

"Going downhill's harder than going up, my chiropractor says; you have to resist your own momentum."

She flicked a look at him that he interpreted this way: *You mean her chiropractor. I couldn't drag you to a doctor, but as soon as you took up with her, it was chiropractor-this and acupuncture-that. Holistic-schmolistic.* Sports *medicine.* "Still. It's been a long time."

One hundred forty-six days (but who was counting?). "Jenny Swale's funeral was this morning." In a cemetery that was a twin of this in Nassau County. Or maybe Suffolk. Same wind, same aging snow, same mud, same limos hiding off behind a scrim of trees, embarrassed at their dirty skirts. Same sea of blue. But no Jo Dante. Why had there been no Jo Dante? Hadn't she said *"Tomorrow. Please?"* "You weren't at that one, were you?"

Connie shook her head. "I know Anita from the support group." Another flick. The support group was for divorced and separated wives of cops, for a few alienated girlfriends. The flick was for his having dropped out of the counterpart group, for the cops themselves, after just a few sessions long ago.

As mature as could be without any pansy support group, Cullen didn't scream at her that they'd been divorced for eleven years, for Christ's sake, and she'd been refuckingmarried for nine, why didn't she give it a goddamn rest? "I didn't realize you still went."

"I didn't for years. I started again after you got shot. . . . Ann came a few times; I guess you know that."

Meaning she was positive he didn't. Why else had she paused before lobbing the tidbit into his laager? It really was a war out there, wasn't it? Women over there, men over here, no-man's-land —no *person*'s—in between; air strikes, artillery barrages, spies, sappers, the whole bit. "Are meetings still at the church in Elmhurst? That's a long round trip for you."

She looked right at him now, finally sure of her ground. "Madison's not that far, Joe. You're the one who thinks it's far."

Madison was twenty miles west of the Hudson, over the Watchung Mountains, and Connie and her husband, Doug Aiello, and her children, James and Tenny Cullen, had moved there last year from Riverdale (notwithstanding its bucolic name still part of the dour Bronx), after Connie's and Doug's cars were both stolen; after Doug was robbed at gunpoint on the subway, Tenny at knifepoint on the street outside her school, James by a posse that swarmed over a hockey game at Lasker Rink in Central Park, assaulted the players and coaches, and made off with sticks, pucks, gloves, jerseys, pads, and helmets. "Well, we've done that," Connie had said at the time. "Now we're going to do something else for a while. Some*where* else."

"Oh, it's not Madison," Cullen said. "It's not the distance. It's the kids, their busy lives. When I come to Madison, Tenny always has someplace she had to be ten minutes ago; if James is home from school he's playing hockey. At least when he wanted to be Hoagy Carmichael, when he wanted to be Bon Jovi, you could find him in his room, under his earphones. Now that he wants to be Wayne

Gretzky, he's always out at some rink. Even in the summer—roller hockey. So I wind up seeing you and Doug. I like you, I like Doug, but I don't like *seeing* you and Doug. Can you understand that?"

Connie nodded. "I can understand that." She took Cullen's arm and they mushed through drifted snow along the roadside to the parking lot.

"They're getting old, the kids," Cullen said.

"Well, they're growing up. *We're* getting old. Look how we plod along, a couple of antiques."

"Hockey makes me feel old."

Connie laughed. "*Hockey?*"

"I used to go to games at the old Garden, Fiftieth and Eighth. There was a Nedick's in the lobby. The players came out the front entrance after a game. We'd hang around and have a hot dog and an orange drink and wait for them. My hero was Bobby Hull. He wasn't a Ranger, he played for the Black Hawks, so I had to idolize him secretly."

"The . . . Detroit Black Hawks?" Connie said.

"Chicago. The Detroit Red Wings. Chicago, Detroit, the Rangers, the Montreal Canadiens, the Toronto Maple Leafs, the Boston Bruins—those were the teams, just six. Now there're twenty-some-thing teams."

"And that makes you feel old?"

"I was listening to WFAN in the car. Brett Hull had four goals and three assists last night. Bobby's son."

Connie cocked her head. "WFAN. I'm surprised. James listens to it, and Doug too, sometimes, but I'd think it would drive you nuts—all that opinionation about *ball* games. Is that a word—opiniona-tion?"

Cullen stopped and sculpted some snow with the side of his shoe. "Neil used to listen to it—and drove me nuts. The first time I drove my car after . . . after . . . the radio was tuned—Neil'd tuned it—to FAN. I've kept it there in his memory, except once in a while I listen to jazz."

Connie humphed. "No, you don't. You listen to Frankie Crocker, to WBL Kicking S, ergonomically correct and listener friendly. Ann was worried, when you started listening to it so much, so I listened a little, to try to understand what she was worried about."

They actually talked to each other, Connie and Ann? Talked about what worried them? Talked about what about *him* worried them? "And?"

"Well, it's pretty *black*. If Doug listened to it, or James, I'd wonder if they were feeling guilty."

"About being white?"

"And middle class. Having *stuff*."

"It's just music," Cullen said. "Frankie Crocker plays Johnny Mathis, Ella Fitzgerald, Louis Armstrong. He plays Lisa Stansfield and Linda Ronstadt and Sinéad O'Connor—white women."

"Linda Ronstadt and Aaron Neville. And 2 Live Crew and Public Enema, as Tenny calls them. She hates rap. Rap is for teeds."

"What are teeds, anyway?"

"That's cinchy, dude. They're tedious people."

" 'Cinchy,' as in 'that's a cinch'?"

"You got it." Connie had let go of Cullen's arm and been standing pretty close, as close as ex-wives are allowed to, maybe, and probably shouldn't. Now she stepped back a half step. She was about to change the subject. To what? "Ann says you're drinking a lot."

Medic! Medic! "I drink some beer."

"A lot of beer. Ann thinks it's funny that you're so conscientious about recycling, since it gives everyone a chance to see how much you drink. In the old days people threw away the evidence."

Funny? Everyone? People? What should he quibble about? "I'm in some pain. It helps me relax. Listen, Con . . . I didn't know Luther Todd. I don't know Anita. I need to talk to her. Five minutes."

There was that flat, frail look in Connie's eye that snitches got (speaking once more of snitches) when they remembered what they never should have forgotten: that you were being nice to them only to collect what they'd sluiced out of the gutter for you to pick over.

In a minute, a second, a flash, you would turn your back on them, maybe even crush them. "You're *work*ing?"

He shrugged. Somebody had to do it.

"Was Luther dirty?"

"Could you please ask her, Connie? I didn't know you'd be here, I was going to ask her myself, but it'll be easier if you ask her."

Connie chewed the inside of her cheek for a moment, then took another step back, a full step, and another and another. She could go either way now; she could go any way. "Wait here."

12

He didn't wait, he followed after her (limped after her). *Never let them get away, not when they don't owe you shit: NYPD Rules, Regs, Helpful Hints, Decorating Tips and Recipes,* Chapter 3, Section IV, Paragraph 6.

Keeping an eye on Connie, per the Regs and Recipes, Cullen walked right into a man in a wheelchair.

"Whoa, there. Anybody get the number of that truck?"

"Sorry. Jesus. I'm really . . . Steve. Hello."

Steve Poole. Once upon a time Stevie Poole, Everybody Out of the Poole, now Steven *Jay* Poole, State Senator Poole, hero cop, wheelchair-jock, Mister Punishment with a capital *P* and it rhymes with *C* and it stands for Chair, Mister Throw-the-Switch-and-Watch-'Em-Twitch. "Good to see you, Joe. *Long* time." Poole had a capital handshake; he reprieved Cullen at the last moment and sized him up. "You look good, Joe. How's the back?"

"Okay. Not bad. Sore. It hurts." Nothing a beer wouldn't help. Or three. Or six. Or nine. How many has it been, Ann? Don't forget to call Connie so she can keep a running count.

"Tough about Zim," Poole said. "Knew the score. Not too many guys do. About themselves, especially. One time—this is funny . . ." Poole didn't look behind him; he didn't have to. All it took was the slightest tip of his head—the above-the-shoulders equivalent of lifting a finger—and his backup singers materialized around him. Three of them, wearing the latest Wise Guy Collection fashions, ready to swim through slime if those were the boss's orders, ready to laugh at something he'd tipped them was funny. One of them was Nick Albert's big guy who'd said hello at the 'Glade to Carlton Woods and Paul Messina, bald as a cue ball, one of those big mustaches, drives Poole around, handles his chair and all, Larry or Harry or something like that.

"Downtown. Last spring. Took some constituents to meet Hriniak. Wanted to see their faces when he told them the good guys were still in first place—"

The backup singers roared, and Poole tipped his head again— jerked it—to stifle them, to let them know *that* wasn't what was funny, what was funny was still to come. "Later, went around the building, said hello. Saw Mas, saw Stathos, Brolin, Richards. In the elevator, ran into Zim. He tell you this? Funny, really funny. I said, 'True what I heard about you, Zim? You're attempting to purchase every high-end consumer product on the market? Unless you're watched carefully you will shop till you drop?' " Poole's head was very still, keeping the backup singers at bay. "Zim said, 'Now that you mention it, I just got an offer to do a Dewar's ad focusing on my twin talents—guardian of law and order and black-belt shopper.' I said, 'No shit?' I mean, it was possible, right? Good-looking guy, interesting job, Dewar's should be kicking themselves they didn't think of it. Zim said, 'Yeah—*Last Book Read: Patagonia catalog.*' Laugh? I thought I'd lose my catheter." And the senator laughed now, discreetly, behind his kid leather glove.

The backup singers looked sick. Then they looked sicker. Their foreheads were rutted with effort as they tried hard and then harder to make the syllables make sense: *Paddle Go Knee Uh? Pat O'Gonnia? Paddy Going, Yuh?* Finally they laughed anyway, too loudly, until Poole cut them off with another jerk of his head.

Cullen smiled. The Dewar's joke, for what it was worth, was Ann's, rubber-tipped with her affection for Neil and aimed ultimately at Cullen, who she thought made too much of Zimmerman's acquisitiveness. "Shopping's a varsity sport in New York," she had said after making the joke, "so why not aspire to be in the starting lineup? The third-stringers—the *scrubs* we called them in high school—they're the ones who're out of step. You're one of them: You go to Moe Ginsburg, you go to Macy's and A&S, you call that shopping. That's not shopping, that's spending. You don't have a special relationship with anything you've bought." [Cullen had felt at this point that she had begun to creep toward *her* point.] "You haven't made a commitment to what you've bought—just the way you haven't made a commitment to a nicer apartment, to a better car—"

("To you?" Cullen had interjected, just to get it over with.

("Now that you mention it," Ann had said. "Neil's a zealot for stuff; when he meets the right woman, he'll be a zealot for her. On the surface he seems a womanizer, but inside, I believe, he's a— good word; I just made it up—a womanist."

("So shopping is destiny?" Cullen had said.

(Ann had laughed, but in her eyes had been disappointment that he had had to try to top her.)

"Good to see you, Steve." Cullen backed away from Poole. "Be well."

"Uh, Joe . . ." The ellipsis was like a noose along the ground; it threatened to pluck Cullen up in the air by an ankle if he moved an inch. "Joe, no bullshit, okay?"

He hadn't been bullshitting. Well, okay, he'd been *semi*-bullshitting: He did wish Poole well, but it was never nice to see him. Cullen could never see *him*, the Poole of the capital handshake, the rich baritone (a stock banality of pieces about Poole, written by those same reporters, oftentimes, who wrote about those *seas of blue*), the movie-star good looks (another commonplace), the steel-trap mind, the rapier wit (ho hum). All Cullen could see was the Poole of the best-selling book ("as told to" one of those reporters) about Poole's . . . well, *Brush with Death* (predictably) was the title, and a brush with Death was what Poole had had a few years back on a street in Bushwick. A traveling man, a soldier home on leave, strapped with a Walther P38 nine-millimeter West German Federal Police pistol, Death had had the crazy, vainglorious idea, along with some of his old buddies, to clean up the neighborhood by taking out the crack dealers doing business on the block. Working undercover and trying to ingratiate himself with those same dealers—mere ouncemen; retailers—so that he could get to know their source, Detective Two Steve Poole had shown up at the wrong place at the wrong time, tried to flee, and was hit from behind by two slugs from Death's Walther (which also felled, fatally, two of the ouncemen, before Death was himself hammered by a patrolman from one of the first whitetops on the scene, a rookie out on the street for only the third night after his probation). (The ironies were abundant, the paperwork an administrative hell.)

One slug embedded itself in Poole's gluteus minimus and did no lasting damage; the other ricocheted off his iliac crest and shattered into three fragments that penetrated the vertebral canal. Poole's spinal cord was cut partway through, and below the first lumbar vertebra his nervous system went out of business. He couldn't piss, he couldn't shit, he couldn't run or skip or hop or jump. Or fuck. Or walk. While doctors labored to figure out what he could do, his body was a pincushion of needles, tubes, IVs, catheters; drugs and nutrients from a blender were pumped into him, waste was pumped out. Computers tracked his heart, his lungs, his brain. They all worked pretty well, considering: His heart beat, his lungs pumped, his brain learned a little Greek: *para,* beside + *plessein,* to strike = *parapleissein,* to strike on one side → paraplegia, complete paralysis of the lower half of the body caused by injury to the spinal cord.

Cullen read *Brush with Death* in paperback in the hospital one week (but who was counting?) after he got winged. He read it in one day, in practically one sitting, and was starting to reread it when Ann noticed it on his bedside table.

"Who *gave* this to you?"

"Maslosky."

"What was he *think*ing?"

"Forewarned is forearmed."

"Did he *say* that? Is that what he *said*? What a horrible thing to *say*."

"He said, 'If worst comes to worst, know you're not alone.' "

"Okay. I'm sorry. He meant well. . . . Still." And she replaced *Brush with Death* with a book she'd brought, David Halberstam's *The Summer of '49*.

Halberstam said in his foreword that he'd interviewed all of the surviving players, and maybe he had; but the old-timers hadn't re-fined their memories, they'd just repeated stories Cullen had been hearing ever since he was a kid and hadn't cared to hear again, so he had retrieved *Brush with Death* from the windowsill behind the radiator where Ann had stashed it and read parts of it again. Up and around by that time, an achy sore grump instead of a full-fledged gimp, he had told Ann he might read a few pages of the book every day for the rest of his life. "It's a reminder."

"That it could've been worse for you?"

"Yes."

"That's a lie, Joe Cullen. What it reminds you is, you had a brush with death and Neil had a head-on collision. It was no fault of yours, he knew it was hot when he volunteered to work in the kitchen, you don't need to do this to yourself, and whenever I see that book, I'm going to hide it, I'm going to throw it away, if necessary, I'm going to burn it."

She had done something with it, all right, but Cullen had found a hardcover copy in the hospital library (misfiled among the fiction mysteries), and read it and read it until finally he stopped flailing himself with Poole's words, though he had not yet absolved himself of his guilt for his partner's death; that would take a few more beers.

"No bullshit, Joe?" Poole repeated.

"No bullshit."

Poole touched his chest with a kid-leather-gloved thumb. "I was there this morning when we buried Jenny Swale. I wanted to talk to you then, but there wasn't a way to do it. I'm grabbing the chance to talk to you now. You didn't bump into me, I got in your way. . . . I have an agenda, Joe. I want to exploit these hammers. In their memory, their honor, for Christ's sake, not for any fucking gain to me. The death penalty—it'll go this time. For sure. Only thing— they've got to be clean, Todd, Swale. You see what I'm saying? If they were dirty—either one, both, whatever—it queers the effort. Makes me look bad. Understand? So I'd appreciate. You know— knowing what's what. Not details—shit. Not that. Just a phone call: 'Back off, Steve-o. Things're heating up and you'll get burned.' That'll do it. I'll owe you with interest. Stay loose, buddy. Watch that back. Doing any P.T.? I have one of the great ones—Liliuoka- lani Weissberg, half-Hawaiian, half-Israeli. Great combo. Great hands. Go figure. She's in the book. Weiss*berg.* Use my name. *Ciao,* babe. Later."

No bullshit? Nothing *but* bullshit. And there was something famil- iar about it. Heard it before. TV, radio. Yes! George Bush! Way he talks. Clipspeak, somebody called it. *Time, Newsweek*—one of the news mags. Life-style piece. Funny. See? He was doing it.

A backup singer who looked like a jockey, tiny and strong, was manhandling Poole's chair through the muck. Nick Albert's big guy, bald as a cue ball, one of those big mustaches, was lagging after.

"Larry, right?" Cullen said.

"Hunh?" the big guy said.

"Harry?" Cullen waggled his fingers, pretending he was trying to call in a name. "Harry, uh . . ."

"Name's Jerry, pal," the big guy said, putting his face close to

Cullen's, dousing him with breath that smelled of mass-produced doughnuts and scorched coffee. "Fuck it's to you I don't know, but name's Jerry. Pal." He swaggered off, checking his attitude in the window of a widowmobile.

"Joe?"

Cullen was startled. "Connie. What? Yes? Okay?"

Connie looked at him nervously. "Come with me. Five minutes is all you get."

"I'm sorry for your loss," Cullen said.

Anita Todd said, "I like Connie and Ann both a lot. Consider yourself lucky, you hear me, to have two such strong women on your side. I don't think Luther was so lucky—I *know* he wasn't—with the bitches he ran with after we split."

Scrunched on the jump seat of a widowmobile, knees up around his chin, facing Anita Todd on the back seat, hugging herself, taking furtive puffs of a cigarette like a teenager sneaking a smoke, the car smelling of disinfectant, menthol, Giorgio, Cullen felt as though the tables were beginning to turn. If Anita Todd had talked with Connie and with Ann about what worried her, talked about what about Luther worried her, then surely they had talked to her about what worried them, about what about *him* worried them. In a minute she would be grilling him. "I appreciate your taking the time to talk to me, Mrs. Todd. I just—"

"You just have a few questions, I know. You can call me Anita, Sergeant. Or maybe you can't—not till you know for sure that Luther wasn't dirty." Luther's widow was small and taut and her voice came from the base of her throat. She reminded Cullen of Eartha Kitt, of whom he hadn't been reminded in years. "*Was* he dirty, Sergeant?"

The single greatest perquisite of police work (the reason Cullen had gone into it, according to Connie Carrera, who had doubtless discussed it with Ann Jones, with Anita Todd, with every other woman in the English-speaking world) was that you didn't have to answer questions like that, you got to ask your own questions. "Women, men, cops, civilians—was there anybody Luther knew, hung out with, got phone calls from, got letters, who you thought he shouldn't?"

Anita Todd began shaking her head before he had finished. "Luther was a big baby. When we split, he moved back in with his parents. That's them over there, the very tall couple getting in the car. They're good people, but they spoiled him rotten. He couldn't make a move without asking their permission. Some wack dude asked him to look the other way while he broke the law, offered him a couple large for his cooperation, Luther'd excuse himself first and call his momma. Luther was dirty, I'm Jane Fonda."

Cullen battled a smile. "I saw you at Jenny Swale's funeral this morning. I didn't see Jenny's roommate. Did you ever meet her? Jo Dante?"

Maybe Anita Todd shook her head and maybe she didn't. She did hug herself tighter and puff faster. She wasn't really listening, she was looking out a side window, looking hard. Cullen looked after her and saw at what: a tight little circle of brass—Chief of Department Ruth, Chief of Detectives Abruzzi, Cummings (known as Short Cummings) from the Bomb Squad, Applegate from Queens D's, First Dep Suzie Price, Martin from Public Information, Hriniak. There was no particular hierarchy to the group's arrangement; they might have convened informally to discuss whether Ruth or Abruzzi had the more elegant double-breasted overcoat (Abruzzi's was belted, if you favored belts). A walkie-talkie tucked in his shoulder, chatting with someone somewhere else similarly equipped, Braverman the bodyguard orbited the cluster.

Why the Bomb Squad? Cullen wondered briefly. What was wrong with the picture was Short Cummings of the Bomb Squad. Then he went back to wondering, *Where was Jo Dante?* Hadn't she said *"Tomorrow. Please?"* Hadn't she said there was a man, and that if she could see him, point to him, she'd feel better about it than if she just told Cullen his name? Hadn't she asked Cullen to indulge her, he who wasn't even in the indulgence business, he was with the

Police, hadn't she assured him it wasn't just smoke, that she wasn't just buying time, that she wasn't going to disappear on him? Hadn't she said *"Tomorrow. Please?"*

Still watching the circle of brass, Cullen saw Hriniak break away from it, break it asunder, turn the circle into a chain, then into disparate beads. Hriniak mucked toward the car—to give Anita Todd his condolences, Cullen wondered, or to give Cullen a piece of his mind for mixing business with grieving, for only doing what he had told him to do—be a pro, handle it like any other investigation, *any* other?

The widowmobile's engine was off and Cullen couldn't use the power switch to open the window, so he opened the door and got out to meet Hriniak. If condolences were what Hriniak had come to give, Cullen would leave him alone with Anita Todd to give them. If chewed out was what *he* was going to get, *he* wanted privacy.

Hriniak nodded. "Sergeant."

Joe no more. Joe had been a detective two, still married, when Hriniak was a DCI with all his hair and his wife was still a blonde. Joe was past tense. "Commissioner."

"Had enough funerals today. You too?"

"Me too."

"Joe? . . ."

Joe again. Reinstated—by the *capo di tutti* cops, who giveth and taketh backeth. "Yes?"

"What is, uh, what is Ann working on?"

Ann? "What happened?"

"She's okay. The last time I watched TV, she was working on—"

"Phil, what *hap*pened?"

"She's okay. Someone wired a plastic explosive to her apartment door. The good news is she didn't open it, the bad news is a driver from her station who brought her home did. He bought it. It was a serious bomb. You know Cummings? Bomb Squad? He says there've been too many magazine articles, too many books, about Mideast terrorists, about the IRA. People who can't hook up their stereos know how to hook up bombs. Ann was by the mailboxes. Like I said, she's okay."

"When was this?" Cullen said.

Hriniak pawed irritably at the mud. "Why do people always ask that? The fuck difference does it make when it was? You weren't there, you weren't there. I thought she was your girlfriend. I thought you, you know, shacked up there. This was early this morning, the bomb was planted sometime last night, you'd've been there, maybe he couldn't've planted it, you'd've heard him. So never mind when was this, where were *you*?"

Home, half standing, half propped against his kitchen counter, listening to WBL Kicking S, to Frankie Crocker (There ain't no other like this brother), to Heavy D & the Boyz, MC Lyte & DJ K Rock, Mr. Lee, Digital Underground, Coleman Hawkins, Smokey Robinson, Michael Jackson, and Paul McCartney, drinking a few Coronas. "Ann's new job . . . We don't see each other much."

"And speaking of her job," Hriniak said, "what was she working on?"

"Didn't you ask her?"

"Yeah, we asked her. And she told us. A hand job on some figure skater flogging skin lotion, so that wasn't it. Anything long-term? Was she moving in on somebody she'd been surveilling for a long time? Her lips said no-no, but there was yes-yes in the way she didn't look at me when she said it."

"You son of a bitch."

Hriniak took the lapel of Cullen's overcoat between his fingertips, as if admiring the quality, as if seeing if it held a candle to Ruth's or Abruzzi's, but not looking at the coat, looking Cullen in the eye. "I could have your badge for that, you insubordinate fuck. Your girlfriend's all right, I told you that. But Robert Kassavian, the driver, ain't all right, he got hammered, and the reason he got hammered is that one more time, once again, back for a return engagement, ladies and gents, due to popular demand, some fucking reporter thought it'd be fun to upfuckingstage the cops. She's in protective custody, your girlfriend, and she's staying there till she tells us what the fuck she's working on that somebody would want to hammer her. No visitors except her lawyer. This means you.

"You want to hear what else I'm really glad about? Jenny Swale's roommate? Jo Dante? Conspicuous for her absence at her best friend's funeral this morning? Her family was there—mom, dad, a brother, a sister, but no Jo. They mentioned it to Swale's parents, Swale's father mentioned it to Conigliaro, Conigliaro mentioned it to Ambach, from the Six. They lived in the Six, on Perry Street. Ambach sent a whitetop around to Perry Street, they found Jo Dante in the bathtub, her wrists filleted with a six-inch chef's knife from the kitchen. They don't make old-fashioned razor blades anymore, Joe, single-edged, double-edged, or maybe they do make them, you just don't notice them 'cause there's always a new kind of high-tech blade, a new kind of razor that leaves your skin feeling like a baby's, you want to go the suicide route you have to remember to stop by the kitchen before you get in the bathtub, or else you have to get up *out* of the tub and track water all over the house.

"I want some answers here. Spread the word. The fuck's your partner? On her honeymoon still? She knows what's good for her, she'll get her ass back in here and get me some answers. Spread it, spread the word. Answers. Not tomorrow. Tomorrow's not good enough. Yesterday's best. I'll settle for today. Answers today."

Hriniak turned carefully in the mud and walked back to his car. Braverman held the door for him, closed it behind him, looked around, gave Cullen a look that said *Today, asshole.*

13

Elvis Polk's born-under-a-bad-sign-if-it-weren't-for-bad-luck-he'd-have-no-luck-at-all-luck was word up changing.

Yo, check it out, here he was turning two she-ras at the same time, one she-ra sitting on his face while the other one went down on him, slurping the love juice out of Renata Kazmeyer's joy slit while Jenny Swale slurped the love juice out of his Louisville Slugger. A little while more of this, then they'd change partners, do-si-do, and he'd do the back-door man on Renata while Renata went down on Jenny Swale. A little while of that, then on to a little of something else, just as toy.

Then, just like that, Elvis's changed luck changed back. Just like that, Renata Kazmeyer slid her knees way apart and sat straight down hard on his mouth, grinding her steely kinky hair into his lips, cutting the corners of his mouth, gagging him with his own tongue, the blood from the cuts filling his mouth, already all sloshy with spit and love juice, damming up his mouth with the wet lips of her joy slit, grabbing his nose with one hand and pinching it hard so he couldn't breathe through it either, using her other hand to fight off his hands trying to gouge her mothering eyes or squeeze her mothering tits or something to get her the mother off him, going after his eyes herself and being in a better position to do it from.

And meanwhile, just like that, Jenny Swale stopped slurping on his Louisville Slugger and started chewing and chomping and gnawing and tearing and snarling till she bit it right off. Blood all over her face, the raggedy end of his Louisville Slugger stuck in her mouth, looking like a cigar butt she'd found in a toilet, Jenny crawled up on her hands and knees right next to Renata. She put her bloody hands on Renata's shoulders, Jenny, and pulled her close to her like she was going to French her the way she Frenched her when the three of them first climbed in the rack together. And Renata opened her mouth and lolled her tongue around like she was hot to get Frenched, except they didn't French this time, they both latched on to the raggedy end of his Louisville Slugger and tugged at it like a couple of dogs, a couple of bitches. They both had their eyes shut and their hands down in their crotches, their fingers going a hundred miles an hour. They both shot their wad at the same time, bucking up and down like they were hooked up to a DieHard.

Then Renata let go of her end of the raggedy end of his Louisville Slugger and Jenny put her face down close to Elvis's and spit the raggedy end in his eye, just the way she'd spit the bloody chunk of his tongue at him when she bit it off after he stuck it way down deep inside her mouth, trying to kiss her heart.

Jerking his head to dodge the raggedy end of his Louisville Slugger, Elvis jerked himself awake. He checked his Louisville Slugger for damage; his Slugger was standing straight up and oozing love juice on his thigh. It took more than a mothering dream of getting chomped off to keep his Slugger down. He checked his mouth for cuts; his mouth was dry and cottony from the mothering radiator that sucked all the wet out of the room's air, his nose, his throat, his eyes. He lifted his head and checked the room for she-ras; he was all alone.

Except for Mabel Parker.

"Shee-it. S'happening, Mabel?" Elvis shoved himself up on an elbow and poked at his hair to spruce it up; he always looked like hell when he woke up, coming out of a dream like that, he probably looked like beyond hell. "Brings you to the Twilight Zone?"

Mabel's mouth moved, but no words sounded. After a while Elvis figured out why and got up out of bed to turn up the sound on the TV. He'd fallen asleep while lying there watching *Geraldo* and before he fell asleep he must've swung over and turned the sound off.

Except he knew he hadn't. Why would he? Why turn the sound off but not the TV?

That meant someone else had. Someone who'd come into the room while he slept.

Elvis looked over his left shoulder and over his right, looking for Jenny Swale, Luther Todd, Renata Kazmeyer—come to pay him back for hammering them, hammered or not.

And there they all were, in the shadows, waiting for him to wake up 'cause hammering him while he was sleeping wouldn't be as toy as waiting till he was awake, cutting off his nuts, his Louisville Slugger, gouging his eyes out, yanking out his tongue and slapping his face with it, buh duh dut, buh duh dut, buh duh dut.

There was no one else in the room, just shadows within mothering shadows.

Then Elvis remembered that Geraldo had had phone-sex she-ras as guests. He remembered that one of the she-ras did her phone-sex rap and his Louisville Slugger stood straight up and lobed real close. He remembered that he started turning Japanese, but the pit bitches in Geraldo's audience were cracking up 'cause they were such uptight tight-ass tight-twat hunkie pit bitches they thought that kind of talk was dirty instead of what it was which was honest and true. He remembered that the laughing distracted him, so he'd turned the sound off and finished while just watching the phone-sex she-ra, who was toy, fact now that you mentioned it she looked kind of *like* Mabel Parker, who was dope toy, even when her mouth was moving and no sound was coming out.

Elvis turned the sound up and sat back on the bed to lobe. His Louisville Slugger was tilting off to the side and he stroked it with his thumb to get it upright.

". . . *My client is very willing to cooperate with the police department. But she can't give them information she doesn't possess. This so-called protective custody I call punitive custody, and I've initiated legal proceedings to put an end to it.*"

Then Mabel was gone and some pit-bitch she-ra with a microphone named Nola or something, standing out on a sidewalk with a bunch of home boys in the background behind her, waving and goofing and voguing, said something about how Mabel's client Ann Jones was a TV news she-ra herself, been reporting on some teenage she-ra who got smacked on the head with a bottle or something. Then the pit bitch was gone and a dope blond she-ra came on the screen long enough to say she'd be right back, then she was gone, and there was a shampoo commercial with a bunch of dope she-ras who looked just like the dope blond she-ra who'd just been there.

Elvis switched channels till he found another news show and lucked in to that show's report on the same story and he figured out that Mabel was working as a defense attorney these days, not as a D.A. like in the old days when she helped put Elvis on ice for trying to make a few bucks selling some mothering computers and shit somebody *gave* him to pay back a lousy mothering favor Elvis did for him that he couldn't even remember doing—computers that turned out to be hot, the mother was he supposed to know that?

Elvis switched back and forth between the two news shows till they were both over. There was nothing on either of them about five-ohs from several jurisdictions scouring the Eastern seaboard looking for him, nothing about the brutal slayings' renewing the debate over the death penalty in the Vampire State, which hadn't had an execution since 1963, nothing about State Senator Steven Jay Poole of Manhattan, former New York Police Department undercover officer paralyzed from the waist down in a 1978 drug shootout, saying he hoped the new year would be an unhappy, unhealthy one for cop killers in the Vampire State.

There was nothing about a clerk in a motel in Nowhere, Pennsylvania, or maybe it was Nowhere, New York, the Vampire State, being missing or getting found rolled up in a blanket in a falling-down potato barn off some road off some other road off some interstate connecting Mars and Russia, a .22 entry wound in her ear, not the one with the diamond stud, the one with the empty pierced hole.

There was nothing about the tattoo artist in Newark, near the train station, being missing or getting found in a Dumpster in back of his shop, a .22 entry wound under his eye, right in the middle of the flower tattoo he'd made out of his four teardrop tattoos—tattooed him*self*, man, ow!—just the way he made a flower out of Elvis's five teardrops.

No news, as his uptight tight-ass tight-twat hunkie bitch mother used to say, is good news.

Especially since yesterday there'd been nothing but bad news, news about Luther Todd's funeral, and Jenny Swale's, millions of cops stretching for miles, looking like a river of blue, and assholes with bagpipes in short mothering skirts and cops shooting off rifles like in the movies and choppers flying back and forth and some dope blond she-ra, not the one he just saw, a different one, standing in front of some building saying Jenny Swale used to live in it with another she-ra (and Elvis wondered if Jenny was a dyke and that's why she was nice to him but not that nice) and that she-ra slit her wrists in the bathtub and died 'cause she was deestrawt over her roommate getting hammered, the blond she-ra said, and Elvis said booshit to himself and out loud said:

"You don't get it, do you? You don't mothering get it. They wanted Jenny hammered so she wouldn't run her mothering mouth, they wanted her roommate hammered too, so she wouldn't run *her* mothering mouth. You don't mothering get it. It ain't about being deestrawt, it's about knowing too mothering *much*."

Elvis got out of bed and went to the window and looked out at the parking lot of the motel that could be anywhere or could be nowhere but just happened to be about six mothering feet from the entrance to the Holland Tunnel, or was it the Lincoln, he could never keep them straight.

There were twelve or fifteen or twenty cars in the lot, toy wheels, some of them, Allantes and Town Cars and Coupe de Villes and even a Benz, just about all of them with Vampire State plates 'cause there was only one reason for a motel like this in a place like this and that was for matinees—brokers and dentists and salesmen and shit taking a break and driving under the river to turn their secretaries, their nurses, their hot-to-trot sister-in-laws.

There's one now—a fat, overweight, potbellied scumbag son of a bitch with a toy she-ra about two-foot-five, she can probably slurp his Slugger without even bending down.

There's another, a skinny dweeb, looks like a bank teller or something, the kind who if you boosted his bank would be stupid enough to press the mothering alarm instead of just handing over the dead presidents, with a big fat she-ra who'd probably kill him if she sat on his face.

Thinking about she-ras sitting on his face made Elvis's Louisville Slugger start twitching. Thinking about she-ras killing him by sitting on his face made his Louisville Slugger want to shrivel up and hide.

But mother the bad dream he just had, there was no question about it, Elvis Polk's luck was definitely changing. I mean, shit, look at it this way. Knowing five-ohs from several jurisdictions were scouring the Eastern seaboard for him, a home boy with born-under-a-bad-sign-if-it-weren't-for-bad-luck-he'd-have-no-luck-at-all-luck would run west, right? Or north or south. Or east if he could go east, if east wasn't Long mothering Island, which didn't go nowhere, if east wasn't the mothering ocean. And the five-ohs would always be breathing down his neck, 'cause there's more of them than there are of him and he's got to sleep sometime and they don't, there's always a fresh one to take over for one who's wacked out and's got to rest. But a home boy whose luck is changing might could say to himself, Shit, brother, why run *away* if *away* is the direction the five-ohs're heading too, west or north or south, after you? Why not slip back past them, slide back past them, back to where you started, more or less, to where they already looked or where they think they don't need to look 'cause what's the point of scouring back where he started for someone who's lamming?

Which was what Elvis had done. And so far, so mothering good. I mean, shit, he had gone out in the street *with* his five tattooed teardrops hanging out for anyone who wanted to to mothering see and no one had noticed a mothering thing. Fact of the matter was, he now realized and he was maybe just a little bit sorry he'd gone and done what he'd gone and done, fact of the matter was more people, home boys and she-ras, seemed to be noticing his flower tattoo, 'cause fact of the matter was you didn't see many flower tattoos on the street, 'specially not on somebody's face, 'specially a home boy's, but the upside, the plus side, the good news was that more she-ras than home boys noticed and the home boys who did notice probably thought he was a faggot, that out? which didn't bother him none, fuck 'em, the she-ras knew he wasn't no faggot, before very long, his luck having word up changed, he'd have a she-ra sitting on his face while another she-ra went down on him, he knew it, he just knew it.

Elvis checked his watch and felt good all over to see it was time for the Evening Bath and he was finally somewhere where he'd be able to hear it, instead of just static. If that didn't mean his luck was changing, what did?

Elvis turned on the box he'd taken from the tattoo artist's shop, who wouldn't be needing it anymore, and he didn't even have to tune it to WBL Kicking S 'cause the tattoo artist already had it set there even though he didn't strike Elvis as a Kicking S–type home boy, he was more a Kiss-FM–type home boy or a Hot 97–type home boy or even a Z-100–type home boy. Another sign his luck was changing. Not only that, but the first time he turned the box on, Frankie Crocker, there ain't no other like this brother, was doing a "box check":

"Check the treble, check the high hat, check the bass. Yo, 'cross the street there, crank it up, *home boy: D Mob with Cathy Dennis,*

'C'mon and Get My Love.' " I mean, shit. Changing? Elvis's luck had word up *chang*ed.

Elvis took the box into the bathroom and put it on the toilet seat and cranked it up so he could hear it over the noise of the shower. It was a mothering bath, mothering relaxing: Lester Young and Billie Holiday, "Fine and Mellow"; then Sarah Vaughan, then Joe Williams, both doing "Embraceable You"; then Aretha Franklin, "In My Solitude"; then Albert King, "The Very Thought of You"; then Stephanie Mills, "The Comfort of a Man"; then Johnny Mathis, "I Can't Help Loving You"; then Little Jimmy Scott, "Someone to Watch Over Me"; then Patti LaBelle, "I Don't Go Shopping"; then something by Tito Puente.

14

Lester Young and Billie Holiday, "Fine and Mellow"; Sarah Vaughan, "Embraceable You"; then again "Embraceable You," Joe Williams this time; Aretha Franklin, "In My Solitude"; Albert King, "The Very Thought of You"; Stephanie Mills, "The Comfort of a Man"; Johnny Mathis, "I Can't Help Loving You"; Little Jimmy Scott, "Someone to Watch Over Me"; Patti LaBelle, "I Don't Go Shopping"; something by Tito Puente.

Half standing, half propped against his kitchen counter, drinking a Corona, two Coronas already in the bag, pretending he couldn't smell the smell of the morgue in his clothes, his hair, his skin, his soul, even though he'd showered and washed his hair and put on clean clothes, Cullen appreciated that Frankie Crocker (There ain't no other like this brother) had drawn a great Bath, but he couldn't get into it. He was too much into wondering who lights the moon, who makes the stars, who does the sun, who does it all, why are there mice, why are there cows, who killed Jo Dante?

Who killed Jo Dante because, as the lisping clipspeaking autopsy teed from the ME's office had put it, holding up the appendages in question even though Cullen had been looking elsewhere, anywhere but *at* Jo Dante, tall and flat-chested still beneath a sheet whiter than her arctic-white skin, whiter than her pale, straight hair, butchered like a martyr in some explicit Flemish Renaissance painting, the teed, taking bites from a ham and Swiss on rye, lettuce, tomato, raw onion, as he clipspoke, making his lithp worthe:

"She killed herthelf, I'm Doogie Howther. Right-handed, according to her perthonnel jacket. Likely, therefore, she would incithe her left writht firtht. Think about it. Left writht inthision tho deep it thevered the *Flexthor carpi radialith,* the palmar antebrachial muthcle that flexeth and abducth the hand. Difficult, maybe impothible, to then incithe the right writht. Un*leth* she grathped the blade in her mouth. No teeth markth, though, on the handle. Crime Thene pulled two printh and two partialth from the handle. One of the printh ith herth, one of the partialth ith her roommate'th, Thwale'th. My guethtimate: thtrong likelihood the wound to the right writht *not,* repeat *not,* thelf-inflicted. Meaning, probably, *nei*-ther wound thelf-inflicted. No thignth of forthed entry, no thignth of a thtruggle, no blood on the floorth elthewhere on the premitheth, nothing thtolen, according to Crime Thene, ecthept maybe a bithycle—there were bithycle thkid markth in the foyer, but no bithycle in the apartment. Thtill. My guethtimate: she wath in the tub, maybe dothing, she wath athaulted by a powerful individual, thkillful with clothe-combat weaponth, who cut her twith almotht before she even had a chanthe to wake up. Time of deceathe, my guethtimate: late Monday night, early Tuethday morning."

Or maybe it was morguespeak, maybe it was how you talked when what you did for a living was guesstimate how people died and when, guesstimated while trying to eat your lunch, while trying to run your life (the autopsy teed had twice been interrupted by phone calls, one from his mother, one from his car insurance company—"Allthate"), while trying to avoid the pleading eyes of cops who wanted you to guesstimate what you couldn't guesstimate—who lights the moon, who makes the stars, who does the sun, who does it all, why are there mice, why are there cows, who killed the victim and why?

"Who killed her and why and, also interesting to me, from my standpoint, what's it to you?" Captain Jake Neuman, the Homicide D who caught the Jo Dante job, said when Cullen stopped by his office at Midtown West.

"She was going to give me a name."

Neuman was famously round and soft and thin-haired, a famously bad dresser (the stripes of his pinstripe brown suit were too wide, the blue stripes of his white shirt too far apart, the red and blue stripes of his necktie too many stripes), and famously disingenuous. "Oh?"

"A man who might've put Jenny Swale up to something that maybe had to do with Swale's getting hammered."

" 'Might've'? 'Maybe'?"

"Yes."

Neuman waited.

Cullen outwaited him.

Neuman had to chuckle. "So."

"I can't tell you any more than that, Captain," Cullen said. "It's sensitive."

"So it would appear to be," Neuman said. "I'm impressed by the apparent sensitivity of it. . . . But what also appears to be true is that you want *me* to tell *you* something."

Cullen shrugged. "I'll owe you."

Neuman swiveled to look out his window at a brick wall on the other side of an airshaft. He was famously dogged too; he had cleared more jobs than many Homicide Ds merely caught in a career—front-page media-circus jobs, many of them, jobs in which villains or victims often acquired catchy appellations that fit nicely in tabloid headlines, that tripped easily from the tongues of first-magnitude TV stars and even of forty-watt supporting players: the Samaritan Killer, Nowhere Man, the Riverside Sniper, the Lady in the Loch, the Alphabet Murders. Books had been written about

Neuman, fictive cops based on him, and he remained famously modest, famously content that that tiny expanse of headers and stretchers be the extent of his view.

"This man Jo Dante was going to give you his name . . ." Neuman swiveled back. "She was going to give you *just* his name, or she was going to point to him and say, 'That's the guy'?"

"She said she'd feel more comfortable pointing him out, yes."

"So in order for her to do that, he had to be there, at the funeral, the guy."

"Yes. Yes, he's probably a cop."

Neuman sagged a little in his chair, as if his artful naïveté wore him out as well, as if relieved he didn't have to go on crafting it. "So you're thinking along those lines too?"

"It hasn't taken me anywhere, but yes."

Neuman moved a pencil from one side of his desk blotter to the other. "I had a partner once who went rogue." He moved the pencil back. "Killed some women. A serial thing. Another time, a D I was teamed up with temporarily turned out to be dirty—dirty from the very same job we caught together."

Cullen nodded. Neuman was famously unlucky in his partners too, famously betrayed by them. It was why he worked alone nowadays—not single-handedly, but without somebody sitting at the office's other desk (his coat on the other hook of the office's coatrack, alongside Neuman's famously dowdy car coat), somebody riding shotgun, somebody always in his face, asking what he was thinking—without somebody always behind his back.

"Looking at those situations now," Neuman said, "which I'm sure you can imagine I do now and then, looking for what was out of whack, what could've been different, what I should've been tipped off by was how they got in places. Hotel rooms, office buildings, apartment houses, whatever. Cops do that better than others, get in places. They badge their way in, they bullshit, they break and enter, they second-story. You lie down with scumbags, you get up in the morning a little bit dirty, you learn things.

"The guy who got in Jo Dante's was a cop. Dante and Swale lived on the top floor of a three-story brownstone on Perry just off Seventh. A baby could get in the street door, a kid who could climb could come down the fire escape from the roof. The apartment door has a good lock, a dead bolt, but who's to say Dante had it locked, even if she was taking a bath, and anyway it's only a lock and locks by definition are pickable. So far, we can't tell how the guy got in. He wasn't buzzed in or let in by a neighbor—that we know. He could've been buzzed in by Dante, before she got in the tub, or even after, if he's somebody she knew—that we don't know. He could've popped the street door, gone up to the roof, come down the fire escape; he could've popped the street door, gone up to the third floor, picked the dead bolt, or used a master key. Whatever he did, however he did it, he didn't leave tracks. That to me says someone who makes his living being a scumbag. Something about the whole MO, though—what, I can't say; it's just one of those things, those, you know, intangibles—says it's not a scumbag, it's a guy who knows scumbags, who maybe's been lying down with scumbags, and got up dirty. Something about the whole MO says cop."

Neuman was above all famously prolix, and though he had stopped, Cullen sensed that he wasn't through.

"I'd say that," Neuman started up again after a moment, "I'd say the guy who got in Jo Dante's was a cop, even if we didn't find the shield—" Neuman waggled his hands, waving off Cullen's forming protest that a shield could *not* have been left behind in Jo Dante's apartment, that such things were a refuge of scriptwriters and novelists with paltry resources. "Not a *shield* shield, a miniature, the doodad for a key ring, the fob or whatever you call it, but not plastic or anything, not junk, something custom-made, something given as a present maybe, to celebrate a promotion or something like that. I actually have something kind of like it, a little lapel pin my wife had made for me when I made detective, about ninety years ago, but who's counting? This, uh, doodad has a rank and other information on it, an indication of where it was made and when, which I'm not going to tell you because, as you freely admitted, you don't have anything for me, you're going to owe me, which is okay, it's fine, it's understandable that you would want to make such an arrangement if at all possible, if I could tell you more I'd be happy to, but, as you said about your investigation, it's sensitive too, my investigation, which is why, by the way, you're not going to say anything to anybody about anything I just told you, I know I don't have to ask you if you understand why that's necessary, I know you understand why that's necessary.

"And, uh, so, it was good to meet you, Sergeant, I've heard good things about you, how long's it been since you were winged, you look like you're getting around okay, sorry about your partner, it's tough, it's always tough, you can find your way out, can't you, just left out the door, then left and then left again, you don't mind if I don't walk you, I've got some calls to make, say, if you should find out anything more about this man Jo Dante—"

"What about the bicycle?" Cullen said. "There were bicycle tire marks on the foyer floor in Dante and Swale's apartment but no bicycle."

Neuman laughed harder than he really wanted to, probably, but he'd been up and out a long time, he was running on fumes. "And you think—what?—a messenger made a delivery—she was in show biz, those people're always getting deliveries—she was running around in her bathrobe or something, he got turned on, she told him to fuck off, he got pissed off, tossed her in the tub, cut her, did a few wheelies around the apartment and split? Or did you maybe have the thought that Swale or Dante had bikes, they kept them in the basement, in a storeroom or something? Did you maybe call the super and ask him, did he maybe tell you Dante had a bike for a long time, she used to ride to work and stuff, it was stolen last summer from out in front of the building where she left it for a while, locked and everything, Swale had one too, it's still down in the basement safe and sound, he forgot all about it when her folks came around to get her stuff? Did you figure maybe one time one of them brought her bike up to the apartment, to fix a flat tire, to raise the seat, to lower it, my wife rides a bike, she's always doing something to it, when she first got it she had it propped against a wall in the living room just so she could look at it, like a kid at Christmas, in the process maybe made a skid mark on the floor?

"So like I said, Sarge, good to meet you, if you should find out anything more about this man Jo Dante was going to give you his name, give me a jingle, will you, you won't owe me anymore, we'll be even."

The street-door intercom buzzed and Cullen guesstimated that it was ecology teeds peddling crunchy candy made of nuts gathered by Stone Age tribes in dampest Brazil. Or entrepreneurial teeds offering free trial memberships in a combination racquet club–coin laundry–video rental parlor–tanning salon. Or religious teeds or magazine subscription teeds or opinion poll teeds. Or Mrs. Berger, his upstairs neighbor, who walked her cocker, Angus, around this time every night and sometimes locked herself out. Or Santa Claus. Maybe it was Santa Claus, more than a week early because Cullen had been so good this year that Santa had more presents for him than he could possibly deliver in one trip on Christmas Eve.

One thing for sure, it wasn't Ann Jones, who in the old days, when she worked for *City* magazine, had around this time of evening a couple of times a week buzzed his buzzer, come upstairs, rung his bell, and he hers. But no more, no longer, *no más* (that was the Coronas talking), *no más*, alas. Ann was in TV now, in TV, on TV, of and by TV, a forty-watt bulb but incandescent nonetheless, brighter than anyone around here, brighter than he; busy, busy, busy, work, work, and more work, her body in demand all the time, up and out at dawn, on the air at six and eleven, up and out at dawn again, doing standups, doing intros and outtros, doing pinch-hit anchoring. The hell with his wanting her at dawn for a few standups, sitdowns, spin arounds, gimme a bale of hay; the hell with his wanting her at six, doing them again, *de más en más;* the hell with his wanting her at eleven, doing them *de más en más o cada vez más.*

So whoever was buzzing, Cullen didn't want to know about it. He wanted *una más* Corona. He wanted to listen to Frankie Crocker (There ain't no other like this brother) right up to his sign-off: *It's been real and you've been regular. May each of you live to one hundred and me to one hundred minus a day, so I'll never know nice people like you have passed away.* He wanted *una más* Corona and to watch *thirtysomething,* rooting for all of them to die of cancer. He wanted *una más* Corona and to watch NewsFocus 14, rooting for Ann Jones to be on introing a standup she'd been out to do at dawn that morning, never mind that someone who couldn't hook up his stereo, probably, had wired a plastic explosive to her apartment door, she might be a forty-watt bulb, but the show must go on.

He wanted *una más* Corona and to stare at Ann's wide thin lips and jerk off to the thought of her wide thin lips on his cock, a white ceiling fan turning slowly, slowly, the sun outside slatted window blinds making an oven of the patio, geckos sizzling up the walls, parrots and cockatoos in a ramshackle zoo halfway down the mountain screaming, cawing, arking; far, far away down the mountain, down the road, around the bend of the bay, on the terrace of one of the high-rise hotels, a bad band fronted by a bad singer doing a bad Doors knock-off: "The End."

That was last October, in Acapulco, a week in a hotel that wasn't a hotel, it was a replica of the shantytowns that dribbled down the mountains above the center city on the other side, the wrong side, of the highway—except that these replicated shanties were air-conditioned and had wet bars, except that instead of sad patches of dirt for yards each of these replicated shanties had its own patio and swimming pool.

The week included October tenth, Ann's thirty-fifth birthday ("But who's counting?"), which was seventy-eight days (but who was counting?) after Cullen was winged and his dear sweet old partner, Neil Zimmerman, hammered. They were there to celebrate, recuperate, copulate. The hotel had screwed up the reservation and didn't have a *casita* at the rate they wanted ("Eef our luck she wahsn't so steenkeen bahd," Ann had said in the *Treasure of the Sierra Madre* accent she lapsed into often during the trip, "we wooden be hahving no steenkeen luck at all"); but the manager made things right by putting them in the *casita,* rented in perpetuity by some Fortune 500 industrialist, stark, raving empty when he wasn't using it, at the very top of the mountain, looking out over all the other *casitas,* the bay, the town, the shantytowns, Heaven. The pool was the size of three or four of the pools in the *casitas* down below. ("Our luck she ees changing," Ann had said.)

Higher than everything else, unseeable except by birds and planes, they wore no clothes by day, only sometimes straw *sombreros* they had bought at the airport. The sunrise woke them and they slipped into the night-chilled pool to stretch out, to wash away the crusted semen and saliva on their limbs and hands and faces. Crouched like monkeys—though who would have seen them *except* monkeys, except parrots and cockatoos and hawks and pilots?— they opened the door in the adobe wall and plucked up the round breakfast tray left by the room-service Jeep that snarled up and down the hotel's service road. They set the round tray on a round table in the first square of sun to reach the patio, arranged chairs in the square of sun to dry and warm themselves, drank sedimentary *café negro* and sour concentrated orange juice, ate congealed eggs and burned bacon and cold soggy toast—all of it delicious—and listened to that part of the world awake to the menace of another paradisiacal day. Long before they'd dabbed up the last crumbs on their fingertips and fed them to each other, they would be hard and wet and ready.

Ann liked to take care of Cullen's first erection by hand, and would spread his semen on her face for its purported benefit to the complexion. While it dried, she would sit on the edge of the pool; he would stand in the deep end, her legs over his shoulders, and lick her off.

They would read (he McPherson's *Battle Cry of Freedom,* she Kristin McCloy's *Velocity*), they would doze, they would swim serious lung-busting laps, they would bathe in the carcinogenic sun till eleven or so, when Ann would phone room service for lunch:

"*¡Hola! ¿Qué tal hoy? Llamo de la casita. . . .* That's right. *Se-*

ñor Frankel's room. *Nos gustaria merienda, por favor.* . . . Uh, *sopa, sopa* cold. *Sopa fria, sí. Y sandwiches*—any, uh, *tipo,* any kind. *Jamón*—perfect. *Y te fria.* . . . *Frio, sí. Una* pitcher, *por favor.* . . . *Sí.* . . . *Sí.* . . . Thank you. Good. . . . Great. . . . *Hasta pronto.* . . . Bye."

They would stand chest-deep in the pool, *sombreros* on, reading, till lunch was delivered. For the few seconds it took to answer the door and exchange the empty breakfast tray for the full lunch tray, they put on matching seersucker robes given them by Ann's best friend, Mabel Parker, as a *bon voyage*—a *buen víaje*—present, then shucked them off immediately and took the tray to a table in the shade. They ate in silence, usually, Ann usually lifting one of Cullen's feet up between her legs, pressing the sole into her crotch. The very first day they tried making after-lunch love on the patio, but it was obdurate even with towels spread out and even in the shade bed-of-coals hot, so they adjourned to the bedroom and subverted routine by putting on each other's bathing suits (his was a pair of striped surfers, hers a one-piece tank that he could get up only around his hips), then undressing each other. They liked that a lot, and looked forward to it, kept on doing it, day after day after day. Afterwards they took a *siesta.*

They woke, they swam, they played in the pool an invented game they called *agua* polo with Kadima paddles they had brought with them from *Nueva York* and a Wiffle ball they found unexpectedly in a closet, they read. Crouched like monkeys, they crept into the shrubbery at the edge of the patio and peeped at occupants of *casitas* down below, pretending to be Crusoe and Friday, kids from *Lord of the Flies,* Butch and Sundance, Burgess and McLean. The other guests were white as fish bellies or so sunburned it hurt to look at them; if any of them saw Ann and Cullen spying, they said nothing, indicated nothing.

Then they took their *paseo,* their half-hour stroll round and round the pool, *sombreros* on or dangling down their backs by the cords, hand in hand, arm in arm, arms around each other's shoulders, each other's backs, hands on each other's asses. This was when most of a day's talking took place: they talked about what they'd been reading, what they'd been thinking, about other sun-infested places they'd been, about sun-infested places they'd always wanted to go—and fog-bound places too, and chill and overcast.

They talked about how it felt to be always penetrable, penetrant. Cullen told how he had been at first frightened but now loved to feel his penis swinging free, his testicles hanging unsupported; Ann told how at first her nipples had ached from being continually tumid but now felt like orchids blooming on her chest, how she wished she had bigger, pendulous breasts, a broad ass—"for the moment. It's great being skinny most of the time, but this is a time I'd like there to be more of me for you to enjoy. You would enjoy it, wouldn't you?"

He would have, though he was always turned on by her spareness, by the ease with which he could take her by the hips and turn her any way at all.

They would swim away the sweat they had worked up. They would shower and order dinner from room service. *("Sí, esta noche también. . . .")* From chairs pulled close to the edge of the patio, they would toast the setting sun with *gin y tónicos*. The sun would still be half a handsbreadth from the mountaintops, their local horizon, when they would start getting goose bumps and would finally dress. They had brought a week's worth of clothes, but Ann always wore a black sleeveless jersey dress, a shawl around her shoulders, Cullen loose white cotton pants, a white cotton sweater. They kept their clothes on when they made love after dinner, Ann lifting the skirt of her dress to sit on Cullen's lap or tying the skirt up around her hips as she stood bent over a chair, her hands on the chair back. They never wore underwear; they never wore shoes; they never quarreled.

The buzzer buzzed again and Cullen put his Corona down and sidled up to the intercom on the kitchen wall. He pressed the Talk button—"Yes?"—then the button marked Listen:

"*Joe?*"

Talk: "Yes."

Listen: "*It's Sam.*"

Sam . . . Spade? Sam Kinison? Sam and Janet Evening (a favorite old joke of Cullen's mother)? Talk: "Samantha?"

Listen: "*Can I come up, Joe?*"

"Uh, sure."

"*Joe?*"

He had forgotten to press Talk. He pressed it now: "Is something wrong?"

Listen: "*Please, Joe. I'm scared.*"

Had he missed an episode, the installment in which he had told her where he lived and invited her to drop over whenever she was in the neighborhood and in trouble?

"*Buzz me in, Joe. Please.*"

"Okay. Come in." Talk: "Okay. Come in." He pressed the button marked Door. He put the empty Corona under the sink. He got *una más* Corona out of the refrigerator and opened it and put it in the bag.

Time passed.

No Samantha Cox, which meant, of course, that it was a different Sam and that she'd realized she had the wrong Joe. Or that it was a leftover Halloween prank, frozen in the snow, then somehow thawed out to do its dirty work like some horror-flick antagonist.

No Samantha Cox. Just a scream.

15

Somewhere in the *NYPD Rules, Regs, Helpful Hints, Decorating Tips and Recipes* was a chapter, a section, a paragraph, on what to do when you heard someone scream:

Shoot to kill?

No, no, no. Come on, *Cullen, wake up and smell the sticky buns. What you do when you hear someone scream is—*

Have una más *Corona?*

For Christ's sake, Cullen. Hit the books, will ya? Anybody know the answer? Zimmerman?

Zimmerman? Neil Zimmerman? My dear sweet old partner, Neil Zimmerman? The fuck does he know what to do when someone screams? He got hammered. *He's* dead.

Could we have a little fucking quiet here, a little respect for your fellow officers? Very good, Zimmerman. You want to run that by us again, please, so your, uh, dear sweet old ex-partner, Cullen, who was running his mouth, can hear you?

Certainly, sir. Glad to, sir. Regs and Recipes, Chapter 12, Section 7, Paragraph 3a: You hear someone scream, you desist what you are doing and haul ass in the direction of said scream.

Very good, Zimmerman. Very, very good. Everybody got that? You desist what you are fucking doing and you haul ass in the direction of said fucking scream. Got that, Cullen?

Uh, yes, sir. I've got that, sir. No problem. Sir.

Well, then?

Sir?

Haul *ass!*

Y-yes, sir. Aye-aye, sir. That's a roger, sir, that's a big 10–4. Hauling ass, sir. Yes, sir.

But first Cullen had to find his goddamn gun, his Smith & Wesson stainless-steel .38-caliber revolver, dull silver nowadays, no more blasic blue-back. . . . Basic. Blue. Black . . . More resistant to rust, requires less maintenance than the old slix-slot metal alloy . . . Six. Shot. Metal alloy . . . Spurless hammer prevents mechanical cocking, must be flired louble-daction . . . Fired. Double. Action. That is, by pulling the trigger, cutting down on accidental dis—

Cullen!

S-sir?

The fuck *are you doing, Cullen?*

Uh, just citing the relevant chapter, sir, or section or paragraph, sir, on sidearms, sir, from the Regs and—

Cullen?

Sir?

Relevant this!

Another scream, and Cullen hauled ass.

Front hall. Coatrack. Shoulder holster. Door. Stairs. No time for the elevator, and anyway, stairs promote fitness, stairs contribute to rust-resistance, to lower maintenance.

All the way down to the basement, through the laundry room—

"Evening, Mrs. Brubach"—the boiler room, out the service door and up the ramp to the street. Along the front of the building to the front door, doing it by the Regs and Recipes: *When interdicting scumbags, whenever possible approach said scumbags from the rear.*

Nothing. No one. The vestibule with the buzzers on one wall, the building directory on the other (his name short two letters—UL EN, J.—looking like an incomplete crossword-puzzle answer: 5 Across: *With the Police*), empty.

"Joe! Here!"

There, down the block, *behind* him: Samantha—sorry, Sam— Cox in a long black opera cape over another trademark red outfit, a little wool number, slim fitted bodice with mock turtleneck and peplum flounce, a slim above-the-knee skirt, ultrablond hair in ultradisarray, ultrared lips and ultralucid skin looking weird, Joker-like, in the ultra-unnatural light of a cobra-head street lamp (the very lamp that stuck its nose into Cullen's bedroom, making making love in it, Ann had said, in the days when they had time for lovemaking, before she got so busy, busy, busy, work, work, and more work, her body in demand all the time, up and out at dawn, on the air at six and eleven, up and out at dawn again, doing standups, doing intros and outtros, doing pinch-hit anchoring, like making love on an expressway off-ramp).

Sam Cox's ultralithe figure was a pretzel of distress as she struggled, desperate hands clawing desperately at her midriff, to . . .

To what?

Cullen's first thought (and he knew it was crazy, he knew it was nuts) was that Sam Cox was trying to rip off her clothes, that she had had the misfortune to go out in public in an outfit that had suddenly been declared démodé and that she couldn't shed fast enough.

Then he figured it out: What Sam Cox was doing was trying to unlatch the finger grip of someone tall and dark and maybe under other circumstances handsome but right now ugly with contorted effort, who had belted himself around her from behind and was trying to yank her into a maroon New Yorker. So it wasn't what she was wearing that distressed her, it was whom.

"Joe!"

"Hey!"

Great, Cullen. Perfect. Be-fucking-eautiful. Where, in the Regs and Recipes, does it say anything about yelling Hey! *to prevent a snatch-in-progress? Cite me, puh-leeze, the chapter, the section, the parafuckinggraph.*

"Hey! Let her go, motherfucker! Police! Po*lice!*"

Nowhere in the Regs and Recipes was a chapter, a section, a paragraph saying that when you shouted *Police!* the bad guys would fold, turn to mush, roll over, throw up their hands, throw down their guns, go straight. But that didn't stop you from devoutly wishing they would: You wished that every time you shouted *Police!*, or said in a conversational tone *Police,* or merely showed up on the scene, the way you walked, the way you dressed, the way you wore your hair, making the statement *Police*—you devoutly wished that the antisocial would become pliant, the violent pacific, that some of the world's worst human beings would break out the peace pipe and offer to make you a cup of tea, to bring you a newspaper, to rub your feet.

As evidence of the high-gossamer content of that wish came the tall, dark, ugly stranger's reply to Cullen's shout: His hands belted around Sam Cox's waist unbuckled, his right hand reached down inside his clothes, reappeared, exploded. There followed the ineffable, unmistakable sound of a bullet passing by at speed, hissing with anger because it had Cullen's name on it and now it was going to go undelivered.

The bullet made a sick *splat* into the side of an innocent parked car.

Some time later, years later, came an echoless blast that hushed all the other sounds of the night, made them harken to this one subsuming sound.

Sam Cox shouted, "Joe! Joe, get down!"

And just as he had called her Sam when she commanded him to, Cullen, commanded to get down, got down, between two parked cars, and felt an ostrich's confidence that the world wasn't such a bad place after all, assured himself that he wasn't really being shot at, not a mere one hundred forty-seven days (but who was counting?) after being not only shot at but winged, one hundred forty-seven days after his dear sweet old partner, Neil Zimmerman, got hammered. One hundred forty-seven days ago and only six more shopping days to Christmas.

Assured, Cullen took a look-see. He saw the tall, dark, ugly stranger pointing at him—*Gotcha!*—saw his hand explode again, saw the windshield of the car he peeped from behind, a Subaru wagon, turn into droplets of glass.

That echoless blast again, 6.8 on the Cullen scale, capable of causing considerable damage in populated areas.

So it *was* happening, nearly Christmas or not. It was happening big-time.

"Jooooe—" Almost a whimper, with discouragement mixed in it and maybe even a dash of anger at him, Sam Cox having gotten the picture that he was as likely to help her as was Woody Allen.

A car door slammed on the whimper, crushing it. Tires yelped. The maroon New Yorker, Cullen didn't have to see to know, shunted around the corner and headed toward Queens Boulevard.

Toward Queens Boulevard, by the way, through streets of the neighborhood—well, not *the* neighborhood, but close by, close enough—where in '64, was it? dozens of people, all snug in their middle-class apartments, glimpsed and heard Kitty Genovese being stalked and stabbed to death right outside their windows and did fuck all about it. You would think, you would hope, that more than a quarter-century later, Kitty Genovese having become synonymic with callous urban indifference, a couple of gun shots in the night would goose the locals into hopping over to the phone and calling 9-fucking-1-1.

No such luck, or so it seemed. No lights going on that weren't already on. No lights going *out* so people could see better and wouldn't be targets themselves. No windows going up. No heads thrust out. No was he all right, did he need an ambulance, was there anything they could do, anyone they should call, should they call for backup, everyone in the global village knew that cops in a jam always called for backup. No would he like a little chicken soup?

So it was up to Cullen, one hundred forty-seven days after being shot at and winged, a few seconds after being shot at and missed *twice,* only six shopping days till Christmas, it was up to him to get up out of his crouch, get in his car—where *was* his car and had he brought his keys?—and haul ass after the maroon New Yorker, giving the tall, dark, ugly stranger still more chances to shoot at him. The tall, dark, ugly stranger and at least one other stranger too, probably, since snatchers didn't go around snatching first-magnitude stars of TV news programs solo, someone had to do the driving while the first-magnitude star was blindfolded, gagged, hog-tied.

Cullen's car, his Valiant, his valiant '81 Valiant, was right across the street, where it almost never was because parking places in this neighborhood were scarcer than neighborliness; his keys were in his pants pocket, which was unusual because he usually hung them on a hook of the coatrack by the front door, next to his overcoat, next to his shoulder holster. But, ah yes, he'd gone down to the basement a while ago, before first-magnitude stars began dropping in, before the shooting started, to dump some bottles into the recycling cans, some Corona bottles, so he'd have room under the sink for the empties if he decided to have a Corona, or *dos* or *tres* or *seis,* so that he wouldn't be driven out of his home by empty Corona bottles (*Ann thinks it's funny,* Connie had said at the cemetery, chatting about what about him worried them, *that you're so conscientious about recycling, since it gives everyone a chance to see how much you drink. In the old days people threw away the evidence*); he had taken his keys with him and hadn't put them back on the hook.

He wished he had taken his overcoat too; he was wearing just a long-sleeve T-shirt he'd put on after his shower, a pair of corduroys, Weejuns with no socks. There were only six shopping days till Christmas. It was cold.

The valiant Valiant started right up, which it didn't always do either, and without letting it warm, without looking for traffic, Cullen pulled out. He went through the stop sign at the end of the block without stopping, without looking for traffic. He would have gone through the red light at Queens Boulevard but it turned green just as he got to it.

Quick looks left and right.

No maroon New Yorker.

He took a guess and went right. Right was east, right was toward the edge of town, toward the burbs, the exurbs, the wilds of Long Island. Right was the way *he* would go if he had just snatched a first-magnitude star—away from Manhattan, where though first-magnitude stars abounded, a good first-magnitude star could still find a way to stand out. Out on the edge of town, in the burbs, the exurbs, the wilds, a first-magnitude star could get swallowed up by the regularity of it all.

Or maybe it was that in Manhattan there were so many star*fuckers,* noses atwitch for the scent of first-magnitude stars, eyes peeled for a glimpse of them, ears cupped for the tremor of first-magnitude footfalls, for the vibrations of first-magnitude vocal cords. Out on the edge of town, in the burbs, the exurbs, the wilds, the musk of a first-magnitude star could be diluted by the perfume of the spheres; its light could be mistaken for the light at the end of a dock, for a firefly; the sounds of a first-magnitude star could be anything at all—a groundswell, an airplane high overhead, distant thunder, surf.

Whatever the fuck, Cullen wasn't even to the Van Wyck yet and there was the maroon New Yorker, slipsliding through medium traffic just at the speed limit, the hand of someone who knew what he was doing, who had probably done this before, on the helm.

It was almost eight o'clock by the valiant Valiant's dashboard clock, a clock with hands that pointed to numbers, a clock that Cullen's dear sweet old partner, Neil Zimmerman, had referred to as an "analog" clock, though what it was analogous to he had never explained. A digital, decimal, high-tech, cutting-edge guy, Zimmerman had been dismayed by analog clocks and watches; he hadn't understood how you could want a watch that told you it was getting close to eight o'clock when you could have one that told you it was 7:58.27 . . . 28 . . . 29, *and* told you the day and the month and the year, the time in three other cities, the altitude, the barometric pressure; that counted down from one week to zero, from twenty-four hours to zero, and from sixty minutes to zero; that had a daily alarm and two reminder alarms; that kept lap times and average speeds for up to one hundred laps; that recorded your pulse rate and stored ten telephone numbers. Could have them in blue, black, red, yellow, and white.

Almost eight o'clock, almost time to hear Frankie Crocker (There ain't no other like this brother) sign off. Cullen switched on the radio and just caught the end.

"*—and me to one hundred minus a day, so I'll never know nice people like you have passed away.*" Then Frankie played "Moody's Mood" and Cullen dialed WINS. Whenever Frankie Crocker wasn't on your radio, your radio wasn't really on, and it was time for a little news.

Cullen had noticed, one hundred forty-seven days ago, that getting shot at and winged had caused him to feel that he was the center of the universe, the point around which everything else pirouetted; getting shot at just moments ago caused him to feel similarly, even though he had been missed, and he was surprised therefore to hear nothing on the news about it, nothing about why Sam Cox had come to his apartment or what she had come to talk about, no speculation on who the tall, dark, ugly stranger was or why he wanted to snatch a first-magnitude star. Surprised and disappointed.

What was on the news was a story about a plane crash in Africa that hadn't killed a Bronx congressman because he had gotten stuck in traffic (Traffic? In Africa?) and missed his flight; a story about a wildcat strike by medallion cabdrivers that had left the streets empty of taxis; a story about a teenager on crack who had raped a woman with MS; a story about a march to the UN on behalf of unhappy Armenians in Turkey or unhappy Turks in Armenia, the reporter didn't seem sure which; a story about a baseball player who shot his girlfriend's sister; a story about a Thoroughbred who kicked his trainer. The usual.

Cullen switched off the radio and pursued the maroon New Yorker onto the Van Wyck.

Well, not *pursued* exactly. *Followed* was more like it, for there was something kind of friendly, kind of flirty, about the way the New Yorker's driver stayed ahead of Cullen, but only just, made faking moves and feigning moves but wasn't fooling anybody. What he was doing kind of made Cullen want to tell somebody about it. Somebody like . . . oh, the boss maybe.

Not because he wanted it, not because he really understood how to use it, not because he was a digital, decimal, high-tech, cutting-edge guy, he was an analog guy, but out of respect, out of homage even, to his dear sweet old partner, Neil Zimmerman, Cullen had had installed in his valiant Valiant, an analog car if ever there was one, a mobile cellular telephone. One thing he had done—though he had forgotten how he'd done it and doubted if he could do it again even looking at the manual—was program the phone to dial ten numbers automatically. One of the numbers was the home number of Captain Richie Maslosky of the Internal Affairs Unit. Cullen even remembered how to punch up Maslosky's home number: press 3 (1 was the office phone downtown that he shared with Maria Esperanza, 2 was Maslosky's extension, 4 was the Department Advocate's Office, 5 was the Public Information Division, 6 was Maria Esperanza's home number, 7 was Ann's home, 8 was Ann's office, 9 was Connie and the kids, 0 was—)

"*Hello?*"

"Jeanie, it's Joe Cullen. Is the captain home?"

"*Hi, Joe. How're you?*"

"I'm fine. Is he there, please?"

"*You know Richie, Joe. He's out jogging. You want him to call you?*"

He did know Richie, and had known Richie would be out jogging. That was why he'd called—so he could say he had. "I'll talk to him tomorrow, Jeanie. Thanks."

"*Sure?*"

"Yeah. Bye, Jeanie." And he hung up. Now he could make the call he wanted to make, to number 0, the number you didn't have to push, to his dear sweet old partner, Neil Zimmerman:

Hi, Joe.

"Zim, listen—are you up to speed on this?"

Of course. I've got nothing better to do than watch you work.

"I didn't mean that. I just meant—"

I know what you meant. It's okay. What's the problem?

"I'm on the Van Wyck, southbound, almost to Jamaica Avenue, following a late-model Chrysler New Yorker, muddy plates, deliberately obscured it looks like. The driver or someone with him took two shots at me outside my apartment building to keep me from helping Samantha Cox, the newscaster. She came to my place uninvited to talk to me about I have no idea what. She resisted, but he or they got her in the car before I could get to her."

You want backup, Joe, you should be calling Communications.

"What I want is to know what Sam Cox wanted."

"*Sam*"?

"Fuck you, Neil."

She wants to know about Hriniak and Jenny Swale, maybe.

"No one knows about that."

I know about it. If I know about it, where I am, there's a good chance she knows about it where she is.

"Maybe. So who're the guys who snatched her? What do they want? How many are there? They want me to follow them, don't they? They're not running, they're leading, aren't they? They weren't on Queens Boulevard when I got on, were they? They waited to see which way I'd go, then they got in the service lane and got ahead of me, didn't they?"

Don't know. Sorry.

"Come on, Neil."

Sorry. Some things I know and some things I don't.

"I don't get it."

I don't either, but that's the way it is. I know who's going to be in the Super Bowl, but not what you're asking.

"Who's in the Super Bowl?"

You don't want me to tell you. You won't enjoy the playoffs.

"Come on, Neil. I can make a few bucks. Doug Aiello, Connie's husband, thinks he's Mr. NFL."

It'd be dirty money. You wouldn't enjoy spending it.

"Try me. Neil? . . . Come on, Neil, don't fade out like that. *Neil!*" But that was the way it went: Sometimes his dear sweet old partner was right there, sometimes he wasn't. Instead of wasting his time asking for winners of football games, Cullen should have been asking who lights the moon, who makes the stars, who does the sun, who does it all, why are there mice, why are there cows, who killed Jo Dante?

But there wasn't time to waste anymore anyway. The maroon New Yorker was getting off the Van Wyck at the exit to the Southern State.

Joe?

"What? You're back? Are they in the Super Bowl, Neil? Are the Giants in?"

I just wanted to say—be careful.

"Yeah, yeah. I'll be careful. Are the Giants in? Make it quick, will you. I'm going to lose them."

You know, I meant to say—I'm impressed at how you know car makes and models. You knew that was a Subaru wagon back there that got its windshield blown away. You didn't used to know a Benz from a Buick.

"It's a tribute to you, my dear sweet old partner. A homage. Now, about the Giants . . ."

Be careful, Joe.

"I'm being careful. I'm being careful."

Be careful, Joe. You're . . . you're drunk.

16

Not so drunk that he didn't know the ass end of Kennedy airport when he saw it: level, muddy, dour; concrete and tarmac and sawgrass protected (from whom?) by chain link and razor tape; smelling of diesel and jet slop, of rot and rust; sounding of banshees having their guts ripped out without anesthetic—where else could it be?

The maroon New Yorker was moving fast now, and the valiant Valiant couldn't keep up. All of a sudden it *was* a chase, and it was no contest.

The New Yorker's taillights were big and aristocratic and easy to follow, but then they got mixed up with runway lights and became characterless. The New Yorker's brightwork glinted now and again, but so did twisted scrap. Cullen rolled down the window to try to hear the New Yorker, but all he heard was the chug of the valiant Valiant's engine and the breath of jets.

He'd lost the New Yorker, so he stopped, right in the middle of a road that didn't seem to have any purpose other than this—to be a conduit for disposing of first-magnitude stars.

The valiant Valiant panted; it creaked and sighed. Cullen switched off its lights and the darkness collapsed around it like a tent whose center pole had been kicked out.

Joe?

"I know, Neil. What the fuck am I doing?"

More to the point, why have they led you all this way just to lose you? I think you were right, I think they did want you to follow. So why lose you now?

"Why does anybody do anything? Neil, I didn't get a chance to ask you, you probably know: Who lights the moon, who makes the stars, who does the sun, who does it all, why are there mice, why are there cows, who killed Jo Dante?"

Come on, Joe. Get a grip. Someone's setting you up. You've got to ask yourself why.

"All right—why?"

Ask yourself. You're getting too close to something—or someone thinks you are.

"I told you, I'm not working on anything like that. The Hriniak-Swale thing, there's no connection between her filing the grievance and getting hammered."

Then who killed Jo Dante—and why? And what about Ann?

Cullen laughed. "Hey, Neil, Ann and I're having some problems, but she wouldn't lure me out here to hammer me."

Someone tried to hammer Ann, asshole. Someone thinks she's getting too close to something. Maybe they think she told you what she knows.

"Ann's been working mainly on Quintana Davidoff."

If Cullen's dear sweet old partner said anything to that it was sucked up by the undertow of a jet groaning down through the clouds like some big fat spoilsport too long on his feet and dying to sit. The crash of sound was so loud—

Joe.

—that it shattered the valiant Valiant's windshield.

Joe!

"Look at that, Neil. It just *evap*orated."

Joe, for Christ's sake, he's shooting again! Get down!

A bullet *ping*ed off the dashboard and broke the window on the passenger's side. Cullen went down to the floorboards, then out the passenger's door. He ran low and broken-field to a mound of snow-covered something and slipped and slid over the top of whatever it was and down the other side, where he planned to remain for the rest of his life, so peaceful was it. He was not so drunk, he was relieved to find, and not so frightened, that he hadn't remembered to bring along his shoulder holster. He slipped the holster on, remembering what it said in the Regs and Recipes: *If you ain't strapped, fucking get strapped.*

Another jet moaned down through the clouds, crushing sense, deranging, confusing. Cullen wanted just to keep his head down, his mind clenched, but he knew that this was the time when the tall, dark, ugly stranger would make another move.

He peeked around the mound of whatever it was and saw a shadow climbing up the valiant Valiant's passenger door. The door was closed; he must have thrust it shut behind him as he ran from the car—why or how he didn't know, it didn't matter, the door was closed.

He thinks you're inside.

"I know. Keep your head down, Neil, for Christ's sake."

I'm dead, Joe. You keep your head down.

"Neil, can you see how many there are?"

Shhh. That jet's long gone.

"There'll be another. Tell me then, tell me where they are."

Shhh.

Cullen peeked again at the valiant Valiant. Nothing. No shadow, no shadow-caster. Nothing.

"Cullen." Behind him. Be*hind* him.

NYPD Rules, Regs, Helpful Hints, Decorating Tips and Recipes, Rule Number One, *Número Uno,* Do Not Repeat Not Break This Rule Under Penalty of Getting Hammered: *When a scumbag who has previously been discharging his weapon in your direction sud-denly throws down on you from behind, hammer the scumbag first and ask questions a whole hell of a long time later.*

Cullen rolled and fired without aiming and kept on firing and kept on and kept on until the chambers of his dull silver stainless-steel-alloy Smith & Wesson .38-caliber six-shot spurless-hammer double-action revolver were empty. He kept on pulling the trigger, pulling and pulling, for a while longer. The Regs and Recipes didn't say it, but you went for your piece infrequently, fired it rarely, once you *had* fired it, you found it difficult to stop. Cullen wasn't having fun or anything—not especially; he was just finding it . . . difficult to stop.

The very first shot punched the scumbag in the neck, which wasn't where the Regs and Recipes said to aim, they said to aim at the scumbag's chest and gut, where there was more of the scumbag. It punched him in the neck and his neck gushed blood like a burst balloon gushes water. The Regs and Recipes didn't say it, but when you punched somebody in the neck and his neck gushed blood like a burst balloon, it was as good as punching him in the middle of his face or the middle of his chest.

But Cullen knew that he had pulled his punch. Sometimes—Ann could go on about this; it was one of the things Ann went on about—you'd slap at a mosquito or a fly or a cockroach with your bare hand, you'd have the varmint dead to rights, but you'd pull your punch, you'd shy your hand away, you'd dread the sharp *squish,* the spurt of bug juice, you'd just graze it, you wouldn't hit it full, you wouldn't hit it solid, and it would buzz off or skitter off and you'd feel like a jerk, a cowardly, inept jerk.

Cullen had pulled his punch.

He hadn't been able to help it.

It's just that he had been so surprised.

He hadn't expected to recognize the scumbag motherfucker.

He hadn't expected to know the scumbag motherfucker.

He hadn't expected the scumbag motherfucker would be a cop.

Paul Messina.

The scumbag motherfucker.

The maroon New Yorker was down the road a ways, the road without purpose, the conduit for disposing of first-magnitude stars.

The first-magnitude star was facedown on the floorboards in the back, hands cuffed behind her, mad as . . . well, as a first-magnitude star somewhat compromised. She was even madder that Cullen didn't have the keys to the cuffs, that he had to go all the way back to where the scumbag motherfucker Messina lay to get them.

Uncuffed, she sat up and jabbed at her ultrablond hair, punishing it for its ultradisarray. "You have a radio in your car, right? I want to call a crew."

Which reminded him: He should call Mystee, tell her he'd killed somebody. He'd pulled his punch, but he'd killed somebody. He sat on the passenger's end of the New Yorker's front seat, the door open, his feet on the ground. "What the fuck is going on?"

Sam Cox yanked at the slim skirt of her little wool number. "How do I know?"

"Was that scumbag motherfucker alone?"

"Who? Oh . . . *Yes,* he was alone."

"All alone?"

"*Yes.*"

"Do you know who the scumbag motherfucker is?"

"*Know* who he is? Of course I don't *know* who he is."

"He's a cop," Cullen said.

Sam Cox shifted to look out the back window toward where the scumbag motherfucker lay. She shifted back and stared at Cullen. "*A cop?*"

"What were you doing at my apartment? How did you get there? What about your show?"

She looked away, at nothing, at anything. "I wanted a story for the eleven. I took a taxi to your place."

"What story?"

"I wanted to know if they were dirty."

" 'They'?"

She crafted a look of supreme irritation. "Todd and Swale."

"You wanted to know if they were dirty."

"Yes."

"You wanted to know if Todd and Swale were—"

"*Yes!* I *said* yes!"

"You wanted to know if Todd and Swale were dirty so you took a taxi all the way out to my house."

Her look now was pitying. "Must you?"

"I just hammered a cop. I can do anything I fucking want."

Sam Cox reached over the seat back and touched Cullen's shoulder. "I'm sorry. I don't understand any of this. He must have followed the cab. I rang your bell, and all of a sudden there he was."

"You don't know him?"

"I *said* I don't know him."

"You never saw him before?"

"I *said*—"

"You didn't, actually. You didn't say a fucking thing one way or the other."

Her voice got soft, childlike. "I'm sorry. This is hard for you, I know. . . . I *don't* know him. I *never* saw him before."

Cullen got up from the New Yorker's front seat.

Sam Cox looked frightened, as though he was going to leave her there. "Where're you . . . ?"

"To my car. I have a phone. Just wait here. You'll be all right."

Cullen walked back to the valiant Valiant.

Joe?

"I know, Neil."

She couldn't have taken a taxi. The drivers're on strike.

"I know."

It was on the news.

"I know." Cullen shook glass dust from the phone and pressed 3. Jeanie Maslosky answered again. *"Hello?"*

"Jeanie, it's Joe Cullen."

"Hang on, Joe. Richie just got out of the shower."

"Cullen? What's up? Where are you?"

"I'm not sure exactly, Captain. Somewhere at the ass end of Kennedy."

17

Decades, it seemed to Ann, had passed since the wedding, in the Tristan~Isolde Room of the vast, strange structure out somewhere near where Queens and Nassau counties blur together, of Detective Two Maria Esperanza and Bronx County Criminal Court bailiff Quincy Ladislaw; so she wasn't altogether surprised at first when through the door of Mabel Parker's office in another odd structure, a building with seven sides on Waverly Place in the Village, walked Maria.

Maria put her hands on her hips, pouted what Joe Cullen called her Neneh Cherry pout, and said, "What the fuck?"

By which time Ann had calculated that Maria ought still to be on some island in some tropical ocean, and not on Manhattan Island in the pincers of two frozen rivers. "Hey. You're on your honeymoon."

Maria grasped her arm inside the elbow. "Honeymoon *this*. Talk to me, would you, please, okay, babe? Bombs? Guns? What? Somebody tries to hammer you, Cullen hammers a cop? What is going *down*?"

Mabel Parker raised her eyebrows. "Ah, you're Joe Cullen's partner. Is this official?"

Maria stuck out her butt, jammed the back of a hand against it,
mocked Mabel's expression. "Who're you?"

Ann got between them and took each by an arm. "Meet Mabel
Parker, Maria. She's a friend, she's my lawyer. Mabel, Detective
Maria Esperanza, Internal Affairs Unit."

Curt nods. Sharp sibilances.

"Ms. Parker."

"Ms. Esperanza."

Ann could feel them resisting each other like two magnets, North
Pole to North Pole. Both were dark-haired: Mabel was pale and
narrow, Maria swarthy and voluptuous. Both dressed somewhat se-
verely on the outside—Mabel in a blue pinstripe suit, Maria in a
banker's gray skirt and navy blazer—but there was a glimpse of
midnight-blue bra at the placket of Mabel's burgundy silk blouse,
and under Maria's ivory sweater a chantilly lace camisole hovered
like the X ray of her soul.

Frenchwomen, Ann recalled Holly Brubach writing in the *New
Yorker,* were "aware of their erotic responsibilities." These two New
Yorkers, one born in Jamaica Estates, the other transplanted from
Asbury Park, were just as hip; each knew that she had it in her to
drive men nuts, each fulfilled her obligation in her own way. Ann
supposed that that would make them in some fundamental way
adversaries, which would explain why they were behaving like longtime rivals who have finally been introduced by the object of their
ardor.

"How's Stacy?" Ann said, to say something. "Stacy's Maria's husband," she explained to Mabel. "How did you know I was here?" If
Abbott or Costello had been there, she would have inquired who
was playing third.

Maria was still sizing Mabel up, leaning back a little to see her
better around the intervening Ann. "You used to work for Leah
Levitt."

Maria usually spoke without accent, without inflection, so Ann took note of the affected *Chew used to work* . . . More Latina equaled more Romance equaled, Ann supposed, greater erotic responsibilities *and* capabilities.

Mabel said only, "Yes." It was a big yes; it answered lots of questions. Yes, Mabel had worked as an assistant prosecutor in the office of New York County District Attorney Leah Levitt. Yes, she had resigned from that position because, yes, the affair she had been having with an arbitrageur named Norman Levitt—yes, Leah's husband—had ceased to be a secret. Yes, Mabel herself had lifted the lid on her own indiscretion; yes, she had been forced to do so by her responsibility as an officer of the court. Yes, from the love-nest apartment where she and Norman met twice a week, Mabel had chanced to see a mysterious stranger leaving, by a back door and through a hole in the fence, a town house on the next street in which one of the town's more sensational recent murders, that of the then police commissioner, Charles Story, had been committed. Yes, after some procrastination, she had told the cops what she saw, and incidentally how she happened to be where she was to see it. Yes, indeed.

Some people knew—and cherished—every detail of Mabel's delicious little tale; some knew a little; some knew nothing. It was one of those stories. Mabel waited to see how schooled Maria was.

Maria had heard bits and pieces. She often resisted knowing too much about the foibles of gringos. Knowing too much made not liking them too easy. Maria looked away from Mabel to Ann, and answered her dangling question. "Bobby Cummings, from the Bomb Squad, said you were staying here." She flicked a look around at *here:* the thirdhand institutional furniture, the brimming file cabinets, the tiers of cardboard file drawers stacked along the walls wherever there wasn't a door or a window; everywhere on the furniture, the cabinets, the drawers, the floor, the remains of meals ordered in by someone who had heard of nutrition the way she had heard of exercise, of a social life, of weekends, nights off, and vacations, of sex that didn't require batteries or alternating current. Drug dealers' lawyers had offices like this: fuck ambiance, just get me kicked. Mabel's rep was for helping beaten, raped, abandoned, misused women who had as little concern, Maria supposed, for decor. "There's an apartment here too?"

Mabel tossed her head. "A room in the back with a bed, a fridge, a microwave." She rolled a swivel chair out from under her desk, swept a stack of unread *American Lawyer*s and *New York Law Journal*s off a leather armchair, liberated a Conran's folding chair from her chesterfield coat and her briefcase. "Sit, sit. You guys want coffee or tea? The coffee's brewed, the tea's from a bag and not-quite-boiling water from one of those bottled water machines."

Ann sat on the folding chair and asked for plain tea. Maria sat on the swivel chair and asked for black coffee. Mabel went down the hall to the office of the architects with whom she shared the cost of the coffeemaker and the water cooler.

"You okay?" Maria said.

"I wasn't hurt," Ann said. "I'm scared."

"You know who did it?"

"Left the bomb?"

"I don't think they 'left' it, Ann. I think they put it there."

"Kind of."

" 'Kind of.' What kind of answer is 'kind of'?"

Ann thanked God she'd been tutored in yuppie-newsbitch evasion tactics. "You didn't come back because you heard about Joe, did you? How could you have heard about him in the islands?"

Mabel reappeared with their drinks and a light coffee for herself. She sat on the lip of the leather chair; to sit deeper in it was to disappear. "So . . ."

Maria tasted her coffee. "This is good."

Mabel smiled slightly, warily. The architects, three men, three tall trim funny good-looking sexy men with T-squares and nifty metal pencils and pleated pants and loud suspenders and wild ties and beautiful shirts and tortoiseshell glasses, three m-a-r-r-i-e-d men, made coffee so much better than her coffee that when they weren't around to make it, when they were out doing whatever it is that architects do when they're not at their drafting tables, surveying sites or being true to materials or wining clients or whatever, Mabel ordered coffee from the coffee shop at Sixth and Waverly. The architects still weren't in this morning, there had been a lot of coming and going already, so Mabel had made a pot herself.

Maria put her cup aside, faced Mabel squarely, opened up her body a little, spread herself. "Stacy, my husband, is a bailiff. Maybe Ann told you. Bronx Criminal. Stacy's brother, Lionel, owns a diner in Newark. He wanted to be a cop, Lionel, but he has double vision from a car crash when he was a kid. He keeps up on crime news though, he's always calling Stacy with his up-to-the-minute theories on whatever murders are in the news. On Tuesday night—he was found Wednesday morning—Joseph Downey, African-American, thirty-six, a hairdresser, was hammered in his shop near Penn Station, Newark. Most of his clients were prostitutes and transvestites, a lot of them junkies, the cash register was empty, so was Downey's wallet, the cops thought robbery for money, for drugs, open-shut.

"But Lionel happened to know, because one of his customers was a customer of Downey's, that Downey also did tattooing. He was hammered with a twenty-two handgun, the same caliber Elvis Polk used to hammer the cops in Rockland, Todd and Swale. Polk had five teardrops—tours in the J—tattooed on his left cheek. Lionel wondered if maybe Polk went in to have his tattoos altered, then hammered Downey to shut him up. He called me, I called Maslosky—my commanding officer," she explained to Mabel. "Maslosky passed it on up the line. *Seguro,* sure enough, both bullets were fired from the same piece. . . .

"After he hammered the cops, Polk got away in Jenny Swale's car, a Plymouth Volare. It turned up Monday at a strip mall in New Milford, Pennsylvania, up by the New York border, kind of near Binghamton. A 1986 Oldsmobile Delta Eighty-eight was boosted that same day from the same mall. It's a good bet Polk boosted it. . . .

"Talking to Maslosky, Ann, to answer your question about did I hear about Joe in the islands, Maslosky told me about him. Stacy understood that I had to come back."

Mabel inched even closer to the edge of her chair. "Elvis Polk's prosecution for possession of computer hardware from the SpeedAir heist was mainly a Queens County case. But there was a New York County end to it, which I handled when I was an ADA. I never spoke a word to Elvis Polk, I never even had a sense that he knew my name, but this morning Elvis Polk called this office. He left a message on my machine, he said he'd call again, he said he had something important to tell me, he said not to call the cops.

"I didn't call the cops, I called Althea Ruth, Powell Ruth's wife, who's a friend. Powell happened to answer." Mabel shrugged, as if to say she couldn't help it if her friend's husband was chief of department. Then she looked pleading, as if to say it worked for her, did it work for them?

Maria wondered, What did it matter? These gringos. A cop killer tells you not to call the cops, so you *don't* call the cops? *¡Caramba!*

Mabel said, "An Emergency Service squad was just here to take the answering-machine tape for analysis and to set up a tap. I think—I've thought from the first—that Elvis is somebody's pawn. Somebody wanted those cops dead, they got Elvis to kill them, they offered him a ride out of the country, a new identity, whatever. But he didn't take it; he's afraid they'll kill him, hammer him, the people who set it up. He was running from them, at first, as well as from the cops. Now I think he wants—"

Mabel turned toward a knock on the door, a knock followed, before she could reply, by the door's opening and in rolling State Senator Steven Jay Poole, just two backup singers in attendance today, one between the handgrips of his wheelchair, another hanging back outside in the hall.

Poole spread his arms, evangelistically. "Mabel. Mabel, Mabel, Mabel. My favorite counselor. Looking forward all morning to this meeting. An unexpected bonus—Ann Jones, my favorite TV journalist. Oh, don't make a face like that, Ann. Yes, you are; yes, you truly are my favorite TV journalist. Trust you're okay, Ann. Horrified to hear what happened. That poor young man. And Maria Esperanza, my favorite gold shield. Maria, Maria, Maria, how could you go and get married like that without at least giving me a chance to plead my case? Hey, best wishes, Maria. Truly. I mean it. *Felicidades*. What a delicious sight the three of you are. They a delicious sight, Jerry? Ever see such a delicious sight?"

Jerry, the backup singer, probably had. He probably thought any three pumped-up oiled blondes in thong bikinis with D-cups a more delicious sight. But he giggled responsively, his bald head bobbling up and down on his gigantic neck, his walrus mustache flapping.

Mabel had taken off her watch and was jiggling it next to her ear, as if it were to blame for her having been taken by surprise. "Everyone knows everyone, I guess. Ann, you've covered the story, Maria, I'm sure you know too that Senator Poole lives on the block where Quintana Davidoff died. He wants to put together some kind of benefit. I've helped with benefits for crime victims before. He wants my input."

"A benefit, I hasten to add"—Poole held up a hand that commanded them to stop thinking what they were surely thinking— "that will not be merely a sleazy attempt to buy off the Davidoffs, but will be an opportunity for the many thousands of New Yorkers moved by this tragedy to express their heartfelt sorrow. . . . Wait outside, will you, Jer?" Poole said to the backup singer without looking at him. "Thanks, buddy. Either you or Eddie go down and get some coffee, okay, pally? I'll give you a buzz when I need you, if these three delicious women get to be too much for me."

Ann had been around Steve Poole more than a few times, had been treated like the flavor-of-the-month every time, and had remarked that in his presence the nonphysically disadvantaged, the undisabled, the . . . the normal were reluctant to stand up. Those standing when he entered a room sat, those seated stayed sitting. Opponents and allies were locked in at Poole's altitude.

So Ann stood, breaking the spell. She hooked her hand at Maria Esperanza. "Come on, let's go get some coffee too. Or breakfast. Waffles. Nice to see you, Senator. We'll be back in a while, Mabe."

18

The coffee shop, unaccountably, was jumping, as if they were giving something away, which they were not. All the booths were taken, there was a long, hungry line for the next empty, Ann and Maria weren't hungry anyway, so they went for a walk, east on Waverly to Washington Square Park, then this way and that, on the paths, the walks, crisscross, down and around, over the so-called grass. The sky was sky blue and brilliant, but a killjoy wind kept shoving onstage dark clumpy clouds that would turn everything solid gray for you would think forever.

"It's officially winter," Ann said. "I don't think I'd realized. When did it get here—yesterday?"

"Which means the days're getting longer," Maria said.

"Ooh. An optimist. You don't have a tan. Were you fucking the whole time?"

"And wearing number-fifteen sunblock. Number-fifteen sunblock should get a Nobel Prize for being one of the few things in the world that actually works."

Just like that, Ann was naked in Acapulco. "The vacation I took with Joe after he got shot? We fucked our brains out. I don't remember what number sunblock we used. There wasn't time for sunblock; we didn't have the energy for sunblock. Have you seen him?"

"Yesterday for a while. He hasn't been charged with anything, but he's confined to Midtown West until whenever. He seems okay. He was legally drunk when he hammered Messina, so he's suspended. Failure to call in a ten-thirteen, failure to get authorization to pursue—it was a real fuck-the-backup-I'm-going-in behavior. Hriniak's been coming down hard on cowboys, he's obliged to come down hard on Joe."

Ann remembered coming down hard on Joe once, in a marina in Port Jefferson (or was it Port Washington?) in the cabin of the boat belonging to a girlfriend of Neil Zimmerman's. Neil and the girl-friend—Rawley, Tawny, Cheney, Lacey; all his girlfriends had had names that could have been first names, they could have been last names, they could have been nicknames, they could have been the names of dogs or small towns—had gone grocery shopping ashore on folding bicycles and Ann and Cullen had stayed aboard and added another location to their life list: Cullen had been on his back on the narrow bunk and Ann had found something to hang on to on the ceiling—or whatever sailors call it—of the cabin, and had been able to come down hard on Cullen, then go back up, then come down hard, then go back up—without hurting him, without hurting her, without hurting either of them one little bit.

And she remembered Cullen's walking out on some movie once after the cop on the screen said, "Fuck the backup, I'm going in." Out on the street he'd explained: "I don't give a shit if the public buys it or not. I'm concerned that some impressionable rookie cop'll see it and think that's the behavior that's expected of him. He'll fuck the backup, he'll go in, and his partner and everybody else involved will be in treble jeopardy as a result."

Should she tell somebody about that, get it into the record? Would it do him any good, or would they only say—whoever *they* were—that naturally she'd want to cover for him, he was her lover, her paramour, her . . . her suitor, her . . . her . . . ?

"So who is this Messina?" Ann said. "I mean, I read about him, I read he's got wise-guy relatives, but he's not the first cop with wise-guy relatives. Was that wise-guy behavior—snatching Sam Cox? What was that all about? I'll tell you what I think: I think Billy Ellis is behind it all. Never heard of Billy Ellis? Billy Ellis is the executive producer of NewsFocus 14, which has gone through the ratings roof thanks first to the bombing of one of its forty-watt bulbs, then to the snatching of its first-magnitude star, all within just a few days of each other. We haven't even been on the air, Sam and I. Sam's holed up no-one-knows-where. I called her house, I called her place in Bridgehampton, but— Oh wait. Of course. How could I not have figured that out?"

Ann had stopped dead. Maria stopped too and turned back to her. " 'Of course' what?"

Ann only shook her head and started up again. "What did Joe say—about Messina?"

"We just talked about the weather, about this and that," Maria said. "As a courtesy, Maslosky let me read the transcript of one of the first IAU interviews. Bobby Colavito caught the job. Bobby's Maslosky's little-bitty pretty one these days—a *primero* ballbreaker. Bobby's got wise-guy relatives himself, so no one's going to be able to say he bought a bill of goods from Joe. . . . Here's what Joe's saying:

"He had a talk with the Queens ADA and the PD who handled Elvis Polk's SpeedAir possession rap and who sat in on Polk's meeting with Todd and Swale. The PD, Margaret Morris, told Joe she thought Polk crammed to know just enough about SpeedAir to make it seem he knew more, that he smoked Todd and Swale into thinking he could roll over on people he couldn't roll over on.

"Joe met the PD and the ADA in a bar on Queens Boulevard, by the courthouse. The ADA, Carlton Woods, was drunk and loud. A cop who happened to be undercover in the bar, on some kind of sting, told Joe he'd seen Woods in another bar a couple of weeks ago—with Paul Messina. One of Messina's wise-guy relatives, I guess you know, a cousin, did points for SpeedAir. And with—"

"Whoa. Wait. Please." Ann stopped again and held up her hands, fingers splayed, trying to keep facts from overwhelming her. "I don't get any of this. I hear the words, I know the names, I can sort of follow the connections, but I don't understand. Polk *did* kill Todd and Swale?"

They were at the southwest corner of the park, near the chess tables, SRO as usual, never mind the weather, never mind the time of day. The émigrés and the prodigies and the patzers and the blitzers and the kibitzers craned like carrion birds over the cement boards, unmindful of the real world, premeditating psychic murders. If the wind wafted Ann's words their way, they might have wondered in some dusty, useless closets of their minds just who this Polk was, and did he annihilate this Todd, this Swale, simultaneously or in succession, had his pieces been black or white, what openings had he played, what variations, what inventions?

"Yes," Maria said. "He killed them."

"With a gun planted in the car?"

"Now that's something else. Woods, the ADA, went on to Joe about Todd and Swale's switching cars. They drove Polk down from Wallkill in Todd's car, they started back in Swale's. He went on about it, Woods, about the cops' not noticing the switch, not making something of it."

"You're a cop. What do you make of it?"

"No dirtbag small-time dickhead punk would have any influence over what car they took."

That was clear, that was direct. Many thousands of dollars in therapy and Ann was still shy of such clarity, such directness. "So, then, if there was no certainty which car they'd take, guns must've been planted in both cars. There must still be one in Todd's car. Have you looked—you, the cops, I mean?"

Maria nodded. *"Nada."*

*"Noth*ing?"

Maria shrugged. "My guess—and Joe's: The piece was planted at the last minute, or whenever it was absolutely clear which car Todd and Swale were taking. Or guns were planted in both cars, and the one in Todd's was unplanted right after they left."

"Unplanted by whoever planted it?"

"Exactamente."

"So are we talking a cop here?" Ann said. "Are we talking a cop wanting other cops hammered, planting guns in their cars where dirtbag small-time dickhead punks would find them and hammer them, the other cops?"

"That's my guess. And Joe's. And probably most everybody else's."

"Okay," Ann said. "I'll bite. What cop?"

Maria took Ann's arm and they started up again, back the way they'd just come, along the west side of the park, heading north. "While I was away, Joe caught a job. Jenny Swale, back last spring, alleged that the PC came on to her sexually."

"The PC?"

"Hriniak."

"I know who the PC is. My boyfriend's a cop."

They had hung a right at the Washington Place entrance and headed east, right into the middle of a drug buy. An ounceman in a Nautica jacket and a customer with an NYU backpack and a copy of Truffaut's *The Films in My Life* under his arm sprang apart on hearing Ann's announcement. They had never seen each other in their lives.

*"Hrin*iak came on to Jenny Swale?" Ann said.

"Allegedly. She thought she was alone in Admin on a holiday, she was goofing, dancing with her shirt off, he walked in on her, he liked what he saw, he asked her for some head. Allegedly. Everything to do with the case has been disappeared—the jacket, the computer disk backups, the tapes, *todo*. That brings us back to Messina again. The alleged harassment happened over the Memorial Day weekend. Messina was part of a skeleton crew on duty Downtown. Joe thinks Hriniak was set up, that he was lured into walking in on Swale, that the jacket was disappeared to make it look like Hriniak was covering up, that Messina was in on it. He thinks maybe—this is where it gets very speculative, very cloud-cuckoo-land—*may*be Messina planted the piece, or had it planted—his wise-guy relatives, their familiarity with Kennedy airport—to make it look like Hriniak wanted Swale hammered.

"Also—I started to say this before—when Joe met the PD and the ADA in the bar on Queens Boulevard, the cop working undercover told Joe he'd seen the ADA, Woods, with Messina, *and* with one of Steve Poole's backup singers, bald Jerry with the big *bigote*."

"*Bigote?*"

"Mustache."

They made a sharp right and headed back toward the chess tables again, past the artificial asphalt hills that some nursery-school kids marched up and then marched down again, chaperoned by two bundled teachers with wind tears in their eyes.

"Jesus," Ann said.

Maria said, "I know. *Muy extraño.*"

"I meant the kids, those teachers," Ann said. "I just realized: Joe met Connie—do you know Connie? His first wife? His *only* wife, for God's sake—he met her *right* here, in 1972. She was a teacher, at the nursery school *those* kids go to, I bet. I think it's around the corner, on West Fourth, in the basement of a church. Joe was a uniform in the Six; the park was on his beat. Nineteen seventy-two. Lord. I was a senior in high school. Our class trip was to New York. We stayed in some dump off Times Square. We saw *The Fantasticks*, we saw *Godspell*, we saw junkies, whores, pimps, transvestites, pushers. We saw a bum—they were called bums then; the homeless hadn't been invented yet—hit by a bus. We saw two drunks in a knife fight. A cop broke it up by hitting one of them in the kidneys with his day stick; the other one started yelling police brutality, so the cop just turned his back and walked away. The boys saw an X-rated movie, with Kitten Natividad. I wanted to go real bad. I was still a virgin, but I had this fear and longing that deep down I was *really* Kitten Natividad.

"What was our school *think*ing? An awful lot of my classmates have never left Michigan, never left Lansing. I think that trip is why.

A bunch of us—the intellectuals—came down to the Village. We went to the Eighth Street Book Shop. We went to the Fig. We walked through the park, looking for cute folk singers. I probably saw Joe Cullen. I probably thought *he* was cute but was afraid to say so to my friends: Cops were pigs in those days. He looked great in a uniform—I've seen pictures.

"Nineteen seventy-two. God. Nixon was president. Watergate was that summer—the break-in. And Fischer-Spassky. And the Munich Olympics: Olga Korbut, guys with balaclavas and machine guns, *Gemütlichkeit*. Is Joe going to wind up in the J, Maria? They hammer cops in the J, don't they?"

"If Messina was dirty," Maria said, and left it dangling there.

They turned back, heading northeast, around the fountain, arid and awash with crack vials and spent poppers.

"So," Ann said, "Joe caught the job of looking into Jenny Swale's allegation. Did he find out anything?"

"He met with Swale's roommate, Jo Dante," Maria said. "She didn't tell Joe straight out, but she indicated Swale was under pressure from someone. A man. She was going to point him out at Swale's funeral the next day. That night, she was hammered."

Ann had seen Jo Dante's picture, had seen that she was beautiful: an ice maiden. She hadn't been able to help herself, she had wondered if Joe Cullen had been made hot by her coolness, wondered what it would be like if they were married: Joe and Jo Cullen, Jo and Joe Cullen. Joe and Jo too. Jo and Joe too. Joe I and Jo II. Jo I and Joe II. By Doctor Seuss. "*Ham*mered? Everyone's been saying she killed herself."

"There were muscles cut," Maria said. "The ME doubts she could've cut both her wrists to the depth she did."

Ann thought about that, then didn't want to think about it. "I used to consider myself a student of human nature, but I've decided to drop the course. Too many surprise quizzes."

Maria tried not to, but she laughed.

They were by the little kids' playground now, chain-link fence to the sky all around it to keep reality at bay. A homeless man, formerly just a bum, had ignored the fence—there was a gate, after all; the highest fences had gates, *Troy* had a goddamn gate—and was asleep under a wooden ziggurat that kids, if there had been kids around, would have climbed up so as to then slide down a wide slide. But there were no kids in the playground, no one whose party had been crashed. Well, wait—there was one kid, on a swing way down at the other end of the playground: a boy, a girl, too bundled to tell, being pushed by a dad who was clearly an expert, who had figured out that he didn't have to give the swing a push at the end of each period, that he could push on every other and take a respite ever so brief but still a respite to look around, to think some thoughts other than about his son or daughter, other than about swinging. She could get interested in a man like that, a man who liked children *and* who liked some time to himself and knew how to get it. Would he like to be her lover, her paramour, her . . . her suitor, her . . . her . . . ?

"Did you know about the drinking?" Maria said.

Ann nodded. Then shrugged. Then shook her head. "He'd have a beer at dinner. Once in a while he'd have several. I said something about it to Connie, to his ex-wife. We both go now and then to a support group, for widows, wives, girlfriends, but I never said anything to him. I guess that makes me a classic codependent."

Maria held Ann's arm tighter. "Joe told Bobby Colavito he never drank on duty, he never drank when he had to drive, when he had responsibilities, when he was going to be with you, to have sex with you."

"He talked about that to another man? To a cop? Hunh?"

"What he did do, he said—"

"Should you be telling me this? Isn't this privileged?"

"Privilege this," Maria said. "He said there were times when he made up excuses about having to stay at the shop, about being tired, because he'd rather drink than be with you. He told about one night, you were supposed to go out with Mabel to hear a friend of hers sing at a club. Joe wasn't going, it was a girls' night out, but you had dinner at his house first. Mabel called to cancel; her friend had gotten sick. You and Joe got in a fight; you assumed you'd just stay over, he said he'd been looking forward to some time alone, that he felt presumed upon, his space was being intruded on, blah blah blah, all that shit, but the fact was, he wanted you out so he could finish the rest of the six-pack without your commenting that he sure was drinking a lot."

Ann felt like crashing the playground gate herself, crawling in under the wooden ziggurat, curling up next to the sleeping bum/ homeless man, sneaking his Aqua Velva out of the pocket of his topmost overcoat, taking a slug, joining him in dreamland. "What time is it? Let's go have a drink."

"Ann."

Ann thrust her fist upward. "Ann this."

"Are you fucking Steve Poole?" Maria said. "Don't look at me like that. You know how people who're doing each other on the side don't look at each other when they're in public, how they give each other too much room, like they're afraid if they brush elbows they'll end up grinding crotches? I know you know what I'm talking about. I've heard you go on about it. That's the way you and Steve Poole acted back at Mabel's office—like lovers."

Ann took Maria's arm and urged her east. "Let's go to the Violet. You don't have to have a drink, you can have coffee. I won't have a drink, I'll tell you a story. I haven't told anybody. Not Mabel, not my mother, not my brother—the people I tell everything . . .

"At your wedding you said you liked my work, the stuff I did about Quintana Davidoff. Quintana Davidoff Still Dead, Quintana Davidoff, the Girl Who Would Not Die. I'll tell you a story about Quintana Davidoff. . . .

"You're right about Steve Poole and me. No, we're not lovers, you're not right about that. But we do have a special relationship. We're . . . accomplices."

19

Quintana Davidoff, the Girl Who Would Not Die, Quintana Davidoff Still Dead: Undying for just twenty-three days, still dead after just twenty-three days, and already the facts of her fourteen-year, six-month, three-week, six-day life were being warped by the distorting pressures of myth.

Though but a freshman, Quintana *had* occupied the first chair of the cello section in the Middlebrooks Music School senior orchestra; she had *not*, however, as you might have thought had you been tuned in exclusively to the local vibes, been a member of an internationally known string quartet; she had *not* been a soloist with a philharmonic; she had *not* recently signed a six-figure recording contract.

Quintana *had* played an enthusiastic right wing on Middlebrooks's coed junior-varsity field hockey team, but she had not played especially well. (Nor, for what it's worth, had the squad's integration of gender been more than nominal: the JV was almost entirely girls, just as the varsity was almost entirely boys.)

Quintana *had* sat at third board on the girls' chess team, but the team had only five members, two of whom had discovered sex and rarely showed up for analysis sessions. Quintana did win occasional intramural matches, thanks to her deliberate play, a necessity made a virtue, for she often lost her way while imagining a series of moves, and had to retrace and trace anew her steps numerous times. Better, more impetuous players became irritated at Quintana's glacial pace and in trying to accelerate things sometimes blundered fatally.

The French, Math, and Biology clubs, and B'nai B'rith Girls, to all of which Quintana *had* belonged, were open to all comers, met only now and then, and were sinecures that existed mostly to award service credits that looked good on college applications.

Quintana *had* been rehearsing the part of Esther (the Judy Garland role) in Play Pro's *Meet Me in St. Louis,* but aspirants for any parts in the show had been few, for Play Pro was regarded around Middlebrooks as passé. (The hip production to be involved with was the Opera Club's mounting of *The Man Who Mistook His Wife for a Hat.*)

To say, as *had* been said, that Quintana looked like Meryl Streep had been a kind way to say she had great hair and a funny face.

Still, no matter how many slips were occurring between the cup of reality and the lip of history, Quintana *had* been an undeniably bright, attractive, talented adolescent, and her death by a strike to her head by a bottle of expensive vodka that fell or was tossed or let slip from somewhere near the top of one of a pair of majestic dowager apartment buildings, luxury liners steaming serenely across the Upper West Side sea of crime, degradation, violence, and corruption, *had* been an undeniable tragedy, a coincidence of victim and opportunity for which just about every New Yorker had empathy.

Judging from chitchat overheard all over town in every language of the polyglot place, just about every New Yorker had at least heard tell of things falling out of windows or off of roofs (a potted plant toppled by a gust of wind; a tomato placed imperfectly on a kitchen sideboard, then finding its way to the windowsill and out by a Rube

Goldberg series of falls, bounces, and rolls; an electric fan that vibrated out of equilibrium and out it went; an aluminum-and-vinyl chair sucked by an updraft from a rooftop tar beach—those were the anecdotes Ann had accumulated), or had wondered about the myriad projectiles with the potential to descend on them from the uncountable sills, ledges, pediments, gables, mansards, architraves, and loggias beneath which they made their vulnerable way every single day.

"When I was in college," Ann had said to the detective lieutenant from the Nineteenth Precinct who had caught the Quintana Davidoff job, "we kept orange juice and milk and soda on the windowsills of our dorm rooms in the wintertime. Nowadays, I gather, college kids have portable refrigerators in their rooms, to go with their microwaves, their stereos, their TVs and VCRs—God forbid a kid should go to college without a VCR—but we used natural refrigeration."

Lieutenant Al Breckman had been a quarter-final victim of Joe Cullen's in the Detectives Endowment Association's *Jeopardy!* Night (in the category What's It Called? he had erred by asking "What are steers?" instead of "What are oxen?" for the answer, "Castrated male cows raised as draft animals") and knew Ann slightly. He looked up from his notebook. "You want to run that by me again?"

Still wearing the Hind Night Blade tights, the Russell Athletic sweatshirt, the New Balance 495s in which she had been out running in Riverside Park in the balmy twilight of the Saturday after Thanksgiving, one of a string of days that had felt more like May than November; in which, as she wound up her four miles and headed back home, she had happened on the first whitetop summoned by witnesses to the fallen Quintana; in which she had gone on the air live just after six, the bar flashers and alley lights and beacons of whitetops and EMS ambulances gyrating behind her, before the yuppie newsbitches—the other yuppie newsbitches—

even knew what hit them, Ann said, "These buildings aren't dorms, their tenants don't chill things on the windowsills. As warm as it's been the past couple of weeks, as many windows as might've been open, they don't hang out the windows and watch the streetscape with a bottle of vodka at their elbows.

"So what happened is this: Someone went up on the roof of one of those buildings to enjoy the sunset. They took the vodka along, maybe they took an ice bucket too, and vermouth or tonic or orange juice or tomato juice or V-8. They put the vodka on the ledge, they toasted, they smooched, they talked dirty, they argued, they debated, they talked about the future, they reminisced about last summer, they stared into space for all I know, they knocked the vodka over the side. I'm sure it was an accident, I don't think they dropped it deliberately. They held their breath, they looked over the ledge, they saw what had happened, they panicked. They're in their apartment right now, terrified. I don't know why, but I think it's a couple."

Breckman said, "Oh? Well, hey, thanks, Ann. Thanks a lot. That'll save us, you know, *weeks* of knocking on doors. We'll go straight up to the roofs, dust the ledges for prints, look for footprints in the dirt and dust and shit. Maybe they smoked a cigarette while they were up there and we'll find the butt. Maybe it has lipstick on it. Maybe the lab'll make the brand, the manufacturer'll tell us what batch it was from, their shipping department'll run us off a list of stores it went to, one of them'll be a drugstore over on Broadway, the girl at the cosmetics counter'll remember selling a tube of it just this morning, the customer charged it, there'll be a credit-card flimsy, holy shit, she'll live in one of these buildings, we'll knock on the door, she'll open it, she'll have her bag all packed, her nightie, comfortable shoes, a book to read, he'll be right there beside her, he'll have a bag too, pj's, some skin mags, some smokes, they'll hold their hands out to be cuffed, they'll say, 'Great collar, guys. We fucking did it.' We should have this wrapped up by ten, ten-thirty, we'll get to watch *Saturday Night Live*. I don't know how we'd've done it without you, Ann, you're the greatest."

"You're right, Al," Ann said. "I apologize. Forgive me."

"Good," Breckman said. "Now go home or something. You'll catch cold in that outfit. Joe Cullen know you run around the streets looking like that?"

She spared him a sisterhood karate kick in the teeth. "I am going home, but I'll be back to do a piece for the eleven. How many tenants do you think you'll have interviewed by, say, ten-forty?"

Breckman slumped. "You may be Lois Lane, I ain't Superman. These things take time, they take manpower. There was a drug ambuscade in a *bodega* at One Oh Three and Broadway. Three perps, five hammered, two of them mushrooms. Greaseguns. Broad fucking daylight. A Mach-9, a thirty-caliber rifle, a nine-millimeter pistol. And get this—before they made doilies out of everybody, they took pictures, Polaroids, of themselves smiling and swagging and shit with their new toys. They left the snapshots on the fucking counter. How stupid is that? So that's where the manpower is at the moment, looking for mugs to go with the mugs in the pix. That's a better story than this, that's where you should be. This is terrible—I got grown daughters; in five months I'll be a grandfather—but in the overall scheme of things, it ain't shit."

Oh, but it was. Ann knew that it was. As much as she liked Breckman (who had known the Q: What is nose leather? to the A: The pad of skin at the tip of a cat's nose), as much as she liked Breckmanese (*swagging, ambuscade*), she knew the mugs with the mugs in the Polaroids would be bagged or they would not be bagged, but the story, in twenty-four hours, would be as dead as the five who'd been hammered. Quintana, though still dead, would not die.

Ann went home, took a fast shower, changed into a turtleneck, slacks, and a blazer, and went back along Riverside to where Quintana Davidoff had lain. Though it had been dark for hours and a wind whipped up off the Hudson, muttering threats of winter, there was still quite a crowd (a bigger crowd, Ann had wanted to bet Breckman, who didn't look happy to see her back anyway, than the crowd right then around the *bodega* at One Oh Three and Broadway): Eyewitnesses were describing to print reporters, to radio reporters, to yuppie newsbitches and meat puppets from network and local, to anyone who would listen how fourteen-year-old Quintana, dressed in jeans, a Middlebrooks sweatshirt, a blue jean jacket with a portrait of Roland Gift hand-painted on the back, had gotten off a number five bus (*What if the bus had been a few minutes earlier, a few minutes later?* witnesses and listeners both were wondering); how she had been returning home from a friend's, a clarinetist's, where they had been playing Mozart, or, as they liked to say, jamming the Wolfman (*What if she had stayed at her friend's a while more, left a while later?*); how she had crossed Riverside at a stoplight (*What if the light had stayed red a little longer, turned green a little sooner?*), had dawdled down the Drive, perhaps enjoying the setting sun's lurid skypainting over the Palisades (*What if she hadn't lazed along, what if the weather had been cloudy, miserable, raining, cold?*); how she had stopped at one point to shift her cello case from one hip to the other (*What if she hadn't been schlepping it, what if she played the flute?*); how she had headed toward the corner where she would have turned and walked to the brownstone near West End Avenue where she lived with her economist mother and children's-book author-illustrator father (*What if they lived on some other block, what if they weren't so successful, what if they couldn't afford a brownstone, they lived in an apartment building on Columbus, on Amsterdam, she wouldn't have taken the Riverside bus, she'd've taken the subway, or a Broadway bus?*), but had never made it.

Ann had a producer, Mary Young (known to everyone at News-Focus 14 as Young Mary), on the scene to help out by that time, and she set Young Mary to winnowing out the true witnesses from the witness wanna-bes. Just as far more baseball fans than there were seats in the Polo Grounds proclaim they saw Bobby Thomson's pennant-winning home run with their own eyes; just as more aficionados of sex, drugs, and rock 'n' roll than even a farm the size of Yasgur's could corral swear they were at Woodstock from the first chord to the last; just as more connoisseurs of the kinky than Nielsen ever toted up assert they were tuned in when Audrey Horne tied the cherry stem in a knot with her tongue on the penultimate episode of the first season of *Twin Peaks,* so more devotees of morbidity and mortality than there were square feet of sidewalk on both sides of Riverside already purported that they had been looking right at Quintana Davidoff before, when, and after she was hit on the head by the liter of eighty-proof Stolichnaya vodka.

Ann interviewed the best of the bunch, a woman straight out of a Koren cartoon—wild and woolly hair, granny glasses, brown corduroy jumper, black turtleneck, black tights, wool poncho, Birkenstocks, the good parts of tomorrow's, Sunday's, *Times* in a Channel 13 tote bag (along with a Margaret Atwood paperback and a container of Mace), the crossword puzzle already ballpoint-penned into submission; rational, thorough, deadpan, fluent in everything, been everywhere, liberal credentials as perfect as the circles of her big hoop earrings, entirely humorless, deficient in irony, by day a word processor, off-duty a poet, teacher two nights a week of rhyme and meter to other word processor/poets at some continuing education emporium (yet *another* continuing education emporium), a native of a city whose natives know only one word for surfaces on which one stands, be they grass, cement, wood, whatever: "Quintana"— already she was on a first-name basis with the victim—"was walking *down* Riverside, heading for the *corner. All* of a sudden, *just* like that, she was lying on the *floor.* I thought she was *shot*—one of those *drug* things. Or she had some terrible dis*ease.* I thought of the awful *pictures*—the children: Ethiopia, Romania, Chernobyl. Then I saw the pieces of *glass,* I had this crazy thought they were bits of costume jewelry. . . ."

Then Ann went over to Broadway to interview the night manager of the discount liquor store where the vodka had been purchased: "When? Who by? You got to be kidding. Stoli is a quality item, yes, but it *moves.* It's not like some wine, you sell a bottle a week, you remember who bought it on account of they were, you know, unforgettable. You're talking an item on which we do a brisk business. Such items, we do not have total recall of the customers' faces."

Back at the scene, Ann nudzhed Breckman and nudzhed him

and nudzhed him until he let her talk to the latent-print specialist from the Crime Scene Unit, who told her for the record but not for attribution that there were dozens of partial prints on the shards of the bottle: "Which is kinda what you'd expect, right, when ten or twenty or fifty or a hundred people've touched it between the distillery and the liquor store, right? But even if they weren't partials, even if they were the best prints in the history of forensics, right, we'd still have to have prints to match them up with for them to tell us more than diddley, right?"

Then Ann interviewed a bunch of tenants—the executive of the American Civil Liberties Union, the environmentalist actor, the Nobel laureate physicist, the city councilman, the folksinger, the screenwriter, a doctor, a professor—passengers of those luxury liners, notwithstanding the turbulence up on deck to face the boarding parties of reporters.

She went on live just after eleven, taking the handoff from Nancy Albright, sitting in at weekend anchor for Samantha Cox, and staying on the air for twelve minutes, a NewsFocus 14 record, winding up with a live interview with a tenant of one of the buildings who had chosen to stay belowdecks, but, because Ann's lover, her paramour, her . . . her suitor, her . . . her . . . was a cop, because he himself was an ex-cop, had agreed to talk to Ann: State Senator Steven Jay Poole.

"Terrible tragedy. Grief-stricken. First and foremost, to the family, my condolences. Second, obviously, I have no proof. However. We have had security problems. Can't elaborate. Obvious reasons. Nevertheless. Both buildings vulnerable to intruders. The narrow alley between them. Just a metal gate, some razor tape. A panic lock, locksmiths call it. Opens with a push. Roofs have been accessed by unauthorized individuals. Alcoholic beverages consumed. Controlled substances. Crack, marijuana, cocaine, and, yes, heroin. Police alerted. Hopeful. Still . . ."

By virtue of Ann's owning the story that night, Young Mary had staked out a corner of the building lobby as the setting for the interviews, and for this last one had commandeered a chair from the doorman's station for Ann to sit on so she wouldn't tower over Poole, in his wheelchair. Sitting in the chair, legs crossed, microphone extended, her good left side presented to the camera that Poole's chair faced head-on, Ann realized fully for the first time since she'd become a yuppie newsbitch the extent to which she could be jerked around by a subject. Aware peripherally of Young Mary, off to the side of the camera, whirlygigging her finger to encourage her to wrap it up, they couldn't hope for any more time, Ann was aware that Poole, no virgin, was aware of Young Mary too, and wasn't going to let Ann have the last word, wasn't going to let her ask if he could prove what he was alleging—that interlopers, not residents, were responsible for the death of Quintana Davidoff, wasn't going to let her ask for dates and times and names of investigating officers, reference numbers of Unusuals, for substance rather than smoke. Poole was in the smoke business, and smoke, Ann realized with something of a jolt, sinuous, sexy, ever-metamorphosing smoke, probably looked pretty good to the viewing audience out there in television land, probably looked better than a stack of documentation, than a list of dates and times and names of investigating officers, reference numbers of Unusuals, close-ups of those Unusuals with the relevant paragraphs highlighted through the miracle of modern technology.

"Again," Poole was saying, "terrible tragedy. Intolerable when not only are the castles that are our homes invaded, but the invaders behave with wanton negligence that leads to this kind of incalculable loss."

And then Young Mary was right down next to the camera, simulating cutting her throat with one short, sharp gesture to let Ann know that was absolutely without question it.

So Ann handed it back to Nancy Albright; chatted for a moment with Steve Poole, ex-cop, about Joe Cullen, her cop lover, paramour, suitor . . . ; consulted with Young Mary about what they might do for tomorrow's follow-up; thanked the camera crew, the remote van crew, the motorcycle messengers; talked with some cops on the scene she knew through Joe and on her own; talked with some fans, a couple of whom weren't *her* fans, they were the fans of other yuppie newsbitches but couldn't tell them apart; went home.

There was a message on her machine from Joe:.He'd seen her on the six, was she okay, call him. Ann called him and met him at Docks. They sat at the bar. It wasn't the Saturday after Thanksgiving anymore, it was the Sunday. Ann told him everything and he listened and said, "I don't want to have any more children. I feel stingy about time and space. I don't have the generosity a parent ought to have. It's important that you know it's nothing personal, but that it is something I feel very strongly."

She didn't ask him what the fuck was he talking about; she didn't ask how could he listen to her talk about her particularly difficult, particularly rewarding night and then just start talking about himself. What he said followed from what she had said; it was relevant, it made sense. She had made a down payment on a substantial investment in Quintana Davidoff because she wanted a child herself: It wasn't very complicated. "You know, you won't believe this, you'll think I'm being a smartass, as usual—"

"I never think of you as a smartass. Smart and sharp—that's how I think of you."

"You won't believe this, you'll think, for the very first time, that I'm being a smartass, but in my junior year in high school, Advanced Biology, Mister Imperato, I sat by the back door, in the spring we kept the doors open, outside in the hall was an especially big, loud clock, the kind with a minute hand that moves a whole minute at a time, with a big *thunk*. It was impossible when things got dull not to be aware of *every single thunk*. I didn't realize it at the time, of course, but of course that's what it was—my advanced biological clock."

Joe gave her a look that said *Smartass*. Then he said, "It must be hard to want to have children and to be seeing, going out with, involved with, whatever we call it—what do we call it?—someone who doesn't."

"I don't know what to call it. I don't know whether you're my lover, my paramour, my . . . suitor, my . . . my . . . And it is hard, yes."

"We need to talk more about it."

"We do, yes."

"But not tonight."

"No. It's been a hard enough night already."

"Tonight we'll spend apart."

"I think that's a good idea."

"I'll drive you home."

"I'll walk."

"I'll walk you home then."

"No need. This is my neighborhood. I'll be fine."

"I insist. I'll worry."

"If you in*sist,* then drive me. Otherwise, you'll have to walk all the way back to Broadway, and *I'll* worry."

Joe drove her home. At Ann's door they kissed and hugged, not perfunctorily but with the dispatch of the preoccupied. Cullen idled at the curb until she unlocked the door and went into the foyer. When he had driven off, Ann came back outside and walked back down Riverside.

The whitetops were gone, the EMS vans, the ambulances, the unmarked but unmistakable squad cars, the TV remote vans, the reporters' cars, the Crime Scene sawhorses and yellow perimeter tape. The onlookers were long gone, the witnesses and the witness wanna-bes.

Ann crossed to the Riverside Park side of the street and sat on a bench that wasn't right under a bishop's-crook street lamp, it was a little bit in shadow. She wouldn't have said it at the time, but in retrospect, 20/20 retrospect, she was waiting, waiting because she had a sense that if the patch of sidewalk across the Drive *was* a crime scene, that if the death of Quintana Davidoff had strictly speaking been a *crime,* then the perpetrator would be unable to resist having a closer look.

A couple of gays walked by, young, but something in the way they moved said together for a long time, seeing each other, going out with each other, involved with each other—whatever they called it. They paused, looked this way and that at street signs, debated quietly, decided that this was the spot, tipped their heads way back and looked up at the two majestic dowager apartment buildings, down at the sidewalk, up at the buildings. Then they walked on. All the while, each kept a hand in a hip pocket of the other's jeans.

A Cairn terrier scuttled by, followed by its scuttling Cairn terrier of a mistress, whining at it—"Heathcliff"—to "do your goddamn duty." Heathcliff sniffed the cornerstone of the northernmost building. *He'll find something,* Ann thought. *He'll find a clue and become a famous dog.*

Heathcliff squirted a couple of drops and scuttled on. His mistress scuttled after: "Good boy. What a gooood boy!"

A stoner and his moll clumped around the corner and up the Drive, dripping anarchy. She screamed at him that he was rotted, he gave her the finger and called her a slag grid drip cunt, she called him a skid and a ted. *Speaking of children,* Ann thought. *Those're somebody's.*

Samantha Cox came out the narrow alley between the two buildings, pushing open the panic lock on the metal gate topped with razor tape. Scuttling like Heathcliff's mistress, scuttling with apprehension, Samantha Cox went north along the Drive and around the corner and just like that was gone, leaving just a sense of her, a sense of a thin blonde in not a trademark red outfit but a little black dress, black pumps, black coat, black bag, where usually she left an *impression:* ultrablond, ultracoiffed; lips ultrared, ultrasucculent; teeth ultraperfect, ultraivory; skin ultralucid, figure ultralithe, carriage ultrasovereign.

Ann got up. Should she follow, should she stay, was that whom she'd been waiting for? Impossible. And yet . . .

Samantha Cox was back—not all the way, just a little, just enough to take a peek, a step toward that patch of sidewalk, a sniff. She peered, she leaned, she straightened suddenly and fled, running now, on the toes of her pumps, around the corner, gone, the impression indelible now.

Ann sat back down on the bench and tried to breathe. She tipped her head back. Through the lattice of bare branches of a hundreds-of-years-old elm tree she saw a man at a high window in the northernmost building, a living-room window of a line of apartments with knock-down, drag-out river views. None of the other living rooms in that line were lighted brightly. Pale lights in some of them indicated that the tenants were still up, but in other rooms, dens and bedrooms, watching television, maybe, watching *Saturday Night Live* along with Lieutenant Al Breckman, except that it was much too late for that now, it was nearly three, they'd be watching *Hee Haw* reruns, *Ebony/Jet Showcase*, paid programming, the Bowery Boys.

The man had the window open and was leaning partway out. He had been watching, there was no doubt in Ann's mind, she was at the time still a student of human nature, she hadn't yet dropped the course, he had been watching Samantha Cox. He had been watching Samantha Cox, there was no doubt in Ann's mind, watching her protectively, watching her with the concern of a host for a departing guest, wishing her safe-home—safe not from muggers or rapists or murderers: safe from being overseen by someone like Ann Jones, who would see her and put it together. The man, there was no doubt in Ann's mind, she was sure from the way he closed the window, now that Samantha was gone, and moved away from it, now that Samantha was gone, that he was not standing but sitting in a chair, a chair that moved on wheels, a wheelchair. The man was Steven Jay Poole.

Maria Esperanza didn't talk at all after she and Ann left the Violet and walked back across the park to Mabel Parker's office in the building with seven sides on Waverly Place. She had talked herself out, Ann figured, as they walked this way and that through the park, on the paths, the walks, crisscross, down and around, over the so-called grass. She was debating too, Ann figured, having long considered herself a student of human nature, whether to drop the course: Too many surprise quizzes.

But it wasn't that kind of course. Enrollment was irrevocable, there were no refunds or exchanges. Ann found out just how true that was when they got to the building with seven sides. Ann felt as though they had been gone for hours, but the backup singer Steve Poole had called Eddie was downstairs, leaning against a black Coupe de Ville with a legislature plate, reading the *News,* bald Jerry with the big *bigote* was sitting on a window ledge in the hallway outside Mabel's office, reading the *Post,* Poole was inside, tipped back in his wheelchair, nonchalant, alongside the thirdhand institutional desk that Mabel sat behind, awkward on her thirdhand institutional swivel chair.

To a student, to a would-be former student, of human nature, those were puzzlements. The surprises were:

Number one, Samantha Cox, in a trademark red outfit once again, a silk Empire-waist dress with a shirred surplice bodice this time, her ultrablond ultracoiffed hair in a tight bun, pacing by the window, her arms pressed tight against her stomach, an emblem of distress and anxiety.

Number two, Maria Esperanza, who had come in the door behind Ann, going around her as she stopped just inside the door, going around her in a way that left Ann alone, cut her loose, abandoned her, going around her and going right up to Steve Poole and touching his shoulder and saying, "She knows," and looking to Samantha Cox and repeating, "She knows."

20

Carlton Woods going down on her was Margaret Morris's favorite thing. So fine did he do it, stretched out on his belly, his butt sticking up out in the jet stream, his hands squeezing the cheeks of her buns, sliding his tongue way in, sliding it out slow, that she called him Glenn Miller. Carlton would slide his tongue way in, he'd slide it out slow, and *Glenn,* Margaret would moan, *Gleeeenn.*

Carlton, when Margaret Morris moaned like that—*Glenn. Glenn. Glenn, Glenn, Gleeeenn*—felt like stopping what he was doing, getting up off his belly, kneeling between Margaret's legs, placing his thumbs side by side in the center of her Caucasian neck, and strangling her. She was dissing him, didn't she fucking understand that, by not knowing the name of at least one African-American trombonist.

No surprise, really:

Margaret, name a jazz singer.

Peggy Lee.

Name a bandleader.

Paul Shaffer.

Let's try another field, Margaret. Name a pro basketball player.

Larry Bird.

Another.

The guy with the glasses—Kurt Rambis.

The sorry, sad fact, though, was that Carlton Woods couldn't be dissed, he already dissed himself by not knowing the name of even one African-American trombonist either. He knew Billie Holiday sang, and Ella Fitzgerald and Pearl Bailey. He knew Charlie Parker played the . . . the sax, Louis Armstrong played the trumpet, Wynton Marsalis played . . . something. But basically, when it came to music, Carlton Woods didn't know diddley.

Carlton knew what he liked, though. What he liked, behind the locked, bolted, chained-up door of his bachelor crib in Kips Bay, was to get out the CDs and the music videos he kept stashed away (along with his porn flicks) in a dresser drawer where his nosy nieces and nephews wouldn't find them, where his moms, always wanting to clean and dust for him, wouldn't find them, where, above all, his pushy righteous doing-it-for-themselves ballbreaking r-e-s-p-e-c-t African-American older sisters wouldn't find them, always wanting to know who he was going out with, what did she do, where did she live, who were her *peop*le (never dreaming for a second her *peop*le might not be black—sorry—might not be African-American), always snooping around looking for a snapshot, snooping to see if she'd left an earring behind, lipstick, a diaphragm —what Carlton Woods *liked* was to lobe the CDs and scope the music videos of white chicks who sang in their undies: Madonna, Joan Jett, Cher, Sheena Easton, Lita Ford, Vanity, Sheila E (who was Hispanic, wasn't she? and played the drums, didn't she? But what a fuckable, tie-uppable body she had—*damn!*).

He tried sometimes, Carlton, to lobe African-American music and African-American musicians—jazz, R&B, blues, soul, even rap (though it seemed to him that not a few of the seventy-five thousand cases handled each year by the Queens DA's office—that works out to two hundred a day—involved individuals who re-

spected the law less and hip-hop more). Sometimes, during a lull
between cases (if you could call a lull the gasp for air between
seventy-five thousand cases yearly, two hundred a day, Carlton
would close the door to his office, put on the headphones of the
Walkman his oldest righteous doing-it-for-herself ballbreaking r-e-
s-p-e-c-t sister Ashanta gave him last Christmas (along with an
Anita Baker tape), and lobe WBLS.

"WBL Kicking S," the deejays called it, the prince of the deejays
being Frankie Crocker, who waxed, "There ain't no other like this
brother," who sometimes came back on the air after the news or the
traffic and ran a "box check" so the home boys in Harlem, in Bed-
Stuy, in Jamaica and Morrisania (places as foreign to Carlton
Woods as Mauritius or Tromsø or Terre Adélie) could set the levels
on their boom boxes, their blasters, the rigs on their Troopers, their
Cherokees, their Samurais, their Monteros:

"Check the treble, check the high hat, check the bass. Yo, 'cross
the street there, crank it *up,* bruhtha: Salt-N-Pepa, 'Expression.' "

WBL Kicking S scared the shit out of Carlton Woods, it spoke to
him, it whispered in his ear that maybe he was on the wrong side of
the bar, maybe he should be chilling out there on the spectator
benches, maybe he should be lamping in the halls with the
ouncemen and the con men and the hit men and the whores and
the whoremasters and the poor sorry fucks, waiting on the un-
derpaid PDs and the overpaid-with-dirty-money-overdressed-
overjeweled scumbag dipshit shyster defense lawyers to cut them a
deal, to cop a plea, to cut them loose, lobing while they chilled,
while they lamped, to their Walkmans, their Aiwas and 'Sonics,
cranked way up so you could hear the tinny music and voices coming out of the headphones, you could cop if you were hip to them,
M. C. Hammer and Queen Latifah and A Tribe Called Quest, the
music and voices sounding like music and voices from another
planet. (Some judges told the ouncemen and the con men and the
hit men and the whores and the whoremasters and the poor sorry
fucks to crank the music the fuck down, other judges didn't mind a

little tinny extraterrestrial music and voices in their courtrooms, they preferred it to a riot.)

The ouncemen and the con men and the hit men and the whores and the whoremasters and the poor sorry fucks lobed Above the Law, "Murder Rap"; Vicious Beat Posse, "Legalized Dope"; Public Enemy, "Welcome to the Terrordome"; Redhead Kingpin & the F.B.I., "Pump It Hottie"; Bobby Jimmy & the Critters, "Somebody Farted"; the Geto Boys, "Trigga Happy Nigga"—wack shit an assistant district attorney with a good grip on the ladder and his sights on the topmost rungs should word up *not* be lobing.

What he should be lobing, Carlton word up knew, was Frankie Crocker's Evening Bath, every weekday from six-thirty to seven or so P.M., some of the night-shift secretaries in the word-processing pool lobed it on *their* Walkmans and Aiwas and 'Sonics, lobed it not to hear wack shit but def sounds. (Kenya Dees was one of them, a stone African-American fox who if Carlton could ever clear his mind of white chicks who sang in their undies would be who would move in and take over, Kenya with the beaded cornrows and the leather miniskirts and the pictures on her desk of Angela Davis and Winnie Mandela, Kenya who never said a word to Carlton but whose eyes, every time she looked at him in his eight-hundred-dollar Geoffrey Beene glen-plaid suit and his hundred-fifty-dollar Charvet pinpoint oxford shirt and his ninety-dollar Chanel necktie and his two-hundred-dollar Allen-Edmonds shoes, said *hunkie-fucker, hunkie-lover, hunkie-ass-hunkie-kisser.*) But six-thirty to seven or so P.M. was for Carlton Woods prime deal-cutting time, time for working the hallways, the elevators, for leaving his door open so the PDs and the scumbag shyster defense lawyers could stop by and mention just in passing, since they were on that floor, oh hey and by the way, almost forgot, remember, uh, what'shisname, looking at reckless endangerment, what it would take to make their ouncemen and con men and hit men and whores and whoremasters and poor sorry fucks cop, roll over, fold up. Six-thirty to seven or so P.M. was no time to be lobing Frankie Crocker housing the foxes, waxing about playing tension-busting tunes, about its being time for working women everywhere to relax and let the cares of the day slip away, about scrubbing their backs, drying off with plush towels, putting on creams and lotions. Waving his dick in the foxes' faces was what Frankie Crocker was wishing he could do—that's what Margaret said one of the few times Carlton got to lobe the Evening Bath, getting home to Kips Bay earlier than usual because it was the night before a holiday or there was a bomb scare in the courthouse or some shit like that. Margaret Morris was there in Kips Bay too and lobed Frankie Crocker waxing about the bathing arrangements, the bubble bath, the creams and lotions and powders and shit, the terry-cloth towels, and instead of getting warmed up, the way Carlton Woods hoped she would, she cooled down, she dissed Frankie Crocker.

So even though he knew he should, that it was a way to learn something about African-American music and African-American musicians, Carlton Woods didn't lobe Frankie Crocker's WBL Kicking S Evening Bath. If seventy-five thousand cases yearly, two hundred a day, left him too weary to wave his dick in any foxes' faces, he didn't want to listen to some brother wave *his,* even if there wasn't no other like that motherfucking brother.

Christmas Eve, out of the office early for a change, no bomb scare this time, a bona fide holiday, Carlton Woods went down on Margaret Morris, her favorite thing, he stretched out on his belly, he stuck his butt up out in the jet stream, his hands squeezed the cheeks of her buns, he slid his tongue way in, he slid it out slow, he did it so fine that Margaret moaned, "Glenn. *Oh,* Glenn."

Margaret Morris called Carlton Woods Glenn because it was safe, Jimmy Stewart played Glenn Miller in the movies, no threat there, no challenge to Carlton's vulnerable cock, to his breakable ego; but in her mind's eye Carlton was whomever she wanted him to be: Paul Newman, Joe Montana, Billy Dee Williams, Mel Gibson, Pat Reilly, Mickey Rourke, Bernie Casey, Michael Keaton, Keith Hernandez, Jeff Bridges, Denzel Washington, Randy Travis, Eric

Clapton, Richard Gere, Kevin Elster, what'shisname who played Bobby Hill on *Hill Street Blues*—Margaret liked all kinds of men.

"Glenn, Glenn, Gle—"

Margaret Morris stopped moaning all of a sudden because all of a sudden Carlton Woods stopped sliding his tongue way in, sliding it out slow, doing it so fine. "Carl?" she whispered, not wanting to topple the tower he was so carefully building if this were just a momentary lacuna, a pause to pluck a pubic hair off his tongue, say.

But it was more than that: Carl had stopped because there was a new ingredient in the mix, something never before experienced, something truly unique and new and strange, something cold and hard and sharp being shoved in his butt, sticking up out in the jet stream the way it was and ever so vulnerable. "M-Margaret?" Carlton asked, as though she somehow some way might could have something to do with it. She had been the owner when he met her of a dildo (his not to ask where she got it or why, hers not to say where or why), and once she had had him strap it on (dwarfing his Bic Biro, which was what Margaret called his johnson, thin and black like her favorite ballpoint pen) and try (unsuccessfully) to enter her vaginally with it and anally with his Bic; she window-shopped at the Pleasure Chest and the Pink Pussycat Boutique. Maybe she had picked out a little Christmas present, something cold and hard and sharp, and hadn't been able to wait to give it to him.

Or maybe not.

"*Carl?*" Margaret said it louder, harder, like Carlton Woods might've done again what he'd done once and she'd never let him forget—fallen asleep in mid-cunnilingus.

"Mmmmargaret?" A whine, a high-pitched wheedling sound Carlton made when he'd lost an argument and was trying to get her sympathy back by what she called "going fragile."

"Carl, what is it? What's wrong? Are you all right?" Margaret didn't doubt that Carl was anything but all right and didn't crane her neck or get up on her elbows to see.

Carlton said, "Muh, muh, muh, muh . . ."

A man said, "Look in the mirror, Carl."

Carlton hated the mirror, which Margaret, who liked to watch, had hung right alongside her bed, not even trying to make it look like it was a mirror to get dressed by. Carlton liked the concept of watching (those porn flicks, those music videos), but he was always afraid that if he looked in the mirror, which long antedated his arrival on the scene, he would see all the studs Margaret had ever done it with, doing it all the ways they'd done it, all the times, every last one of the studs more acrobatic than he, more creative, in better shape, better looking, better jobs, probably—private-sector jobs, better hung.

But Carlton did as he was told and looked in the mirror and saw a man holding a pistol to his butt.

"Peekaboo, Carl." Elvis Polk cocked the hammer.

"Jesus, no!"

"Merry Christmas." And pulled the trigger.

21

"No!"

But Elvis Polk had pulled the trigger on an empty chamber, and instead of dying Carlton Woods vomited between Margaret Morris's legs.

Elvis Polk slipped off his Triple Fat Goose and hung it on the knob of the bedroom door. With a foot (with one of Luther Todd's mothering Reebok Twilight Zone Pumps), he hooked a chair out from under Margaret Morris's dressing table. He straddled it, arms over the back, wrists crossed, the .22 dangling from the tip of his right middle finger, smiling at Margaret Morris. She wasn't Elvis's type of she-ra (she had the kind of wide load he liked, but her hooters were the droopy kind with big brown tips like plumber's helpers), but she was the only she-ra on hand and she wasn't scrunching up none neither, she had her legs spread so she wouldn't get puke on them and her hands were down at her sides still gripping clumps of sheet the way they'd been gripping them when Carlton was having himself a little box lunch. Elvis had even stopped turning Japanese lately, for he couldn't keep his day- or nightdreams of Jenny Swale and Renata Kazmeyer from switching into day- or nightmares of his Louisville Slugger getting chomped off. So Elvis was thinking he wouldn't mind turning Margaret, even with Carlton right there watching. Especially with Carlton right there watching. It would teach Carlton a thing or two, maybe; it would teach him that being a home boy was more than skin-deep. "S'happening, you two? S'been going down? . . . Carl, you know what you remind me of?"

Carlton Woods had scrunched way over in the corner of the bed, as far from both Elvis and Margaret as he could get. He had his elbows and his forearms and his hands jammed down in his crotch, hiding his Louisville Slugger from view (but not before Elvis scoped it and saw that it was more like a Little League model). He had puke on his chin. He was dripping sweat and glaring at Margaret, who wouldn't look at him.

"My whining old-fool moms used to have these monkeys. Ceramic monkeys. Up on the chiffonier. See-no-evil, hear-no-evil, speak-no-evil monkeys. S'what you look like. You look like a mothering do-no-evil-with-your-Louisville-Slugger monkey, 'cept that thing of yours don't look like no Louisville Slugger, looks like a Little League model."

Slowly, carefully, so as not to jostle his stomach more, Carlton Woods said to Margaret Morris, "Didn't you lock the door? Didn't you lock the *fucking* door?"

Margaret Morris didn't answer. Instead she did something that was very interesting to Elvis Polk: She let go of the clumps of sheet she'd been gripping while Carlton was having himself a little box lunch and rolled onto her side and swiveled her hips and bent her legs so her legs and hips were clear of the puke in the middle of the bed.

At least that's what it *looked* like Margaret had done, but what she'd *really* done was she'd turned her back on Carlton Woods while continuing to present Elvis Polk with the opportunity, should he choose to accept the mission, of scoping every inch of her front side. No question about it: Elvis Polk's born-under-a-bad-sign-if-it-weren't-for-bad-luck-he'd-have-no-luck-at-all-luck had *changed*.

"S'happening, Elvis?" Margaret said. "I'll tell you s'happening. You're in deep shit, that's what s'happening. Deep, deep shit."

Elvis copped that she was dissing him, and had it been just the two of them, he would have smacked her—smacked her, then turned her, up her ass and in her mouth, just to keep her in line. But it wasn't just the two of them, and he didn't trust sorry sweaty pukey Carlton not to make a leap for his piece while he turned Margaret and he knew that who Margaret was really dissing was sorry sweaty pukey Carlton, who had dissed her by puking in her box practically, then dissed her again by jawing at her for not locking the door when it was the window Elvis came in anyway, for mothering Christ's sake, down from the mothering roof.

He had got up to the roof by pressing all the buttons on the intercom in the foyer of Margaret Morris's building on West Twenty-third Street, in Chelsea or whatever they call it (all the buttons except Margaret's button, you don't press the button of the she-ra you're coming to surprise). Some asshole buzzed him in, some asshole was word up certain to always buzz you in, he took the elevator up to the top floor and walked up to the roof and through the fire door with just a slide bolt on it (to keep someone *on* the roof from getting *in* the building but not keeping someone already *in* the building from getting *on* the roof, which made no mothering sense at all to Elvis), and came down the fire escape and in the kitchen window. People were weirder than shit, they never locked the fire escape window—not unless they'd been cleaned out, in which case they locked the fire escape window and put a gate on it, which was like putting up a billboard announcing that they'd replaced all the shit they'd been cleaned out of, so you just ripped the front door off its hinges with a crowbar and cleaned them out again.

('Course, maybe Margaret Morris left her fire escape window open so Santa could get in, her not having no fireplace, no chimney or anything. That case, though, her and her neighbors might could have left unbolted the fire door to the roof, so Santa could land *on* the roof, then get *in* the building.)

"Deep shit," Margaret said again. "Deep, deep shit. Was it before you killed those cops, Elvis, or was it right after, or a while after— *when,* is what I'm asking you, when did you see the light? When did it come to you that you were the sorry little monkey in the middle? Every cop east of Chicago has your doleful face burned in his brain, every one of them would give up his pension and his shooting arm to take you out—that's bad enough. What's worse, you finally realized—or maybe you knew it all along—that your clients weren't going to be there for you the way they'd said they'd be, were they? Europe, Tahiti, Hong Kong, South America—hanging out on the pampas with the former SS men—is that what they said they'd do for you, Elvis? Bullshit, right?

"When did you get the picture? I'm really curious. Was there a meet set up a day or two after the hit? Was that when you'd get your money, they'd get you started out of the country on a small boat, a light plane, you'd hook up with a bigger boat, a bigger plane, to take you to Europe, to Tahiti, to the pampas—was that the way it was supposed to work? Along the way you'd get some plastic surgery, maybe, someone would take care of that tattoo—was that part of the plan? Whoever *you* got to take care of it, Elv, did a shitty job. What the fuck is that thing on your face supposed to be? People aren't supposed to notice, you're supposed to blend the fuck in? You should've gone along with that part of the setup, Elv, that part you should've gone along with.

"So was that it, Elvis? There was a meet set up and you were all set to go and then you had a revelation—I always have to be careful not to call them *rel*evations—you saw yourself walking into the meet and never walking out? Is that what happened? Or are you just flat smarter than I give you credit for, Elv? Did you kill those cops knowing—*knowing*—that from that moment on you were on your own, you were solo, that if you went for help to the people who swore up and down you could trust them, they'd be there for you,

you were their main man, they'd be your main men—*knowing* that if you went anywhere near them you'd be dead meat?"

Elvis was only half paying attention to Margaret Morris. He was more interested, right this minute, that his Louisville Slugger (speaking of dead meat) was trying to stand up and holler in spite of his tight 501s. Elvis liked having a she-ra talk to him like this for a change, it was getting him hot and bothered. He liked having a she-ra telling him what went down, instead of, as per mothering usual, the same old story, so what else is new, axing *him* what went down, axing him what was he *think*ing about, what was he *feel*ing.

"Carl and I had an interesting talk with a cop the other day." Margaret Morris didn't look at Carlton Woods as she said that; she didn't tip her head in his direction, she didn't flick a thumb or even move her eyes or any of that. Carlton Woods might as well have not even been on the bed, in the room, in Margaret Morris's apartment, on the face of the mothering planet. "He wasn't the first cop we've talked to since your little rampage, I'm sure you can imagine. I would've said we'd be asked a million questions, but the fact is we were asked a very few questions dozens of times. Hundreds of times.

"This cop was good, this cop knew about that, about very few questions getting asked hundreds of times; this cop asked us to think about what we *hadn't* been asked. That's something I'm going to try to use in my work, Elv. In my work I talk to people, I question people, I ask them the same things over and over; when I get stuck, when things just won't move forward another inch, I shouldn't demand over and over to know what they're not telling me, which is what I usually do, unfortunately; I shouldn't accuse them of not cooperating, which is what I usually do, unfortunately; I should say to them, 'What am *I* not asking you?'

"Carl told this cop that we hadn't been asked about the car switch. You know better than anyone that Todd and Swale drove you down from Wallkill in Todd's Geo and started back up in Swale's Volare. Did the switch mean anything? Did the switch mean that piece in your hand was planted in Swale's car, and that someone interceded to make sure the five-ohs *took* Swale's car? That is the same piece, isn't it?

"The switch *didn't* mean anything, did it, Elvis? Pieces were planted in both cars, weren't they—or just the one piece was planted after it was certain which car the five-ohs were going to take, wasn't it? You don't know by whom or when or how the piece or pieces were planted, do you? That wasn't for you to know. All that was for you to know was that a piece would be there, in a predetermined spot, in whatever car they took."

Which would happen first? Elvis wondered. Would his 501s split at the crotch or would his Louisville Slugger break in two, the way Bo Jackson broke his in two sometimes after he fanned? Was *that* for him to know? Would Bo know?

Margaret had had her head propped up on a bent left arm and she was starting to lose the circulation in her left wrist. She rubbed her wrist to get the blood going and reached around behind her for a pillow. She shifted around onto her belly and plumped the pillow and folded it in half and rested her chin on it, one arm on each side. She looked kind of like a dog and she looked kind of cute, especially with her wide-load butt sticking up in the jet stream. "Another thing we talked about, Elv, this cop and Carl and I, was how Todd and Swale brought you in to talk about the SpeedAir heist's having the same handwriting as the Mercury heist, but when the time came you didn't know squat about SpeedAir. You ended up with some hot hardware from SpeedAir, period. How it got hot you had not a clue."

All of a sudden, out of nowhere, there were Jenny Swale and Renata Kazmeyer down on their hands and knees between Elvis's legs, drooling and snarling, on the trail of his Louisville Slugger. Elvis pressed the heel of one hand into his lap protectively. Just like that, his Louisville Slugger stopped shouting and shriveled up and hid. Elvis made sure not to look at Carlton Woods over there in the corner of the bed, because he knew he probably looked a lot like Carlton Woods right now, not sorry and sweaty and pukey, but like a mothering do-no-evil-with-your-Louisville-Slugger monkey, 'cept it probably looked like a Little League model now, his Louisville Slugger.

Margaret, reminding Elvis a little of his whining old-fool mother in the way she was enjoying the sound of her own pit-bitch voice: "So your clients knew Todd and Swale caught the Mercury job, they contacted you, they told you to call me, to pretend you knew something about a SpeedAir-Mercury connection, they told you to have me arrange a meet with the five-ohs. And with Carl."

Still no look Carlton Woods's way on Margaret Morris's part. Carlton was an afterthought, Carlton might as well have been in Europe, in Tahiti, in South America, hanging out with the old-fart Nazis on the Pampers. If Jenny Swale and Renata Kazmeyer would just get the mother out of there, would just stop drooling and snarling after his Louisville Slugger, Elvis would be able to turn Margaret Morris, he was sure of it, turn her right there in front of Carlton Woods and Carlton Woods wouldn't be able to do a mothering thing about it. But Jenny Swale and Renata Kazmeyer *were* there, drooling and snarling, so Elvis's born-under-a-bad-sign-if-it-weren't-for-bad-luck-he'd-have-no-luck-at-all-luck hadn't changed a bit, had it?

"So who's your client, Elv?" Margaret Morris said. "There aren't a lot of possibilities. . . . This cop and I—Carl was indisposed by that time, he was off puking his guts out"—still no look at Carl, Carl might as well be puke—"this cop and I talked about Roy Reagan, about your day-room fight over what radio station to play. I told the cop what I thought: Someone wanted Todd and Swale hit. So the cops' guard'd be down the job should be done by a con without a violent record. Roy Reagan was doing points because some wise guys dropped a dime on him, his final payment for getting them off his back was to start a fight with you, your parole was canceled, you were vulnerable to an approach.

" 'Who's the someone?' the cop asked me.

"I said, 'Beats me.'

"He said, 'Answer: "Beats me." Question: "Who's the someone?" ' I didn't know what he was talking about, but he was talking about *Jeopardy!* I realize now: They give you the answer, you give them the question. So let's play *Jeopardy!* Elv. I'll give you the answer, you give me the question. The answer is, Carl Woods, so come on, Elv, what's the question?"

The question, Elvis Polk knew in the split-fraction flash pulse of a second it took for Carlton Woods to uncoil snakelike from over there in the corner of the bed where he'd been looking sorry and sweaty and pukey and grab pluck snatch suck the .22 off Elvis's finger and juggle it for a beat, then come up pointing its cold hard sharpness right at Elvis's forehead, hammer cocked, ready, the question was: Who is going to see to it that Elvis Polk's born-under-a-bad-sign-if-it-weren't-for-bad-luck-he'd-have-no-luck-at-all-luck don't never change?

"Shit, Carl," Elvis said. "Put that thing down."

"Know any black trombone players, Elvis?" Carlton Woods said. "Any *African-American* trombone players?"

Elvis giggled. "Say what, Carl?"

"Aren't you the big jazz fan, Elvis?" Carlton said. "Aren't you always listening to the radio—to WBL Kicking S, to Frankie Crocker?"

Elvis was sweating; he felt like puking. "Shit, brother. Word up. Frankie's def. There ain't no other like *that* brother." Try as he might to block his ears, Elvis could hear Frankie Crocker signing off: *"It's been real and you've been regular. May each of you live to one hundred and me to one hundred minus a day, so I'll never know nice people like you have passed away." Try as he might to block his ears, Elvis could hear the Neville Brothers singing:*

> *"Undertaker, undertaker, won't you please drive real slow.*
> *That's dear sweet Elvis Polk. I hate to see him go."*

Try as he might to block his ears, Elvis could hear Bukka White singing:

"I'm lookin' funny in my eye
I believe I'm fixin' to die."

"You're such a big jazz fan, Elvis," Carlton said, "tell me some African-American trombone players."

Some civilians who get their hands on pieces have no intention of firing them—you can tell by the scaredy-cat crooked way they hold them, pointing them off to the side, flinching even though they ain't even pulled the trigger yet. Carlton Woods was not one of those civilians; he held the gun like a pro—steady, cool, unblinking. "Trom*bone* players? *Slide* trombone players? You want me to name some trom*bone* players?"

"Some trombone players, yes, Elvis," Carlton said. "Some African-American trombone players."

"Well . . ." Elvis said.

"Carl?" Margaret Morris said.

"Uh . . ."

"*Carl.*"

Elvis snapped his fingers. "I know. I know one. Glenn—"

"*Glenn!?*" Carlton Woods roared. "Fuck you talking about, *Glenn?* Doan chew fuck wit me, *Glenn.* I'll blow your fucking head off, *Glenn.*"

"Hey, chill out, brother, sheee-it. Damn. Damn. Tyree Glenn is a brother who plays the mothering trombone. I cain't do nuffin about it, shee-it."

"Tyree Glenn?" Carlton Woods said.

"Word up."

"Name another."

"Another brother who plays the trombone?"

For an answer Carlton Woods just pressed the barrel of the .22 against Elvis Polk's forehead. He still hadn't blinked.

"Chill, brother, chill . . . C-C-C-Curtis Fuller plays the trombone. Curtis Fuller. Grachan Moncur the Third plays it. Grachan Moncur the Third. J. J. Johnson. J. J. Johnson, J. J. Johnson, J. J. Johnson is a brother plays the trombone. Word up, word mothering up. Uh, Tyree Glenn, uh, C-Curtis Fuller, uh, Grachan Moncur the Third, uh, J. J. Johnson, uh, uh, uh . . ." *Undertaker, undertaker . . .*

"That it, Elvis?" Carlton Woods said.

"Carl?" Margaret Morris said.

"That *it,* Elvis?"

Won't you please drive real slow . . . "Uh, yeah. I guess that's it. Yeah, yeah. That's it." *Lookin' funny in my eye, believe I'm fixin' to die.*

"Thanks, Elvis," Carlton Woods said. "Merry Christmas to you too." And Carlton Woods shot Elvis Polk in the forehead. Then he turned the .22 on Margaret Morris—

"Carl, no! *No!*"

—and shot her in the chest.

22

Sergeant Bobby Colavito, Maslosky's little-bitty pretty one, a *primero* ballbreaker, wise-guy relatives himself, no one could say he'd bought a bill of goods from Joe Cullen, was a world-class sentence finisher. Confronted with a sentence that had half a dozen words or more still to come, that was wending its way through dependent clauses, that awaited an apodosis, Colavito didn't hesitate to leap in and take it over.

"Uh, Bobby . . ." Cullen looked at the time (four-forty-five P.M.) on the clock over the door of the room off the squad room of the Midtown West station house, at the date on the *Penthouse* calendar on the wall (the day, December 24; the pet, a brunette with red high-lights, Lyndzee), back at Colavito forming his careful script on a yellow legal pad with a royal-blue Le Pen. A friendless bachelor who lived in an apartment, according to the few who had seen it, that resembled a serial killer's, Colavito was manifestly willing to forgo yuletide cheer and keep on grilling Cullen for the rest of Christmas Eve, the rest of the holiday season, till Memorial Day or Labor Day or however long it took. "I haven't had a chance—"

"To do any Christmas shopping." Colavito was, as well, a nodder, one of those people (you went to school with one; we all did) who, as you speak, moves his head vigorously up and down to communicate to you his perfect understanding of and agreement with what you're saying. The Carl Lewis of nodders, Colavito was so quick off the blocks that he began nodding while you were still I mean–ing and you know–ing and getting up to speed; it was as if English were your second language and you needed all the encouragement you could get. Since, of course, Colavito terminated your sentence for you whenever possible, he wound up nodding along with himself, affirming with each jerk of his chin that there was only one destination that could have been reached by the path you set out on; congratulating you for selecting that path; praising himself for knowing how your mind worked, for being out there along with you on the cutting edge.

Had Colavito been deputized, Cullen wondered, had he deputized himself, to round off the articulations of others against the chance that one of them might suffer a fatal heart attack, a bout of aphasia, mid-sentence? The responsibility, whoever had empowered him, must exhaust him—to never rest, to never space out as do the rest of us while others yammer on. Cullen was exhausted, that was for sure, to discover that each and every time he opened his mouth he had nothing original to say. When he hammered Colavito, as he was going to do as soon as he got back his piece and his shield, he wasn't going to so much as peep. Unable to interrupt, Colavito would die with his trap shut.

Cullen: "Any chance—"

"We could go to Macy's?" *Nod, nod, nod.* "I think they're open till ten tonight. Let me check with the captain."

Midtown West was known familiarly as Midwest, not only because of the departmental urge to abbreviate, but because the nameless, characterless neighborhood in which it sat, though just a few blocks from Macy's, from Madison Square Garden, from the comings and goings of Penn Station, from the bustle and shmooze of the garment district, looked as if it had been transplanted from, oh, Omaha. There was a midcontinental quality to the vicinity, the quality not of the end-of-the-line but of the middle of the journey.

Nearby the station house was the maw/anus of the General Post Office: tractor-trailers and semis full of mail rolled in, step vans and little *putt-putt* cubes rolled out. Down the block gaped the incision through which one could study the exposed intestines of the Penn Station yards: Amtrak and Jersey Transit trains clicked at half-throttle over the snarl of points; passengers inbound and outlooked anxiously up from the cut, fearful, whether they had come all this way or had just set out, that they were now altogether lost. Around the corner was the eerie eight-block thoroughfare without a single edifice fronting on it, connecting Thirty-fourth Street to Forty-second Street, the *Jeopardy!* answer to the question: What is Dyer Avenue? (Young, hip cops called the street Dyer Straits.)

Cub reporters just out of journalism school and just off the bus from upstate New York or rural Delaware, writing careless articles in newspapers and magazines whose editors and fact-checkers lived in the suburbs or didn't give a damn, sometimes located Midwest "near Chelsea," but what the hell *was* Chelsea but a not-terribly-interesting place to visit and do you know *any*one who lives there? No main street, no clear boundaries (was the Hudson River Chelsea's western edge, or did it end much sooner, at Tenth Avenue, at *Ninth* Avenue? Did Chelsea extend east all the way to Fifth, or only to Seventh? The General Theological Seminary, the ILGWU houses, Barneys, FIT, belly-dancing row, M.K., the Joyce—were they *all* in Chelsea?), its best-known landmark a dowdy residential hotel that one could stroll right past without noting. No nucleus, no membrane, no cytoplasm, no There there. With the entry into evidence the observation that roster-makers of famous Chelsea residents, past and present, always include Clement Clarke Moore of "A Visit from St. Nicholas," Sid Vicious of the Sex Pistols, and Anthony Perkins of *Psycho,* the prosecution rests.

So what? So these were a few of the things Joe Cullen got to think about while sitting around Midwest, trying to beat Bobby Colavito to the punch in describing how it had come about that he, Cullen, hammered Paul Messina, the scumbag motherfucker.

"So, uh, one more time," Colavito said, one more time. "Any connections between you and Paulie? Ever catch a piece of the same job? Ever get tapped for the same task force, pulled out for any of the same refreshers—firearms, procedure, whatever?"

Sometimes Cullen said, "No." Or he might just shake his head (smiling slyly) and mutter, "Un-unh," trying not to give Colavito anything to chew on.

"You, uh, wanna elaborate?" Colavito might say, smiling too, the smile of a mouse who has seen mousetraps come and mousetraps go and nothing new under the sun. This time, before Colavito could say anything, Cullen elaborated: "Except that three years ago, Neil Zimmerman and I—"

"Checked Paulie out," Colavito said, "after his cousin, Nickie, took a tumble on the SpeedAir job."

Cullen could live (at least until he got his piece back) with the sentence-finishing, with the nodding, with Colavito's appetite for junk food (new menus from fast, faster, and fastest food joints went up on the wall every day, slowly surrounding Lyndzee, who had been there when they got there, reaching eternally for the slit between the legs of her red fishnet bodysuit); the *Paulies* and the *Nickies* made him nervous. The flip side of Colavito's not buying a bill of goods from Cullen, on account of his wise-guy relatives, was that he wouldn't be able to see around and past and through his wise-guy relatives to the truth. "Yes. We interviewed him twice face-to-face, we talked to him—"

"Four or five times on the phone. He came up clean."

"He came up clean," Cullen agreed—agreed with himself, after all. "Other than that, I saw him—"

"At a few—"

"Yes," Cullen blurted, interrupting the interrupter.

Off balance, Colavito looked at Cullen sideways. " 'Yes' what?"

"Other than that, yes, I saw Messina at a few funerals—as you just anticipated I was going to say." Cullen should have said *funerals,* he realized, finishing the sentence Colavito was attempting to finish. He'd been late, he'd been inadequate, there was no making it up, no second chance.

A storm front had gathered on Colavito's brow. "What're you saying, Cullen?"

"Nothing."

"You saying I'm putting words in your mouth?"

Reaching in and yanking them out was more like it. "No."

"Good."

". . ."

". . ."

Cullen got lost in thoughts on the orthography of the Christian names of pinups: Was Lyndzee a *nom de guerre*? Had she been born Lindsey or Lindsay and did screwing around with the vowels make it easier to face the lens? Did she know Traycee, who hung on a wall of Midwest's basement locker-room bathroom, half submerged in a marble bath, the surface of the water littered with rose petals, or Mairee, who peeked out from behind coats in the squadroom coat closet, wearing just a pair of chaps, lizard cowboy boots, spurs, a Stetson? Did she know Mystee, over at VU Sound Magic, and would she be impressed that he had hammered someone? He finally heard Colavito saying: "One more time, you and Paulie had *no* connection?"

"First of all, Bobby," Cullen said, "with all due respect, what you—"

"Should be axing is, Why did Samantha Cox lie about taking a taxi to your place? Did she have some connection with Paulie, did she, like, know him? What's to her being out at Kennedy, right near Air Cargo, the very day Todd and Swale got hammered?"

Cullen flexed his trigger finger. "That's right."

Colavito flipped backward through his legal pad, pretending to need refreshing on what he'd known before Cullen had finished saying it so he must know it by heart, *mustn't* he? "Samantha says you're right, there were no medallion cabs on the street on account of they wildcatted, a medallion might not've taken her all the way out to Queens anyway, she took a gypsy, she offered the driver fifty bucks, she offered him another fifty to wait while she went upstairs, but he wanted to get home before the boogieman came out.

"Samantha says she never saw Messina in her life, the first good look she got at him was after you hammered him, the rest of the time he was behind her with a choke-hold on her, or up in the front seat, her down on the floorboards in the back.

"Samantha says she was at Kennedy, near Air Cargo, because that's where she just happened to be, doing a story on dopeheads in the tower. Her and her crew heard about the hammer, they moseyed over to Air Cargo. We axed her all this shit, Joe. We axed her more than once."

"She's—"

"Lying." Colavito was *so* fast. "You been saying that. You been saying she's—"

"Full of shit." Cullen smiled.

Colavito didn't smile. "Fuck're you trying to prove, Cullen? Finishing what I'm saying before I get through saying it, grinning like a fucking monkey? I'll tell you the God's honest truth, Joe, the way things are going for you right now, you want to finish what somebody's saying before they say it, you should try finishing what Samantha Cox is saying, 'cause it's her word against yours. You say you were set up, you say she was putting on an act, you say she was pretending to struggle with Paulie; she says it was no setup, it was no act, she was struggling her ass off with him. The business she's in, the ratings she's got, the audience, she's got a lot of—"

"Credibility," Cullen said.

Colavito slammed his hand down flat on the table between them, making his pad jump, his Le Pen, an empty Burger King Styrofoam coffee cup. "Don't *do* that."

"Sorry." Cullen put his hand to the corners of his mouth and assassinated a grin.

After some consideration, since he hadn't said it, Cullen had,

Colavito said, "*Yes,* credibility. And on top of that, cops, sometimes, you know, the public—"

"Doesn't believe us."

Colavito breathed in through his nose and very, very slowly breathed out, counting to himself, probably. Then: "That's exactly right. That's exactly motherfucking right. The public sometimes, a lot of the time, and who can blame them, you know that, I know that, you work in IAU, you see the crap that goes down, *I* work in IAU, I see the crap that goes down, doesn't fucking believe us."

Cullen tried to think of a way to say what he wanted to say that Colavito wouldn't anticipate. *Fuck it,* he thought, and said, "So it's her word—"

"Against your word."

"And her story is, she came out to my place—"

"To find out if Todd and Swale were dirty."

"Messina tailed her—"

"Because he was in on the scam to set up the PC."

"He didn't want Samantha—"

"To find out a scam was what it was."

"Swale was in on it, maybe—"

"Todd, maybe others."

"Not Braverman," Cullen said, while Colavito said in near unison, "Not Braverman."

A pause, during which they studied each other. Finally, remarkably, Colavito struck out on his own: "There's something else, Joe, you should be keeping in mind. It's not only Samantha Cox's word against yours, it's not only that she's got *mucho cred*ibility; the other thing to keep in mind is a lot of people have got the idea that maybe, just maybe, maybe it's a surprise to them, maybe it's not such a surprise, maybe, just maybe, you're—"

"A drunk."

No nonsense, Colavito flipped his pad to the top page. He centered it on the tabletop. He laid down his royal-blue Le Pen and lined it up on one of the pad's ruled lines. "That's right. That's fucking A one-hundred-percent right. You said it, Joe, I didn't. A drunk. I mean, in two minutes, you're going to go talk with the Department headshrinker, right? You talked to him already a couple of times. Doesn't he say you're a drunk?"

Bernstein (precisely, the Department psychologist) didn't say what he thought Cullen was, he wasn't "in the label business." Then, after a pause, he said, "How would you describe yourself?"

Cullen smiled. "I've done a few interrogations, Doc. When someone protests he's not guilty, I ask him how he'd describe himself."

Bernstein smiled too. He was a nice guy. Cullen felt a little guilty that, when he had come back on duty after he had been winged and his dear sweet old partner, Neil Zimmerman, hammered, he hadn't returned the messages Bernstein had left, messages suggesting Cullen might want to come and see him. Cullen hadn't returned the messages because he had been busy, Bernstein had been busy, Bernstein had been on his floor, Cullen on his, or out in the street. Their paths had crossed every couple of months, getting in or out of an elevator, Cullen usually with a buddy or his partner, which made it hard for him to just stop and breeze with Bernstein because whoever he was with got nervous, Bernstein *was* the Department headshrinker, Bernstein with his secretary running after him yelling what he'd forgotten to do because he was hurrying to what he was already late for.

I talked to him doctor-patient, Hriniak had said to Cullen on the faux Shaker bench. And Cullen, reluctant to have *a therapy session with a headshrinker,* had thought that it might be a piece of cake, no sweat, hey, no problemo, to *talk* to Bernstein *doctor-patient.* It *was* a piece of cake, Cullen had found out for a fact these afternoons, for you could talk, doctor-patient, about anything at all:

"You asked before about times when I've felt really good about myself."

Bernstein craned his neck a little, seemed to sit forward without actually sitting forward, in anticipation of what Cullen was about to say. His expectations were so high it was hard to look right at him, especially since Cullen wasn't going to give him much.

"What I keep coming back to aren't days like, say, my wedding day, like the day I made detective. I come back to days like the day I saw Jackie Robinson. It was a Saturday afternoon the summer between my freshman and sophomore years at City College. I was walking, I don't remember why, on Madison Avenue in the Thirties, near the Morgan Library. It's not a neighborhood I've been in more than a few times in my life, before or since. Jackie Robinson was walking the other way, wearing a business suit, carrying a briefcase, with a couple of other men in suits. This was after he quit baseball, he was working for Chock Full o'Nuts, I guess. Our eyes met, he saw that I recognized him, he said hello, I walked on. I felt elated. I wasn't a Dodger fan, I liked the Yankees. Mickey Mantle was my hero, and Joe DiMaggio before that. . . .

"Another time, years later, I don't remember the year but it was before I got married, Connie and I were still dating, so before 1974, spring or summer, I was walking on Fifty-ninth Street, by the Plaza Hotel, probably going to meet Connie to see a movie or something. I was wearing a madras jacket I loved—patchwork, almost like a quilt —but almost everybody else, Connie included, thought was too loud. Phil Hriniak—a fellow cop, not the PC then—thought it was too loud. It was late afternoon, people were getting out of work, the sidewalk was very crowded. All of a sudden I was face-to-face with Buddy Rich. He checked out my jacket, said, "Great coat," went around me and was gone. Again I felt elated. I'm not a Buddy Rich fan; I wasn't even a jazz fan then; I listen to some jazz now. Hriniak was the jazz fan, still is. I told him Buddy Rich liked my coat, he said I must've been mistaken, he must've been talking to someone else."

Bernstein waited until he was sure there was no more. "You felt elated because . . . these two celebrities singled *you* out, recognized *you*."

It wasn't a question. Bernstein wasn't in the question business either. "I suppose."

"You have fantasies about being a celebrity. You are a celebrity of sorts; you often catch high-profile jobs."

Other not-quite questions. "I never know whether to agree with you or argue with you."

"You feel argumentative," Bernstein said.

Cullen said, "Fuck you."

Later, watching Cullen watching Lyndzee, Bernstein said, "You find her attractive."

"If *you* find her attractive," Cullen said, "say so. I find her frighteningly vulnerable."

"Jo Dante," Bernstein said.

"What about her?"

"You spent—what?—ten minutes with her, twenty minutes, an hour—whatever. Yet she attained a reality for you. You believe that you had some kind of relationship with her."

To which Cullen said anything at all: "There've been two women in movies—two actresses, but really two characters—who've knocked me out to such an extent that I actually went looking for them. Jennifer Warren in *Night Moves* and Arielle Dombasle in *Pauline at the Beach.*"

Bernstein shook his head. "I don't go to movies much."

"Even if you did," Cullen said, "these're obscure movies."

"But vividly real to you."

"You know, Bobby Colavito puts words in my mouth, but most of the time they're my words. The thoughts you put in my mind aren't ever necess*a*rily my thoughts."

"Went looking for them where?" Bernstein said.

"The setting for *Night Moves* was generic shabby Florida Gulf Coast, for *Pauline* generic French beach town. I took a vacation in Sarasota and another in Deauville, convinced I'd meet those women."

"The women represented . . . freedom, irresponsibility."

"Yes."

"You weren't married, or involved, when you took those vacations."

"No."

"Marriage and involvement mean to you an absence of freedom."

"Yes."

Bernstein smiled. "That's progress, recognizing that."

"Vacations," Cullen said.

Bernstein cocked his head. "Sorry?"

"Vacations, holidays, I just thought of something." He hadn't thought of it as much as it had been brought to his attention, brought by his dear sweet old partner, Neil Zimmerman. It was something Zimmerman had been saying when the shooting started six days ago back out at the ass end of Kennedy airport, and that Zimmerman had been trying to get Cullen to address ever since:

Someone tried to hammer Ann, asshole. Someone thinks she's getting too close to something. Maybe they think she told you what she knows.

Cullen hadn't known what to make of it then, and he didn't know what to make of it now, but he knew this: Talking to Bobby Colavito wasn't the way to find out anything; it was time to talk to someone who was capable of being surprised.

Cullen was on his feet.

"You're leaving," Bernstein said.

"Yeah. Maybe we can do this again sometime."

"Talk doctor-patient," Bernstein said.

"Yes."

Bernstein said nothing at all. He laced his fingers together, ready to continue talking doctor-patient, or ready for the patient, the impatient patient, to break things off.

23

"Captain Neuman?"

"Cullen. I heard you were in the building. Tough, what happened. I mean, I don't know the details, I just hear talk, but it sounds tough. . . . Christmas Eve, they going to let you go home, or—"

"Captain, that key-ring doodad you found at Jo Dante's, the replica shield." Cullen didn't finish others' sentences, he elbowed them out of the way. "You know whose it is, don't you?"

Neuman swiveled suddenly, as if someone might be trying to rearrange the headers and stretchers outside his window. There was no one in the air shaft, so he swiveled back. "Like I said to you in our previous conversation, Sergeant, the, uh, doodad has engravings on it that—"

"It's Hriniak's. It was left at Jo Dante's, planted by her killer, to incriminate him. It was lifted from his office by someone who has business there, someone he knows and trusts enough to leave alone while he steps out to take care of some other matter. That's not too many people, and a lot of them're cops. The guy who got in Jo Dante's was a cop—that's what you said. Cops do that better than other people, you said—get in places. They lie down with scumbags, you said, they get up a little bit dirty, they learn things. Ex-cops have had that kind of instruction too. Don't forget ex-cops."

Swiveling his chair this way, swiveling it that way, his fingertips on the edge of his desk top, his ankles flexed so his feet were a little off the floor, Neuman looked like a kid on a stool at a soda fountain counter, salivating for his idiot's delight. "When you say 'ex-cops,' do you, uh—"

"Steve Poole," Cullen said.

Neuman stopped swiveling and Cullen didn't feel dumb anymore. Hanging around with Bobby Colavito, listening to Bobby Colavito finish every last one of his sentences, he had come to feel very, very dumb—as dumb as Bobby. Talking to someone who listened and reacted and didn't bob his head up and down like one of those fucking bobblehead dolls in the rear windows of assholes' cars (Bobby Colavito had a Jets bobblehead doll in the rear window of his rusty sprung Dodge Dart, a serial killer's car if ever there was one), he found that he could string ideas together, make small leaps of logic, entertain two thoughts at the same time, pat his head and rub his stomach.

"I ran into Poole at Luther Todd's funeral," Cullen said. "He told me a story about a conversation he had with my partner"—*my dear sweet old partner*—"Neil Zimmerman, last spring. Poole'd gone Downtown to introduce some constituents to Hriniak, he ran into Neil in the hall. I'm not saying Poole took the doodad on that visit; I'm sure there've been other visits. He has access to Hriniak."

"Yeah, well, access," Neuman said. "Access is, you know, one of those things. My wife reads detective stories. You read detective stories? I never read them, but a lot of people do, I guess. My wife does. She's trying to figure me out or something. She's always saying she can't understand how I can do this shit year after year, year in, year out. I don't know the answer, that's for sure; some writer's figured out how, I'd like to read it.

"Anyway, some detective story my wife was reading, the detective
—I guess it was the detective; maybe it was the perp, maybe it was a
victim or a potential victim, maybe it was somebody on the sidelines, a reporter, like, or a lawyer or something; I don't know, like I
said, I didn't read it—my wife, she tells me at dinner how somebody
in the story was always talking about 'motive and opportunity,' did
real-life cops talk a lot about 'motive and opportunity' too? Every
perp's got 'em, I guess the writer's trying to say—the motive and the
opportunity. Opportunity is, you know, it's what you're talking about
—*acc*ess. Motive is . . . Well, you know what motive is.

"So what I'd like to know is, maybe you can tell me, let's say Poole
did have *acc*ess to the PC's office, to his desk, to the *drawers* of his
desk, what was his *mo*tive for lifting the doodad, what was his *mo*-
tive for planting the doodad at Jo Dante's? Plus, are you also saying
Poole planted the doodad at Jo Dante's? 'Cause if you are, then you
maybe ought to rethink that part of it, 'cause since you recall I said
the guy who got in Jo Dante's was a cop, since you recall I said cops
get in places better than other people, they lie down with scumbags,
they get dirty, they learn things, since you recall all that, you may
also recall I said the guy who got in Jo Dante's could've been buzzed
in by Jo Dante; he could've popped the street door, gone up to the
roof, come down the fire escape; he could've popped the street
door, gone up to the third floor, picked the dead bolt, or used a
master key. But he couldn't've done any of those things, or a lot of
them anyway, in a wheelchair.

"But let's say, Joe, just for the sake of discussion, that you're *not*
saying *Poole* planted the doodad, you're saying someone planted the
doodad *for* Poole, one of his staff, one of his associates, one of
his—"

"Backup singers," Cullen said.

Neuman laughed. "Okay. All right. One of his backup singers. So
you're *not* saying *Poole* planted the doodad, you're saying one of
Poole's *back*up singers planted it *for* Poole. The question *I* have, the
thing I still don't—"

"The death penalty," Cullen said. "Poole's staking his career on the death penalty. It's an issue people feel strongly about and then they forget they feel strongly about it. They need headlines to remind them how they feel. When cops get hammered—"

"People start screaming capital punishment."

"Without that kind of front-page exposure, there's no—"

"Juice."

"The bandwagon has no—"

"Grease."

Bobby Colavito seemed to get no pleasure from his interruptions, even when he was, as it were, right; there was a sense of duty to them, of obligation. Neuman looked like he was having fun, the fun of . . . well, of simultaneous orgasms. But having come together, they were now affected by classic postcoital estrangement. Neuman looked over Cullen's premise and sniffed at it and pushed it arm's length away. "Poole framed Hriniak for Jo Dante's hammer—that's supposed to bring back the electric chair? I can't buy that, Cullen."

Turning to look out at the air shaft himself, Cullen could hear the pieces slipping and sliding around in the front of his mind, like the pieces—God help him, cliché or no cliché, it's *just* what they were like: all about the same size, the same shape, the same configuration, each unimportant in itself, all part of the big picture—like the pieces of a jigsaw puzzle. He hadn't tried to order them lest he discover how many more than he'd anticipated were missing, lest he find that the design that was beginning to be revealed be a squiggle signifying nothing. He didn't try to order them now, to fit locks into keyholes, salients into indentations; he just set them out, one by one, in more or less chronological order:

"Jenny Swale filed a grievance against Hriniak for sexual harassment. Memorial Day weekend. Hriniak thinks he was set up. The jacket, everything on the computer about the case, was disappeared —to make it look like he disappeared it, Hriniak thinks . . .

"Thanksgiving Day, hijackers hit Mercury Freight at Kennedy. The next week Elvis Polk calls his PD, proposes a serenade, the lyrics of which are similarities between the Mercury job and SpeedAir, May '88. Swale and Luther Todd bring Polk down from the J. The PD, Margaret Morris, says Polk didn't know shit about SpeedAir, he learned the words but not the meaning. Also listening to the serenade is a Queens ADA, Carlton Woods, who right after Thanksgiving was in a bar on Queens Boulevard with Paul Messina and a guy named Jerry. Messina was on duty Downtown on Memorial Day, when Hriniak allegedly hit on Swale. Messina has a cousin who took a tumble for SpeedAir. The guy named Jerry is one of Poole's backup singers. . . .

"Jo Dante got hammered before she could name a man she said knew why Swale was hammered. Hriniak's doodad was planted in her apartment. . . .

"Messina—maybe Messina took the doodad; he's got the motive, he's had lots of opportunities—Messina tried to hammer me. . . ."

There they were; those were the pieces. Now for making the joins:

"There're two things going on here. Three actually.

"The first is: Poole wants Hriniak out. He sets up the harassment charge, he sets up a cover-up that'll be pinned on Hriniak.

"The second is: Poole wants a front-page murder case. He finds a dirty DA—Woods—to find him a con with parole problems—Elvis Polk—to hammer a couple of cops. That one of the cops happens to be the cop involved in the Hriniak matter will turn out to be either an irrelevant coincidence or a big bonus. Hriniak will be guilty to some degree by association. Poole's backup singer hammers Jo Dante, and Hriniak's fucked coming and going. Also, think about this—the bicycle tire marks. Maybe they're wheelchair marks. Wheelchairs fold up. His backup singers could've carried Poole upstairs. That night, some other night—he must've known Swale or Dante or both. He could've been there—once, a dozen times. Ask the super about a man in a wheelchair . . .

"The third thing is . . . The third is . . . You know Ann Jones, don't you, Captain?"

Neuman frowned, then brightened. "Reporter. TV now, used to be with *New York*. No!" He snapped his fingers twice. "*City*. She was with *City*. You and her are, uh . . ." Neuman signed with his hands, his fingers going every which way.

"Involved, yes," Cullen said, though a better translation might have been *entangled*. "Ann's been working on the Quintana David-off story, the girl who was killed by the falling bottle. Steve Poole lives in a building the bottle's suspected of falling from. He's been trying to take some of the heat off the tenants—and off himself—by getting the girl's parents involved in the death-penalty thing. Ann knows who's responsible. She hasn't said so to me, but I know she does. Her apartment was booby-trapped; a driver was killed. A scumbag did it, or a cop who's lain with scumbags. Or an ex-cop. I'm involved with Ann, I must know what she knows. Messina came after me to muzzle me. . . .

"One more thing: If Poole knew Swale or Dante or both, maybe they'd been to his place. Ask his super, ask Poole's super; show him pictures. There's a connection. It's all connected. I'm . . . I'm sure of it."

Neuman swiveled, slowly, three hundred sixty degrees. It was something he'd practiced. He did it all with one push. He wanted to grin at the accomplishment, but he kept his face straight. "First of all, I knew about Swale's grievance, Maslosky briefed me. Second of all, the problem you're having with all this is, Hriniak's your well-known longtime buddy. I don't have that problem; I don't have a problem with any of it. The PC hits on a lady cop, instead of her being frightened or flattered, which is what he expects, she gets feisty, blows not him but the whistle. He disappears the jacket, he diddles the computer, that's simple enough, people're always losing things, everyone's got a computer horror story. But he knows as long as the lady cop's alive disappearing records isn't going to be a long-term solution, the only long-term solution is a long-term so*lut*ion. He finds a con with parole problems, offers him a new life in, you know, Costa Rica or one of those places, nobody's quite sure where it is, the, uh, you know, the bad-guy version of witness relocation, the

con effects the long-term so*lu*tion to which I referred. The lady
cop's partner, unfortunately, must be hammered too, and the
lady cop's roommate. It works for me, I don't need to drag Poole
into it, politics, the chair, all that."

Cullen could see how it would work for a lot of people. "What
about Messina? Messina came looking for me. Messina and Sam
Cox. I didn't *drag* them into it, they—"

The interruption this time was something tangible, made to mate-
rialize by Neuman, with the flourish of a third-rate magician, from
the middle drawer of his desk—the old incriminating photograph,
the eight-by-ten glossy, full-frame with a border, color these days
instead of that old-time grainy, contrasty black-and-white, the photograph that when it's introduced in a movie you roll your eyes, you
slump down in your seat, you think about slipping out for another
popcorn, you say to yourself that these things just don't happen in
real life, in real life people don't permit their indiscretions and per-
versions to become trapped, fossilized, in celluloid.

Yet there it was—trite, mundane, incontrovertible, valued at one
thousand words and a few lives. Homemade porn, autobiography
with an auto-timer: badly lighted, poorly framed, awkwardly posed,
erotic in conception maybe, but by the time it had been staged,
realized, captured, nothing more than a piece of sleaze, a dirty piece
of sleaze. You could never feel nostalgia for the pictured caresses;
you would wince at the remembered pain.

Pallid, out of shape, presenting to the camera in profile an erection made pathetic by slabs of flesh hanging above it, imperiling it,
like eaves of snow poised to avalanche over an alpine village; not
wearing black ankle socks, thank God, not wearing black shoes but
with the same furtive bearing as the men in black ankle socks and
black shoes in blue movies (you'd think they'd be pleased with
themselves, proud of themselves, that a woman would do this with
them, to them, for them; instead, they're embarrassed, uneasy, reluctant, as though it was all someone else's idea); wearing a wristwatch though, with a stainless-steel bracelet band, on his left arm,
and on his left hand a gold wedding band, a man who didn't have a

lot of time or a lot of opportunity for activities like this, who had places to be and a wife at home, the Commissioner of the Police Department of the City of New York, the *capo di tutti* cops, Philip Warren Hriniak.

Standing facing the camera, beside him but slightly behind him, legs wide apart like a superheroine, like a babe on a James Bond movie poster, wearing a merry widow and matching garters and g-string, red with black lace trim, black stockings with embroidered roses up the sides, red spike heels, black over-the-elbow fingerless lace gloves, a worn leather shoulder holster (Hriniak's, his well-known longtime pal Cullen recognized), its wooden counterweight polished from years of handling, decades of handling; her right hand cupping her partner's testicles, her left rather amateurishly, girlishly, on the grip (the tip of the barrel was provocatively, danger-ously thrust in the crotch of her g-string) of a Smith & Wesson stainless-steel .38-caliber revolver, dull silver nowadays, no more blue-black, more resistant to rust, requires less maintenance than the old six-shot metal alloy, spurless hammer prevents mechanical cocking, must be fired double action by pulling the trigger, cutting down on accidental dis—

"Cullen?"

"Jenny Swale had a roommate, a woman named Jo Dante," Hriniak, shoulders slumped, elbows down between his knees, hands wringing each other, had said to Cullen on the faux Shaker bench. *"Works at a sound studio, which I'm not exactly sure what it is, something to do with movies, TV. It's in the West Fifties somewhere, Maslosky has the address if you can't find her at home. You should probably talk to her."*

"Cullen?"

Had a roommate, indeed. *Something to do with movies,* indeed. *In the West Fifties somewhere,* indeed. *If you can't find her at home,* indeed. *Should probably talk to her,* indeed.

"*Cullen!*"

Cullen looked up at Neuman. "Sir?"

Neuman raised his hands and let them fall. "Come on, Joe, don't 'sir' me. I'm sorry about this. I wish I could make it go away, I wish Crime Scene'd never found it. It was in a book on a shelf in her bedroom, *Great Masterpieces of Art of the Western World,* or some shit like that. Hriniak knows I've got it. He's, uh, you know—embarrassed. What can he say? It doesn't prove he hammered her. It doesn't prove a connection with Jenny Swale's hammer. There's no sign whoever hammered her tried to find it, or anything else; it was staged to look like a suicide, remember? 'Course you remember. I'm just . . . I'm *sorry.*"

Cullen lifted the photograph closer to his eyes (he would normally have bent over it, but he was afraid he would keel forward); if he squinted, if he made a scrim of his eyelashes, the pale hair, straight as straw, framing her face like a helmet of white-gold mail, the sky-blue eyes, the tall, flat-chested figure that he didn't know but that was so familiar—everything looked . . . different.

Schmuck, he would say to Neuman. *You're supposed to be so famously dogged. You've cleared more jobs than some Ds catch in a career. Books've been written about you, fictive cops based on you, and you can't tell that this isn't Jo Dante, it's an imposter, a fraud, a hoax, a look-alike, a brunette in a blond wig, a black woman in white-face? Come on, Neuman. Jesus.*

Or: *It's a fake, Neuman. Can't you see that? Can't you see this is Hriniak's head on somebody else's body? A child can see it. Look at the head, the shoulders, the angle, the way this goes this way and that goes that way. Are you blind, Neuman? Jesus. Don't you go to the movies? Don't you know that every incriminating photograph's been doctored? Every one.*

Cullen tossed the photograph on Neuman's desk. "How does he know her? Where did he meet her?" That had been a favorite question of his ex-wife, Connie Carrera; and Ann liked to know too how couples had come to be together. Cullen thought that how and where men and women met was insignificant; what counted was what fantasy they had of where they would be together next—like, oh, his fantasy of getting married to Jo Dante: Joe and Jo Cullen, Jo and Joe Cullen. Joe and Jo too, Jo and Joe too. Joe I and Jo II, Jo I and Joe II. By Doctor Seuss.

"Some, you know, film company made a PD recruiting movie," Neuman said. "She worked on it. Hriniak recorded a sound track for it. They met."

Cullen studied his knees; they were bent. The legs of his pants had creases in them. There were shoes on his feet. "Ann Jones"— (snap, snap)—"told me a story once, about when she was a kid, nine or ten. She went to her father's office on some school holiday. She was sitting at his desk, playing with one of those plastic cubes people keep pictures in, family pictures, six pictures, one on each side of the cube."

Neuman nodded—not a smug Bobby Colavito kind of nod, but an impatient nod, like: *Okay, already. Yes, I understand what you're talking about. One of* those *cubes. Yeah? So?*

"She was fiddling with one of the pictures and took it out of the cube, and underneath was a picture of a woman in a bikini. A babe in a bikini. She was stunned. Without knowing that people did things like that, she was absolutely certain that her father had a girlfriend. Should she tell her mother, her brother, an aunt or uncle? She didn't know what to do, and what she finally did was suppress it. She just forgot that it had happened. Years later, buying such a cube for herself, she remembered the incident and realized that the picture had been a display picture that came with the cube. On another side there might've been a landscape, on another a picture of . . . Troy Donahue."

Neuman laughed. Then he sighed and shook his head. "This ain't that kind of picture, Joe. It's—"

"Unfuckingreal," Bobby Colavito said, opening Neuman's door, thrusting in his head and shoulders, blurting the word. He wasn't interrupting, for once, he was bearing tidings. "Downstairs, Cullen. It's your friend."

Ann? Here? "Friend?"

"*Margaret* . . . what'shername," Colavito said.

Margaret? "Margaret M—"

"Morris. Better hurry. It's bad. Somebody winged her."

"Margaret?"

"Hey, Cullen. Stop saying 'Margaret,' will you, and move your ass."

On the stairs Colavito said, "She live near here or something?"

"Margaret? Uh, yeah, I think she does. Chelsea." That not terribly interesting place to visit and it now turned out he *did* know someone who lived there.

"Hunh. Probably explains why she's bare-assed. Looks like she dragged herself all the way up here, winged and completely fucking bare-assed."

"Joe?"

"Maggie, don't talk."

"Oh, yeah. I better."

"Don't. Don't. You need to rest."

"Apartment. Elvis."

"Your apartment? Elvis Polk?"

"Dead. Or hurt bad."

"Strapped, yes?"

" 'Strapped'?"

"He has a gun?"

"I . . . He . . . he had one."

Cullen, on his knees on the marble Midwest vestibule, looked up at Neuman, who was already nearly through the door to the lobby, shouting orders. He turned back to Margaret Morris, putting his arms down beside her, resting on her elbows, protecting her, among other things, from Colavito, who hovered like a vulture. From the outside door up two steps to the place where she lay was a wide path of her blood. Blood and . . . pieces of her, parts of her. "Warm enough?"

"He shot me in the tit, the fuck," Margaret said.

"You'll be okay. Emergency Services has a unit here. They're bringing their van around."

"N-not Elvis."

"What's not Elvis, Mag?"

"Uh, Cullen?" Colavito said.

"Elvis didn't . . ."

"Didn't what, Mag?"

"Cullen, listen up."

"He . . . he didn't . . . Carl did."

"Carl . . . ?"

"Cullen? *Cullen!*"

". . ."

"Carl . . . shot you?"

Margaret Morris nodded.

Cullen whirled on his knees. "Get Neuman. Tell him the armed and dangerous is a male African-American, mid-thirties, medium build. Carlton Woods."

Colavito placed the tips of his fingers against his chest. "Hey, I'm supposed—"

"Carlton. Woods. Tell. Neuman." Cullen covered Margaret Morris again. "Hang on, Mag."

She smiled. "Mag."

"Yeah."

"M-monkey in . . . in . . . in the—"

"Maggie, shut up. Please."

"Monkey in the . . . the middle. Elvis."

Cullen saw a layer of her life peel away like onion skin and disappear.

"Tahiti. South America. The pampas. SS men. Drastic surg— Stra— Spastic surgery. *Pla*stic surgery."

"Maggie."

"And the switch. Listen. The switch. The switch?"

"I know what you mean, Mag. The car switch."

Margaret Morris managed the tiniest shake of her head.

"There was no switch? There were pieces in both cars?"

Margaret Morris shut her eyes and nodded once and smiled.

"Maggie, open your eyes."

She opened her eyes.

"Carl planted them?"

She nodded.

"Carl and who?"

"The fuck. My tit."

"Carl and who, Mag?"

She died.

"Maggie . . . Margaret . . . Margaret? *Maggie!* Shit."

Cullen got his overcoat off the hook behind the door in the room off the squad room. It was five after seven by the clock above the door, still December 24 by the calendar on the wall. Lyndzee still reached for the slit between the legs of her red fishnet bodysuit; as bare as she was, as vulnerable, she didn't seem to Cullen half so naked as Jo Dante in her merry widow and garters and g-string and stockings and spike heels and gloves and shoulder holster and .38, didn't seem as *farblondjet.*

"The fuck're you . . ." Colavito began, getting between Cullen and the door.

Cullen took him by the shoulders and tossed him aside and went out the door and down the stairs.

Left to finish his own sentence, Colavito said, ". . . going?"

24

Cullen hit the street running, which didn't make him stand out much, there were cops hauling ass every which way out in front of Midwest: Emergency Service cops banging a stretcher out of an ambulance and tooling it alongside the vivid path of blood, pieces, parts of Margaret Morris, across the sidewalk, up the steps, in the big heavy double doors; TPF cops saddling up to swing down to Chelsea after the armed and dangerous Carlton Woods; cops going off duty and hoping to make it to their cars before the desk officer decided, Fuck Christmas, everyone on O.T.; cops coming on duty figuring they had to work Christmas Eve anyway, at least there was a little action, hurrying to get dressed, get fucking strapped, get in on it.

Beyond the corner, though, the sidewalks were Omaha-empty, and a runner would be remarkable. On Thirty-fourth Street there would be some street life to dive into and swim along under the surface of, and Cullen struck out north toward it. He hadn't gone half a block when, even though he'd read Genesis 29, even though he'd read *Lost Horizon,* even though he'd seen *Brigadoon,* cautionary tales all of them about the perils of looking back, he couldn't help it, he slowed enough for a quick peek.

There was Colavito, bucking the tide to get out the In door, struggling with his overcoat; the collar was bunched into a hump in back and the sleeves flapped like Dopey the Dwarf's. Colavito was shouting to someone; he was being ignored by everyone. Frustration or just dumb luck made him lift his eyes above the tumult right in front of him; he saw Cullen, who turned and ran.

Thirty-first, Thirty-second, trying not to think about running, trying not to think that running wasn't something he did a lot of these days. He allegedly did twenty minutes of rowing every day on the Precor 610 in his bedroom, the television on to distract him from the monotony and the discomfort, the discomfort and the monotony, but more often it was fifteen minutes every other day, or ten minutes every third, or so long between ordeals that he couldn't remember the last one; stood on end, for convenient storage, the Precor had become a handy clothes hanger. The days when he'd done a lot of running had been, oh, forty years ago, back before running was a fad, a cult, an addiction, a social grace, all it was was an eight-year-old's locomotion of choice.

Thirty-third.

Ann was a runner, speaking of addictions, speaking of Ann. Remember Ann? Ann (snap, snap) Jones. Busy, busy, work, work, her body always in demand, up and out at dawn, on the air at six and eleven, standups, intros and outtros, weekend pinch-hit anchoring. She didn't have time for him at dawn anymore, time for a few standups, sitdowns, spin arounds, gimme a bale of hay; she didn't have time at six or eleven or any other time. Yet she still had time to run. Sometimes, when she didn't have to be out on the street at dawn for a standup, or on weekends when she went in a little later to pinch-hit anchor, she ran to work; she'd call a radio cab company where she had an account and pack her anchorwoman's dress in a garment bag and any other stuff she was taking with her in an L. L. Bean duffle bag; she'd give the bags to the driver when he showed up and arrange for him to leave them with the security guard at the station. She'd run south through Riverside Park to Seventy-third Street, east to Central Park West, into the park at Seventy-second, down the West Drive and around and up the East Drive to Wollman Rink, along the path past the rink, into the zoo, out onto Fifth Avenue, north to Sixty-ninth Street, east to the NewsFocus 14 studio just off Second. Sometimes she ran home, using a radio cab or one of the station's cars to ferry the duffle and the garment bag. Prudent after dark, though too feisty to avoid Central Park altogether, she ran across the Seventy-second Street transverse and had the cab or the car tag alongside her.

Some days, after the morning editorial meeting, or at lunchtime, or in mid-afternoon if her piece for the six was in the can early, she ran in Central Park or over to Carl Schurz Park and John Finley Walk, then up alongside the FDR to the Ward's Island Bridge. Once in a while, in pouring rain or drifting snow or shriveling heat, she ran at the West Side Y, joining the giant headless-tailless centipede that pounded around the twenty-fourth-of-a-mile track. When she was going to be at her apartment for any length of time, one of the first things she did was get out of the apartment and go for a run in Riverside Park. If Cullen had spent the night, she would make sure she didn't wake him (he who was so deprived of standups, sitdowns, spin arounds, gimme a bale of hay, that he didn't even bother to brush his teeth before attempting a few) until she had gone for her run. Against the chance that she would spend a night at Cullen's, a rarer and rarer event all the time, she kept tights, a sweatshirt, a running bra, socks and shoes in his closet. She found paths to run on in Forest Park that he, who had lived near the park for more than a decade, since his divorce, didn't know existed.

What made Annie run? Bernstein, in a session on another day, had asked the question when Cullen had complained about Ann's busy, busy, busyness, her work, work, working, her run, run, running—had asked in his not-quite-question way: "You feel that her running is a technique for avoiding you."

"She ran before she knew me," Cullen had said. "At one point, years ago, she was considering competing in triathlons."

"Which involve a considerable investment of time for training."

"Yes."

"But she didn't compete in them."

"No."

"She's no longer considering competing in them."

"No."

"And her investment of time for running isn't unreasonable."

"Okay, Doc. What's the point?"

"There are men and women both who exercise to extremes, whose behavior is similar to that of anorexics."

"I'm not saying Ann's one of them."

"If she didn't run, if she worked less, you feel that the time saved would be time applied toward your relationship."

"Meaning, if I drank less, that time would be applied to our relationship?"

Bernstein didn't bite.

"Would it?" Cullen said.

"You feel it would," Bernstein said.

"But I'm just an amateur. You're the professional. You tell me. Would it?"

The expert's nostrils flared a little. In his last job, at a state prison, dealing with sociopaths, psychopaths, experts in dissimulation and disorder, Bernstein would win a few, he would lose a few. Every last inmate began by claiming to be innocent; sooner or later, they gave up the pretense. Cops, he was finding, used their uniforms and their shields as proof against culpability and responsibility. They never admitted wrongdoing. Against such experts at evasiveness, Bernstein was still learning to settle for standoffs.

Thirty-fourth Street. No miracles here, not tonight, Christmas Eve or no Christmas Eve. Middling weather, not cold enough to make pedestrians scurry, not warm enough to encourage dawdling. Not many of them, pedestrians, not much cover. A few straggling shoppers—the absentminded, the forgetful, the procrastinating, the willful. Bargain hunters and those desperate for anything to fill a stocking, to distract a hard-to-please aunt, squabbled halfheartedly over what remained on shelves, in bins, on tables out in front of bargain emporia. Salvation Army grunts labored cheek by jowl with skirmishers from Satan's legions—three-card monte dealers, vendors of merchandise fallen from trucks, ouncemen, porno leafleteers; the grunts' weary oompahs vied with the beat of house music from the opportunists' blasters. Lean and hungry Santas, roly-poly Santas, indifferent Santas, Santas with style worked their last shows of the year. Sharing curb space with the Santas and the opportunists and the grunts and the shoppers and the vendors were the usual pesky homeless. (At some point in some summer of the era of living without walls, some benefactor had handed out to homeless people folding aluminum and vinyl chaise longues, and all over town ever since people who had once squatted on cardboard mats or directly on the cold cold ground now reclined, lounged, lolled, swaddled in everything they possessed, or so it seemed, looking like passengers on deck chairs on some cruise to Hell.)

Cullen wanted to slow down, to amble, to saunter, to browse and peruse and bargain. He *hadn't* done his Christmas shopping, after all. But his feet were in a moving mood and the chill he felt on the back of his neck wasn't just from evaporating sweat.

The traffic signal at Seventh Avenue was flashing Don't Walk as Cullen neared the corner, and from uptown a substantial flash flood of traffic was washing toward the intersection. If he missed the light, and if Colavito was still on his tail, he risked being overtaken. And why wouldn't Colavito still be on his tail? Cullen hadn't done anything particularly elusive, anything wily, sly, foxy, crafty, anything that would be written up in subsequent editions of the Regs and Recipes: *Great Escapes: See: Cullen, Joseph (Sgt.), from Colavito, Robert (Sgt.).*

If Cullen missed the light, he could make a left and go north along Seventh. Or he could cross Thirty-fourth and go south. Either way, he would forsake what little camouflage he had.

As a native he knew that lights at most major intersections flash ten times before going red. Having seen the very first flash and having counted four more, Cullen slowed a little, hoping to trick Colavito (the assumed Colavito) into slowing too.

Six, seven, eight.

Then he sprinted with all he had, which wasn't much, it had been forty years since he'd done a lot of running, back before running was a fad, a cult, an addiction, a social grace, back when all it was was an eight-year-old's locomotion of choice.

A gypsy cab nipped at Cullen's heels as he leaped for the easterly curb, but that could have happened to anyone, he didn't take it personally, he didn't imagine that the driver was in league with Colavito.

He'd made it. And having made it, he looked back and saw Colavito, back in the west gutter, chest deep in the river of cars, sometimes over his head amid vans and trucks, swinging his arms, trying to accelerate the sweep of traffic past him, hopping from foot to foot as he repeatedly dipped his toes into the current and each time found it too treacherous.

Cullen hopped into a revolving door and hopped out back in the past.

The place was the same, the southwest entrance to Macy's, a vestibule with a bank of pay phones, a set of revolving doors to the street, another set to the store itself; but the time was a dozen years ago, Christmas 1979, and Cullen was taking his son, James, five years and three months old, to see Santa at Macy's for the first time. (His daughter, Tenny, at two, was still too young.) A friend, a neighbor, a sister-in-law, *some*body had counseled him to get there just as the store opened at ten on one of the Sundays in December, to take an elevator straight up to Santaland on nine, to march right in with hardly a wait. Joe and James had come out of the subway at the northeast corner of Seventh Avenue and Thirty-fourth Street (the southwest entrance to Macy's), at about ten minutes to ten. They had gone through the revolving door and found a place to stand among the crowd of fifty-odd early-bird shoppers. James had sized up the situation in silence for a while, the unmoving crowd, the unrevolving doors, the bank of pay phones, a few of them occupied, then had said, loudly enough for many right nearby to hear and chuckle and smile at, "Dad, are all these people waiting to use the *phones?*"

Oh, well, maybe you had to have been there.

That same Christmas, 1979, was coincidentally the last time Cullen could remember having had dinner, wives included, with his well-known longtime buddy, Philip Warren Hriniak, the Commissioner of the Police Department of the City of New York, the *capo di tutti* cops. As Cullen had recalled on the faux Shaker bench, right after Hriniak had said Cullen was a pro, he should treat the allegation that Hriniak had asked Jenny Swale to give him a blow job like any other investigation, right after Hriniak had said Cullen's Integrity Rating (IR) was in the ninety-ninth percentile, people trusted him, the dinner was at Hriniak's house, Cullen was a detective two and still married to Connie, Hriniak was a DCI with all his hair, Beryl Hriniak was still a blonde. Hriniak had laughed, rocking back on his buttocks on the faux Shaker bench till his feet were off the floor, punching a thigh with a fist. He had said, "A DCI with all my hair. Beryl still a blonde," and had laughed and rocked and punched again, though it hadn't been that funny; it had very nearly been insubordinate.

"Things all right with Beryl, Phil?" Cullen had asked, and Hriniak had stared at him. And no wonder. Things had clearly not been all right with Beryl.

Cullen went through the revolving door into the store, past the information desk, right onto the up escalator. He walked up the escalator to two and walked through men's suits to the escalators in the middle of the store. He rode to five, walked around the corner to the elevators, pressed up, waited, wondered if there was a section in the Regs and Recipes about evasive techniques to be used in department stores when being pursued by a *primero* ballbreaker world-class sentence finisher with wise-guy relatives—a *primero* ballbreaker world-class sentence finisher with wise-guy relatives *cop.*

An up car stopped and Cullen got in, keeping his eyes down the way he always did when he got in elevators, being a native, not wanting to frighten anybody, not wanting to come on too strong, not wanting to seem like a tourist. There were eight or ten passengers in the car, five of them kids. The parents smelled irritable and exhausted; the kids smelled like McDonald's or Burger King or Roy's —french fries and pickles and ketchup. The car was not even to six when Cullen smelled Colavito, ragged and pissed off.

The car stopped at six. People got in, people got out. The doors closed, the car went up.

The car stopped at seven. It was a local. People got in, people got out. The doors closed, the car went up.

The car stopped at eight. People got in, people got out. The doors closed, the car went up.

The car stopped at nine. Santaland. Cullen stepped aside to let people out. Everyone else on the car was getting out. Everyone except Colavito. There was a big crowd waiting to get on. Colavito stepped to the door and held his hands up. "Sorry, folks. Sorry. This car's going out of service. Please wait for the next one. This car's going out of service. It'll just be a minute or two. Thank you for your patience. Sorry, folks, sorry. This car's—"

Cullen hit Colavito in the spleen with his fist. Colavito slumped in his arms, sucking for air. Cullen let him down to the floor and stepped over him and off the elevator. "Going out of service," he said to the people waiting and wondering.

25

"Hi, I'm Ginny. What's your name?"

"Uh . . . Joe." You didn't fib to Santa's elves, not on Christmas Eve, not when, having made their list and checked it twice, Santa's staff still entertained a reasonable doubt whether this had been a year in which you had been nice or very, very naughty. Not when the Santa's elf had big brown eyes and big brown curls and looked the way your daughter was probably going to look in about three years, when she was seventeen, way beyond compare.

"All by yourself this evening, Joe?"

"Uh, yes." Cullen took a look behind him, to make sure *that* was the truth. Whatever he'd done to Colavito —it wasn't something he'd learned in the Regs and Recipes; he'd just made it up on the spot—wouldn't have disabled him, just inconvenienced him. Colavito would be along any minute now, more ragged, more pissed off. "Uh, my son. My son's sick. I told him I'd come see Santa for him. To tell him what he wants for Christmas. Tell Santa what he wants. What my son wants."

Ginny cocked her head unsuspiciously, held her arms out as if she wanted to hug him. His pronoun problems made him only more poignant. *"Aw,* that's *nice.* Here, I'll tell you what I'll do. *This* line's to *talk* to Santa, *that* one's to take just a *peek* at him. It's *kids,* right, who want to *talk* to him, so *this* line goes past all the electric trains and the mechanical elves and everything, and *that* one just goes straight around to a window where you can *peek* through and *see* Santa. You don't want to see the trains and the elves and everything, *do* you? You just want to *talk* to Santa so you can tell your son, so if you take *that* line, I'll meet you at the other end, where the Santas are, and *sneak* you in. Anybody complains, well, tough on them. There's *more* than one Santa, I guess you *know* that; we don't tell the *kids* that, but there *is* more than one. I mean, there'd *have* to be, wouldn't there, there're so *many* kids—"

"Ginny?"

"Y-yes?" Just the slightest quaver, as though she had suddenly remembered the cryptic warning in the orientation lecture about a few people—*men*—who didn't love Santa, who didn't think it was cute that he shook like a bowlful of jelly when he laughed, who might try to pass themselves off as, oh, caring fathers coming to see Santa on behalf of their ailing sons, who in reality were psychowacko Santa-dicers, schizo-weirdo elf-rapers.

"Is there a back way out, Ginny, an exit . . ." But before Cullen could ask if there was an exit all those Santas used to come and go, so the kids wouldn't chance to see them and get all disillusioned, would it be okay if he went out that exit, because, yes, she was right, he wasn't really a caring father coming to see Santa on behalf of his ailing son, he was a secret agent on a most sensitive mission, he wished he could tell her more about it, but national, even *international* security, was at stake—before he could say any of that, he saw Colavito. The heel of one hand pressed into the small of his back to try to push out the pain left behind by Cullen's improvised blow, the palm of his other hand flat against the wall for support, Colavito looked even more ragged, more pissed off, than Cullen had foreseen.

Before Colavito saw him, Cullen ducked down the path that would take him past all the electric trains and mechanical elves and face-to-face with Santa.

The path zigged and zagged, it went up and down. The path was terribly familiar. And why not? After taking James to see Macy's Santa for the first time a dozen years ago, Christmas 1979, Cullen had returned six more times. He brought Tenny along for the first time in 1981, when she was four. Both kids last went in 1985, after which Christmas (James was eleven and had a Madonna fan magazine secreted in his closet) he declared Santa Claus if not a fiction at least an undependable, unpredictable source of stuff. Born a skeptic, Tenny, though only nine, had probably been an influence on, rather than merely influenced by, her brother; she had been profoundly moved earlier that year to learn that Natalie Wood, converted to a belief in Santa Claus in *Miracle on 34th Street,* had grown up only to die prematurely, accidentally.

Above all else about those outings, Cullen remembered how fucking hot it got: all those little warm sticky bodies, sherpa-ing their goddamn coats and boots, refereeing their disputes, wrangling them when they sneaked ahead or lagged behind, pooh-poohing their claims of near death by starvation or thirst, disabusing them of their conviction that they had to pee, they had *just* peed. It was hot work.

This Christmas Eve was hotter than all those other visits put together. Fleeing from the law, lying to a Santa's elf (he had lied, hadn't he, barely hesitating?), having little or no genuine Christmas spirit—they all generated a few Btus. Cullen's face was slick with sweat, the shirt under his sport coat under his overcoat was wet through front and back, his jockey shorts were damp and clinging, the backs of his knees dripped.

There were only a dozen or so, uh, family units—fathers and kids, mothers and kids, mothers and fathers and kids, grandparents and kids, older siblings and kids—waiting on line to confront Santa face-to-face. Enough is enough, after all; there comes a time when you have to stop anticipating Christmas, and actually celebrate Christmas, stop shopping and start partying. Cullen turned sideways and scooted through.

"Excuse me, please. Security. Coming through, please. Security. Watch your backs, please. Security, Security."

At this hour, on this night, *Security* didn't generate a lot of respect. To wit:

"Be careful, mister. You be careful of these children."

"Security? Security *this.*"

"Hey, don't push."

"Stuart, be careful. Stuart! *Stuart!*"

Finally: "I'm sorry, sir." A blond elf this time; her nametag said *Dawn.*"You'll have to go back to the end of the line."

Suddenly everyone was on his side:

"It's okay, honey. He's Security."

"Let him through. Security."

"Security, Security. Come on, hunh? Hey, girlie, Se*cur*ity."

Beyond Dawn was a dimly lighted antechamber, off which several doors opened. Each door, Cullen the Santaland veteran recalled, was attended by an elf who took visitors over from the elf at Dawn's post and introduced them personally to the Santa in the room behind the door. The doors were wood (or maybe faux wood) and were supposed to be replicas, Cullen guessed, of the doors of Santa's actual house. But Santa lived at the North Pole, didn't he, a treeless place, and Macy's clearly hadn't thought *that* through. In fact, the doors looked more like the doors to outhouses—though what Cullen knew about outhouse doors he knew from seeing Hollywood's versions in movies and on television.

Or maybe the apparent resemblance to outhouse doors was born of Cullen's sudden and violent need to pee.

"Are any of the Santas on a break, Dawn?"

"A *break?*" Dawn yelled. She remembered the orientation lecture on psycho-wacko-schizo-weirdo-Santa-dicer-elf-rapers only too well.

"Just show me where, Dawn. Then go back to your work."

The crowd was changing sides again:

"Hey, buddy! Hey, hey! Who says *you*'re next? How come *you*'re next? We've been on this line forty-five minutes. *We're* next."

"Just show me, Dawn. Don't worry about these people."

"Uh . . ."

"Just show me, Dawn."

She showed him after a fashion, waving at the door at the far left side of the antechamber while she backed away from him into the gloom on the far right side. Cullen tried the latch of the door and finding it open went in without knocking.

A Santa sat on a folding chair eating a tunafish sandwich, heavy mayo, on whole wheat bread off a napkin spread out in his lap. A pint container of Tropicana orange juice was open on the floor beside his shiny black boots, a straw peeking out. His red coat was off and hung from a hook on the back of the door, his white beard and wig and mustache lay on the bench where he sat to dandle children on his knees. His suspenders were down around his hips. He wore a plain white cotton T-shirt and over it some foam padding, with straps, like a catcher's chest protector, to give him extra girth, for he was tall and lank for a Santa, long-nosed and pointy-chinned. He wasn't even all that old—early fifties, maybe, not much older than the sweat-slick psycho-wacko-schizo-weirdo-Santa-dicer-elf-raper who stood before him, wet shirt, damp shorts, drippy knees, eyeing his sandwich, for his stomach was as empty as his bladder was full.

"Evening, Santa," Cullen said.

"Howdy," Santa said. "Macy's?"

"Uh, no. I'm, uh—"

"A cop." *Another* sentence finisher. Cullen would've hammered him if only he'd been strapped. Which reminded him—maybe he should ask Santa for a gun.

"Done points?" Cullen said.

Santa nodded mournfully. "Bounced some checks. Long ago, far away. Might lose this gig if they found out. You won't be telling them, will you?"

Cullen shook his head. "Listen, Santa, I need—"

"Harry. Harry Fain." Santa wiped the fingertips of his right hand on the napkin in his lap and extended his hand.

Cullen shook it. "Joe Cullen. Is there a back way out of the store, Harry, a basement route, some way I won't be seen?"

Harry Fain scratched his chin. "None of my business who's after you, but there can't be any shooting. The children."

"I have children. There won't be shooting."

Harry Fain looked doubtful. Santas attended the orientation lectures too and knew about the many guises Santa-dicer-elf-rapers came in. He sighed though and nodded once. He folded up what was left of his sandwich in the napkin, closed the top of the pint of orange juice, and got up out of the folding chair. He put the sandwich and the juice in a small cupboard concealed behind a pile of gift-wrapped boxes that lent verisimilitude to his quarters. From deep in a side pocket of his baggy red pants he extracted a wristwatch with no strap. He consulted the time, put the watch back, and went to a door opposite the door Cullen had come in. He put a hand on the latch and motioned to Cullen with his head.

Cullen went to him.

"Said you got kids. Ever been here before?"

"Out there's a counter where they sell pictures," Cullen said, relieved to have some test to pass. "Pictures of the kids and the Santas."

Harry Fain looked a little relieved himself. "To the left of the counter's the way out to the elevator bank. To the right there's a staircase. It's marked Exit, but they don't make a big thing of it; they want people going back out to the selling floors. The stairs go all the way down to the street, for sure. If there's a flight to the basement, I've never noticed, but there might be."

Cullen put a hand on Harry Fain's shoulder. "Thanks, Harry."

Fain shrugged. "Ever need a favor, need to look you up, where'll I find you?"

"Call the main number, ask for the Locator Wheel. They'll find me." Cullen put his hand on the latch, then took it off. "Also, Harry, these kids of mine, I've been jammed up, I haven't had a chance to do any Christmas shopping. You have any influence with the . . . the real guy?"

Fain bobbed his head. "Maybe, maybe not. What do you need?"

"My son wants hockey gloves—CCM's. I'm not sure what my daughter wants. I guess that means there's not much chance of getting what *I* want, is there? Not if I don't even know what my own daughter wants."

"What is it you want, Joe?" Fain said.

Cullen thought for a moment. "My daughter . . ."

"Yeah?"

"Years ago, when she was six—she's fourteen now—my daughter wrote a poem . . . 'Who lights the moon?/Who makes the stars?/ Who does the sun?/Who does it all?/Why are there mice?/Why are there cows?' "

Fain chuckled. " 'Why are there mice?' "

"I have a close friend," Cullen said, "another cop."

"Your partner?" Fain said.

"Not my partner. A superior—but an old friend nonetheless. He's done something that I don't understand and I—"

"Want to know why?"

"Yes."

Fain shook his head. "Can't help you. Neither can the real guy. It ain't our thing. You should know that. Don't mean to be harsh with you, buddy, but it ain't our thing."

"No. I guess not."

"The shit you people want—stuff, things, possessions—that we got. Answers? Sorry."

"Okay. I get the point."

Fain poked Cullen in the chest, hard. "Hey, listen, buddy. You came asking me questions. I didn't go looking for you. Didn't make no claims. So fuck off. There's a button back there calls Security. I've got a mind to press it, see your ass in stir."

Cullen opened the latch. "Thanks for everything, Harry."

"Yeah, well, fuck you."

"Merry Christmas."

"And the horse you rode in on."

26

"Not counting this one," Ann said, "what's the worst Christmas you ever spent?"

"Nineteen seventy . . . six or seven," Mabel said. "Seventy-*six*, definitely, because I'd just turned thirty and I suppose I should've known better, I went to Aspen for what was supposed to be two weeks with Gary Greenstein, Dr. Gary Greenstein, radiologist, The New York Hospital-Cornell Medical Center. Very good-looking, kind of a Jewish Robert Redford, but brunet. Smart, funny, athletic—a beautiful skier and not a show-off. Nice dresser—preppy, but Paul Stuart preppy, not Brooks Brothers preppy. I was his first *shiksa,* and maybe his last. He was on the rebound from a long relationship with a woman he'd met in med school, an ophthalmologist. She got the holiday blues, I guess, tracked him down through his answering service in the middle of our first week there and demanded that he come back to New York. He went for two days. He told me it was a medical emergency, that she needed a consultation on a diagnosis.

"While he was gone, I slept with a guy on the ski patrol. That was the great thing about the seventies: Somebody pissed you off, you fucked somebody else. Skip Gaines. Is that a ski-patrol name or what? I saw Skip's picture last summer in one of those ridiculous triathlon magazines you read. He's like a major professional triathlon star, Skip. He certainly was swift in bed. He spent more time combing his hair afterwards than he did on foreplay. His name should be Skip Foreplay.

"Doctor Gary came back Saturday afternoon. He wanted to fuck. I could smell her on him. I bit his cock—not as hard as I wanted to, not *off*, but hard enough that he knew I knew he was a lying scumbag. I flew home that night—Christmas night. Everyone on the plane was really nice to me; I guess they knew. We had a little party —there were only twenty or thirty people on the whole big plane; it was pathetic, I guess, but it was sort of nice.

"Doctor Gary got married a couple of years later; I saw it in the *Times*. Not to the eye doctor, to a woman who has a small chain of boutiques on the East Side and in the Hamptons. I can't think what they're called, but you've seen them. . . . And you?"

"Nothing so dramatic," Ann said. "I often go home at Christmas. My mom cooks, my brother and I eat and play gin, my dad watches football."

"I guess Joe spends Christmas with his kids," Mabel said. "Or aren't we talking about Joe?"

"We can talk about whatever and whomever we want," Ann said. "We're going to be dead soon. I mean, isn't that the scenario? When I first saw that word as a kid, I thought it was pronounced see-nuh-*ree*-oh."

They had evaded speculating about the scenario, expending their energy instead on guessing where they were. All that was clear was that where they were was cheerless—a sterile cube of an office, fairly new industrial carpet on the floor, faux redwood paneling on the walls, an ugly metal desk with matching ugly metal chair, a metal folding chair, ugly in a different way, against one wall, and that was all, nothing else: no phone, no file cabinets, no desk or wall calendar, nothing in any of the desk drawers except in the wide shallow top drawer the usual rubber band, penny, packet of Sweet 'n Low, and paper clip that are in the wide shallow top drawers of all ugly metal desks everywhere. No windows, just a heavy metal door, great for banging on, great for keeping in those who wanted to get out. In a ceiling light fixture two one-hundred-fifty-watt bulbs, operated by a chain-pull switch lengthened by a piece of dingy string. That was too much light, thanks, and Ann had stood on the folding chair to unscrew one of the bulbs.

Oh yes, and two thin grungy exercise mats and two rancid blankets—"Stolen from the homeless," Ann bet—for sleeping on.

That it was Christmas Day, Wednesday, they knew from Ann's Tridor Oyster Perpetual Lady Datejust Rolex. Otherwise, it could still have been Monday, the day they were brought to this place from Mabel's office in the building with seven sides on Waverly Place in the Village; it could have been Friday, it could have been February, or June.

They had been fed, so to speak, three so-called meals: pizza—large plain pies, cut into six slices; two-liter plastic bottles of Coke. The first pie was delivered just after they arrived, about eleven-thirty Monday night, the second just after noon on Tuesday, the third at nine-thirty Tuesday night. They came in generic pizza delivery boxes with this boast on the top: "Our Ingredients Are Guaranteed Fresh," and small squares on one end for checking off the appropriate additional (fresh) ingredients:

☐ Mushrooms   ☐ Peppers   ☐ Anchovies   ☐ Sausage
☐ Pepperoni   ☐ Extra Cheese ☐ Spinach   ☐ Other

No address, no phone number, no check, no identifying marks.

"So what do we know?" Mabel said after the second pie arrived—arrived the same way as the first: the heavy metal door was unlocked, bald Jerry with the big *bigote* opened the door wide enough for the box, dropped the box on the floor, tossed the plastic soda bottle in after it, on it, he didn't give a fuck, pulled the door to and locked it. Two or three seconds, max. All they saw over the shoulder of bald Jerry with the big *bigote* was the blackness of a big dark empty space—a room, a warehouse, an interplanetary void, they couldn't estimate.

"We know . . . it's an Italian neighborhood," Ann said. "Maybe." The pizza could have been classic or it could have been a catastrophe—they were starving, they didn't know the difference, they ate the congealed cheese that stuck to the lid and the sides and the bottom of the box.

"Maybe," Mabel agreed. "We know the pizzeria's close by, though. This pie is warm, and so's the box. So there must be people living close by, is what I'm saying."

"There could be a kitchen somewhere in this building," Ann said.

"Right. And they warmed the pie up for us."

"Right. 'Cause they're warmhearted."

"Right."

"Right. We know," Ann said, "we know, we know . . . I heard trucks. Did you hear trucks?"

"When? Just now?"

"Last night. When we were trying to sleep."

"I couldn't sleep. You slept?"

"A little. So did you."

"I did?"

"I was watching you," Ann said. "Thinking, 'How can she sleep?' You were having a dream; your eyelashes were fluttering."

"What kind of trucks?" Mabel said.

"Not highway trucks. Trucks making pickups, deliveries, stopping and starting."

"We're in a UPS depot," Mabel said. "We'll be sent home along with stuff we ordered from J. Crew, from Victoria's Secret. . . . Were they garbage trucks?"

"Garbage trucks? Maybe . . . No. No crashing and banging, just stopping and starting . . . How long did it take us to get here from the Village? An hour? An hour and a half?"

"When somebody points a gun at me and tells me to do what they tell me, it doesn't occur to me to look at my watch," Mabel said.

"I wanted to time the trip, that's all, but I couldn't see my watch. I was down on the floorboards under a blanket. Were you covered up too?"

Mabel nodded. "Were there just the two cars, or was there a third?"

"Bald Jerry with the big *bigote* drove the car I was in," Ann said. "It was some kind of Dodge or Chrysler."

"Big what?" Mabel said.

"Mustache. Maria sat in the front seat. She kept reaching over to check the blanket. She . . ."

"She what?"

"Nothing. Who was in the Cadillac?"

"The little one—I think his name is Eddie."

"Yes, Eddie."

"He drove, Eddie. Sam Cox and Poole were in the front seat. Eddie put Poole's wheelchair in the trunk. It kept thudding around; at first I thought it was you. . . . What?" Mabel leaned closer to Ann to try to see her eyes. "What, Ann, what?"

"Nothing."

"You already said 'Nothing.' "

"I don't want to get your hopes up."

"Go ahead. I can take it."

"Okay, I don't want to get *my* hopes up."

Mabel shrugged. "I can understand that. So how long did it take us to get here? An hour? An hour and a half?"

"At least. I tried to get a sense of bridges or tunnels, but I just couldn't. We started out going south, I'm fairly sure, down Seventh Avenue, but after that, I just don't know. I think it's safe to say we're not in Manhattan, but other than that, we could be anywhere."

After a while Mabel said, "Go ahead. Get our hopes up."

Ann said, "Maria put her hand on my shoulder, my hips. It felt . . . reassuring, comforting."

Mabel snorted.

"Okay, maybe not," Ann said. "But how do you explain the stuff she told us about the murdered hairdresser?"

"What did she tell us? I don't even remember."

"Elvis Polk killed a hairdresser in Newark who also did tattoos. He changed Elvis's tattoo, then Elvis killed him. Maria was tipped off by her brother-in-law. She called Maslosky, Rickie Maslosky, Internal Affairs. Why would she do that if . . ."

"If what?"

"I don't know. I don't know what's going on."

"If she was a crook?" Mabel said. "I'll tell you why. Everybody wants Elvis Polk dead. The cops want him dead, the crooks want him dead. The cops want him dead because he killed two cops, the crooks want him dead because they hired him to kill the cops and now they don't need him anymore, in fact, they emphatically *un*-need him. Maria's one of the crooks."

Crooks? Crooks was so quaint. Did Mabel used to call them *crooks* when she was an ADA? Was she calling them *crooks* now to make them less fearsome? "Elvis called your office. You called Powell Ruth. He sent an Emergency Services Unit. Poole showed up. Is Ruth in cahoots with Poole, or does Poole have someone inside Emergency Services?" Listen to her: *cahoots*. What the hell *were* cahoots? Was there such a thing as *one* cahoot? Ann wanted her mother. "At her wedding, Maria brought up Quintana. It seemed . . . inappropriate. Now I understand."

Over the first pizza Ann had explained her reasons for not having told Mabel, her lawyer as well as her best friend, what she had seen after leaving Joe Cullen early on the Sunday after Thanksgiving, walking back down Riverside Drive to where Quintana Davidoff died, the whitetops gone, the EMS vans, the ambulances, the unmarked but unmistakable squad cars, the TV remote vans, the reporters' cars, the Crime Scene sawhorses and yellow perimeter tape, the onlookers long gone, the witnesses and the witness wanna-bes, crossing to the Riverside Park side of the street, sitting on a bench that wasn't right under a bishop's-crook street lamp, it was a little bit in shadow.

("It was all speculation," Ann had said. "I couldn't prove anything."

("Bullshit," Mabel had said. "What *power* you have over these people, knowing what you know. You wanted that power over all of us—the whole city, the whole world. You wanted to be the most powerful person on earth. When you were ready, you'd let us in on it, and how we'd admire you, how we'd kiss your goddamn feet, your all-knowing ass. Is there anyone more powerful in this town than Sam Cox, by virtue of her ratings, by virtue of the things people do to get on her show? There isn't. So just think what a double whammy dose of power you have by knowing something *about* Sam Cox."

(Ann hadn't been able to refute that, so she hadn't let the matter come up again till now, and Mabel hadn't brought it up.)

"Now I understand," Ann repeated, as if she did, but she didn't, not really. All she understood was that Mabel was right, knowledge was power, and there existed a group of people who feared her because of what she knew and that that group of people intended to expunge their fear by expunging her.

"I'm hungry," Mabel said. "Where's the fucking pizza?"

"Mabel," Ann said.

"What?"

"Two things. First of all, I read only one triathlon magazine."

Mabel just shook her head wearily.

"Second, let's give ourselves a Christmas present."

"Great idea. I'd like Godiva chocolates."

"Let's get out of here."

"Oh, Ann."

"I mean it. They're not as smart as they think they are, these . . . these crooks. They're dumber than they know."

27

Carlton Woods wished his pushy righteous doing-it-for-themselves ballbreaking r-e-s-p-e-c-t African-American older sisters could scope him now, in his Reebok Twilight Zone Pumps, his Triple Fat Goose, gold toothcaps on his front teeth, one cap with a pair of dice etched on them (six the hard way), one with a crown, lobing WBL Kicking S on his Seiko box, AM/FM cassette recorder, five-band equalizer, sixteen-step random access program and display CD player, lobing Morris Day and the Time, "Jerk Out," lamping with Kenya Dees, stone African-American fox, beaded cornrows, devotee of Angela Davis and Winnie Mandela. They would have to word up confess they had never scoped such a toy B-boy, the bitches. The bitches would be mothering housed.

Kenya Dees had been word up mothering housed, it was written all over her face, when Carlton Woods buzzed the buzzer of her crib on the parlor floor of a brownstone on Prospect Place off Flatbush in Park Slope, Brooklyn, the borough of ouncemen and con men and hit men and whores and whoremasters and poor sorry fucks, when she buzzed him in, when he rapped on the door of her crib with the barrel of his .22—*da da dadit da, da da.* "Carlton?"

Carlton had shoved the .22 under the Triple Fat Goose into the waist of his Jordache jeans while she was throwing locks and slip-sliding chains (he'd tried to fit himself into Elvis Polk's 501s, but he had a few pounds on Elvis, he couldn't get them over his hips), so it wasn't the heat that housed Kenya, it was word up certain that instead of the Geoffrey Beene suit and the Charvet shirt and the Chanel necktie and the Allen-Edmonds shoes, that instead of them she scoped the Twilight Zones, the Goose, the toothcaps, the box. "S'happening, Kenya? S'up?"

"Carlton, you know what time it is? The sun's not even up. Where'd you get those clothes? What're you doing here? How'd you know where I live? What is that in your *mouth*?"

Bitches. Nothing just ever *is,* they always got to know the reason *why.* "Merry Christmas, Kenya. I came to wish you Merry Christmas."

"Merry Christmas this, you jive motherfucker." And Kenya Dees closed the door in his face.

But Carlton got a Twilight Zone Pump across the sill before Kenya Dees could get the door all the way closed. He worked an elbow around the doorpost and with his hand shoved the door open and slip-slided inside. He shut the door and stood with his back against it, his Seiko up alongside his ear, voguing to Jay Williams now, "Sweat," so Kenya would get the point that while she and the other night-shift secretaries in the word-processing pool had all this time been lobing the def sounds of Frankie Crocker's Evening Bath on their Walkmans and Aiwas and 'Sonics, unbeknownst to her all this time toy B-boy Carlton Woods had been lobing those def sounds too. "Chill, Kenya. Chill, baby. Don't dis me, sweet thang."

Kenya stood with her feet wide apart and her hands on her hips and shook her head from side to side over and over and over and over. She wasn't wearing a leather miniskirt, she was wearing a worn terry-cloth bathrobe that had probably once been red but had been washed to a pale pale pink. Under the robe, which was belted but only loosely, Kenya wore a pair of baggy gray sweatpants and a black Nike T-shirt: *Just Do It.* "You are the sorriest-looking thing I have ever seen. You poor pathetic man. You look ridiculous. You *sound* ridiculous. You *are* ridiculous. What're you *doing* here? I let you in 'cause I thought it was some kind of emergency at work, but you're just trolling for pussy, you sorry motherfucker. You get my address from Personnel? I'll bring your ass up for harassment, I swear to God I will. You'd've called me on the phone, I'd've brought you up, for dragging your ridiculous ass all the way out here I will word up certain bring you up."

This wasn't going down the way it was supposed to go down. Word. The way it was supposed to go down, Kenya Dees was supposed to answer the door in her leather miniskirt and some kind of tank top or maybe one of them fishnet things, she was supposed to have a glass of wine in her hand and maybe a big fat joint, she was supposed to say, *Why, Carlton, Christmas morning or no Christmas morning, I thought you'd be hard at work, or are you just*—and here she'd rub up against him with her thigh, with the back of her hand, with her leather-covered butt, no undies underneath maybe, or maybe just some kind of thong bikini panties—*or are you just hard?* "Chill, bitch. You can word up 'fess you're housed."

Kenya stared at Carlton for a moment, then took a step toward him and put her face close to his. "Don't you *ever* call me bitch, you hunkie-fucker, hunkie-lover, hunkie-ass-hunkie-kisser. I'll scratch your fucking eyes out, I'll rip your balls off and flush them down the motherfucking toilet. You dig, *bro*ther? Now get out of here, 'cause I'm calling the big boys." And she took a step to her right to a phone on a table by the couch and picked up the handset and punched in 911. A stone African-American woman of action: no threats, no warnings, just do it. She should be the prosecutor, locking up the ouncemen and the con men and the hit men and the whores and the whoremasters and the poor sorry fucks, he should be the secretary in the word-processing pool, typing, tapping, filing, merging, mailing, inserting, deleting, repeating, repeating, repeating, lobing

Frankie Crocker's Evening Bath on the headset of the Walkman his oldest righteous doing-it-for-herself ballbreaking r-e-s-p-e-c-t sister Ashanta gave him last Christmas (along with an Anita Baker tape).

Carlton Woods hot-footed it to the phone and put a thumb on the plunger. Keeping the plunger down, with perfect mothering timing he swung the Seiko box up on the table next to the phone and cranked up the volume just as a sweet-voiced African-American WBL Kicking S fox started reading the news:

"A bizarre and violent story tops the headlines early this Christmas morning. Alleged cop-killer Elvis Polk is dead. The object of a manhunt that scoured the Eastern seaboard since he killed two New York City Police detectives nearly two weeks ago, Polk was found shot to death last night in an apartment in the Chelsea section of Manhattan. The occupant of the apartment, Margaret Morris, Polk's Legal Aid attorney, was also fatally wounded. Miss Morris managed to stagger naked through temperatures around the freezing mark to the Midtown West police precinct. Before she died, she reportedly identified the assailant who shot both her and Polk as Carlton Woods, an assistant Queens County district attorney. The thirty-four-year-old Woods was described as quote an outstanding criminal lawyer with an unblemished record unquote by his boss, District Attorney Ralph—"

It was Kenya Dees who turned the radio off. "Poor Margaret. I always said—"

"What you always said is of absolutely no interest, Kenya." Carlton dropped the hip-hop, not merely dropped it but hurled it into a corner, hurling after it first the gold toothcap with the pair of dice etched on it—six the hard way—then the gold toothcap with the crown. He shrugged his shoulders and let the Triple Fat Goose fall to the bare parquet floor of Kenya Dees's living room. He kept the Reebok Twilight Zone Pumps on, lest his feet get cold on the bare parquet floor. "All that concerns me now is getting the fuck out of the fucking country. And you . . . are going to help me."

Kenya Dees laughed.

Carlton Woods drew the .22 from the waist of his Jordache jeans and pointed it at her face.

She didn't move, she didn't flinch, she didn't blink.

Carlton laughed and tried to twirl the .22 and did it badly and put the .22 back in his waist. "Get dressed, Kenya. We're going to the office. There're some confiscated passports in Property. We're going to pick out a couple, then we're going to take a little trip."

Kenya Dees put her hands on her hips. "Why me?"

Carlton took her by the elbow and turned her around and marched her down the hall toward her bedroom. "This is a nice place, Kenya. Take a last look around, you won't be seeing it again."

Kenya jerked her arm free and walked ahead of him. "Why me?" she said over her shoulder.

There was a rocking chair in the bedroom, and Carlton sat in it, hooking his ankles around the legs, resting his Twilight Zone Pumps on the rockers. He took the .22 out of his waist and waggled it at Kenya. "Get dressed. Get packed. One small suitcase. Your bathroom shit. Oh, and, uh, your diaphragm." Carlton giggled.

Kenya stood hipshot for a long time, looking right at Carlton Woods, looking into him, seeing *him*. She scared the shit out of him. Finally she sighed, "Lord," and bent and dragged a red nylon duffle bag out from under the bed. She tossed the bag on the bed and went to the closet.

"Uh, Kenya," Carlton said. "Wear that leather miniskirt of yours. And wear some kind of tank top or something."

Kenya didn't say a word. She slammed hangers back and forth, yanked clothes down, tossed some in a pile on the bed. Somehow, in the middle of doing all that, way back in the closet, she got herself out of her robe and her sweatpants and her Nike T-shirt and into a pair of corduroy slacks and a black wool turtleneck sweater. Black Adidas workout shoes. No *How 'bout if . . . ?* Just do it. Then just like that she had the clothes on the bed stuffed in the bag and the bag shut and zipped up. She went into the bathroom and in about half a second came out with a toilet bag. She jammed it into a side pocket of the red nylon bag, zipped the side pocket shut, stood up straight, hands on hips, looking right at Carlton, right into him. "My coat's in the front hall." Then just like that, just do it, she hefted the bag off the bed and yanked it down the hall, leaving Carlton Woods sitting all snarled up in the rocking chair.

This wasn't going down the way it was supposed to go down. Word. The way it was supposed to go down, Kenya Dees was supposed to do a kind of reverse striptease, slip-sliding out of her robe, her sweatpants, her Nike T-shirt, slip-sliding on a pair of thong bikini panties, her leather miniskirt, a skimpy tank top or one of them fishnet things. Slip-sliding them on so Carlton could get an idea of what it was going to be like later when Kenya slip-slided them off.

Carlton unsnarled himself from the rocking chair, unrested his Twilight Zone Pumps from off of the rocker, unhooked his ankles from around the legs. He went down the hall after Kenya Dees.

She was standing in the middle of the living room, wearing a big black down coat, her hands clasped in front of her like she was standing around a schoolyard waiting for the nuns to say it was okay to go in or something. She looked right at Carlton Woods as he came into the room from the hall, looked right into him. " 'M ready."

"Don't you have any curiosity, Kenya, about what has transpired?" Carlton said. "Or isn't your mind capable of curiosity? Has it been so anesthetized by WBL *Kick*ing S, by Frankie Crocker, there ain't no other like that brother, by the wack shit you listen to, you and the ouncemen and the con men and the hit men and the whores and the whoremasters and the poor sorry fucks—Above the Law, 'Murder Rap,' Vicious Beat Posse, 'Legalized Dope,' Public Enemy, 'Welcome to the Terrordome,' Redhead Kingpin & the F.B.I., 'Pump It Hottie,' Bobby Jimmy & the Critters, 'Somebody Farted,' the Geto Boys, 'Trigga Happy Nigga'? Is that it, Kenya? *Is* that it?"

Kenya Dees sighed and shrugged out of her big black down coat and let it fall on top of the red nylon bag next to her on the floor.

She put her hands on her hips and looked right at him, right into him. "Yo, Carlton—what the fuck trans*pir*ed?"

She was dissing him, he knew that, but he was chill, didn't let it get to him. "Remember Tiger Monroe Garr?"

Kenya Dees folded her arms under her breasts and shook her beaded cornrow head.

"Tiger Monroe *Garr*?" Carlton Woods said.

Kenya Dees shook her beaded cornrow head.

"Weren't you working for us when Tiger Monroe Garr was buy-and-busted by Steve Poole?"

Kenya Dees sighed and slumped, slumped and sighed. "Just tell me the motherfucking story, *Carl*. Don't try to make me an unindicted co-conspirator in the motherfucking telling of it."

"Tiger Monroe Garr—" Carlton began.

"Tiger Monroe Garr, Tiger Monroe Garr," Kenya sing-songed.

". . . Tiger Monroe Garr was a major roller in Far Rockaway. Twenty-second and Seagirt. A roller is a drug dealer."

Kenya Dees rolled her eyes.

"Steve Poole, nowadays State Senator Steven Jay Poole, in those days Detective Steve Poole, Brooklyn Vice, Brooklyn Homicide, Brooklyn Major Cases, on loan at this particular time to Queens Narcotics. Being on loan, being something of a cowboy anyway, an independent, a free spirit, someone who didn't take kindly to the dictates of authority—"

Kenya Dees pawed suddenly and impatiently at the bare parquet floor with one of her Adidas gym shoes.

"I'm getting there, Kenya," Carlton Woods said. "It's not a long story, it's a short story. Short and simple and sweet. Here it is. Here's the rest of it, then we'll go, then we'll be moving out. Steve Poole buy-and-busted Tiger Monroe Garr in Tiger's Cadillac at the corner of Twenty-second and Seagirt, discovering in the trunk, after obtaining a probable-cause search warrant, ten keys of scutter, twenty-two thousand a key at the time, two hundred twenty K street value. Yours truly was assigned to prosecute. Scutter is cocaine."

Kenya Dees looked away from Carlton Woods, looked out the window at the brightening day.

"You listening, Kenya?" Carlton Woods said.

She glared at him, glared right into him. "Listening? Fuck should I listen to this jive smoke? Hear you say it was Poole put the scutter in Tiger Monroe Garr's Cadillac? Hear you say somebody ratted Poole out, before you could put Poole away Poole got to you, he offered you a piece of some action, a slice of the pie, money, scutter, whatever the fuck? You went down with him, Carlton, you went down into the black hole, he didn't have to drag you, you were hot to trot. Everything was cool, you were living high, then Margaret found out about it, so you killed her. Is that it, Carlton? Is that all? Is it over? I mean, shit, you don't have to be a motherfucking fortune teller to figure all this the fuck out."

That wasn't it at all. It was so much more complex, more complicated, more convoluted.

"It's not that simple, Kenya."

Kenya Dees looked away.

"Kenya, it's not that simple. It's not what you think. It's complicated."

"Complicate this, Carlton." Kenya Dees gave Carlton Woods the finger.

Carlton lunged for it, intending to break it off, to stuff her finger up her pushy righteous doing-it-for-herself ballbreaking r-e-s-p-e-c-t African-American ass. He missed and fell against the phone table, fell onto it, broke it. The phone table broke under him, and he went down on his knees on the bare parquet floor.

There was a brass banker's lamp on the phone table too, and it crashed down onto the bare parquet floor along with the phone, the notepad and pencil for phone messages, the phone books on the shelf under the tabletop, along with Carlton Woods. Kenya Dees took a step—*Just Do It*—to the fallen lamp, picked it up, and hit Carlton Woods with the heavy base on the back of the head. He didn't move. She felt for the pulse in his neck and found it and was glad there was one *and* glad he wasn't moving.

Kenya Dees used the lamp cord to tie Carlton Woods's feet together, first tugging off his ridiculous Reebok Twilight Zone Pumps, using a reverse surgeon's knot she had learned as a Girl Scout. She unzipped the red nylon bag and reached in among the clothes and felt for the belt from her worn terry-cloth bathrobe. She hauled Carlton Woods's hands behind him and tied them together with the belt, making a figure eight of the belt and ending it off with a reverse surgeon's. She got up and got her breath and picked up the phone. She flicked the plunger until she got a dial tone, then punched in 911.

28

"Merry Christmas," said the big man in the blue double-breasted suit.

Fuck you, Cullen thought, *and the horse you rode in on.* He stirred his coffee, though it was plenty cool, it was downright cold. He'd been drinking coffee at one Greek coffee shop after another for hours or maybe days or was it weeks (this one, on Astoria Boulevard, looking out on a ramp to the Triborough Bridge, was for some reason called the Paris Coffee Shop, though on a couple of walls there were what you might call murals of what you might call Greece), he'd had enough.

"You, uh, *are* Cullen, right?" said the big man in the blue double-breasted suit.

That Cullen. "Sorry, friend, you have the wrong . . . Nick?"

Nick Albert held out his big hand. "I *knew* it was you, right? But you acted like you'd never seen me. I was starting to think, 'He *did* call me, right?' I guess, uh"—he gestured at his suit, his white French-cuffed shirt and off-white silk tie, his freshly cut hair, combed straight back and moussed, late eighties Wall Street corporate-raider style—"I guess I look a little different than the last time, right?"

"The last time," Cullen said, at O'Boyle's Tap House on Queens Boulevard across from Borough Hall, with the tattoos, the ponytail, the T-shirt with the condom with the smiling face and the slogan *Poking Fun,* "you looked like a recovering biker, a born-again biker, a Krishna biker. Now you look . . . you look like an NBA coach."

Nick Albert laughed. "Yeah, well. We're wrapping up the O'Boyle's thing, I'm moving on, moving out, I have to dress a little, you know, different, right?" He sat on the stool to the right of Cullen's and motioned to the counterman. "Coffee, please, and a warm-up for my friend here."

Cullen kept his hand over his cup and shook his head no thanks at the counterman. When he had gone away, Cullen said, "Problem?"

Nick Albert looked down between his legs and Cullen looked after him and saw on the step between Albert's feet a navy-blue canvas duffle bag, red trim, red shoulder strap. "SIG Sauer twelve-shot nine-millimeter. Rack the slide to cock it, right? Recocks after discharge. Faster muzzle velocity than a thirty-eight, very accurate. Slugs on the light side, though; they've been known to go through who you're shooting at and hit who you're not, so watch out guys you like aren't around in back of guys you don't. They do not tend to knock people down, right? You shoot, you should be shooting to hammer. Tell me to go fuck myself if you know all this, these're fairly new pieces, not everybody's hip to them. There's a hip holster in there too. I don't know how you like to get strapped, I didn't know what you'd be wearing, I figured that was the safest bet. None of it's traceable without a shitload of work, you want to know where it came from, I'll tell you, otherwise I never saw it in my life either, must've fallen off a truck. Oh, yeah, there's three extra clips in there too. You going to do any more shooting than that, you should probably ask the Pentagon for backup, right?"

"You're sticking your neck way out for a stranger, Nick," Cullen said.

"Nah. You got a good rep, Joe." Albert used a napkin to mop up the coffee the counterman had spilled in his saucer. He added a little cream, a little sugar, to his cup. He stirred delicately, his pinky crooked. "Besides, you'll owe me in a major way, right? And I got an ulterior motive. You know Nancy Albright, right?"

Cullen at first didn't think he did, and was afraid Nick Albert would leave, taking the duffle he rode in with, taking the SIG Sauer, the holster, the ammo, the update to the Regs and Recipes. Then he remembered: Nancy Albright. TV. Works with Ann. A forty-watt bulb at NewsFocus 14, but incandescent nonetheless, brighter than anyone in the Paris Coffee Shop on Astoria Boulevard. "Nancy, sure."

"Works with your friend, Ann Jones. She's like your old lady, right, Ann?" Albert had stopped stirring and had put down the spoon, but his finger was still crooked.

"We, uh, yeah. You know. Yeah. I don't *know* Nancy. I mean, I've talked to her at a couple of parties. She's nice, very nice. Funny. They work hard, on television." Busy, busy, busy. "Long hours." Up and out at dawn, on the air at six and eleven, up and out at dawn again, standups, intros, outtros. "Doing extra work"—weekend pinch-hit anchoring—"is a way of getting ahead."

"They're not always around when you could use them around is what you're saying, right?" Nick Albert's finger was still crooked.

"They're not always around when you could use them around is what I'm saying," Cullen said. Not at dawn, for a few standups, sitdowns, spin arounds, gimme a bale of hay; not at six, doing them again, not at eleven, doing them again and again. "I'll mention it, though. I'll see. Right now, Nick, I have to get moving." Cullen reached down and hooked the duffle's shoulder strap. "Thanks again. Means a lot. I owe you. I'll get your coffee. Merry Christmas."

Nick Albert put a hand out flat in the air, holding Cullen in place the way a dog trainer holds a dog. He stuck his chin out and pulled his stomach in and drank off his coffee, his shirt and tie out of harm's way from dribbles, finger still crooked. He blotted his lips with a fresh napkin from the dispenser on the counter, finger still crooked. He touched the knot of his necktie, finger still crooked, checking his reflection in the mirror behind the counter. He got off the stool and buttoned the jigger button of his suit coat, then the lower right button, finger still crooked. "Very bad idea to do this alone, babe. Very bad idea. Christmas, you should be with your, you know, your friends, right?"

"This'll cost me my badge, Nick. It's not worth yours."

Nick Albert waved a hand, finger still crooked. "Hey, no risk, no razzle-dazzle, right? Besides, I know a couple of things you don't and should." His camel overcoat was on the hook of a coatrack of a booth near the cash register; he unhooked it and swung it on. He pulled from a pocket a car key on a doodad and tossed it in the air for Cullen to catch. "The blue Reliant. You know where you want to go, you drive, I'll talk. I'll get the check, right?"

"When you made me back at O'Boyle's last week," Nick Albert said, "all I could say was we were after dirty court personnel. Dirty ADAs is more like it, and dirty cops. Can't tell you why it wasn't an IAU investigation, can't tell you why 'cause I just don't know. One of those things, I guess, where it was better not. Or maybe it was a jurisdictional thing and the DA's office won.

"Carlton Woods, Steve Poole, Tiger Monroe Garr—some trifecta, right? The Tiger, maybe you know, maybe you don't, was a semibig roller in a rinky-dink pond—Far Rock, Arverne, Belle Harbor, Neponsit. It's like Mississippi out there, man, you should see it, it's scary. He was buy-and-busted by Steve Poole, Tiger, in like '83, right? Poole was Brooklyn Major Cases at the time, on loan to Queens Narcotics, so this is before he got winged, obviously, before he got seriously fucked up.

"Poole got a search warrant for Tiger's El Dorado, found ten keys of scutter in the spare tire well. Tiger said it wasn't his scutter, but what would he say looking at a ten-year mandatory, right? A grand jury indicted him, a jury of thank God not his peers but his betters convicted him, a judge gave him an express ticket to Attica. He hammered a guard, Tiger, had his ticket upgraded, he's at Marion now, doing hard-hard time, gets out of his cell an hour a day. He is out of the loop for a long time. . . .

"Last March, Officer Calvin Webster—you never heard of him, right?—Queens Property, has a heart attack, nearly checks out. Remorse, guilt, all that. He writes a letter to the Queens DA, tells him that around the time of Tiger Monroe Garr's bust, a narcotics D paid him a grand, Webster, to fail to notice that two suitcases of scutter from a bust in Howard Beach never made it to Property. Twenty fucking keys, at the time worth twenty-two K each. He gave Webster the grand, the D, without even asking if he wanted it, he just handed it to him, Webster was in without even a chance to be out. He's a decent guy, Webster, it ate him up, he developed ulcers, back pains, classic shit, he told a Queens ADA, a soul brother, about the twenty keys, told him his theory that ten of those keys made their way into the spare tire well of Tiger Monroe Garr's El Dorado, that the Tiger took the frame so Steve Poole, who was the D in question, could score a major collar.

"Webster told the soul brother ADA all this and then he waited. Nothing. No would he wear a wire? No grand jury subpoena, no blue ribbon this, no special investigation that. Nothing. The ADA is Carlton Woods, right?

"We can't make it stick, we just can't make it stick, but a pattern developed, right? Poole cut a corner, Woods smoothed it out. A perp said Poole didn't Mirandize him, Woods swore he was there in the holding cell and that yes Poole did. We can't make it stick, but it looks ever so much like Poole and Woods and a, uh, understanding, a, uh, pact.

"Then Poole got winged, got seriously fucked up, went into politics. End of pattern, right? Wrong. The pattern becomes Poole has a friend who needs this or an associate who definitely *doesn't* need that, that there's a very important individual whose son was on the premises when a girl was raped and sodomized by a number of individuals with among other things the butt of a hockey stick, but Junior certainly didn't have anything to do with it, right? We can't make it stick, right, but it looks like case after case after case of 'Do me a favor, Carl.' 'I need a big favor, Carl.' 'Carl, I gotta say the F word again, I gotta ask you one more time for a big, big favor.' My personal theory—some of the guys buy it, some don't—is Woods originally set out to blackmail Poole, but by having done so gave Poole the chance to blackmail *him*. Either way, it's like they were stuck—a couple of dogs fucking.

"Meanwhile—I didn't catch this part of the job, so I only know what I hear at task-force briefings and shit, right?—meanwhile, Poole is working this thing where any time a new cop does something a little bit dirty, a little bit bent, IAU flags him, the Advocate's Office hauls him in, he even just gets desk duty for a while at precinct level—or she—Poole finds out about it, recruits the poor sorry fucker, wines him, dines him—or her, offers the promise of big bucks, glamorous life-style, all the blow he can toot, all the loot he can carry—"

"Or she." Cullen finished Nick Albert's sentence. "Jenny Swale."

"Among others," Albert said. "Among quite a few others."

"Paul Messina," Cullen said.

"For instance," Albert said. "This is not a gang of thieves or anything, a pack of rogue cops roving the streets with ski masks over their faces. These are guys—and gals—who stay in uniform, get ahead, get connected, get noticed, get promoted, all with the idea that one day, probably, they will run the Department, run it the way Poole—who knows what Poole will be by this time, right? He could be president or something—the way Poole says run it. We call them Poole's Brat Pack. Hey, it's not original, I know, but it, uh, you know, tells the story, right? . . . Like I said, we're a ways from making it stick. We bag Carlton Woods, that'll be a big help." Albert checked a street sign. "Myrtle Avenue? The fuck are we?"

"We're coming up on Woodhaven Boulevard," Cullen said. "Woodhaven turns into Cross Bay."

"Howard Beach," Albert said. "So you figured it out. You didn't need me at all."

Cullen spoke, but it was Margaret Morris talking, in the booth in the back at O'Boyle's: "Elvis Polk got a parole hearing canceled after he stabbed a con at Wallkill. The con, Roy Reagan, was doing points for running a chop shop in Ozone Park, too close for optimum competitive business comfort to a Howard Beach chop shop run by a couple of brothers with *links* to organized crime—"

Albert laughed. " 'Links.' "

"The brothers not only dropped a dime on Reagan, they kept the heat on him in the J. Their price for turning it off once and for all was Reagan should start the fight with Polk. With his parole canceled, Elvis was vulnerable to an approach to hammer Jenny Swale, who must've been about ready to rat out Poole's dirty little network. Carlton Woods was the intermediary. Paul Messina. It all connects. It's not pretty, but it connects." Cullen checked a street sign. "Down at the end of this block there should be a warehouse, the one Messina's wise-guy relatives used for the SpeedAir thing. Just beyond it is an old gate to Kennedy, a proposed access road that never got built. I'll get out there and you can take off."

Albert snorted. "What? And spend Christmas by myself? You been listening to me, right? We're in this together, bro. I got to make sure you come out upright and unventilated so I can get my intro to Nancy Albright."

Cullen made a left and slowed down to get the lay of the land. Attached houses suffocating in lianas of Christmas lights, a stretch of gray sky, far up ahead of them the ass end of Kennedy airport: level, muddy, dour; concrete and tarmac and sawgrass, chain link and razor tape. "Where's *your* family, Nick? *Your* friends?"

"I'm, uh, you know, a few years behind you when it comes to getting divorced, being on my own. It's tough: She got the house, the Toyota, the dog, the friends."

"No kids?"

"No kids. You have two, right?"

"Right."

"What'd you get them for Christmas?"

"Hockey gloves for my son," Cullen lied. "For my daughter . . ."

Nick Albert put a hand on Cullen's shoulder. "Hey, you've been jammed up. Cut yourself some slack."

29

Don't pull your punch, Ann pep-talked herself. *Do not for the love of God and the sake of your unborn children pull your punch.*

And Mabel's sake, and the sake of her unborn children.

Ann could go on about this; it was one of the things Ann went on about: You'd slap at a mosquito or a fly or a cockroach with your bare hand, you'd have the varmint dead to rights, but you'd *pull your punch,* you'd shy your hand away, you'd dread the sharp *squish,* the spurt of bug juice, you'd just graze it, you wouldn't hit it full, you wouldn't hit it solid, it would buzz off or skitter off and you'd feel like a jerk, a cowardly, inept jerk.

Ann wasn't marching off to war bare-handed; she was armed—with a pizza box, the box in which the first of their three so-called meals had been delivered. Muttering *Don't pull your punch, don't pull it,* she hefted the box, holding it lightly between her fingers, juggling it a little, jiggling it, getting the feel of it, getting a feel for it.

The way a guy would:

A guy in the dugout, plucking a bat out of the bat rack, stepping up out of the semigloom into the loud glare of the on-deck circle, glomming the bat handle with the pine-tar rag, slipping on the metal doughnut, jamming his hard hat down, rolling his neck around, swinging the bat in big figure eights, down and up and around, down and up and around, swinging it in small circles down between his shoulder blades.

Or a guy on the sidelines, hauling on his helmet, snapping the chin strap, yanking the face mask, stretching, flexing, quickstepping in place, butting shoulder pads with another guy, butting heads; or a guy at courtside, unzipping his warm-up pants, tearing off his warm-up jacket, double-knotting his Reebok Twilight Zone Pumps, pointing a finger like a pistol at the guy he was coming in for, giving him high-fives, or maybe just a forefinger, hip high, real cool.

A guy out on the court, the course, the diamond, the gridiron, the rink, down on the track, up in the ring—or just a guy on the street, in a parking lot, in an elevator, turning a corner on the sidewalk, looking a little embarrassed that you caught him at it, but not a whole *lot* embarrassed—caught him grooving an imaginary back-hand, an imaginary sixty-yard spiral, an imaginary seven-iron onto the green, backspinning the ball up to the lip of the cup; caught him drilling an imaginary field goal from the midfield stripe, an imaginary slapshot from the blue line; caught him going low over an imaginary hurdle, planting an imaginary pole in an imaginary pit, planting-lifting-handstanding-pushing-off-clearing an imaginary bar nearly twenty feet in the air, the imaginary air; caught him following up an imaginary straight left with an imaginary right uppercut, lifting the soles of his imaginary opponent's fringed shoes off the canvas, making the opponent's jeweled loincloth quiver and tremble. And all the while accompanying his imaginary performance, the guy, with a simulated play-by-play broadcast, complete with color commentary and sound effects—bat on ball, echoing public-address announcements, enthusiastic crowd, maybe even, if he were really good at this, vendors: *Hot dog, hot dog, who wants a hot dog? Hey, getcher beer, getcher beer, getcher ice-cold beer here.*

There were undoubtedly girls who performed these little rituals too, their versions of them, but Ann bet they did because they had seen guys perform them, because they had been taught (by guys) that these little rituals were kinetic drills that instructed muscles and nerves and bones and tissue what the real thing was going to feel like. A guy didn't have to be taught this stuff; it came to him naturally, not by means of art or artifice. A guy's facility at it, Ann had argued from time to time when the subject came up (usually in discussions with her brother, who had put himself to sleep until late adolescence by calling fictive games suited to the season: *At the top of the key . . . Fakes left, puts it up . . . Yessss! . . . Brings the puck over the blue line, down into the corner, two men on his back, he's still got it, behind the net, a backhander, he scores! . . . Here's the windup, the kick, the pitch. Swung on, a drive deep to left. It's going, going, boom, off the wall. Rounding first, going into second, around second, heading for third. Here comes the throw, here comes the runner. He slides . . . He beat the ball! He beat the ball! . . . It's as quiet as a cathedral here at Augusta National as this huge crowd on the eighteenth green . . .*), a guy's facility was related to the ease and frequency with which guys masturbated. A guy didn't need a giant electric jerk-off machine, for God's sake, he didn't need to go to a consciousness-raising group to get per*miss*ion, he used his hand, a magazine, his mind's eye. A guy could fuck *any*one he wanted; he could be a star in any sport he wanted. It followed, Ann was quite sure, that a guy could kill anyone he wanted, using any weapon.

Ann wanted to kill only bald Jerry with the big *bigote.* For now, at any rate. She wanted to kill bald Jerry by driving the corner of the pizza box into one or the other of his nostrils, driving it up and up, back and back, driving whatever the hard parts of bald Jerry's nose were called up and back into whatever the front of bald Jerry's brain was called, if not killing him at least turning him into a bald vegetable with a big *bigote.*

That the corner of the pizza box was a surprisingly lethal-seeming weapon (great high-concept idea for a movie, Ann: *Lethal-Seeming Weapon,* starring, oh, Rick Moranis and, uh, Spike Lee) had been discovered by Mabel while trying to stuff the box into one of the drawers of their sterile prison's ugly metal desk. Tidying up a little, using the drawer since the sterile prison didn't have a wastebasket, Mabel had stabbed herself in the palm with the corner of the pizza box, and had given Ann an idea.

Ann had checked out the box, which Mabel abandoned half in the drawer and half out—fuck cleanliness, they were prisoners, for Christ's sake; examined it, studied it, and noted that it had double-strength corrugated cardboard around the edges so that it could be carried with one hand, even fully loaded with a pie (even a pie with [fresh] mushrooms, peppers, anchovies, sausage, pepperoni, extra cheese, spinach, or other [fresh] ingredients), without sagging or buckling. It was a strong son of a bitch, and by folding the box in half, thereby reinforcing the corners with an additional layer of cardboard, Ann was able to make it even stronger, *and* make it more manipulable, more . . . lethal-seeming.

"I'm hungry," Mabel said. "Where's the fucking pizza?"

Ann looked at her Tridor Oyster Perpetual Lady Datejust Rolex: two-thirty, Christmas afternoon. Yesterday's, Christmas Eve day's, so-called lunch had come just after twelve, so today's was either a little later or a lot late or it wasn't coming at all, there was no way to know, no one to ask. They were worse than prisoners, they had no guards, no fellow inmates from whom to learn the drill, the routine, the ropes. "I have a feeling . . ."

"What?" Mabel said.

"I just have a feeling today's the day."

"Moving day?"

"Yeah."

"Getaway day?"

Ann nodded.

"Judgment day?"

"Mabel." Ann put the pizza box back down on top of the ugly metal desk and went to where Mabel sat on the ugly metal folding chair. She leaned over and put her hands on Mabel's shoulders. "Look. We're going to make it. It's going to be all right. Don't—"

Mabel battled her way out of the little cage Ann had made of herself. "I hate it when people put their hands on me and get right in my face. I hate it. Men do it. It's patronizing. Don't do it ever again."

Ann went back to the ugly metal desk and stood with her fingertips on its edge, her back to Mabel. "I'm sorry."

After a while Mabel said, "I'm sorry."

"No, you're right," Ann said. "You're right."

"Oh, Christ." The ugly metal folding chair squealed as Mabel shifted irritably. "Are we going to argue about who's sorrier? Let's *not* argue about who's sorrier, okay? *Okay?*"

"Okay."

"What time is it?" Mabel said.

"Two-*thirty*," Ann said.

"Don't get snippy. I just wanted to *know*."

"I just *told* you. I told you *five* minutes ago."

"An hour." Mabel grasped her elbows. "I asked you an hour ago."

Ann entered her watch into evidence, tapping the crystal with a fingernail, boxing the compass: "One-fif*teen*, one-*twen*ty, one-thirty-*five*, one-*for*ty-five, one-*fif*ty-five, two-ten, two-fif*teen*—"

"Fuck you," Mabel said. "And the watch you rode in on."

Ann laughed.

Mabel laughed. "Is this what they call the Stockholm syndrome? The hostages turn on each other."

Ann faced Mabel and sat on the edge of the ugly metal desk, legs dangling. "When in Stockholm, hostages fall in love with their captors."

Mabel shuddered. "With these creeps?"

Ann looked at her watch. Two thirty-six. "Christmas Day, maybe an Italian neighborhood—what're we thinking? There won't be any pizza parlors open."

"They'll bring Chinese," Mabel said. "I'm starving. Being a captive is hard work. Did you ever meet Andy Keith? An old boyfriend. He writes about movies for obscure publications. We talk on the phone every couple of months. Just last week, *last* week, he was telling me about a piece he wrote about the 'ubiquity'—his word—in contemporary Hollywood movies of climactic action scenes in abandoned warehouses. *Total Die Harder RoboTerminator*—those movies. He did a whole hilarious routine about the watchman of an abandoned warehouse getting phone calls wanting to book the space: 'Sorry, I can't give it to you Thursday. We've got some Colombians coming in on Wednesday and it always takes twenty-four hours to clean up after them. . . . Friday's good, unless you're planning to use explosives, 'cause that'll take us into the weekend.' I laughed and laughed, and here we the fuck are. I think they'll bring Chinese."

Ann was miffed. *She* had a hilarious routine about the motherfucking u*biq*uity—a word she would *never* use; she used *lots*—there were *lots* of climactic abandoned-warehouse action scenes in contemporary Hollywood movies; she could go on and on about it. But she wouldn't go on about it now; she could hear the panic in Mabel's voice, see the panic in her eyes. "Bringing Chinese, bringing Thai, bringing anything, having anything delivered, means calling attention to themselves. The pizza parlor, I would not be surprised, is probably fam-uh-lee."

Mabel said nothing, just shifted irritably again, making the ugly metal chair squeal.

Neither said anything for a long time.

"Hear that shuffling noise?" Mabel said.

"Mice," Ann said.

"And what about that rumble?"

"That's your stomach."

Mabel laughed.

"Shhh."

"I mean, we're probably out of our minds, right?" Mabel said. "We're probably stark, raving mad. We probably lost it somewhere yesterday afternoon, somewhere between our so-called lunch and our so-called—"

"Mabel, shush."

"Oh, stop, I can talk all I want. What're you afraid of, someone's going to *hear* me?"

Ann got off the desk and took three quick crossover steps toward the door.

Mabel stared. "Do you . . . ? Is it . . . ?"

Ann put her finger to her lips. She tiptoed back to the desk, got the pizza box, and tiptoed back to the door.

"Ann—"

"Shhh."

"Ann, what if—"

Sotto voce: "Shut *up*, Mabel. I'm not staying here another minute. No one, I mean *no* one, knows we're here, so the chances of anyone other than us doing anything to get us out of here are nonexistent. So *I'm* going to do something. So shut *up*, Mabel."

They waited two hours, though somehow only four minutes went by on Ann's watch.

Shoes scraped outside the heavy metal door.

Ann hefted the pizza box, held it lightly between her fingers, juggled it, jiggled it, got the feel of it, got a feel for it.

Don't pull your punch, don't pull it. For the love of God, for Mabel's and your unborn children, for Mabel, for you, for democracy, for a world free from tyrants and . . . and crooks.

Ann looked at Mabel, glared at her, her eyes said, *Okay, Mabel, this is it, this is fucking it, do your part now, do it!*

And Mabel did her part. She got up off the ugly metal chair, slipped her shoes off, and stood on the chair. She licked the tips of her thumb and middle finger to insulate them and turned the light bulb until it went out.

Ann heard Mabel get down off the chair and slip her shoes back on.

Ann heard a key ring. She heard jingles.

Maybe it was Santa, running late.

A key in the door. It wasn't Santa.

A space, between jamb and stile. The blackness of a big dark empty space—a room, a warehouse, an interplanetary void. But not so black as the blackness of the sterile office. Lights here and there, not close by, but doing their job, making things less black.

In the space, a face.

Bald Jerry with the big *bigote*. Looking up, squinting up, toward the ceiling light fixture, somewhat suspicious but not totally suspicious, trying to remember if the light had ever been off before, if maybe he'd turned it off, not sure the light's being off meant things were out of the ordinary, not *sure* of anything.

No pizza. No Chinese. No nothing in bald Jerry's hands. It *was* moving day, getaway day, judgment day. It was . . .

"Showtime, ladies," said bald Jerry with the big *bigote*. "Let's—"

Before he could say *let's* what, Ann stepped up out of the blackness of the sterile office and drove the corner of the pizza box at the center of Jerry's face, hoping to engage a nostril, either one, not pulling her punch, *not* pulling it, driving the box up and up, back and back, trying to see in her mind's eye the box driving whatever the hard parts of bald Jerry's nose were called up and back into whatever the front of bald Jerry's brain was called. Driving, driving, driving.

Bald Jerry went down. Bald Jerry went down against the heavy metal door, crashing it all the way open, crashing the door against the wall of the sterile cube of an office, the doorknob burying itself in the plasterboard wall. Such noise. Then echoes of the noise. Then . . . nothing.

Then: "You stupid fucking cunt."

It was little Eddie, little Eddie the forgotten man, the forgotten crook, little Eddie, I think his name is Eddie, yes, Eddie. Little Eddie coming in from the blackness of the big dark empty space and standing in the doorway with a very big gun looking down at bald Jerry with the big *bigote,* the smashed-in nose, the staring eyes.

"You stupid fucking cunt, you hammered him."

Ann took a step toward little Eddie, but he stopped her without even looking at her, looking still at bald Jerry, by raising the barrel of his very big gun half an inch. He finally did look at her and shook his head sadly at the sheer pathos of it all; he waggled his gun at her and lifted his chin at the pizza box. "Put that fucking thing down, will you."

Ann thought about throwing the pizza box at him, spinning it killer Frisbee-style, killer martial-arts throwing star–style, but little Eddie saw her thinking and spread his hands and shrugged his shoulders, like, *What am I, wood?*

Ann put the fucking thing down.

"Turn the fucking light on, will you," little Eddie said, not looking at Mabel but waggling his very big gun in her direction.

Mabel didn't move.

Little Eddie looked right at her. "Turn. The fucking light on."

Mabel slipped her shoes off and stood on the metal chair. She screwed the bulb back in until it lighted. She got down off the chair and slipped her shoes back on.

Little Eddie poked at bald Jerry with his toe, as if to prod him awake. He reached down to feel for a pulse in bald Jerry's neck. He felt several places and clearly didn't know if any of them was the right place. He stood straight. "Let's get out of here, the botha yez. It's showtime."

Little Eddie stepped backwards out the door into the blackness of the big dark empty space, pointing the very big gun first at Ann's midriff, then at Mabel's, then at Ann's, then at Mabel's, gesturing at them with his left hand as he backed away, making circles, ellipses, loops, *Come on, come on, come on.*

Then stopping, little Eddie, stopping backing away, stopping making that gesture, *Come on, come on,* stopping pointing his very big gun first at Ann, then at Mabel, pointing the gun down at the floor, then letting it fall to the floor, as though he'd converted, been born again, was a crook no more, as though he'd seen the light, heard his mother calling him home to dinner.

Then little Eddie walked back toward them, out from the black-ness of the big dark empty space, into the sterile cube of an office, his hands not up exactly, but out, out in front of him, like a begin-ning ice skater's, like a sleepwalker's. Behind him, a smaller gun, but still a gun, held against the place where little Eddie's head rested on his neck—there was a name for that place. What *was* it? Ann had learned it the time she'd taken a lesson in Alexander Tech-nique, learned to free her neck—behind little Eddie walked Joe Cullen. Super Joe, Wonder Joe, how-could-she-ever-for-a-moment-have-doubted-her-feelings-for-him Joe, the Most Valuable, the Most Wonderful, the Best, the Brightest, the . . . the . . . What was he *do*ing? What was he—Oh, shit.

"Just put the piece down, Joe, down on the floor. Down on the floor. Now kick it this way. Kick it this way. Don't look at me, just kick it this way. Now over in the corner there, and down on your face. Down on your face, hands behind your head. Hands be*hind* your head. Good. Ann, Mabel, same way. Down on the floor, hands behind your head. Good. Eddie—here's your piece back. Here's Cullen's. Where'd you get this piece, Joe? You have it squirreled away? SIG Sauer, very nice."

Maria Esperanza, looking good, looking in control, looking pissed at little Eddie for letting Cullen get the drop on him, looking really pissed at bald Jerry for getting killed or made into a vegetable with a big *bigote*.

"Okay. *Mira*. One at a time, first Ann, then Mabel, then Cullen, on your hands and knees, not all the way up, hands and knees, crawl backwards—have you got it? *Back*wards—out the door. Back-wards. Ann. Now. *Now*, Ann. It's showtime."

30

There's nothing about it in the Regs and Recipes, but you get to know when you're expected, when someone's looking forward to you: You can feel the buzz of anticipation, you can sense the blend in the air of anxiety and excitement.

No one was waiting for them, for Joe Cullen and Nick Albert, no one was giving them a thought.

They had made it from Albert's Reliant, parked in front of a candy store shuttered with a metal gate for the holiday, maybe forever, across a street connecting nothing to nothing, to the chain-link fence, topped with razor tape; they had made it through the steel-chain gate, bound shut by a thick chain fastened with a heavy combination lock but old and bent and battered and sagging away from the tension bars, leaving room to squeeze through, so they had. They had made it across an open patch of frozen crud dusted with snow; they were crouched on their heels behind a stack of packing skids covered with a smelly holey canvas that billowed and flapped in the bitter wind that infests such places whatever the season, waiting to see if anyone in or around the cement-block building they were creeping up on had noticed that they'd gotten that close, waiting to see if anyone minded, before they tried getting closer still.

In the Regs and Recipes, under *Partners and Colleagues, Communication with,* it says something about clearly articulating perceptions and conclusions so that there will be no mistaking your intended course of action, ya dada ya dada. But what Nick Albert said was, "You get the feeling that, uh . . . ?" and what Cullen answered was, "Yeah."

There is undoubtedly a section in the Regs and Recipes about *Tire and Tread Marks, Identification and Classification of* (only an enthusiast, a grind, would read it unless the situation demanded). But there's nothing in there about the feeling you get when you see fresh herring bones in the slop but don't see any cars around that the cars haven't come and gone, the feeling that's more than a feeling it's a certainty that the cars are under wraps close by.

"Feels kind of like, uh . . ." Albert said.

"Like moving day?" Cullen said.

"Right. Like getaway day, right?"

"Right."

The Regs and Recipes are chock-full of admonitions to proceed with caution and with backup; the *Gray Areas,* the *Situations Where You Don't Know Quite What to Expect So You Can't Say for Sure Just How Many People You Need to Help You and to What Extent and in What Manner,* are not addressed.

"We could call this in, but, uh . . ." Albert said.

"But what would we tell them?" Cullen said.

"Right. So let's look around some more, right?"

"Right."

They pushed up off their heels and ran low across more frozen snow-dusted crud to a corner of the cement-block building, which reminded Cullen more than anything (though this one was smaller and grungier and less extravagant) of the building, looking like a vast bowling alley, or maybe a discount-appliance dealership, out somewhere near where Queens and Nassau counties blur together, in which his dear sweet young partner, Maria Esperanza, was married.

His dear sweet young dirty partner, for the last thing Nick Albert had told Cullen before they got out of Albert's Reliant, the last of the couple of things he knew and Cullen didn't and should, was that among the cops recruited by Steve Poole for his Brat Pack was Maria Esperanza.

"Right after she got her shield, she worked in clothes for the Bronx DA," Nick Albert had said, a hand on Cullen's arm momentarily to keep him from bolting. "It's where she met her husband, I guess, right? He's a clerk at County Criminal, right?"

"A bailiff," Cullen said.

"A bailiff . . . The Bronx," Albert said, "is, you know, the Bronx. You come up out of the subway on the Concourse, you drive by Co-op City, through Throgs Neck, Kingsbridge, Hunts Point, it doesn't matter, wherever, you get hit in the kisser with this smell of corruption, some people maybe don't know what it is but if you've smelled it once you never forget it, your clothes start stinking of it, you've been there five minutes you feel like you've been on the pad your whole life, on two or three payrolls, some roller's, some pol's, some pimp's.

"It's the only borough that's on the mainland of the continental United States of America, the Bronx, you know that? I was born there, is how I know it, Bedford Park, East One Nine Six, right near Fordham. I was a kid, I felt good knowing that, knowing it was connected to the mainland, the Bronx, it was like the Bronx was, you know, solid, the rest of the city was, you know, shaky. People joke sometimes about cutting New York City loose from the rest of New York State, the rest of the country, letting it fend for itself, making it a separate country; I used to think, But not the Bronx, bro, the Bronx stays put, the Bronx is solid, the Bronx is part of the mainland. But it doesn't mean shit, does it? The Bronx sucks, just like everyplace else. . . .

"Anyway, Maria Esperanza, she was working in clothes for the DA in the Bronx, she's a piece of ass, guys were hitting on her *all* the time, it's a tough fucking thing to handle, I wouldn't want to be a good-looking woman, I've thought about it and I wouldn't want to be one. One of the guys hitting on her was Bennett Weinstein, the real estate guy, right? He had the brainstorm, Weinstein, he would leverage a venture here, a venture there, by selling a little scutter, a little soda, to his friends in Riverdale, he got in with people he had no business getting in with, he got hammered.

"Before he got hammered, Weinstein, maybe because he didn't understand rollers aren't as patient as your usual creditors, or maybe because he didn't understand customers, even in Riverdale, don't like their scutter stepped on, before he got hammered he wrote Maria Esperanza a few checks, bought her a few dinners, opened a few charge accounts in her name, stupid stuff, harmless stuff maybe, maybe she kidded herself he was in love with her, we'll never know, he's hammered, Weinstein, we've got only her word for it, right?

"This is only a couple of months old, Joe, this info, I'm talking about it like it's gospel, like it's ancient history, but you shouldn't be asking yourself how it is you never got wind of it. Ronald Levine, maybe you read about him or heard about him, an accountant who rubbed up against Weinstein and got very, very dirty, got collared by the feds. He's been giving people away right and left and one of the givees is Maria Esperanza. Poole, Steve Poole, seems to have known she was vulnerable for a long time. How, we don't know, that's one of the things we don't know about him, how he knew cops were already on the bubble. Getting someone inside IAU, I gotta tell you, you can probably imagine, that was one of the best things that ever happened to him, Poole. We don't think she's done a lot of damage, Maria, not yet anyway, but we don't know. . . ."

Nick Albert put his hand on Cullen's arm again. "I'm sorry, Joe. It's, you know, it's one of those things, right?"

Cullen looked at Albert's hand, bare, the brown leather glove that had been covering it during the drive held in the grip of his other, gloved, hand. Not a big hand, not small, a normal hand, a nice-sized hand, a hand that could get the job done, resting, the hand, on Cullen's forearm, resting there to assure him that just because his dear sweet young partner was dirty didn't mean Cullen was dirty, not to this cop anyway, not to Nick Albert. "Right," Cullen said.

A little of everything that had ever fallen off a truck in the borough of Queens, a borough not connected to the mainland of the continental United States of America, the borough Cullen was born in, was inside the cement-block building, stored according to no rhyme or reason, stored as it had come in, probably, you can't control what's going to fall off trucks, you just have to take it as it comes, put the fucking Canon portable copiers over here, if we have to move them to get the Nikon Teletouch Deluxes out, well, we'll have to fucking move them, that's all:

Boxes, boxes, boxes, cubes and rectangular solids, big ones, little ones, huge ones, slim ones. Cardboard, miles of it. Acres. Inside: televisions, VCRs, stereos, CD players, microwaves, computers, printers, typewriters, modems, air conditioners, refrigerators, stoves, faxes, stationary bicycles, telephones, answering machines.

"See anything you need?" Nick Albert whispered as they made their way along a haphazard aisle between boxes piled precariously high.

Cullen pointed with the barrel of his SIG Sauer at, down at the end of the aisle, the light at the end of its tunnel, the frosted-glass door of an office, a storeroom, something. There was a light on in the room, silhouettes slipped and slid across the frosted glass, just like in film noirs, voices squirmed under the bottom rail of the door and danced around among the contraband.

Nick Albert nodded and pointed down a tributary aisle to say that he would go along it and converge with Cullen farther along, closer to the busy little room.

Cullen nodded back.

It's not in the Regs and Recipes, it's just not: *How to Make Yourself Perfectly Understood with Only a Look, a Twitch, a Flicker.* Check the table of contents, check the index, you won't find it.

Before Cullen had moved very much farther, before he'd moved from the Epson Equity LT laptops to the Sony DTC-700 digital audio recorders to the Norelco 825RX rechargeable electric shavers, the silhouettes on the frosted-glass door came together in a dark, unruly shape that signified purpose, change; the voices stopped chatting idly and asked and answered questions, gave commands, aye-ayed, popped-to.

Cullen waited, hoping to fucking God that Nick Albert was waiting too. (Nothing about that in the Regs and Recipes, either—no *Hoping to fucking God—See: Thinking, wishful.*

The door opened. Lights, camera, action, movement. Coming and going.

Steve Poole's big backup singer, bald as a cue ball, big mustache. Big Jerry.

Poole's other backup singer, who looked like a jockey, tiny and strong. Never did get his name.

Poole himself, Steven *Jay* Poole, State Senator Poole, hero cop, wheelchair jock, Mister Punishment with a capital *P.*

And, hello, who's this? Samantha—sorry—*Sam* Cox, NewsFocus 14's first-magnitude star. Trademark red outfit—natch—but with a difference: cashmere tunic sweater, cotton tights, Manolo Blahnik boots, alpaca kimono coat. Casual, sporty. Other changes? Lips still ultrared, ultrasucculent; teeth ultraperfect, ultraivory; skin ultralucid; figure ultralithe; carriage ultrasovereign. Here! Big change! Ultrablond hair cut ultrachic ultrashort. This was a woman dressed and coiffed for speed, for flight, for getting the fuck out of town.

The backup singers closed the frosted-glass door behind them and went where Cullen couldn't see them anymore but could hear them.

"It has twenty-four valves," said the tiny backup singer. "It has wishbone suspension."

Big Jerry said, "Wishbone this, Eddie."

Cullen moved to the end of the aisle and looked the way they had gone, along a wall of the warehouse, past boxes and boxes and boxes. He looked the other way, looking for Nick Albert, and saw nothing. He waited. Still nothing. He went after the backup singers, looking back often for Albert, always seeing nothing.

A right turn through boxes and boxes and boxes, a left turn. Oops, a little too fast, there they were, right there, the backup singers, heads bent over a ring of keys, picking out the key that fit the metal door, no window, that they stood in front of.

Their shoes scraped on the concrete floor.

A light shone under the door.

The light went out.

The backup singers didn't notice. They were still fussing over the keys.

"It's that one, Ed, it's that one."

"It's *not* that one, it's *this* one."

Cullen looked behind him for Nick Albert. Nothing.

Big Jerry put a key in the lock of the metal door. He turned the key and opened the door and stuck his head inside.

"Showtime, ladies," big Jerry said. "Let's—"

Big Jerry went crashing down and back and landed on the floor inside the door. His fall slammed the door against the wall and the doorknob went into the wall with a *crump,* you could hear it, you didn't have to be there to see it.

Eddie took a step back, his feet fluttered, he almost ran. Then he remembered he was strapped and he reached inside his coat and came out with a pistol. Cullen couldn't tell what kind, what caliber, but it had bullets in it, he was sure of that.

Eddie stepped up to the door and said, "You stupid fucking cunt." He stepped over big Jerry into the room. "You stupid fucking cunt, you hammered him." Looking down at big Jerry, he raised the barrel of his pistol half an inch, at somebody who'd looked like he—

like she—was going to make a move at him, you could tell, you didn't have to be there to see it. He looked up, looked at . . . at her, and shook his head sadly. He waggled his pistol at her and lifted his chin. "Put that fucking thing down, will you."

You could tell, you didn't have to be there to see it, that she, the woman, was thinking about not putting the fucking thing down, but about throwing it at him, sticking it in him, dousing him with it—whatever it was. Eddie saw her thinking and spread his hands and shrugged his shoulders, like, *What am I, wood?*

You could tell, you didn't have to be there to see it, that she put the fucking thing down.

"Turn the fucking light on, will you," Eddie said, waggling his pistol.

No action, no compliance. He extended his neck a little and said, "Turn. The fucking light on."

You could tell, you didn't have to be there to see it, that the woman—except maybe it was a different woman, another woman—took her shoes off and stood on a metal chair.

The light came back on.

Eddie poked at big Jerry with his toe, as if to prod him awake. He reached down to feel for a pulse in his neck. He didn't know where to feel and felt several places. He stood straight. "Let's get out of here, the botha yez. It's showtime." He stepped backwards out the door, pointing his pistol from side to side, gesturing with his left hand as he backed away, making circles, ellipses, loops, *Come on, come on, come on.*

Cullen put the barrel of his brand-new fell-off-a-truck SIG Sauer behind Eddie's ear. Eddie stopped backing away, stopped making that gesture, *Come on, come on,* he let his pistol fall to the floor, as though he'd had a change of heart. He whimpered, as though he wanted his mother.

Cullen made Eddie go back in the room. Coming in after him, Cullen saw Mabel Parker standing there, saw Ann Jones, a folded-up pizza box between her feet and in her eyes a look that told him he was for her Super Joe, Wonder Joe, how-could-she-ever-for-a-

FIXIN' TO DIE   297

moment-have-doubted-her-feelings-for-him Joe, the Most Valuable, the Most Wonderful, the Best, the Brightest.

The look lasted about as long as an elementary physical particle, a quark, a lepton. It transformed itself into another look, a look of *Oh, shit,* when she, when he, when they all heard Maria Esperanza say, "Just put the piece down, Joe, down on the floor. Down on the floor. Now kick it this way. Kick it this way. Don't look at me, just kick it this way. Now over in the corner there, and down on your face. Down on your face, hands behind your head. Hands be*hind* your head. Good. Ann, Mabel, same way. Down on the floor, hands behind your head. Good. Eddie—here's your piece back. Here's Cullen's. Where'd you get this piece, Joe? You have it squirreled away? SIG Sauer, very nice. . . . Okay. *Mira.* One at a time, first Ann, then Mabel, then Cullen, on your hands and knees, not all the way up, hands and knees, crawl backwards—have you got it? *Back-wards*—out the door. Backwards. Ann. Now. *Now,* Ann. It's show-time."

31

Eddie the little backup singer came through the door first, backing, backing, as he'd meant to do in the first place, pointing his pistol, Cullen still couldn't tell what kind, what caliber, but it had bullets in it, he was sure of that, waggling it back and forth.

After Eddie, on hands and knees, degraded, humiliated, terrorized, terrified, sure they were going to get shot in the ass if they didn't defecate all over themselves first, came Ann Jones, Mabel Parker, Joe Cullen.

Cullen's dear sweet young dirty partner, Maria Esperanza, came last, her Smith & Wesson stainless-steel .38-caliber revolver pointed right at the crown of Cullen's, her dear sweet old partner's, head.

"Maria," Cullen said.

"What the fuck," Steve Poole said, "is going on?" He rolled his wheelchair up alongside the weird little procession, looked it over, shook his head in sharp, disbelieving jerks. He was dressed for speed too, for travel, for getting the fuck out of town, in blue jeans, cowboy boots, a leather jacket, a turtleneck. In his hand was a Glock nine-millimeter. "Where's Jerry?"

"Hammered," Eddie said. "One a the cunts."

Steve Poole raised his eyebrows. "Really?"

Eddie put the toe of his shoe against Ann's thigh. "This one."

Ann tried to bite Eddie's thigh and he danced back.

Samantha Cox came up beside Poole, dressed for speed and, Cullen could tell at a glance, on it, on something that dilated her pupils and made her breath come fast and heavy. She giggled. "Hello, Ann. What's new at the station?" She giggled again.

"Station this," Ann said.

Eddie, longing for approval from Samantha, probably approval and a blow job, kicked Ann in the ass.

Ann got up on her knees and lunged for Eddie's balls.

Eddie danced back, laughing.

Nick Albert came out of somewhere and shot Eddie in the back of the knee. Eddie went down clutching and screaming.

Maria Esperanza fired at where Nick Albert had been, between the Motorola PT500 Flip Phones and the Olympus VX803 camcorders, but he wasn't there anymore.

Eddie screamed.

Steve Poole rolled his wheelchair right up next to Eddie and shot him behind the ear with the Glock. Eddie stopped screaming.

Poole scooped up Eddie's pistol, wheelchair-jock style. "On your feet. Everybody. *Now!*" And Poole and Maria Esperanza rushed Mabel and Ann and Cullen along the aisle of contraband and back to the office with the frosted-glass door. Samantha Cox ran after them, drugged, flat-footed.

Maria Esperanza shut the door and turned the lock. "Down on the floor, everybody. Down. *Down!*"

Mabel and Ann and Cullen got down on their knees. Mabel went down flat on her face, but Ann and Cullen stayed upright.

Poole rolled his wheelchair right up to Cullen. He held Eddie's pistol an inch from Cullen's nose. It was a SIG Sauer too. Had it fallen off the same truck?

"How many with you?"

Cullen was calculating. From Wednesday, July twenty-fourth, the day he was winged and his dear sweet old partner, Neil Zimmerman, hammered, to today, Wednesday, December twenty-five, Christmas, was one hundred fifty-four days. Or was it only one hundred fifty-three? Should he count today as a day, or had he already counted it? And, anyway, who was counting?

Poole put the barrel of the SIG Sauer against Cullen's Adam's apple. "How. Many?" He leaned down to see Cullen's eyes and didn't wait for an answer. "There's just the one. Sam, bring the car around. Maria, get on the phone to Jack and tell him we're coming over, to get clearance from the tower. We've waited long enough for Woods, we can't wait any longer. Sam, *bring* the car around."

Samantha Cox was trying to remember the last time anyone had given her an order. Her eyes were foggy with the effort, her forehead rutted. She couldn't remember. "But . . ."

Poole rolled his eyes, sagged his shoulders. "Sam, there's one fucking guy out there. Just take him out." He held out Eddie's SIG Sauer.

Samantha Cox whimpered, sounding like Eddie wanting his mother, wanting her mother. Her mommy. "He's a cop. . . . Isn't he?" She looked to Cullen for verification. "He's a cop, isn't he?" Looked to Cullen for verification too that if she went out that door, when she went out that door, she would die.

Maria Esperanza was on the phone. "Jack, bring the plane out. We're coming over."

"Isn't he?" Sam Cox said to Cullen. *Won't I?*

Cullen was calculating. On Wednesday, July twenty-fourth, the shooter who winged Cullen and hammered his dear sweet old partner, Neil Zimmerman, got hammered himself, by Maria Esperanza, who was already dirty then, according to Nick Albert, had already been perfused with the venal air of the Bronx, had already been written a few checks, been bought a few dinners, had a few charge accounts opened in her name by some real estate slimeball who she maybe kidded herself was in love with her, we'll never know, he's hammered, the slimeball, we've got only her word for it.

Already dirty, yet she hammered the shooter who winged Cullen and hammered his dear sweet old partner, Neil Zimmerman— didn't that count for something?

Sam Cox screamed, *"Isn't he?!"*

Maria Esperanza was off the phone. She went to the door, put a hand on the knob. "I'll get the car."

Didn't it?

Poole rolled his eyes, sagged his shoulders. "Get it."

Maria Esperanza stood to the side of the door, turned the lock, held her dull silver .38 Smith at the ready, put her hand on the knob. "Give me two minutes."

The Glock was on Poole's lap, the SIG Sauer in his hand, but Cullen had never fired a Glock, he'd been given an update to the Regs and Recipes on the SIG Sauer, so Cullen went for it, coming up off his knees, throwing his hip against the wheel of the wheel-chair, forcing it off balance, forcing Poole to reach for air to keep from toppling out of the chair, shouting, "Nick! Coming out! Strapped!"

He must have been right by the door, Nick Albert, he must have been crouched down by the bottom rail, trying to hear, maybe hearing everything. As the door cracked, he hit it with his shoulder, popped it open, came through it.

Came through it too fast, expecting resistance and getting none, panic on his face because he was out of kilter and could do nothing about it, because he wasn't going to stop until he slammed into something bigger and harder than he was.

Cullen let the wheelchair fall back, he thrust himself out and caught Nick Albert by the hips, tackling him to stop his career, to keep him on his feet, trying to turn him even, so he'd be facing Poole, who had both fucking guns up and out and blasting, blazing, exploding.

Cullen caught him all right. He tackled him all right. He also knocked Albert's gun, his dull silver .38 Smith, from his hand with his shoulder. It skittered across the floor and under a desk.

Cullen was up on his feet now, he and Nick Albert side by side, Cullen empty-handed, Nick Albert disoriented, empty-handed. Some team.

Ann was curled against a desk. Mabel was flat on the floor, her arms over her head. Samantha Cox whimpered in a corner.

Poole raised the Glock; he raised the SIG Sauer. He smiled. "Hello, Nick. . . . Good-bye, Nick."

Maria Esperanza shot Steve Poole in the head.

Maria Esperanza put the barrel of her dull silver .38 Smith in her mouth and pulled the trigger.

Cullen looked away as she pulled the trigger, so he didn't see that Maria Esperanza blew out the back of her head.

Ann looked away too as Maria Esperanza pulled the trigger, so she didn't see that Maria blew out the back of her head.

Looking away, Cullen and Ann looked at each other.

Then they looked away.

32

"Happy New Year," Hriniak said.

"Phil," Cullen said.

"Mind if I sit?"

Cullen made a gesture that might have been welcoming or might simply have called attention to the fact that the only two places to sit in the congested little office were the empty desk that had belonged to Maria Esperanza and a plain hard chair with a stack of files on it.

Hriniak thought about it for a moment, then took the files off the chair and put them on a corner of Cullen's desk. He sat. "Just got back from the Hall. Mayor asked me to stay on."

"There's no reason you shouldn't," Cullen said, trying to think of something other than Hriniak's pathetic erection, his pallid slabs of flesh, his furtive bearing, something other than Jo Dante cupping Hriniak's testicles, pointing a .38 Smith at her crotch. *Any*thing other.

Hriniak shrugged. "Maybe, maybe not. He never saw

the photograph, the mayor. . . . Beryl's still down in Miami. At her sister's. I don't know if you knew that or not. Grapevine."

Cullen nodded, though he hadn't known it, the photograph plastered everywhere he looked now, unable not to see it.

"I want her back," Hriniak said. "Beryl."

Cullen nodded again, though he thought wanting would have little to do with it. He lifted the top file. "This just came over from Neuman at Midwest. A print on the handle of the knife that killed Jo Dante was Jerry Vargas's, Poole's backup singer's. No record, so we'd never've gotten a match, unless we ran the print against military records. Vargas was a marine and the assistant ME was thinking military training." *"Thkillful with clothe-combat weaponth,"* the ME had said.

Hriniak nodded. "Neuman called me last night. I'm a lucky guy, it was a frame that almost took if Jake Neuman nearly bought it."

Cullen tossed the file back on the pile. "I guess he would let you know right away, wouldn't he? I guess I'd be one of the last to know."

Hriniak sighed. "You're right to be pissed, Joe. I should've told you about Jo." He paused. There was just a little flicker in his eye, as if he was going to make a joke about it, about Joe and Jo, Jo and Joe, Joe I and Jo II, Jo I and Joe II; he let the ember die. "If I'd known Swale was using Jo, I would've told you. If I'd known Swale was using Jo, the whole thing would've gone down differently."

"If I had a million dollars," Cullen's uncle Bill, his mother's brother, liked to say, and say and say and say, *"I'd be a millionaire."* "I'm not pissed, I'm tired. Is every cop in town dirty? *I'm* dirty now, I'm part of the cover-up to keep you in your job, to bury that photograph—bury it, burn it, obliterate it, turn it into a fantasy I'll be considered crazy for insisting it ever existed. The mayor's part of the cover-up, Maslosky's part of it, Ruth and Abruzzi and Novak and Suzie Price must be part of it. Is Neuman part of it? I hope Neuman's not part of it, Neuman knows what it's like having a partner roll over on you, I hope he's not part of it, he doesn't deserve it.

"You lie down with scumbags, you get up in the morning a little bit dirty, you learn things—that's what Neuman likes to say, he's talking about the bad guys. You lie down with cops, you get up in the morning just as dirty, just as schooled in deceit and dishonesty and disloyalty. There's an interesting word: loyalty. I was thrown down on four times last year—but who's counting?—and the scumbags throwing down on me were not bad guys, they were cops or ex-cops. Blond Tommy, Paulie Messina, Steven Jay Poole, my dear sweet young partner, Maria Esperanza. Does that make a lot of sense to you, does that make you think of loyalty? So I'm not pissed, I'm tired."

"You're right to be pissed," Hriniak said. "Neuman asked about working with you."

"Believe me, Homicide'd be a vacation after Internal Affairs. Internal Affairs always takes the rap, the heat. Scumbags, here come the IAU scumbags, the rats, the traitors, the turncoats, the snitches. Weasels. Fuck that shit. Homicide'd be a vacation."

"You're being facetious, but you should think it over. Neuman knows what it's like having a partner roll over on him, you know what it's like. You'd be good with each other."

"Facetious this," Cullen said.

Hriniak got up. "Samantha Cox is giving people up right and left, but the fact is, for a news, uh, person, she doesn't know shit. It's too bad Maria Esperanza hammered Poole. He'd've taken a very heavy fall for all this shit, a very heavy fall. I'd've liked to see who he'd pull along with him."

Cullen just hung his head and breathed out a big tired breath.

"You're right to be pissed," Hriniak said.

"I've never been in your office," Ann said. "How is that possible?" She sat in the plain hard chair and put a small gift-wrapped box on top of the pile of files. "Your Christmas present. You might as well have it, nothing would be proven by not giving it to you."

Cullen put a hand on the box but didn't take the box off the pile. "Shall I open it?"

Ann sighed. "No, Joe. Shove it up your ass."

Cullen unwrapped the box and opened it. Inside was the faux classic watch with yesterday's style and today's accuracy that he had seen advertised in the *Times*. He had clipped the ad and given it to Ann after receiving her ultimatum that he tell her what he wanted for Christmas or he would get ankle socks and boxer shorts; he had given her the ad on the way to Maria Esperanza's wedding. "I'd forgotten about this."

"Yeah, well, so had I. I found it while I was packing. As I said, nothing's served by not giving it to you."

Packing. Now there was an unexpectedly ominous word. "Packing?"

"I'm going to California. The coast. El Ay. I'm famous. I killed a man. With a pizza box. I can write, I have discovered, my own ticket. The phone rings and rings and rings. Program directors, station managers, news directors. The *sal*aries they talk about. Zero after zero after zero. The ABC affiliate in Los Angeles—or maybe it's NBC; I'm not really cut out to work in television, I just can't tell the difference—*some* affiliate offered me an anchor job, so I'm going out there for a week to hang out and be seduced. Mabel's going with me, as my agent. We're going to stay at the Beverly Hills and suck a lot of movie-star cock. . . .

"Oh, did I hurt your feelings? Did I make you jealous? You disappeared, Joe, you vanished. The drinking, hunh? Or is it just the solitude you crave, the bottle's a handy place to crawl inside and curl up? Maria"—Ann looked around at the empty desk—"are we allowed to say her name in here? Maria said you told somebody, some cop somewhere, that you never drank on duty, you never drank when you had to drive, when you had responsibilities, when you and I were going to be together, when we were going to fuck. That sounds semi-encouraging, except you also said there were times when you made up excuses about having to work late, about being tired, because you preferred drinking to being with me.

"You told her about the night—remember?—when Mabel and I were going to hear her friend, Aimée, sing at the Bitter End. You weren't going, it was a girls' night out, but I had dinner at your house first. First we fucked, so you didn't drink, you waited till dinner. Mabel called to cancel; Aimée'd gotten sick. We had a fight: I assumed I'd just stay over, you said you'd been looking forward to some time alone, you felt presumed upon, intruded on, all that bullshit, but the fact was—this is you telling this cop—the fact was you wanted me gone so you could finish the rest of the six-pack you'd started without having to listen to me say you sure do drink a lot.

"Maria confessed to me," Ann went on, barely taking a breath. "Not in so many words, but she really did tell me everything, just leaving herself out, her role. We were walking around Washington Square Park. Rex Reed. Back in the days when he wrote profiles and interviews, someone asked Rex Reed how he got people to tell him their intimate secrets. He said first he told them his. Maria told me everything, not in so many words, leaving herself out, her role, so I'd tell her I knew who killed Quintana Davidoff. I guess—what?—Maria wanted out. She certainly took the earliest opportunity—the Smith and Wesson express, I heard some cop call it. Costa Rica. What were they all going to *do* in Costa Rica? Grow vegetables? Weave blankets? What was Samantha going to do—anchor *Los Avisos de las Seis*? Where would she have shopped? I can't help wondering if Maria isn't better off dead than in Costa Rica. I called her husband. Poor fucker. I have no idea what I said. What's to say?"

Ann switched tracks again, skimming over the points: "Your buddy, Nick Albert, called Nancy Albright the other day and invited her out to dinner. Is he crazy? He must be, he gave you as a reference. Might as well give Charles Manson. She liked him, Nancy, she's seriously considering going out with him. Go figure. Maybe she likes that she won't have to change her monogram.

"I'm lonely, Joe, and I'm really really ticked off. You lied to me. You're a drunk and you lied to me by pretending that you're not. I fell for it, I lied to myself by pretending that you weren't. It's classic stuff, classic shit. I won't be part of it anymore, include me out. Mabel says I should help you. If I love you, I should help you. Mabel *loves* codependency, she swears by it, it's the only dependency worth a damn as far as she's concerned.

"I do love you, but I can't help you. You have to help yourself, and I can't stand around and watch and hold your hand, hold your head. . . . Are you drinking now? I don't mean *now,* I mean These Days?"

"No," Cullen said.

"I suppose that's something. Or are you lying? And would you tell me? How long has it been?"

"I guess I should be counting, but I'm not. Since before Christmas, the thing at Kennedy, with Samantha Cox, with Paul Messina, since then."

Ann counted in her head but wasn't sure of her sum. "Are you still grounded?"

"Yes. Pending this and that."

"Samantha wanted you dead, the cunt, didn't she? Just because she thought you knew what she thought I knew. The cunt. Why *aren't* you counting?"

"I guess I should be."

"You're taking it a day at a time."

"I guess."

"I suppose that's all you can do."

". . . If you went to work in California," Cullen said, "when would you start?"

Ann shrugged. "It's all subject to negotiation. It's the California state sport—after beach volleyball: negotiation." She looked over her shoulder at the empty desk. "Is that where she sat?"

"Yes."

"Is it where Neil sat?"

"Yes?"

"Poor Neil."

"Poor Maria."

"I guess." Ann moved some stuff around and unearthed a Realistic Chronomatic 245 clock radio. "Where'd you get that?"

"Fell off a truck," Cullen said.

Ann laughed. She turned it on. "Who's that?"

"Lisa Stansfield."

"You do know your music. Do you still listen to Frankie Crocker?"

"Yes."

"The Evening Bath?"

"Yes."

"Is it time for the bath?"

Cullen looked at the faux classic watch with yesterday's style and today's accuracy. "It's a little early."

"If I . . ." Ann shook her head. "Nothing."

"What?"

"Nothing."

"Thanks for the watch."

"You're welcome." Ann got up suddenly. "I was going to say 'If I invited you over, would you show me where to find the Evening Bath on my radio?' But that's ridiculous, isn't it? Anyone can find it. Any idiot. Idiot. Idiot, idiot, idiot."

She meant him.

She left.

After a long time Cullen got up and shut the door and turned up the radio. It was Foxy Brown's cover of Tracy Chapman's "Baby Can I Hold You."

Sorry, is all that you can't say.
Years gone by and still words don't come easily.
Like sorry, like sorry.
Forgive me, is all that you can't say.
Years gone by and still words don't come easily.
Like forgive me, forgive me.